THE VIRAGO BOOK OF
Wanderlust
&Dreams

Edited and Introduced
by

Lisa St Aubin de Terán

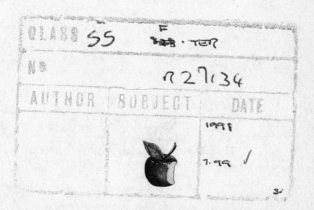

A *Virago* book

Published by Virago Press 1999
First published by Virago Press 1998

This collection and introduction copyright © Lisa St Aubin de Terán 1998

Copyright Acknowledgements on pp. 313–314 constitutes an extension
of this copyright page

The moral right of the editor has been asserted

A CIP catalogue record for this book is available from the British Library

ISBN 1 86049 534 6

Typeset by Solidus (Bristol) Ltd, England
Printed and bound in Great Britain by Clays Ltd, St Ives plc

Virago
A Division of
Little, Brown and Company (UK)
Brettenham House
Lancaster Place
London WC2E 7EN

CONTENTS

CONTENTS

FLIRTING WITH LIFE

When you flirt with another, you are courting; when you flirt with life you are courting danger. This is a collection of writing about travelling: whether that travel is across a dirt track, a field, a desert or an ocean, a cellar in war-torn Berlin or a hedge in London's suburbia. Travel, like poetry, 'is a way of taking life by the throat'. I present here an essence of wanderlust and dreams and flights of fancy along life's tightrope. This is a travelling circus with a programme of literary performances: some are lion tamers, some are jugglers. The ringmaster, the one who cracks the whip, is the yearning, be it imaginative or geographical, for another world, another experience. The reader is part of the audience in the big top who has had the chance to peek into the caravans and see not just the acts themselves but what lies behind them.

Women by no means have the monopoly on travel; in fact, the greatest explorers have nearly all been men. Yet there is nothing competitive about female travellers, the Isabella Birds, the Mary Kingsleys and the Karen Blixens, travelled through sheer curiosity and to pay homage to the glories of life, not through any search for glory or national pride. Thus, races like the one to the South Pole by Scott and Amundsen are hard to imagine between two rival groups of women of whatever nationality: the milk of human kindness is there to be shared, and places exist to be seen and known, not owned. The only flags planted by the heroines in this troupe are ones of personal achievement, of understanding, of passion fulfilled, and often, of liberation from a repressed status in the society that is left behind.

Travelling is like flirting with life. It's like saying, 'I would stay and love you but I have to go; this is my station.' Despite the apparent superficiality of this, travel contains an element of gambling, of dicing with life itself. Lord Byron (who was one of the world's great travellers) wrote, 'There is a tide in the affairs of women,/ Which taken at the flood, leads – God knows where.' In Marilynne Robinson's *Housekeeping*, the tide laps at the shore of the small lakeside settlement of Fingerbone, washing up a hobo aunt to care for her two orphaned nieces, curling round the edges of insanity and eccentricity, dragging the aunt and one of the girls away to a life of travelling and railroads, to a life of freedom far from the petty intolerance that would prise them apart. For Liane de Pougy, one of France's most notorious courtesans, it leads to marriage to a Romanian prince to whom she remains strictly faithful 'from the waist down' while trying to cross the border from sinner to saint.

None of the authors or heroines here is running a race, but they are all running, be it away from or in search of something or someone. The scarlet letter that they all wear or carry in their carpet bags is not the A of an adulterer but the A of adventurer: the search for adventure is branded on their spirit. Doña Catalina de Erauso, the seventeenth-century nun-cum-serial killer, runs headlong into hers. As Zora Neale Hurston (1891–1960), the black American novelist whose philosophy embodies the spirit of this collection, says, 'Just because my mouth opens up like a prayer book, it does not just have to flap like a Bible. And then again, anybody whose mouth is cut cross-ways is given to lying, unconsciously as well as knowingly.'

Harriet Wilson's novel *Our Nig* takes its place here not for its historical merit as being the first ever book in English by a black woman, but for its intrinsic wit and charm and the wild streak that carries the half-white, half-black heroine through the drudgery of her indentured labour with an irrepressible *joie de vivre* despite her blighted childhood.

Several of the journeys are more through time than place. The past is the foreign country that New Zealander Janet Frame travels through in *To the Is-Land*, emerging from the chrysalis of her pain to a mastery of words and emotions. In *Their Eyes Were Watching God*, Zora Neale Hurston's narrator travels through love in what must be one of literature's most profound evocations of its stations. Elizabeth Smart's love of the Irish poet, George Barker, is an incantatory celebration born of the despair of separation. From the kitchen tap dripping to the trickling stream, to the river and then the sea itself, there is a universality of longing. It is the same longing that drove the young Jessie Kesson from the labour of a bleak farm in north-east Scotland to the relative freedom of a life of penury writing in London. When she died in 1994, aged seventy-four, she left behind her a rich understanding of human nature. Apart from her initial flight from Scotland, Jessie Kesson was an armchair traveller. In this collection, Sue Tatt from *Glitter of Mica* is travelling on a local bus, yet she could be anywhere because she has dipped her cup into the drinking well of life.

There is a blues lyric which says 'my baby bought a ticket as long as my right arm'; reading through the many books that have gone to make up this anthology, and the many others that have been excluded only because of the lack of space here, I see more than ever that there are tickets and tickets. Some of them are for bus rides, and some of them are so long they cross continents. For most people, *Out of Africa* conjures up Karen Blixen (Isak Dinesen) more than Pliny the Elder and his 'There is always something new out of Africa'. Part of her narrative is timeless. She walks a financial tightrope of a different girth than some of the other heroines, but the trail she blazed has not grown over.

As disparate as the entries may seem at first sight, coming from five different continents and spanning nearly four hundred years, they are all about or by women who have put their lives on the line together with their prose. The flirtation, the invitation or acceptance of attentions merely for amusement, is a visible patina of dust that sits on the water's surface: underneath is the water itself. The old cliché of women being always fickle and changeable fails to take into account the persistency and universality of their dreaming. There are spangled costumes here and silken wrappings, ribbons and home-spun shawls, but they are all draped over a need to go beyond the narrow parameters of whatever restrictions time and place have imposed on them.

Few women travel with a fanfare of trumpets; they tend to hitch up their skirts and get on with it. Fewer still have written about their journeys. From those who have, we know that many have cross-dressed as a protection of their sex. The two cross-dressers I have chosen both did so for other reasons. Flora Tristan (1803–44) the social and political reformer, dressed as a man to gain access to the male domain of the British Houses of Parliament, skirting a taboo. Doña Catalina de Erauso, the homicidal nun, was, on her own admission, a predatory trans-vestite: easing her way through Latin America as a man, the better to indulge in the courtship of pretty girls.

There have been only a handful of actual women flyers from the past. Most notable as a writer would be Beryl Markham, who also came out of Africa. The flyers here do so in their fantasy; they are escapologists and escapees. Their flight paths are complex, and some flee to embrace what others are struggling to avoid. The dream exodus from Europe to Africa contrasts with a fantasy in reverse when Buchi Emecheta describes a Nigerian lady longing to escape from the eventual comfort of her wealthy African home to the apparent glamour of a squalid bed-sitting room in a London suburb and the vagaries of the life of an immigrant condemned for ever by the colour of her skin to be a second-class citizen.

Enough daydreamers have ignited the spark of travelling from no matter where to show that it can be done, by anyone, man or woman, who merely wants it enough. And enough have stayed put and travelled in their mind to show that such journeys can also be made vicariously. The exotic can be found in the commonplace, and the commonplace is the weft of life, its thread weaving through every person and every place. Great writers like Emily Brontë, Carson McCullers and Virginia Woolf have mapped out some of the foreign countries of the mind. It is more important to navigate such maps and charts than how this navigation is achieved. From the comfort of an armchair or the discomfort of a ditch or kitchen, a woman's daydreaming, her fantasy and escapism, is like Cathy's love for Heathcliff in *Wuthering Heights*: 'it resembles the eternal rocks beneath – a source of little visible delight but necessary'.

This book attempts both to delight and to disturb the dust on the becalmed ocean's complacency; to clear a view of the swirling sea and the fountain hidden somewhere in it. One of the main unifying threads is courage in all its forms. It is about people who have had the courage to say 'yes' to life, whether that meant daring to go or daring to stay.

> *For some people the day comes*
> *When they have to declare the great Yes*
> *or the great No. It's clear at once who has the Yes*
> *ready within him; and saying it*
>
> *he goes from honour to honour, strong in his conviction.*
> *He who refuses does not repent. Asked again,*
> *he'd still say no. Yet that no – the right no –*
> *drags him down all his life.*

C.P. Cavafy

Lisa St Aubin de Terán

AH'LL BE GONE

ANGELA CARTER

Angela Carter (1940–1992) was born in Eastbourne and brought up in south Yorkshire. One of Britain's most original and disturbing writers, she read English at Bristol University and wrote her first novel, *Shadow Dance*, in 1965. *The Magic Toyshop* won the John Llewelyn Rhys Prize in 1969 and *Several Perceptions* won the Somerset Maugham Prize in 1968. More novels followed and in 1974 her translation of the fairy tales of Charles Perrault was published, and in the early nineties she edited the *Virago Book of Fairy Tales* (2 vols). Her journalism appeared in almost every major publication; a collection of the best of these were published by Virago in *Nothing Sacred* (1982). She also wrote poetry and a film script together with Neil Jordan of her story 'The Company of Wolves'. Her last novel, *Wise Children*, was published to widespread acclaim in 1991. Angela Carter's death at age fifty-one in February 1992 'robbed the English literary scene of one of its most vivacious and compelling voices' (*Independent*).

SHE SIGHS

from *Black Venus*

Sad; so sad, those smoky-rose, smoky-mauve evenings of late autumn, sad enough to pierce the heart. The sun departs the sky in winding sheets of gaudy cloud; anguish enters the city, a sense of the bitterest regret, a nostalgia for things we never knew, anguish of the turn of the year, the time of impotent yearning, the inconsolable season. In America, they call it 'the Fall', bringing to mind the Fall of Man, as if the fatal drama of the primal fruit-theft must recur again and again, with cyclic regularity, at the same time of every year that schoolboys set out to rob orchards, invoking, in the most everyday image, any child, every child, who, offered the choice between virtue and knowledge, will always choose knowledge, always the hard way. Although she does not know the meaning of the word 'regret', the woman sighs, without any precise reason.

Soft twists of mist invade the alleys, rise up from the slow river like exhalations of an exhausted spirit, seep in through the cracks in the window frames so that the contours of their high, lonely apartment waver and melt. On these evenings, you see everything as though your eyes are going to lapse to tears.

She sighs.

The custard-apple of her stinking Eden she, this forlorn Eve, bit – and was all at once transported here, as in a dream; and yet she is a *tabula rasa*, still. She never experienced her experience *as* experience, life never added to the sum of her knowledge; rather, subtracted from it. If you start out with nothing, they'll take even that away from you, the Good Book says so.

Indeed, I think she never bothered to bite any apple at all. She wouldn't have known what knowledge was *for*, would she? She was in neither a state of innocence nor a state of grace. I will tell you what Jeanne was like.

She was like a piano in a country where everyone has had their hands cut off.

On these sad days, at those melancholy times, as the room sinks into dusk, he, instead of lighting the lamp, fixing drinks, making all cosy, will ramble on: 'Baby, baby, let me take you back where you belong, back to your lovely, lazy island where the jewelled parrot rocks on the enamel tree and you can crunch sugar-cane between your strong, white teeth, like you did when you were little, baby. When we get there, among the lilting palm-trees, under the purple flowers, I'll love you to death. We'll go back and live together in a thatched house with a veranda overgrown with flowering vine and a little girl in a short white frock with a yellow satin bow in her kinky pigtail will wave a huge feather fan over us, stirring the languishing air as we sway in our hammock, this way and that way ... the ship, the ship is waiting in the harbour, baby. My monkey, my pussy-cat, my pet ... think how lovely it would be to live there ...'

But, on these days, nipped by frost and sulking, no pet nor pussy she; she looks more like an old crow with rusty feathers in a miserable huddle by the smoky fire which she pokes with spiteful sticks. She coughs and grumbles, she is always chilly, there is always a draught gnawing the back of her neck or pinching her ankles.

Go, where? Not *there*! The glaring yellow shore and harsh blue sky daubed in crude, unblended colours squeezed directly from the tube, where the perspectives are abrupt as a child's drawing, your eyes hurt to look. Fly-blown towns. All there is to eat is green bananas and yams and a brochette of rubber goat to chew. She puts on a theatrical shudder, enough to shake the affronted cat off her lap. She hates the cat, anyway. She can't look at the cat without wanting to strangle it. She would like a drink. Rum will do. She twists a flute of discarded manuscript from the waste-paper basket into a spill for her small, foul, black cheroot.

Night comes in on feet of fur and marvellous clouds drift past the windows, those spectral clouds of the night sky that are uncannily visible when no light is there. The whim of the master of the house has not let the windows alone; he had all the panes except the topmost ones replaced with frosted glass so that the inmates could pursue an uninterrupted view of the sky as if they were living in the gondola of a balloon such as the one in which his friend Nadar made triumphant ascents.

At the inspiration of a gust of wind such as now rattles the tiles above us, this handsome apartment with its Persian rugs, its walnut table off which the Borgias served poisons, its carved armchairs from whose bulbous legs grin and grimace cinque-cento faces, the crust of fake Tintorettos on the walls (he's an indefatigable connoisseur, if, as yet, too young to have that sixth sense that tells you when you're being conned) – at the invitation of the mysterious currents of the heavens, this well-appointed cabin will loose its moorings in the street below and take off, depart, whisk across the dark vault of the night, tangling a stillborn, crescent moon in its ropes, nudging a star at lift-off, and will deposit us—

'*No!*'she said. 'Not the bloody parrot forest! Don't take me on the slavers' route back to the West Indies, for godsake! And let the bloody cat out, before it craps on your precious Bokhara!'

They have this in common, neither has a native land, although he likes to pretend she has a fabulous home in the bosom of a blue ocean, he will force a home on her whether she's got one or not, he cannot believe she is as dispossessed as he is ... Yet they are only at home together when contemplating flight; they are both waiting for the wind to blow that will take them to a miraculous elsewhere, a happy land, far, far away, the land of delighted ease and pleasure.

After she's got a drink or two inside her, however, she stops coughing, grows a bit more friendly, will consent to unpin her hair and let him play with it, the way he likes to. And, if her native indolence does not prove too much for her – for she is capable of sprawling, as in a vegetable trance, for hours, for days, in the dim room by the smoky fire – nevertheless, she will sometimes lob the butt of her cheroot in the fire and be persuaded to take off her clothes and dance for Daddy who, she will grudgingly admit when pressed, is a good daddy, buys her pretties, allocates her the occasional lump of hashish, keeps her off the street.

Nights of October, of frail, sickle moons, when the earth conceals the shining accomplice of assassins in its shadow, to make everything all the more mysterious – on such a night, you could say the moon was black.

This dance, which he wanted her to perform so much and had especially devised for her, consisted of a series of voluptuous poses one following another; private-room-in-a-bordello stuff but tasteful, he preferred her to undulate rhythmically rather than jump about and shake a leg. He liked her to put on all her bangles and beads when she did her dance, she dressed up in the set of clanking jewellery he'd given her, paste, nothing she could sell or she'd have sold it. Meanwhile, she hummed a Creole melody, she liked the ones with ribald words about what the shoemaker's wife did at Mardi Gras or the size of some fisherman's legendary tool but Daddy paid no attention to what song his siren sang, he fixed his quick, bright, dark eyes upon her decorated skin as if, sucker, authentically entranced.

'Sucker!' she said, almost tenderly, but he did not hear her.

She cast a long shadow in the firelight. She was a woman of immense height, the type of those beautiful giantesses who, a hundred years later, would grace the stages of the Crazy Horse or the Casino de Paris in sequin cache-sexe and tinsel pasties, divinely tall, the colour and texture of suede. Josephine Baker! But vivacity, exuberance were never Jeanne's qualities. A slumbrous resentment of anything you could not eat, drink or smoke, i.e. burn, was her salient characteristic. Consumption, combustion, these were her vocations.

She sulked sardonically through Daddy's sexy dance, watching, in a bored, fascinated way, the elaborate reflections of the many strings of glass beads he had given her tracking about above her on the ceiling. She looked like the source of light but this was an illusion; she only shone because the dying fire lit his presents to her. Although his regard made her luminous, his shadow made her blacker than she was, his shadow could eclipse her entirely. Whether she had a good heart or not underneath, is anybody's guess; she had been raised in the School of Hard Knocks and enough hard knocks can beat the heart out of anybody.

Though Jeanne was not prone to introspection, sometimes, as she wriggled around the dark, buoyant room that tugged at its moorings, longing to take off on an aerial quest for that Cythera beloved of poets, she wondered what the distinction was between dancing naked in front of *one* man who paid and dancing naked in front of a group of men who paid. She had the impression that, somewhere in the difference, lay morality. Tutors in the School of Hard Knocks, that is, other chorus girls in the cabaret, where, in her sixteenth summer, she had tunelessly croaked these same Creole ditties she now hummed, had told her there was all the difference in the world and, at sixteen, she could conceive of no higher ambition than to be kept; that is, kept off the streets. Prostitution was a question of number; of being paid by more than one person at a time. That was bad. She was not a bad girl. When she slept with anyone else but Daddy, she never let them pay. It was a matter of honour. It was a question of fidelity. (In these ethical surmises slumbered the birth of irony although her lover assumed she was promiscuous because she *was* promiscuous.)

Now, however, after a few crazy seasons in the clouds with him, she sometimes asked herself if she'd played her cards right. If she was going to have to dance naked to earn her keep, anyway, why shouldn't she dance naked for hard cash in hand and earn enough to keep herself? Eh? Eh?

But then, the very thought of organising a new career made her yawn. Dragging herself around madames and music halls and so on; what an effort. And how much to ask? She had only the haziest notion of her own use value.

She danced naked. Her necklaces and earrings clinked. As always, when she finally got herself up off her ass and started dancing, she quite enjoyed it. She felt almost warm towards him; her good luck he was young and handsome. Her bad luck his finances were rocky, the opium, the scribbling; that he ... but, at 'that', she snapped her mind off.

Thinking resolutely of her good luck, she held out her hands to her lover, flashed her teeth at him – the molars might be black stumps, already, but the pointed canines still white as vampires' – and invited him to join in and dance with her. But he never would, never. Scared of muzzing his shirt or busting his collar or something, even if, when stoned, he would clap his hands to the rhythm. She liked it when he did that. She felt he was appreciating her. After a few drinks, she forgot the other thing altogether, although she guessed, of course. The girls told over the ghoulish litany of the symptoms together in the dressing room in hushed, scared voices, peeking at the fortune-telling mirror and seeing, not their rosy faces, but their own rouged skulls.

When she was on her own, having a few drinks in front of the fire, thinking about it, it made her break out in a horrible hag's laughter, as if she were already the hag she would become enjoying a grim joke at the expense of the pretty, secretly festering thing she still was. At Walpurgisnacht, the young witch boasted to the old witch: 'Naked on a goat, I display my fine young body.' How the old witch laughed! 'You'll rot!' I'll rot, thought Jeanne, and laughed. This cackle of geriatric cynicism ill became such a creature made for pleasure as Jeanne, but was pox not the emblematic fate of a creature made for pleasure and the price you paid for the atrocious mixture of corruption and innocence this child of the sun brought with her from the Antilles?

For herself, she came clean, arrived in Paris with nothing worse than scabies, malnutrition and ringworm about her person. It was a bad joke, therefore, that, some centuries before Jeanne's birth, the Aztec goddess, Nanahuatzin, had poured a cornucopia of wheelchairs, dark glasses, crutches and mercury pills on the ships of the conquistadores as they took their spoiled booty from the New World to the Old; the raped continent's revenge, perpetrating itself in the beds of Europe. Jeanne innocently followed Nanahuatzin's trail across the Atlantic but she brought no erotic vengeance – she'd picked up the germ from the very first protector. The man she'd trusted to take her away from all that, enough to make a horse laugh, except that she was a fatalist, she was indifferent.

· She bent over backwards until the huge fleece of a black sheep, her unfastened hair, spilled on to the Bokhara. She was a supple acrobat; she could make her back into a mahogany rainbow. (Notice her big feet and huge, strong hands, capable enough to have been a nurse's hands.) If he was a connoisseur of the beautiful, she was a connoisseur of the most exquisite humiliations but she had always been too poor to be able to afford the luxury of acknowledging a humiliation as such. You took what came. She arched her back so much a small boy could have run under her. Her reversed blood sang in her ears.

Upside down as she was, she could see, in the topmost right-hand window-pane he had left unfrosted, the sickle moon, precise as if pasted on the sky. This moon was the size of a broad nail-paring; you could see the vague outline of the rest of its surface, obscured by the shadow of the earth as if the earth were clenched between the moon's shining claw-tips, so you could say the moon held the world in its arms. An exceptionally brilliant star suspended from the nether prong on a taut, invisible leash.

The basalt cat, the pride of the home, its excretory stroll along the *quai* concluded, now whined for readmittance outside the door. The poet let Puss in. Puss leapt into his waiting arms and filled the apartment with a happy purr. The girl plotted to strangle the cat with her long, agile toes but, indulgent from the exercise of her sensuality, she soon laughed to see him loving up the cat with the same gestures, the same endearments, he used on her. She forgave the cat for its existence; they had a lot in common. She released the bow of her back with a twang and plumped on the rug, rubbing her stretched tendons.

He said she danced like a snake and she said, snakes can't dance: they've got no legs, and he said, but kindly, you're an idiot, Jeanne; but she knew he'd never so much as *seen* a snake, nobody who'd seen a snake move – that quick system of transverse strikes, lashing itself like a whip, leaving a rippling snake in the sand behind it, terribly fast – if he'd seen a snake move, he'd never have said a thing like that. She huffed off and contemplated her sweating breasts; she would have liked a bath, anyway, she was a little worried about a persistent vaginal discharge that smelt of mice, something new, something ominous, something horrid. But: no hot water, not at this hour.

'They'll bring up hot water if you pay.'

His turn to sulk. He took to cleaning his nails again.

'You think I don't need to wash because I don't show the dirt.'

But, even as she launched the first darts of a shrew's assault that she could have protracted for a tense, scratchy hour or more, had she been in the mood, she lost the taste for it. She was seized with sudden indifference. What does it matter? we're all going to die; we're as good as dead already. She drew her knees up to her chin and crouched in front of the fire, staring vacantly at the embers. Her face fixed in sullen resentment. The cat drew silently alongside, as if on purpose, adding a touch of satanic glamour, so you could imagine both were having silent conversations with the demons in the flames. As long as the cat left her alone, she let it alone. They were alone together. The quality of the separate self-absorptions of the cat and the woman was so private that the poet felt outmanoeuvred and withdrew to browse in his bookshelves, those rare, precious volumes, the jewelled missals, the incunabula, those books acquired from special shops that incurred damnation if you so much as opened the covers. He cherished his arduously aroused sexuality until she was prepared to acknowledge it again.

He thinks she is a vase of darkness; if he tips her up, black light will spill out. She is not Eve but, herself, the forbidden fruit, and he has eaten her!

> *Weird goddess, dusky as night,*
> *reeking of musk smeared on tobacco,*
> *a shaman conjured you, a Faust of the savannah,*
> *black-thighed witch, midnight's child.*

Indeed, the Faust who summoned her from the abyss of which her eyes retain the devastating memory must have exchanged her presence for his soul; black Helen's lips suck the marrow from the poet's spirit, although she wishes to do no such thing. Apart from her meals and a few drinks, she is without many conscious desires. If she were a Buddhist, she would be halfway on the road to sainthood because she wants so little, but, alas, she is still pricked by needs.

The cat yawned and stretched. Jeanne woke from her trance. Folding another spill out of a dismantled sonnet to ignite a fresh cheroot, her bib of cut glass a-jingle and a-jangle, she turned to the poet to ask, in her inimitable half-raucous, half-caressing voice, voice of a crow reared on honey, with its dawdling accent of the Antilles, for a little money.

Nobody seems to know in what year Jeanne Duval was born, although the year in which she met Charles Baudelaire (1842) is precisely logged and the biographies of his other mistresses, Aglaé-Josephine Sabatier and Marie Daubrun, are well documented. Besides Duval, she also used the names Prosper and Lemer, as if her name was of no consequence. Where she came from is a problem; books suggest Mauritius, in the Indian Ocean, or Santo Domingo, in the Caribbean, take your pick of two different sides of the world. (Her *pays d'origine* of less importance than it would have been had she been a wine.) Mauritius looks like a shot in the dark based on the fact that Baudelaire spent some time on that island during his abortive trip to India in 1841. Santo Domingo, Columbus' Hispaniola, now the Dominican Republic, a troubled history, borders upon Haiti. Here Toussaint L'Ouverture led a successful slave revolt against French plantation owners at the time of the French Revolution.

Although slavery had been abolished without debate throughout the French possessions by the National Assembly in 1794, it was reimposed in Martinique and Guadeloupe – though not in Haiti – by Napoleon. These slaves were not finally emancipated until 1848. However, African mistresses of French residents were often manumitted, together with their children, and intermarriage was by no means a rare occurrence. A middle-class Creole population grew up; to this class belonged the Josephine who became Empress of the French on her marriage to the same Napoleon.

It is unlikely that Jeanne Duval belonged to this class if, in fact, she came from Martinique, which, since she seems to have been Francophone, remains a possibility.

He made a note in 'Mon Coeur Mis à Nu': 'Of the People's hatred of Beauty. Examples: Jeanne and Mme Muller.' (Who was Mme Muller?)

Kids in the street chucked stones at her, she so tall and witchy and, when she was pissed, teetering along with the vulnerable, self-conscious dignity of the drunk which always invites mockery, and, always, she held her bewildered head with its enormous, unravelling cape of hair as proudly as if she were carrying upon it an enormous pot full of all the waters of Lethe. Maybe he found her crying because the kids in the street were chucking stones at her, calling her a 'black bitch' or worse and spattering the beautiful white flounces of her crinoline with handfuls of tossed mud they scooped from the gutters where they thought she belonged because she was a whore who had the nerve to sashay to the corner shop for cheroots or *ordinaire* or rum with her nose stuck up in the air as if she were the Empress of all the Africas.

But she was the deposed Empress, royalty in exile, for, of the entire and heterogeneous wealth of all those countries, had she not been dispossessed?

Robbed of the bronze gateways of Benin; of the iron breasts of the amazons of the court of the King of Dahomey; of the esoteric wisdom of the great university of Timbuktu; of the urbanity of glamorous desert cities before whose walls the horsemen wheel, welcoming the night on trumpets twice the length of their own bodies. The Abyssinia of black saints and holy lions was not even so much as a legend to her. Of those savannahs where men wrestle with leopards she knew not one jot. The splendid continent to which her skin allied her had been excised from her memory. She had been deprived of history, she was the pure child of the colony. The colony – white, imperious – had fathered her. Her mother went off with the sailors and her granny looked after her in one room with a rag-covered bed.

Her granny said to Jeanne: 'I was born in the ship where my mother died and was thrown into the sea. Sharks ate her. Another woman of some other nation who had just still-born suckled me. I don't know anything about my father nor where I was conceived nor on what coast nor in what circumstances. My foster-mother soon died of fever in the plantation. I was weaned. I grew up.'

Nevertheless, Jeanne retained a negative inheritance; if you tried to get her to do anything she didn't want to, if you tried to erode that little steely nugget of her free will, which expressed itself as lethargy, you could see how she had worn away the patience of the missionaries and so come to inherit, not even self-pity, only the twenty-nine legally permitted strokes of the whip.

Her granny spoke Creole, patois, knew no other language,

spoke it badly and taught it badly to Jeanne, who did her best to convert it into good French when she came to Paris and started mixing with swells but made a hash of it, her heart wasn't in it, no wonder. It was as though her tongue had been cut out and another one sewn in that did not fit well. Therefore you could say, not so much that Jeanne did not understand the lapidary, troubled serenity of her lover's poetry but, that it was a perpetual affront to her. He recited it to her by the hour and she ached, raged and chafed under it because his eloquence denied her language. It made her dumb, a dumbness all the more profound because it manifested itself in a harsh clatter of ungrammatical recriminations and demands which were not directed at her lover so much – she was quite fond of him – as at her own condition, great gawk of an ignorant black girl, good for nothing: correction, good for only one thing, even if the spirochetes were already burrowing away diligently at her spinal marrow while she bore up the superb weight of oblivion on her amazonian head.

The greatest poet of alienation stumbled upon the perfect stranger; theirs was a match made in heaven. In his heart, he must have known this.

The goddess of his heart, the ideal of the poet, lay resplendently on the bed in a room morosely papered red and black; he liked to have her make a spectacle of herself, to provide a sumptuous feast for his bright eyes that were always bigger than his belly.

Venus lies on the bed, waiting for a wind to rise: the sooty albatross hankers for the storm. Whirlwind!

She was acquainted with the albatross. A scallop-shell carried her stark naked across the Atlantic; she clutched an enormous handful of dreadlocks to her pubic mound. Albatrosses hitched glides on the gales the wee black cherubs blew for her.

The albatross can fly around the world in eight days, if only it sticks to the stormy places. The sailors call the huge birds ugly names, goonies, mollyhawks, because of their foolish clumsiness on the ground but wind, wind is their element; they have absolute mastery of it.

Down there, far down, where the buttocks of the world slim down again, if you go far south enough you reach again the realm of perpetual cold that begins and ends our experience on this earth, those ranges of ice mountains where the bull-roaring winds bay and bellow and no people are, only the stately penguin in his frock-coat not unlike yours, Daddy, the estimable but, unlike you, uxorious penguin who balances the precious egg on his feet while his dear wife goes out and has as good a time as the Antarctic may afford.

If Daddy were like a penguin, how much more happy we should be; there isn't room for two albatrosses in *this* house.

Wind is the element of the albatross just as domesticity is that of the penguin. In the 'Roaring Forties' and 'Furious Fifties', where the high winds blow ceaselessly from west to east between the remotest tips of the inhabited continents and the blue nightmare of the uninhabitable ice, these great birds glide in delighted glee, south, far south, so far south it inverts the notional south of the poet's parrot-forest and glittering beach; down here, down south, only the phlegmatic mono-chrome, flightless birds form the audience for the wonderful *aerielistes* who live in the heart of the storm – like the bourgeoisie, Daddy, sitting good and quiet with their eggs on their feet watching artistes such as we dare death upon the high trapeze.

The woman and her lover wait for the rising of the wind upon which they will leave the gloomy apartment. They believe they can ascend and soar upon it. This wind will be like that from a new planet.

The young man inhales the aroma of the coconut oil which she rubs into her hair to make it shine. His agonised romanti-cism transforms this homely odour of the Caribbean kitchen into the perfume of the air of those tropical islands he can sometimes persuade himself are the happy lands for which he longs. His lively imagination performs an alchemical alteration on the healthy tang of her sweat, freshly awakened by dancing. He thinks her sweat smells of cinnamon because she has spices in her pores. He thinks she is made of a different kind of flesh than his.

It is essential to their connection that, if she should put on the private garments of nudity, its non-sartorial regalia of jewellery and rouge, then he himself must retain the public nineteenth-century masculine impedimenta of frock-coat (exquisitely cut); white shirt (pure silk, London tailored); oxblood cravat; and impeccable trousers. There's more to *Le Déjeuner sur l'Herbe* than meets the eye. (Manet, another friend of his.) Man does and is dressed to do so; his skin is his own business. He is artful, the creation of culture. Woman is; and is, therefore, fully dressed in no clothes at all, her skin is common property, she is a being at one with nature in a fleshly simplicity that, he insists, is the most abominable of artifices.

Once, before she became a kept woman, he and a group of bohemians contrived to kidnap her from her customers at the cabaret, spirited her, at first protesting, then laughing, off with them, and they'd wandered along the streets in the small hours, looking for a place to take their prize for another drink and she urinated in the street, right there, didn't announce it; nor go off into an alley to do it on her own; she did not even leave go his arm but straddled the gutter, legs apart, and pissed as if it was the most natural thing in the world. Oh, the unexpected Chinese bells of that liquid cascade!

(At which point, his Lazarus arose and knocked unbidden on the coffin-lid of the poet's trousers.)

Jeanne hitched up her skirts with her free hand as she stepped across the pool she'd made, so that he saw where she had splashed her white stockings at the ankle. It seemed to his terrified, exacerbated sensibility that the liquid was a kind of bodily acid that burned away the knitted cotton, dissolved her petticoat, her stays, her chemise, the dress she wore, her jacket, so that now she walked beside him like an ambulant fetish, savage, obscene, terrifying.

He himself always wore gloves of pale pink kid that fitted as tenderly close as the rubber gloves that gynaecologists will wear. Watching him play with her hair, she tranquilly recollected a red-haired friend in the cabaret who had served a brief apprentice-ship in a brothel but retired from the profession after she discovered a significant proportion of her customers wanted nothing more of her than permission to ejaculate into her magnificent Titian mane. (How the girls giggled over that.) The red-haired girl thought that, on the whole, this messy business was less distasteful and more hygienic than regular intercourse but it meant that she had to wash her hair so often that her crowning, indeed – she was a squint-eyed little thing – unique glory was stripped of its essential, natural oils. Seller and commodity in one, a whore is her own investment in the world and so she must take care of herself; the squinting redhead decided she dare not risk squandering her capital so recklessly but Jeanne never had this temperament of the tradesperson, she did not feel she was her own property and so she gave herself away to everybody except the poet, for whom she had too much respect to offer such an ambivalent gift for nothing.

'Get it up for me,' said the poet.

Albatrosses are famous for the courtship antics they carry on throughout the breeding season. These involve gro-tesque, awkward dancing, accompanied by bowing, scrap-ing, snapping of bills, and prolonged nasal groans.

Birds of the World, Oliver L. Austin Jnr

They are not great nest-builders. A slight depression in the ground will do. Or, they might hollow out a little mound of mud. They will make only the most squalid concessions to the earth. He envisaged their bed, the albatross's nest, as just such a fleeting kind of residence in which Destiny, the greatest madame of all, had closeted these two strange birds together. In this transitory exile, anything is possible.

'Jeanne, get it up for me.'

Nothing is simple for this fellow! He makes a performance worthy of the Comédie Française out of a fuck, bringing him off is a five-act drama with farcical interludes and other passages that could make you cry and, afterwards, cry he does, he is ashamed, he talks about his mother, but Jeanne can't remember her mother and her granny swapped her with a ship's mate for a couple of bottles, a bargain with which her granny said she was well satisfied because Jeanne was already getting into trouble and growing out of her clothes and ate so much.

While they had been untangling together the history of transgression, the fire went out; also, the small, white, shining, winter moon in the top left-hand corner of the top left-hand pane of the few sheets of clear glass in the window had, accompanied by its satellite star, completed the final section of its low arc over the black sky. While Jeanne stoically laboured over her lover's pleasure, as if he were her vineyard, she laying up treasure in heaven from her thankless toil, moon and star arrived together at the lower right-hand window-pane.

If you could see her, if it were not so dark, she would look like the victim of a robbery; her bereft eyes are like abysses but she will hold him to her bosom and comfort him for betraying to her in his self-disgust those trace elements of common humanity he has left inside her body, for which he blames her bitterly, for which he will glorify her, awarding her the eternity promised by the poet.

The moon and star vanish.

Nadar says he saw her a year or so after, deaf, dumb and paralysed, Baudelaire died. The poet, finally, so far estranged from himself that, in the last months before the disease triumphed over him, when he was shown his reflection in a mirror, he bowed politely, as to a stranger. He told his mother to make sure that Jeanne was looked after but his mother didn't give her anything. Nadar says he saw Jeanne hobbling on crutches along the pavement to the dram-shop; her teeth were gone, she had a mammy-rag tied around her head but you could still see that her wonderful hair had fallen out. Her

face would terrify the little children. He did not stop to speak
to her.

The ship embarked for Martinique.

You can buy teeth, you know; you can buy hair. They make
the best wigs from the shorn locks of novices in convents.

The man who called himself her brother, perhaps they *did*
have the same mother, why not? She hadn't the faintest idea
what had happened to her mother and this hypothetical, high-
yellow, demi-sibling popped up in the nick of time to take
over her disordered finances with the skill of a born
entrepreneur – he might have been Mephistopheles, for all
she cared. Her brother. They'd salted away what the poet
managed to smuggle to her, all the time he was dying, when
his mother wasn't looking. Fifty francs for Jeanne, here; thirty
francs for Jeanne, there. It all added up.

She was surprised to find out how much she was worth.

Add to this the sale of a manuscript or two, the ones
she hadn't used to light her cheroots with. Some books,
especially the ones with the flowery dedications. Sale of cuff-
links and drawerful upon drawerful of pink kid gloves, hardly
used. Her brother knew where to get rid of them. Later, any
memorabilia of the poet, even his clumsy drawings, would
fetch a surprising sum. They left a portfolio with an
enterprising agent.

In a new dress of black tussore, her somewhat savaged
but carefully repaired face partially concealed by a flattering
veil, she chugged away from Europe on a steamer bound
for the Caribbean like a respectable widow and she was not
yet fifty, after all. She might have been the Creole wife of a
minor civil servant setting off home after his death. Her
brother went first, to look out the property they were going
to buy.

Her voyage was interrupted by no albatrosses. She never
thought of the slavers' route, unless it was to compare her
grandmother's crossing with her own, comfortable one. You
could say that Jeanne had found herself; she had come down

to earth, and, with the aid of her ivory cane, she walked perfectly well upon it. The sea air did her good. She decided to give up rum, except for a single tot last thing at night, after the accounts were completed.

See her, now, in her declining years, every morning in decent black, leaning a little on her stick but stately as only one who has snatched herself from the lion's mouth can be. She leaves the charming house, with its vine-covered veranda; 'Good morning, Mme Duval!' sings out the obsequious gardener. How sweet it sounds. She is taking last night's takings to the bank. 'Thank you so much, Mme Duval.' As soon as she had got her first taste of it, she became a glutton for deference.

Until at last, in extreme old age, she succumbs to the ache in her bones and a cortège of grieving girls takes her to the churchyard, she will continue to dispense, to the most privileged of the colonial administration, at a not excessive price, the veritable, the authentic, the true Baudelairean syphilis.

The lines of page 9 are translated from:

SED NON SATIATA

Bizarre déité, brune comme les nuits,
Au parfum mélangé de musc et de havane,
Oeuvre de quelque obi, le Faust de la savane,
Sorcière au flanc d'ébène, enfant des noirs minuits,

Je préfère au constance, à l'opium, au nuits,
L'élixir de ta bouche où l'amour se pavane;
Quand vers toi mes ésirs partent en caravane,
Tes yeux sont la citerne où boivent mes ennuis.

Par ces deux grands yeux noirs, soupiraux de ton âme,
Ô démon sans pitié! verse-moi moins de flamme;
Je ne suis pas le Styx pour t'embrasser neuf fois,

Hélas! et je ne puis, Mégère libertine,
Pour briser ton courage et te mettre aux abois,
Dans l'enfer de ton lit devenir. Prosperpine!

Les Fleurs du Mal, Charles Baudelaire

ZORA NEALE HURSTON

Zora Neale Hurston (c.1891–1960) was born in Eatonville, Florida, the first incorporated black town in America. The nine secure years she spent there ended when her mother died and her father remarried. She characterised her life from then on as 'a series of wanderings' – occasional work, intermittent schooling, time as a wardrobe assistant with a travelling theatre troupe – until she enrolled at Baltimore's Morgan Academy. Moving to Washington D.C. in 1918, she became a part-time student at Howard University and began to write. She also earned a scholarship to Barnard College, where she studied Cultural Anthropology under Franz Boas. Her collection of tales, songs, games and voodoo practices was published in *Mules and Men* (1935). Her first novel about black life, *Jonah's Gourd Vine* (1934), was followed by the acclaimed *Their Eyes Were Watching God* (1937). Her standing as the most accomplished figure in Afro-American letters in the 1930s has endured as a new generation of black women writers, Alice Walker and Toni Morrison among them, have acknowledged their debt to her work.

AH ALWAYS DID WANT TUH GIT ROUND

from *Their Eyes Were Watching God*

It was after the picnic that the town began to notice things and got mad. Tea Cake and Mrs Mayor Starks! All the men that she could get, and fooling with somebody like Tea Cake! Another thing, Joe Starks hadn't been dead but nine months and here she goes sashaying off to a picnic in pink linen. Done quit attending church, like she used to. Gone off to Sanford in a car with Tea Cake and her all dressed in blue! It was a shame. Done took to high-heel slippers and a 10 dollar hat! Looking like some young girl, always in blue because Tea Cake told her to wear it. Poor Joe Starks. Bet he turns over in his grave every day. Tea Cake and Janie gone hunting. Tea Cake and Janie gone fishing. Tea Cake and Janie gone to Orlando to the movies. Tea Cake and Janie gone to a dance. Tea Cake making flowerbeds in Janie's yard and seeding the garden for her. Chopping down that tree she never did like by the dining-room window. All those signs of possession. Tea Cake in a borrowed car teaching Janie to drive. Tea Cake and Janie playing checkers; playing coon-can; playing Florida flip on the store porch all afternoon as if nobody else was there. Day after day and week after week.

'Pheoby,' Sam Watson said one night as he got in the bed. 'Ah b'lieve yo' buddy is all tied up with dat Tea Cake shonough. Didn't b'lieve it at first.'

'Aw she don't mean nothin' by it. Ah think she's sort of stuck on dat undertaker up at Sanford.'

'It's somebody 'cause she looks mighty good dese days. New dresses and her hair combed a different way nearly every day. You got to have something to comb hair over. When you see uh woman doin' so much rakin' in her head, she's combin' at some man or 'nother.'

''Course she kin do as she please, but dat's uh good chance she got up at Sanford. De man's wife died and he got uh lovely place tuh take her to – already furnished. Better'n her house Joe left her.'

'You better sense her intuh things then 'cause Tea Cake can't do nothin' but help her spend whut she got. Ah reckon dat's whut he's after. Throwin' away whut Joe Starks worked hard tuh git tuhgether.'

'Dat's de way it looks. Still and all, she's her own woman. She oughta know by now whut she wants tuh do.'

'De men wuz talkin' 'bout it in de grove tuhday and givin' her and Tea Cake both de devil. Dey figger he's spendin' on her now in order tuh make her spend on him later.'

'Umph! Umph! Umph!'

'Oh dey got it all figgered out. Maybe it ain't as bad as they say, but they talk it and make it sound real bad on her part.'

'Dat's jealousy and malice. Some uh dem very mens wants tuh do whut dey claim deys skeered Tea Cake is doin'.'

'De pastor claim Tea Cake don't 'low her tuh come tuh church only once in a while 'cause he want dat change tuh buy gas wid. Just draggin' de woman away from church. But anyhow, she's yo' bosom friend, so you better go see 'bout her. Drop uh lil hint here and dere and if Tea Cake is tryin' tuh rob her she kin see and know. Ah laks de woman and Ah sho would hate tuh see her come up lak Mis' Tyler.'

'Aw mah God, naw! Reckon Ah better step over dere tomorrow, and have some chat wid Janie. She jus' ain't thinkin' whut she doin', dat's all.'

The next morning Pheoby picked her way over to Janie's house like a hen to a neighbour's garden. Stopped and talked a little with everyone she met, turned aside momentarily to pause at a porch or two – going straight by walking crooked. So her firm intention looked like an accident and she didn't have to give her opinion to folks along the way.

Janie acted glad to see her and after a while Pheoby broached her with, 'Janie, everybody's talkin' 'bout how dat Tea Cake is draggin' you round tuh places you ain't used tuh. Baseball games and huntin' and fishin'. He don't know you'se useter uh more high time crowd than dat. You always did class off.'

'Jody classed me off. Ah didn't. Naw, Pheoby, Tea Cake ain't draggin' me off nowhere Ah don't want tuh go. Ah always did want tuh git round uh whole heap, but Jody wouldn't 'low me tuh. When Ah wasn't in de store he wanted me tuh jes sit wid folded hands and sit dere. And Ah'd sit dere wid de walls creepin' up on me and squeezin' all de life outa me. Pheoby, dese educated women got uh heap of things to sit down and consider. Somebody done tole 'em what to set down for. Nobody ain't told poor me, so sittin' still worries me. Ah wants tuh utilise mahself all over.'

'But, Janie, Tea Cake, whilst he ain't no jail-bird, he ain't got uh dime tuh cry. Ain't you skeered he's jes after yo' money – him bein' younger than you?'

'He ain't never ast de first penny from me yet, and if he love property he ain't no different from all de rest of us. All dese ole men dat's settin' round me is after de same thing. They's three mo' widder women in town, how come dey don't break dey neck after dem? 'Cause dey ain't got nothin', dat's why.'

'Folks seen you out in colours and dey thinks you ain't payin' de right amount uh respect tuh yo' dead husband.'

'Ah ain't grievin' so why do Ah hafta mourn? Tea Cake love me in blue, so Ah wears it. Jody ain't never in his life picked out no colour for me. De world picked out black and white for mournin', Joe didn't. So Ah wasn't wearin' it for him. Ah was wearin' it for de rest of y'all.'

'But anyhow, watch yo'self, Janie, and don't be took advantage of. You know how dese young men is wid older women. Most of de time dey's after whut dey kin git, then dey's gone lak uh turkey through de corn.'

'Tea Cake don't talk dat way. He's aimin' tuh make hisself permanent wid me. We done made up our mind tuh marry.'

'Janie, you'se yo' own woman, and Ah hope you know whut you doin'. Ah sho hope you ain't lak uh possum – de older you gits, de less sense yuh got. Ah'd feel uh whole heap better 'bout yuh if you wuz marryin' dat man up dere in Sanford. He got somethin' tuh put long side uh whut you got and dat make it more better. He's endurable.'

'Still and all Ah'd ruther be wid Tea Cake.'

'Well, if yo' mind is already made up, 'tain't nothin' nobody kin do. But you'se takin' uh awful chance.'

'No mo' than Ah took befo' and no mo' than anybody else takes when dey gits married. It always changes folks, and sometimes it brings out dirt and meanness dat even de person didn't know they had in 'em theyselves. You know dat. Maybe Tea Cake might turn out lak dat. Maybe not. Anyhow Ah'm ready and willin' tuh try 'im.'

'Well, when you aim tuh step off?'

'Dat we don't know. De store is got tuh be sold and then we'se goin' off somewhere tuh git married.'

'How come you sellin' out de store?''

''Cause Tea Cake ain't no Jody Starks, and if he tried tuh be, it would be uh complete flommuck. But de minute Ah marries 'im everybody is gointuh be makin' comparisons. So us is goin' off somewhere and start all over in Tea Cake's way. Dis ain't no business proposition, and no race after property and titles. Dis is uh love game. Ah done lived Grandma's way, now Ah means tuh live mine.'

'What you mean by dat, Janie?'

'She was borned in slavery time when folks, dat is black folks, didn't sit down anytime dey felt lak it. So sittin' on porches lak de white madam looked lak uh mighty fine thing tuh her. Dat's whut she wanted for me – don't keer whut its cost. Git up on uh high chair and sit dere. She didn't have time tuh think whut tuh do after you got up on de stool uh do nothin'. De object wuz tuh git dere. So Ah got up on de high stool lak she told me, but Pheoby, Ah done nearly languished tuh death up dere. Ah felt like de world wuz cryin' extry and Ah ain't read de common news yet.'

'Maybe so, Janie. Still and all Ah'd love tuh experience it for just one year. It look lak heben tuh me from where Ah'm at.'

'Ah reckon so.'

'But anyhow, Janie, you be keerful 'bout dis sellin' out and goin' off wid strange men. Look whut happened tuh Annie Tyler. Took whut little she had and went off tuh Tampa wid dat boy dey call Who Flung. It's somethin' tuh think about.'

'It sho is. Still Ah ain't Mis' Tyler and Tea Cake ain't no Who Flung, and he ain't no stranger tuh me. We'se just as good as married already. But Ah ain't puttin' it in de street. Ah'm tellin' *you*.'

'Ah jus lak uh chicken. Chicken drink water, but he don't pee-pee.'

'Oh, Ah know you don't talk. We ain't shame faced. We jus' ain't ready tuh make no big kerflommuck as yet.'

'You doin' right not tuh talk it, but Janie, you'se takin' uh mighty big chance.'

''Tain't so big uh chance as it seem lak, Pheoby. Ah'm older than Tea Cake, yes. But he done showed me where it's de thought dat makes de difference in ages. If people thinks de same they can make it all right. So in the beginnin' new thoughts had tuh be thought and new words said. After Ah got used tuh dat, we gits 'long jus' fine. He done taught me de maiden language all over. Wait till you see de new blue satin Tea Cake done picked out for me tuh stand up wid him in. High heel slippers, necklace, earrings, *everything* he wants tuh see me in. Some of dese mornin's and it won't be long, you gointuh wake up callin' me and Ah'll be gone.'

DOÑA CATALINA
DE ERAUSO

Catalina de Erauso spent her childhood locked in a convent, became a nun at fifteen and then fled, disguised as a soldier of fortune, adventurer and traveller. Under various names and disguises she was renowned for her valour, daring and capricious aggression. Today she would be called a serial killer. Her story, written by herself, lays bare her predatory lesbianism, her fights, murders and trials in a manner so matter of fact the reader has to keep remembering that this is the journal of an aristocratic nun at the end of the sixteenth century. Having run away from the convent, she travelled in Spain for three years dressed as a boy before embarking for America where she spent the next twenty years. Her own manuscript ends in c.1626 in Naples. However, in 1630 she was in Seville and in 1645 she was accompanied from Veracruz to Mexico by a priest together with her 'train of mules and the black slaves she owned and trafficked in, dressed as a man and calling herself Don Antonio de Erauso'. It is supposed that she died in Mexico where she had become as notorious as she was in Spain.

STORY OF THE NUN LIEUTENANT

from *Historia de la Monja Alferez*

I, Doña Catalina de Erauso, was born in the town of San Sebastian de Guipuzloa, in the year 1585: daughter of captain Don Miguel de Erauso and of Doña Maria Perez de Galarraga y Arce, both born in, and residents of, that town. My parents brought me up in their house with my brothers and sisters 'til the age of four. In 1589, they put me in the Dominican convent of San Sebastian el Antiguo in the above town, where my aunt Doña Ursula de Unza y Sarasti, my mother's cousin, was abbess of that convent. I was there until the age of fifteen when it was time for my ordination. Close to the end of my novitiate year I had a fight with an 'ordained' nun called Doña Catalina de Alirr, who entered the convent as a widow and took her vows. She was strong and I was a young girl and she used to hit me, which I resented. On the night of 18 March 1600, the day before the festival of St Joseph, everybody got up in the middle of the night for prayers. I went into the choir and found my aunt kneeling; she called me over and gave me the keys to her cell, asking me to bring the Breviary. When I went to fetch it I saw the convent keys hanging from a nail: I left the cell and gave my aunt the key and the Breviary. With all the nuns in the choir and the matins in progress, during the first part of prayers I asked my aunt for permission to leave because I did not feel well. My aunt, touching my head with her hand, said, 'go on, go to bed'. I left the choir, stole a pair of scissors, and a needle and thread, some money that was there, and the convent keys and left. I opened each door and closed it after me; at the last one, the one to the street, I left my escapulary and went outside, not having seen it or knowing which way or where to go; I do not know in which direction I went, but I ended up in a chestnut grove close to the back of the convent, and stayed there. I remained three days in the grove, designing, cutting and fitting something to wear.

From a blue woollen skirt I cut and made a pair of trousers; from a green underskirt I had I made a top and leggings; I had abandoned the habit there, since I did not know what to do with it. I cut my hair and scattered it. On the third night, I left, I knew not whither, through roads and various places to get far away (from the convent) and ended up in Victoria, which is nearly twenty leagues from San Sebastian, walking, tired, and having eaten only the herbs I found on the way.

On arrival in Victoria I was at a loss as to where to go; a few days later I found Doctor Francisco de Gerralta a professor there; who took me in readily without knowing me, and fitted me out: he was married to my mother's cousin, as I later discovered, but I didn't say who I was. I was with him about three months, during which, seeing that I read Latin well, he favoured me and wanted me to study; when I refused he laid hands on me in his anger. Consequently I determined to leave him which I did thus: I stole some money from him and made a deal with a carter who was leaving for Valladolid to take me with him for the sum of twelve reales; I left with him and travelled forty-five leagues.

Entering Valladolid where the Court was then held, I found a position as a page of D. Juan de Idiaquez, the king's secretary, who clothed me. And there I was, calling myself Francisco Loyola, established seven months. At the end of the seven months, one night when I was at the door with another page, my father arrived and asked us if Señor D. Juan was at home. My colleague answered 'yes'; the other page went upstairs, I remained with my father without uttering a word or being recognised. The page came back telling him to go upstairs, and up he went, with me after him. Don Juan came out to the stairs, hugged him and said, 'Captain! What a welcome visit this is!' My father spoke in such a way that D. Juan knew he was upset; he went in and took his leave of a visitor whom he had been with, and came back. Sitting down he asked my father what news he had and my father told him how his young daughter had escaped from the convent and how he was now searching for her. D. Juan was very sorry to see my father upset, also on account of his great affection for me and for the convent, founded by his family, of which he was a patron. Upon hearing the conversation and of my father's intentions, I went to my room, took my clothes and left, taking eight doubloons that I had and I spent the night at an inn. There I learned a carter was leaving for Bilbao in the morning; not knowing what to do or where to go, other than let the wind take me like a feather, I went along. After a long way, I think of forty leagues, I arrived at Bilbao where I could find neither lodgings nor comfort.

In the meantime I was bothered by some boys, who surrounded me. They upset me so that I had to pick up some stones and throw them at them. One was hurt, but I don't know how as I didn't see him; they arrested me and kept me in jail for a long month 'til he got better and I was set free, with a fine. From there I travelled to Estella de Navarra, which I believe is a distance of twenty leagues.

I went into Estella, where I was established as a page for D. Cárlos de Arellano, of the order of Santiago in whose house I served for two years, well dressed and well treated. After this time, for no reason but my whim, I left this comfortable spot and went to S. Sebastian, my homeland, ten leagues from Estella, and was there without being recognised by anybody. Smart and well-dressed, one day I attended mass in my convent, a mass in which my mother was also a communicant. I saw her looking at me without recognition. After mass some nuns called me to the choir. I pretended it was nothing to do with me and left courteously. This was in the year 1603. From there I went to the port of Pasage, a league from S. Sebastian: there I found the captain Miguel de Berroiz, leaving by ship for Sevilla. I asked him to take me with him, and we agreed on forty reales; I embarked and we left, soon reaching San Lucar.

Disembarking in San Lucar, I went to see Sevilla, staying only two days despite wanting to stay longer, before returning to San Lucar. There I found the captain Miguel de Echazarreta, from my own part of the country, in charge of a group of ships under the generalship of Don Luis Fernandez de Córdova, forming part of the armada of D. Luis Fajardo; the year was 1603. They were leaving for the Punta de Araya. I settled down as a cabinboy in the ship of Esteram Eguiño, my uncle; my mother's cousin, who today lives in S. Sebastian. We embarked and left S. Lucar on holy Monday, 1603.

I had difficulties on the way as I was new to the trade. My uncle, without knowing who I was, came to me and paid his compliments, having heard where I was from and the names I had given as those of my parents, that he didn't know, and I had some support from him. We arrived at la Punta de Araya and found there a small force fortified on land, from where they were repelled by our army. Finally we reached Cartagena de las Indias.

I started walking along the coast, having great difficulties and lacking water; on the way I found two fugitive soldiers and the three of us continued together, resolving to die rather than be taken prisoner. We had our horses, swords and firearms, and the grace of God. We continued into the mountains, ascending for more than three leagues without finding even a bite of bread there or in the other three hundred leagues we travelled, only sometimes we found water; sustained by roots, weeds and the occasional small animal. We had to kill one of our horses for dried meat, but found only bones and skin. As we travelled on, slowly, we had to do the same thing with the other horses. We came to a very cold land, so cold we were freezing. We were pleased to find two men beside a rock and greeted them, asking what they were doing there. They made no reply and when we reached them we found they were dead, frozen, mouths open as if laughing. This terrified us. We carried on and on the third night as we approached a rock one of us could no longer hold out and perished. The two of us who were left continued, and at about four o'clock the following day my companion, crying, let himself fall, unable to walk further and expired. In his pocket I found eight pesos and continued on my way, not knowing where I was going, carrying the arquebus and a piece of dried meat I had left, awaiting the same fate that had befallen my colleagues. I was afflicted, tired, my bare feet hurt. I stopped by a tree, wept, and I think for the first time, counted my rosary, commending myself to the Virgin Mary and the glorious St Joseph her husband, rested a bit then got up again and started walking. It seems as if I left the kingdom of Chile and entered that of Tucumán. I was walking the next morning, shattered by fatigue and hunger when I saw two men approaching on horseback. I didn't know whether to be joyful or fearful; not knowing if their intentions were peaceful I prepared my arquebus, though unable to hold it. They arrived and enquired as to where I was going in such a remote place.

I recognised that they were Christians and the heavens smiled on me. I told them I was lost and knew not where I was, that I was exhausted and starving and couldn't stand on my feet. They were sorry for me, dismounted and gave me what food they had. They put me on a horse and took me to a property three leagues from that place, where they said their mistress was. We arrived about five in the afternoon. The lady was of mixed race, daughter of a Spaniard and an Indian woman, a widow and a good woman. Seeing my defeated and abandoned condition she pitied me and then provided me with a comfortable bed; after a good dinner, she let me rest. The next morning she fed me well and gave me a fine cloth outfit seeing that I needed it, and treated me well, loading me with presents. She was quite well off, and had many animals, and as seemingly there were not any Spaniards in those parts she thought of me for her daughter. After eight days she invited me to stay there to run the house. I showed her I was grateful for her kindness in taking me on when I was forsaken, and offered to serve her in any way I could.

A few days later she said she wanted me to marry her daughter, who was there with her and was very black and ugly like a devil, whereas my taste had been always for handsome faces. I showed great joy at this undeserved favour, and on my knees begged her to dispose of me as she would. I served her as well as I could, dressing very well, and she gave me the run of the house and property. After two months we went to Tucumán for the wedding; for another two months there I postponed the event with different pretexts, until at last I could postpone it no longer. I took a mule and left, and they have not seen me since.

Leaving Potosí for Los Chuncos, we arrived at a town called Arzaga, inhabited by peaceful Indians, where we stayed for eight days; we took guides for the roads onwards, but still got lost. There was great confusion when fifty mules, laden with food and provisions, plunged from a cliff together with twelve men. We headed inland and found flatlands covered with an infinite number of almond, olive and fruit trees, like those of Spain. The governor wanted to sow the fields there to make up for our lack of food, but footsoldiers came and told us that our aim was not to sow but to conquer and find gold, and that food could be found. We went on, and after three days discovered a town of Indians who later armed themselves; on our arrival they felt the arquebus and fled in panic, leaving some dead. We entered the place finding not one Indian who knew the way. When we left, the field-marshal Bartolomé de Alva tired of wearing his helmet, took it off to clean his sweat, and a devil of a boy, of about twelve, who was opposite the exit in a tree threw an arrow at him which pierced his eye and unhorsed him, he died on the third day.

We made ten thousand pieces of the boy; in the meantime the Indians returned, more than ten thousand of them. We came back in such a rage, and made such a slaughter, that a stream of blood ran through the square like a river, and following it we carried on killing until we reached the Rio Dorado. Here the governor ordered us to retire, which we did only reluctantly, as in the houses of the locality they had found more than sixty thousand pesos in gold-dust. By the riverbank, others had found an infinity with which they filled their hats, and we knew later that the tides commonly left more than three fingers' thickness of gold there. For this reason many of us asked the governor's permission to conquer that land, and, for reasons that I wouldn't give if I had them, left at night. When we reached the Christian town we seized the population. I went to the province of Los Charcas with some 'realejos', which bit by bit, and in a short while I lost.

I went to La Paz, where I stayed a few days. Without a care in the world, I stopped one day at the door of Don Antonio Barraza, the chief magistrate, to speak to a servant of his, who, prompted by the Devil, accused me of telling untruths and struck my face with his hat. I drew my sword and he fell dead on the spot. Many made to attack me, and arrested me wounded, then put me in jail. There I was being simultaneously cured (of the wound he gave me) and charged (with the crime of his murder): for which the chief magistrate sentenced me to death. I appealed, but to no avail. I spent two days confessing, and the next day there was a mass in the prison and the saintly priest gave me the sacrament and returned to his altar. I at once returned the host from my mouth into the palm of my right hand, screaming, 'Church is my name, Church is my name'. There was a great mayhem and accusations of heresy: the noise brought the priest back, who ordered that nobody should approach me. The mass ended and just then Bishop Don fra Domingo de Valderrama, a Dominican, walked in with the governor. Priests and many others gathered; lights were lit, the 'palio' arrived and I was taken in procession. When we reached the altar, everyone kneeling, a priest took the host from my hand and put it in the coffer, I paid no attention as to exactly where. They then took my hand, washed it several times and rinsed it. The church emptied and the important people left, while I stayed on, and a stern warning was given to me by a Franciscan monk who had advised me in prison and finally heard my confession.

For a month the governor had the church cordoned off, with

me inside, at the end of which time the guard was removed and a local clergyman, as I guessed, sent by the bishop, checked the environs and the road before giving me a mule and some money, with which I departed for Cuzco.

WAITING FOR THE RISING OF THE WIND

BERNICE RUBENS

Bernice Rubens was born in Wales and later read English at the University of Wales where she holds an Honorary Doctorate and is a fellow. Her writing career began when she was thirty and around the same time she started work in the film industry. For some time, she alternated between writing novels and making films. For the last twenty years she has concentrated solely on writing. She has written over a dozen novels including the Booker Prize winner *The Elected Member* and *Madame Sousatzka*. Her other love, apart from writing, is playing the cello. In *Birds of Passage*, a biting comedy of manners, she cruises through a chilling backwater of suburbia with Mrs Pickering and Mrs Walsh who didn't want their husbands to die but they did want to survive them for the cruise.

ONCE DECENTLY WIDOWED

from *Birds of Passage*

A CERTAIN LACK OF SYNCHRONICITY

Neighbours. That's what they were, Ellen Walsh and Alice Pickering, with a thin wall between their sitting rooms and an even thinner one between their bedrooms on the first floor. An eavesdropping house of which both the Walshes and the Pickerings took full advantage. And had been so doing for nigh on forty years. It could fairly be said that they knew each other pretty well, in the private as well as the public domain. Sometimes they confused those facts that were officially known with the information they had gleaned from bricks-and-mortar echo. But, since the pursuit of eavesdropping was common to both sides, each overlooked the others' indiscretion. In all respects, they were good neighbours, and what sealed their togetherness was the hedge that joined their two terraced estates. It stretched from the Walshes' front gate to the Pickerings' with no outward sign of hesitation at its centre as to a change of ownership. It was straight as a die from one holding to the other. Every Saturday morning, Mr Walsh would stand at his gate, shears at the ready. And Mr Pickering likewise. The two men would nod to each other, and silently shear their way to a central encounter. They worked at the same efficient pace, arriving simultaneously at the halfway point, where they would pause and exchange morning greetings. And when one day, late in the spring, their other neighbours noted that the Walsh hedge was growing untamed, towering over the Pickering holding with a certain helpless impudence, they took it as a sure sign that Mr Walsh was indisposed. But it was more than that, as further enquiries and certain visible evidence proved. Mr Walsh had gone to his Maker, and his holding in the hedge was orphaned.

Now, Mr Pickering had never coveted his neighbour's wife, even when Mr Walsh was alive and shearing; now that he was dead, he coveted her even less. Even so, to shear his late neighbour's portion would, in his mind, have been tantamount to a delayed and public adultery. So he refrained, much as their common frontage now displeased him. He would have to wait until Mrs Walsh herself invited him to husband her hedge. But Mrs Walsh issued no such invitation. As the hedge grew, shadowing her sitting room and the mourning within, she harboured a deep resentment of Mr Pickering simply because he was still alive. She didn't care how high her hedge grew, or how untidily. It would be a constant reminder to Pickering that he had outstayed his welcome. Let him depart as her Walsh had done, and let Alice's hedge reach for the skies like her own. For, over a year ago, she and Alice had made plans as to how to disport themselves together once decently widowed. Now, with Pickering's survival, those plans would have to be delayed. Nowadays she could hardly acknowledge him, and the poor and innocent Pickering ascribed her rudeness to her bereavement.

It had been their custom, on New Year's Eve of every year, to celebrate in each other's houses, each taking the rites in turn. In the beginning, when both families were new to the street, their children had gathered together and listened to the bells on the wireless. Later it was television, but, by that time, the children had married and left home. A year ago, the celebrations were conducted in the Walsh house, in the days when the hedge did not trellis the windows and all was reasonably well between the paper-thin walls. They had a roast beef supper, Mrs Walsh's speciality – Mrs Pickering went in for roast lamb. The champagne stood on the sideboard awaiting the midnight bell. At the stroke of twelve, according to the television, Mr Walsh aimed the cork at the floor and filled their glasses. Their eyes watered, a prelude to nostalgia, and the neighbours linked arms, and along with their television hosts, they sang 'Auld Lang Syne'. That done, Mr Pickering kissed his spouse, and Mr Walsh likewise. Then the ladies clasped each other tenderly, while the men waited on the sidelines in deference to that law which endorses the male embrace only after a goal scored in a football match. Then Mr Pickering would kiss Mrs Walsh on her cheek, and Mr Walsh would do his New Year's duty by his neighbour's wife. Then together they would reminisce, with laughter, longing and infinite sentimentality. To recall the past, the first meetings, marriage, the birth of children was a reliable defence against the corroding boredom of familiarity. On each New Year's Eve, the recollections of loving, of the youth and beauty of the past, diluted the present reality of the whispering behind walls, the sobbing at bedtime and the morning rage. It would see them through another year. Thus formalities were observed and, after their journeys into the past, the gentlemen would watch television, while the ladies cleared the table.

On their last celebration, Ellen and Alice had not rejoined their spouses. They had remained in the kitchen. Ellen sat at the table and poured the freshly brewed tea. Alice sat beside her. It had seemed quite natural to both women that there was a need to be with each other for a while, a mutual recognition, perhaps, in view of all their talk of the past, that the future was diminishing. Walsh's asthma was worsening and Pickering's ulcers were no better. It did not occur to either woman that their husbands would survive them. It was time to think of their approaching widowhood.

Ellen looked across at her friend. She noticed how Alice was fingering the cloth of her dress, rubbing the material between her fingers, smoothing it on to her flesh. She's getting old, Ellen thought, and then noticed that she was doing exactly the same herself. And Alice looked at her friend and thought that, though they were more or less the same age, Ellen was wearing less well.

Alice sipped her tea. 'Ellen,' she said, and she laid her hand on her friend's arm. She picked a tuck of the sleeve and rubbed it between her fingers.

'What is it, Alice?' Ellen said and found her own fingers straying to a pleat on Alice's skirt. To finger one's own clothes is to test one's mortality. To finger the clothes of others is to acknowledge that that mortality is shared. It was a moment of deepest intimacy. It was a moment to suggest a cruise.

Which Alice did. 'When we're both widowed,' she added.

'Oh that will be fun,' Ellen said, then clapped her mouth on the blasphemy lest the fun was heard to refer to her husband's demise. But she had to admit to herself that widowhood would indeed be a diversion; that already, on each successive New Year, it was more difficult to recollect the joys of the past, filtered as they were by the passionless present. Indeed she could hardly remember them at all. Yet they must have been, those glad days, since her Walsh seemed to recall them with ease. Or did he too invoke them only as a principle? She didn't want him to die, but she wanted to survive him. She wanted a little time without him, a chance to come into her own. She would not have been surprised to know that Alice's thoughts dwelt on the same lines.

'We must be decently widowed,' Ellen said, and 'decent' referred to time. Time to let the grass grow, time to dry out the tears, time to exhaust others' sympathy and patience.

Thus they had come to an agreement, and it did not occur to either of them that their achievement of widowhood might not be simultaneous. As it turned out, synchronicity did not oblige. Mr Walsh had departed in the following spring, leaving Ellen widowed and Alice still pinned to her wifehood.

On the following New Year's Eve, Ellen had gone to the Pickerings alone. It was an irritable evening. A quartet is not adaptable to trio-playing any more than 'Auld Lang Syne' is orchestrated for one. Mr Pickering was embarrassed, Ellen ashamed, Alice tetchy. Mr Walsh's demise had thrown out the arrangement of her supper table. For a moment she wished that by next year her friend would have married again, but then quickly withdrew that wish, in fear or hope of her own widowhood, and a further postponement of their cruise.

By the spring of that year Ellen had already served her 'decent' year, while Mr Pickering still flourished. And, moreover, showed no signs of wilting. His hedge-holding, clipped to a leaf's-breadth, was infuriating proof of his stubborn survival, and the foliage that now shrouded her windows served only to darken the already black rage in Ellen's heart.

Each time Alice saw her friend, she felt she had to apologise for her continuing wedlock. Occasionally she offered Ellen a little hope, though her spirit balked at the treachery. 'His ulcers are very bad today,' she would say; and when Ellen did not sufficiently react, she would specify her prognosis: 'I don't know how much longer he can go on,' and, as she said it, she resented Ellen for her unspoken demands on her own disloyalty. Ellen was really a bit of a bully, Alice thought, and Alice would return to her kitchen and seethe. 'It's not my fault she lost her husband,' she would mutter, 'and it's not my fault that I kept mine.' She dreaded their next New Year's gathering.

It was Ellen's turn. The roast beef era had passed, along with its carver. Ellen did a strogonoff from a recipe she'd heard on the wireless. It was foreign and would make an impression not only on her neighbours but on Mr Thomas, a newcomer. The Pickerings were much unnerved by his presence. Especially Alice. Was her friend on the point of marrying again? Thomas was a robust-looking man and, from his large appetite, clearly without ulcers, and threatened yet again the simultaneity of their joint widowhood. The prospect of the cruise was considerably dimmed. That year it was Mr Thomas who popped the champagne as they raised their glasses to the television choir. But they did not sing. Mr Pickering hummed a little for old times' sake, but Thomas was an outsider, who was not allowed to sing their tune. Ellen avoided the kitchen-chat after supper and the evening broke up early. Alice took the unasked question into her own sitting room.

'Who was that Mr Thomas?' she said. 'I've never seen him before.'

Mr Pickering was unhelpful, and then, as an afterthought, without any notion of its relevance, he said, 'I do wish she'd get that hedge cut.'

For relevant it was, because Mr Thomas had made his first appearance on Mrs Walsh's doorstep with the request that he might clip her hedge. Mrs Walsh was astonished. She felt assaulted, as if the stranger were making a certain suggestion, a proposition perhaps, for which the hedge-clipping was only a cover. Over the years since her husband's demise, the green foliage had seemed to corset her, to straitjacket her body into a repaired virginity. She had grown intact, as it were. Which was why she was glad Pickering had never touched her hedge. And now this stranger was on her doorstep with his suggestion, and, in Ellen's mind, it was a request to bed her. She looked at him hard, and found him not unattractive. She decided the hedge would remain intact. He would have to marry her before he deflowered it.

After that New Year's Eve, the Pickerings were accustomed to seeing Mr Thomas, who was now a daily gentleman caller. Ellen kept their wedding very quiet, so Mr Pickering was astonished, to say the least, when, one Saturday morning, as was his wont, he took up his hedge-post and saw, through the jungle of foliage, a very positive human shape on the other end. And heard the unmistakable clipping of shears.

Ellen Walsh looked through her net curtains, shuddering with each thrust of the blade, and, like a bride, she thrilled to a second coming. She now belonged to Thomas as legally as she had once belonged to Walsh.

Alice Pickering, whose head had been shamefully bowed since Mr Walsh's passing, now lifted it, and felt a lot less guilty. She no longer apologised for her husband's survival and, when she did refer to his ulcers, it was with confidence and no shame that they were getting better. She rather looked forward to their next New Year's celebration.

But poor Thomas never made it. Robust as he was, and ulcerless, it is possible that he died simply of his rude sound health, too rude, and too sound perhaps, for his own good.

Whatever, one Saturday morning, on reaching for his shears, while Ellen waited at the net-curtained window, he collapsed and cheated her. She couldn't understand it. No one could. It was his heart, the doctor said, but Ellen didn't believe him. There was nothing wrong with Thomas's heart. Some people survived, she decided, with a terrible glance in Pickering's direction, and others simply died. Her Thomas had died of death, and that was all there was to it.

Her neighbours watched the hedge grow once more, and wondered what on earth it was that Ellen Walsh did to her men. Ellen Walsh she still was to them. They hadn't yet grasped the Thomas handle in her connection, and now it was hardly worth their pains. The hedge grew and grew, shrouding Ellen's windows once more. Poor Alice. She could hardly make a public appearance, so ashamed was she of Pickering's survival.

That year, they celebrated New Year's Eve not at all. Ellen went to her daughter up north, and the Pickerings watched television on their own. That year Mr Pickering didn't even hum 'Auld Lang Syne'. It never worked without the presence of a third party, single or otherwise. It was silly singing it just to Alice. It would have embarrassed them both.

When Ellen came back shortly after the New Year, the hedge had grown with a vengeance, and she was obliged to keep the light on in her living room during the daylight hours. But not again, she decided. Not another hedge-cutter. She would let it grow, curl around her rooftops, and shroud her in its evergreen balm. And she would wallow within it, waiting for old Pickering to die.

She had no intention of serving a 'decent' year for Thomas. There was hardly any point in mourning a man for longer than you had known him. As soon as Pickering popped off, she would persuade Alice to curtail her 'decent' year. It was the least Alice could do. Nowadays Ellen could hardly look at Pickering, and Alice had become her apologetic worst. Pickering's ulcers were no better, and she understood less and less, at each meeting, how he managed to survive at all.

Sometimes Alice looked at her husband and the thought

occurred to her that she might not even outlive him, that he and Ellen were the great survivors, and that it would be she who would earn the 'decent' year, and Ellen and Pickering the cruise. Then she began to dislike Ellen and she kept herself indoors for a long time.

It was during this period when Ellen saw little of her friend that, one Saturday morning, the clipping did not awaken her. She opened her eyes to mid-morning on the clock, and dashed out of bed to the window. The usual flat-sheared edge of the Pickering hedge was rudely unbalanced by a week's growth. No tell-tale clippings lay on the path, and hope surged in Ellen's heart. She put her ear to the common wall between, and the silence from that direction fed her hopes. Illness was never silent. A groan, a whisper or a scream were tokens of pain or indisposition. Even resignation merited a sigh. But that quality of silence from behind the wall, the silence without echo, the silence of footsteps that were never taken, of sighs that stayed in the throat – that silence was reserved for Death alone.

She dressed and knocked on Alice's door. Alice opened it almost immediately, and the two women stared at each other for a long while.

'Yes,' Alice said at last, and Ellen followed her into the house.

They sat at the kitchen table. A lone tear dropped from Alice's eye. 'I think there's something about that hedge,' she said. 'It's got the devil in it.'

'What happened?' Ellen said, after a pause.

'He collapsed. Just fell down on the hall floor. The shears were in his hand. A heart attack, the doctor said.'

He died of hedge, Ellen thought, like the rest of them. 'Let's cut it down,' she said suddenly. 'Let's poison the roots of it.'

Alice smiled. She was thinking of the cruise, and she crushed Ellen's apron between her fingers. Ellen did likewise with Alice's shawl. It was a moment of forgiveness, a mutual pardon for the curses that each woman in her time had laid on the other.

'Can I see him?' Ellen said. Alice had offered to see her Walsh, and she felt bound to do the same duty by Pickering.

She followed her up the stairs. Pickering lay in that silence that Ellen had heard through the wall. He looked deeply ashamed and Ellen was suddenly very sorry for him. He was entitled to a 'decent' year, she thought, and as if Alice was reading her, she said, 'We'll take our cruise in the spring.'

They clasped each other and wept together, both for the losses of the past and the possible joys of the future.

After the funeral, an odd-job man came and poisoned the hedge on both sides. Its demise was slow and possibly painful, for it took some months to die, and it was almost spring before it shed its last offended branch. And then, astonished at the sudden light, the daffodils and irises stretched their necks to view the unaccustomed street and the figures of two women of a certain age, arm in arm, suitcases at their feet, waiting for the taxi to pull into the kerb. Between them they added up to the total of 126 years, though neither would admit to the sum of her own share. One lies about one's age only when one is not proud of it. A little girl will boast her calendar as proof of her growth; an old woman will trumpet her years in pride of her survival. Ellen Walsh and Alice Pickering dwelt in that no man's land between, a land that idled between the reachable borders of innocence.

As they settled themselves in the back of the taxi, Alice said, 'Pickering would have loved a cruise.' And Ellen felt obliged to offer a similar token of regret, though she was undecided as to the target. Thomas would have been more fun, but Walsh was more worthy, simply because he had served longer. 'So would Walsh,' she said.

It was a formality, for both women knew that their pursuit was never considered a coupled one. It belonged to widowhood, a status in which both women, after a series of unfortunate ill-timings, were now amply qualified.

ROSETTA LOY

Rosetta Loy, an Italian novelist, was born in Rome in 1931. Much of her writing focuses on the years she spent growing up during the war and spending the holidays in the old Piedmontese family house which inspired *The Dust Roads of Monferrato*, her best known work. First published in 1987, it won literary prizes in Italy and has been widely translated. In it, Loy describes the lives of a family of farmers in nineteenth-century northern Italy.

DANCING BEFORE IT'S TOO LATE

from *The Dust Roads of Monferrato*

For a long time, that summer, the object of their jokes was Bastianina. Tall, built like Sacarlott, Bastianina seemed born to be an abbess. And she felt she was an abbess, even though she was a mere novice and the nuns constantly sent her back to the family, to 'test her vocation'.

As the cart with the young novice turned, swaying, into the driveway, everyone was impelled by a sudden need to do some job and only Gonda remained on her chair in the sun as Bastianina's voice was raised, loud, to call everyone to come for her numerous and cumbersome cases. And her face, framed by the veil, pretty perhaps, was turned solemnly, like that of an heir to the throne.

Bastianina, impassive at the announcement of a hailstorm or a lightning bolt that sets a haystack afire. Not even seeing a rabbit's throat slit causes her the slightest shudder; but the moment she hears the sound of an organ or breathes the smell of incense, she flings back her veil with a burst of pride, radiant, freeing her round girlish cheeks. She doesn't like the *Messa prima*, the opalescence of dawn and the cold church; she is for the *Messa granda*, the pomp of the bells, the glittering copes, the altarboys dressed in red. The throb of the organ pipes.

She gives orders, checks, organises, from her broad mouth,

always moist with saliva, comes a delicate and hoarse voice where the purest Italian vibrates like the metallic strings of some toy guitars. No one understands, but they are forced to understand. The inflexible, piercing eyes, a speckled grey, set brains in motion, forcing them to decipher what seems impossible. So she is obeyed. Not infrequently with the most sensational errors.

No one knows if she ever grasped, even once, her brothers' irony. No one ever noticed any sign, not even a darkening of her gaze when they would make her repeat certain expressions over and over. She submitted to their jokes and their feigned stupidity, not deigning to give them a moment's attention. *Fratelli, porcelli*, she used to say: brothers, piglets; and in the evening they heard her reciting the *Officio* in a falsetto voice. From her room the notes crept out, arrogant, implacable in their monotony: they reminded that penance must be done for sins, that God's punishment is prompt to strike the wicked, and where his justice arrives, there weeping and gnashing of teeth will be heard. The closer she came to the final part, the more feverish and shrill her voice grew. Until, in the darkness of the looming night, it became something like the howl of an animal.

She was rich, nobody in the family had the ready money she had. Everything that Fantina had earned and still earned was earmarked for Bastianina's dowry, her trousseau, the habits of the novice who would one day be abbess. And instead of helping her mother in the house she sat in the living room, painting at a monumental easel, which required half a day just to set up, plus strong arms to raise and lower the wooden pieces, turn them in the right position for the sun as the clogs of the farm-hands echoed shyly over the waxed floor.

She painted aquatic birds for the most part: cranes, geese, herons standing on one leg in the water. She loved to copy tropical fauna from the illustrations of a book that had belonged to Gioacchino, and against the great leaves of the banana palms and the tangle of lianas she set her swans in profile, the eye outlined in black. Once finished, the pictures were wrapped in great lengths of white canvas and no one was to touch them, as they were ready to travel with her, to be dispersed later among various convents of the realm. Some would perhaps navigate, with billowing sails, towards the islands; and one, the most beautiful, with a life-size swan, would perhaps reach Rome, not far from the Pope.

The brothers were rarely granted access to the room: their shadow was irksome on the canvas, and their voices disturbed the serenity of the mind. At times they appeared beyond the window among the pear trees and apples of the garden, and Luìs would doff his hat. Gavriel would deferentially bow his head to the young novice seated at the easel. With her palette supported by her thumb, an ample smock over her habit, Bastianina looked at them without seeing them, her lips pursed into a pink cherry, to ask for silence. At times, lost in awed contemplation, Fantina would sit beside her. And she, who had embroidered copes now legendary, allowed sighs of admiration to escape her, contemplating those canvases painted with broad layers of colour, strong hues without nuance, few shadows.

Bastianina cannot recall a summer this hot, and, motionless, she waits for a cool bit of shade; a shiver of wind on her face and neck. She yawns, and is so sleepy she cannot even hold the brush in her hand. Then she stands up and asks Fantina to accompany her to the sulphur spring that cures intestinal ailments, hot flushes. And once there, she takes off her shoes and stockings, rolls up her skirt and steps into the pool of clear water enclosed in a circle of trees and from there she calls to her aunt: 'Come in, *Magna*!' she says to her. 'Aunt! You come in, too!'

Fantina shakes her head; she has sat down on the bank in the shade of a locust and she tells how, when she was a girl, a water snake once seized her ankle, coiled around it, slapping its tail against her legs, and Maria had to pull it away with her bare hands, and afterwards they ran off, forgetting their clothes. Ever since then neither of them has gone bathing, and to this day she is afraid even to drink that water where it flows from the spring.

Bastianina shrugs, in the shade of the acacia Fantina's broad face is scattered with spots, some are the leaves' shadows but others are on her skin and it seems impossible to the girl that Fantina can have been young, have had legs white and strong like hers, silvered by the flowing water that disappears into the ground. Bastianina looks at her, seated on the grass in her patched dress, her neck bloated from drinking, and an inexplicable irritation vexes her. Fantina has become stingy, for herself she would not buy so much as a button, even pennies must serve, to make Bastianina rich, the richest of all the novices. For a moment Bastianina closes her eyes, she would like to forget, she doesn't herself know what. Forget. She trickles water down her bosom, and in the silence, now that Fantina is dozing off, she thinks of Fracin's Rosetta, who will soon be married, and of Luìs, when he used to come back with his jacket all rumpled. Once he lost that jacket, he didn't know where, then Gerumin found it, and Gerumin laughed ... 'Enough,' she says, in a hoarse voice, 'I want to go home.' She wakes Fantina, she is rude, she slips her shoes on again and grumbles because now they have to walk under the sun, her dress is uncomfortable.

Fantina has risen obediently and they walk along past the parched blackberry bushes. The peasant girls have climbed on to the wagons, wearing great hats with holes in them, the oxen struggle, chasing away the flies with their tails, the children's hands and faces are seared with erysipelas. Fantina has opened an umbrella to protect herself from the sun. 'Ven chì sutta,' she says, 'Come under here', to Bastianina, who stubbornly walks on, her throat tight. The peasants doff their hats, the children look at her, intimidated. Already they call her *la Munja*, which means the Nun. Fantina responds to the greetings with a slight nod in the black shade of the umbrella, she replies for herself and for Bastianina, unperturbed in the dust raised by her long strides. In this way they cross the town and, under her veil, Bastianina's hair, soaked with sweat, sticks to her head; it itches, but she doesn't move a muscle of her face, doesn't raise a hand to scratch herself. In the square the mayor is about to get into

Signora Bocca's carriage to go to Casale and wait upon King Carlo Alberto, who is breaking his journey at the Hotel Mogol. Signora Bocca peers curiously through the yellow curtains at this novice so like Gavriel in the strength of her body. Bastianina goes past, head high, without so much as a glance; her anxiety makes her breathless at the memory of the evening when Gavriel left home amid the cries of Sacarlott. She has never learned what it was that made her father yell like that, what dark conscience drove Gavriel into the night, but she remembers that name shouted by her father like some obscenity. And in a flash she understands, she understands without understanding, in the torture of that day. Further on, she stops; Fantina is still beside the carriage, bowing to Signora Bocca, almost prostrating herself as if she were before the Blessed Sacrament. '*Magna*!' Bastianina calls. '*Magna*!' She has forgotten all her manners and her voice re-echoes in the square, from beneath the umbrella Fantina looks at her aghast, Signora Bocca leans forward between the yellow curtains. 'Magna, andumma!' she cries, 'Come on.' Only the dialect can express her desperation and her blushes blind her, she wants to cry in shame, sweating down to her thighs.

'Why don't you come dancing, at least once?' Luìs asks her. 'You could give it a try, before it's too late.'

'Dance? Me?' Bastianina puts her hand to her bosom to stay her heart.

'Yes, dance. Dance ... wouldn't you like to, at least once?'

A flash in Bastianina's eyes, the memory of the smell when, as a girl, holding her mother's hand, she crossed the square on fair days. The music and the dust. One afternoon she stood spell-bound by all that swirling and her mother couldn't drag her away. She looks at him: a novice dancing, with a veil on her head?

As if he understood the unspoken question in that gaze Luìs gently touches her veil. 'Take it off,' he says to her. Instead of flushing, she turns pale: if now, with a sudden movement, she were to slip the veil from her hair, her life could be different. Who knows how, who knows to what extent? Her legs are straight and sturdy, they seem made for dancing, the passion she puts into her painting is a force in her blood, the same as in Sacarlott's. As in the Great Masten's.

Luìs insists. 'Just this once ...' As children they played together, he was the knight wearing his father's cape, she was Saint Geneviève, besieged by wild animals, and he always came to save her, knelt beside her, stroking her long hair spread out on the floor.

'... No, no, what *tabalori*! How stupid!' What little feminine grace left her is lost in the sharp turn she makes, she will not fall into the trap, she will not end up like her mother, like Luison; she will not end up like Fantina.

That afternoon, late, Bastianina was seen walking through the fields with her long stride, her white habit standing out against the dark of the hedges, her veil, which she constantly threw back. Fantina, who had come into the living room to bring her a slice of watermelon, found a barely begun picture on the easel and the chair empty. Bastianina walked for a long time, almost submerged by the stalks of corn beginning to turn yellow, she passed through the clover wilting in that August heat and through the rye that brushed, pale, against her skirt, far from the barnyards where the peasant women were tending the silkworms. She went as far as the high road to Giarole. From Braida, where they were dancing, some people saw her, with her white veil and dress, and thought she was lost. She stopped in the shade of a mulberry: all that walking, dressed as she was, must have tired her, sweat made everything on her smell, skirt and petticoats, bodice, wimple. She was not yet twenty and she rested her back against the mulberry's trunk and stayed there a long time, looking at the dancing couples. Their distant voices reached her, and their laughter. The music of the instrument played by Zanzìa.

From Braida Luìs recognised her, too, and suddenly felt remorse for all the times he and Gavriel had made fun of her. A deep sorrow made him almost blind for a moment; he didn't want her to stay there, he wanted her to go away; but at a certain point Bastianina took off her veil because of the heat and her head, down there in the distance, was a wooden puppet's, her hair had been cut so short. Then, as a mazurka began, Luìs forgot her. When he looked down again, the distant shadow of that mulberry was already blended with the countryside, the moon was rising to light the empty high road to Giarole.

BUCHI EMECHETA

Buchi Emecheta was born in 1944 near Lagos, Nigeria where she attended school and later married. Since 1967 she has lived in London with her five children. A graduate in sociology from London University, she has been a teacher, librarian and community worker. She writes journalism, poetry, plays and for television as well as her highly acclaimed novels. *Second-Class Citizen* looks from the inside at immigrant England through the eyes of young, clever Adah who leaves prosperity in Lagos for her dream of becoming a 'been-to' – a Nigerian who has visited London. When she finally joins her husband there, she discovers that London is not the kingdom of Heaven she was brought up to believe.

DETERMINATION

from *Second-Class Citizen*

It had all begun like a dream. You know the sort of dream which seems to have originated from nowhere, yet one was always aware of its existence. One could feel it, one could be directed by it; unconsciously at first, until it became a reality, a Presence.

Adah did not know for sure what gave birth to her dream, when it all started, but the earliest anchor she could pin down in this drift of nothingness was when she was about eight years old. She was not even quite sure that she was exactly eight, because, you see, she was a girl. She was a girl who arrived when everyone was expecting and predicting a boy. So, since she was such a disappointment to her parents, to her immediate family, to her tribe, nobody thought of recording her birth. She was so insignificant. One thing was certain, though: she was born during the Second World War. She felt eight when she was being directed by her dream, for a younger child would not be capable of so many mischiefs. Thinking back on it all now that she was grown up, she was sorry for her parents. But it was their own fault; they should not have had her in the first place, and that would have saved a lot of people a lot of headaches.

Well, Adah thought she was eight at the time when her mother and all the other society women were busying themselves to welcome the very first lawyer to their town, Ibuza. Whenever Adah was told that Ibuza was her town, she found it difficult to understand. Her parents, she was told, came from Ibuza, and so did many of her aunts and uncles. Ibuza, she was told, was a beautiful town. She had been taught at an early age that the people of Ibuza were friendly, that the food there was fresh, the spring water was pure and the air was clean. The virtues of Ibuza were praised so much that Adah came to regard being born in a godforsaken place like Lagos as a misfortune. Her parents said that Lagos was a bad place, bad for bringing up children because here they picked up the Yoruba-Ngbati accent. It was bad because it was a town with laws, a town where Law ruled supreme. In Ibuza, they said, you took the law into your own hands. If a woman abused your child, you went straight into her hut, dragged her out, beat her up or got beaten up, as the case might be. So if you didn't want to be dragged out and beaten up you wouldn't abuse another woman's child. Lagos was bad because this type of behaviour was not allowed. You had to learn to control your temper, which Adah was taught was against the law of nature.

The Ibuza women who lived in Lagos were preparing for the arrival of the town's first lawyer from the United Kingdom. The title 'United Kingdom' when pronounced by Adah's father sounded so heavy, like the type of noise one associated with bombs. It was so deep, so mysterious, that Adah's father always voiced it in hushed tones, wearing such a respectful expression as if he were speaking of God's Holiest of Holies. Going to the United Kingdom must surely be like paying God a visit. The United Kingdom, then, must be like heaven.

The women of Ibuza bought identical cotton material from the UAC department store and had it made into *lappas* and blouses of the same style. They dyed their hair, and straightened it with hot combs to make it look European. Nobody in her right senses would dream of welcoming a lawyer who had come from the United Kingdom with her hair left naturally in curls. They composed songs, weaving the name of the new lawyer into them. These women were so proud of this new lawyer, because to them it meant the arrival of their very own Messiah. A Messiah specially created for the Ibuza people. A Messiah who would go into politics and fight for the rights of the people of Ibuza. A Messiah who would see to it that Ibuza would have electricity, that Ibuza would have a tarred road (which Adah's mother called 'Kol tar'). Oh, yes, Lawyer Nweze was going to do all sorts of things for the people of Ibuza.

Adah's mother was a seamstress, so she made most of the blouses. Adah was very lucky, because she had some remnants from the material made into a frock for her. She still remembered the frock; it was so big for her that she more or less swam into it. Her mother would never dream of making her a dress that was exactly her size because, you see, she would soon outgrow it. So even though she was a small girl, too skinny for her age, whatever that might be, she always had dresses three or four sizes bigger. That was one of her reasons for liking old dresses, since by the time her dresses were old, they fitted her. She was so happy with this new 'Lawyer dress' that she begged her mother to let her go with the women to the Apapa Wharf on the great day. It pained her so much when she realised that she was not going to be allowed to go because it fell on a school day.

School – the Ibos never played with that! They were realising fast that one's saviour from poverty and disease was education. Every Ibo family saw to it that their children attended school. Boys were usually given preference, though. So even though Adah was about eight, there were still discussions about whether it would be wise to send her to school. Even if she was sent to school, it was very doubtful whether it would be wise to let her stay long. 'A year or two would do, as long as she can write her name and count. Then she will learn to sew.' Adah had heard her mother say this many times to her friends. Soon, Adah's younger brother, Boy, started school.

It was at this time that Adah's dream started to nudge her. Whenever she took Boy to Ladi-Lak Institute, as the school was called, she would stand by the gate and watch all her friends lining up by the school door, in their smart navy-blue pinafores looking clean and orderly. Ladi-Lak was then, and still is, a very small preparatory school. Children were not taught Yoruba or any African language. This was why it was such an expensive school. The proprietress was trained in the United Kingdom. At that time, more than half the children in the school were Ibos, as they were then highly motivated by the middle-class values. Adah would stand there, filled with envy. The envy later gave way to frustration, which she showed in many small ways. She would lie, just for the joy of lying; she took secret joy in disobeying her mother. Because, she thought to herself: if not for Ma, Pa would have seen to it that I started school with Boy.

One afternoon, Ma was sitting on the veranda of their house in Akinwunmi Street. With Adah's help, she had cooked the afternoon meal and they had both eaten. Ma started to undo her hair, ready to have it re-plaited. Adah had seen her do this a million times and was bored with watching her. There was nothing for her to do, there was nobody to play with; there was not even any mischief to plan. Then the thought suddenly struck her. Yes, she would go to school. She would not go to Ladi-Lak, because Boy was there and they might ask her to pay, it being such an expensive school. She would go to the Methodist School round the corner. It was cheaper, her ma had said that she liked the uniform, most of her friends attended it, and Mr Cole, the Sierra Leonian neighbour living next door to them, taught there. Yes, she would go there.

Her dress was clean enough, though it was too big, but she thought of something to smarten it up. She went into their room, got an old scarf, twisted it round and round, so much so that it looked like a palm-tree climber's rope, then tied it round her little waist, pulling her baggy dress up a little. Other children went to school with slates and pencils. She had none. It would look ridiculous for her to march into a classroom without a slate and pencil. Then another thought struck her. She had always watched Pa shave: Pa had a broken slate, on which he usually sharpened a funny sort of curved knife. Adah often watched him do this, fascinated. After sharpening the knife, Pa would rub some carbolic soap lather on his chin and then would shave away. Adah thought of this slate. But the trouble was that it was so small. Just a small piece. It would not take many letters, but a small bit of slate was better than no slate at all. She then slipped it into the top of her dress, knowing full well that her scarf-belt would hold it up. Luck was with her. Before she left the room, one of Ma's innumerable friends came for a visit, and the two women were so engrossed in their chit-chat that they did not notice when Adah slipped past them.

Thus Adah went to school. She ran as fast as she could before anyone could stop her. She did not see any of Ma's friends, because it was past midday and very hot; most people were too tired to walk the streets at this time. She got tired running and she started to trot like a lame horse; tired of trotting, she walked. She was soon at the schoolroom. There were two buildings in the compound. One was the church, and she had heard from her friends that the church was never used as a classroom. She knew which was the church because, even though she had not started school, she attended Sunday school in the church. With her head up, in determination, she walked down the centre looking for Mr Cole's class. This was easy for her because all the classes were separated from each other by low cardboard-like partitions. It was easy to see all the classes by simply walking down the middle.

When she saw Mr Cole, she walked into his class and stood behind him. The other children looked up from their work and stared at Adah in wonder. At first there was a hush, a hush so tangible that one could almost hold and feel it. Then one silly child started to giggle and the others followed suit, until almost every child in the class was giggling in such an uncontrollable way that Mr Cole glared at the children who had all gone crazy, for all he knew. Then it happened. The child who started the giggle covered her mouth with one hand and pointed at Adah with the other.

Mr Cole was a huge African, very young, very handsome. He was a real black man. His blackness shone like polished black leather. He was a very quiet man, but he used to smile at Adah every time he passed her on his way to school. Adah was sure Mr Cole would give her that reassuring smile now, in front of all these giggling idiots. Mr Cole spun round with such alacrity, that Adah took a step backwards. She was not frightened of Mr Cole, it was just that the movement was so quick and so unexpected of Mr Cole, with his great bulk. Only God above knew what he expected to find behind him. A big gorilla or a wandering 'masquerade' perhaps. But all he saw was Adah, staring at him.

God bless Mr Cole. He did not laugh, he took in the situation immediately, gave Adah one of those special smiles, held out his hand, and led her to a boy who had craw-craw on his head, and gestured her to sit down. Adah did not know what to make of this gesture. She felt Mr Cole should have asked her why she came, but being reassured by his smile, she said in her little loud voice:

'I came to school – my parents would not send me!'

The class went quiet once more, the boy with the craw-craw on his head (he later became a lecturer in Lagos City Hospital) gave her a bit of his pencil, and Adah scribbled away, enjoying the smell of craw-craw and dried sweat. She never forgot this smell of school.

The day ended too soon for Adah's liking. But they must go home, Mr Cole assured her. Yes, of course she could come again if she liked, but if her parents would not allow her to come he would take it upon himself to teach her the alphabet. If only Mr Cole would not bring her parents into it. Pa would be all right: he would probably cane her, you know, just a few strokes – six or so, not much – but Ma would not cane, she would smack and smack, and then nag and nag all day long.

She thought that it was these experiences with Ma so early in life that had given her such a very low opinion of her own sex. Somebody said somewhere that our characters are usually formed early in life. Yes, that somebody was right. Women still made Adah nervous. They had a way of sapping her self-confidence. She did have one or two women friends with whom she discussed the weather, and fashion. But when in real trouble, she would rather look for a man. Men were so solid, so safe.

Mr Cole took her to the stall of a woman selling *boli*, which is the Yoruba name for roasted plantain. These women usually had open pots in which they made a kind of coal fire. These fires were covered with wire gauze; and on the gauze were placed peeled plantains, ready for roasting. Mr Cole fed her with a big *boli* and told her not to worry. It was another story when they got home; at home things had got out of hand.

In fact there was a big hullabaloo going on. Pa had been called from work, Ma was with the police being charged with child neglect, and the child that had caused all the fuss was little

Adah, staring at all of them, afraid and yet triumphant. They took Ma to the police station and forced her to drink a big bowl of *gari* with water. *Gari* is a tasteless sort of flour made from cassava. When cooked and eaten with soup, it is delicious. But when uncooked, the watered type Ma was forced to drink, it became a torture, purgatorial in fact!

Those policemen! Adah still wondered where they got all their unwritten laws from. This happened at the police station near Sabo Market. Ma told them with tears in her eyes that she could swallow the *gari* no more. She must drink the whole lot, she was told, and told in such language that Adah hid behind Mr Cole. If Ma did not finish the *gari*, the policemen went on, they would take her to court. How they laughed at their own jokes, those horrid men; and how they scared Adah! Ma went on gulping, her eyes dilating. Adah was scared; she started to howl, and Pa, who had said very little, begged the policemen to stop. They should let Ma go now, he explained, for she had learned her lesson. She was a great talker, very careless, otherwise Adah would not have been able to slip away as she had. Women were like that. They sat in the house, ate, gossiped and slept. They would not even look after their children properly. But the policemen should forgive her now, because Pa thought she had had enough *gari*.

The chief policeman considered this plea, then looked once more at Ma, cupping the *gari* to her mouth with her fingers, and smiled. He took pity on Ma, but warned her that if such a thing should happen again, he personally would take her to the court.

'You know what that means?' he thundered.

Ma nodded. She knew court meant two things: a heavy fine which she would never be able to afford, or prison, which she called 'pilizon'. They advised her to sell one of her colourful *lappas* and send Adah to school, because she looked like a child who was keen to learn. At this point Ma gave Adah a queer look – a look that contained a mixture of fear, love and wonder. Adah shrank back, still clutching Mr Cole.

When they got home from the station, the news had already got round. Adah had nearly sent her mother to 'pilizon'. So frequently was this sentence repeated that Adah began to be quite proud of her impulsive move. She felt triumphant, especially when she heard Pa's friends advising him to make sure he allowed Adah to start school soon. This discussion took place on the veranda, where the visitors were downing two kegs of palm-wine to wet their parched throats. When they departed, Adah was left alone with her parents.

Things were not as bad as she thought they would be. Pa fished out the cane and gave her a few strokes for Ma's benefit. Adah did not mind that because they were not hard strokes. Maybe Pa had been mellowed by the talks with his friends, because when Adah cried after the caning, he came and talked to her seriously, just as if she were a grown-up! He called her by her pet name, 'Nne nna', which means 'Father's mother', which was not so far from the meaning of Adah's real name. How she came by that name was a story in itself.

When Pa's mother was dying, she had promised Pa that she would come again, this time as his daughter. She was sorry she could not bring him up. She died when Pa was only five. She would come again, she had promised, to compensate for leaving him so young. Well, Pa grew up and married Ma at the Christ Church in Lagos, which was a Christian church. But Pa did not forget his mother's promise. The only reservation he had was that he did not want a girl for his first child. Well, his mother was impatient! Ma had a girl. Pa thought Adah was the very picture of his mother, even though Adah was born two months prematurely. He was quite positive that the little, damp monkey-like thing with unformed face was his 'come back mother'. So she was loaded with strings of names; 'Nne nna', 'Adah nna', 'Adah Eze'! Adah Eze means Princess, daughter of a king. Sometimes they called her Adah Eze, sometimes Adah nna and sometimes Nne nna. But this string of names was too long and too confusing for Adah's Yoruba friends and playmates and even more so for impatient Ma. So she became just 'Adah'. She didn't mind this. It was short: everybody could pronounce it. When she grew up, and was attending the Methodist Girls' High School in Lagos, where she came in contact with European missionaries, her name was one of the first ones they learned and pronounced correctly. This usually gave her a

start against the other girls with long names like Adebisi Gbamg-
bose, or Oluwafunmilayo Olorunshogo!

So that was how Adah started school. Pa would not hear of her
going to the Methodist Primary; she was to go to the posh one,
Ladi-Lak. Success in life would surely have come earlier to her
if Pa had lived. But he died soon after, and Adah and her brother
Boy were transferred to an inferior school. Despite all this,
Adah's dream never left her.

It was understandable that Ma refused to take her to see the
new lawyer, because Adah had started school only a few weeks
before the preparations for the great man's arrival. Ma got really
furious with Adah for asking such a thing.

'You made me drink *gari* only last month until I nearly burst my
stomach, all because you said you wanted school. Now we gave you
school, you want the wharf. No, you won't go. You chose school. To
school you must go from now until you go grey.'

How right Ma was! Adah would never stop learning. She had
been a student ever since.

Adah's face had fallen at this. If only she had known before,
she would have staged her school drama after the arrival of
Lawyer Nweze. But as it turned out, she missed little. The
women practised their songs several times and showed off their
uniform to which they had given the name *Ezidiji ji de ogoli, ome
oba*, meaning: 'When a good man holds a woman she becomes
a queen.' They wove the name of the uniform into the song, and
it was a joy to hear and see these women, happy in their
innocence, just like children. Their wants were simple and easily
met. Not like those of their children who later got caught up in
the entangled web of industrialisation. Adah's ma had no
experience of having to keep up mortgage payments: she never
knew what it was to have a family car, or worry about its innards;
she had no worries about pollution, the population explosion or
race. Was it surprising, therefore, that she was happy, being
unaware of the so-called joys of civilisation and all its pitfalls?

They went to the wharf that day, these happy women, to
welcome someone who had been to have a taste of that civilisation;

the civilisation which was soon afterwards to hook them all, like opium. That day, they were happy to welcome their man.

They went in their new uniform. Adah still remembered its colour. It had a dark velvety background with pale blue drawings of feathers on it. The headscarf was red, and it was tied in such a way that it displayed their straightened hair. The shoes they wore were of black patent leather called 'nine-nine'. No one really knew why, maybe it was the rhythm of the repetition. In any case they wore those 'nine-nine' shoes with their *Ezidiji ji de ogoli ome oba* and bought new gourds which they covered with colourful beads. When these gourds were rattled, they produced sounds like the Spanish samba, with a wild sort of animal overtone.

They had had a good time, Adah was told later. They danced happily at the wharf, shaking their colourful gourds in the air. The European arrivals gaped at them. They had never seen anything like it before. The climax of it all was when an Englishman took their photographs. He even singled out women with babies on their backs and took several shots of them. Ma and her friends were really happy to have their pictures taken by Europeans! These were the days before Nigerian independence when nearly every boat from England brought hundreds of English graduates and doctors to work in the schools and hospitals of Lagos.

The few gaps in the magical story of Nweze's arrival were filled in by Pa. All the Ibuza men went to welcome him the following Sunday. They could not leave their places of work during the week. Pa said that the lawyer could not swallow pounded yam any more; he could not even eat a piece of bone. The meat they cooked for him had to be stewed for days until it was almost a pulp. 'I felt like being sick,' Pa said as he spat on the floor. 'It reminded me of the sickly, watery food we ate in the army. There is one thing, though,' Pa went on: 'he did not bring a white woman with him.' All Pa's friends agreed with him that that was a good thing. If Nweze had brought a white woman to Ibuza, Oboshi would have sent leprosy on her!

Remembering all these taboos and superstitions of the Western Ibos of Nigeria, Adah could not help laughing to herself. She had been brought up with them, they were part of her, yet now, in the seventies, the thought of them amused her. The funniest thing about all these superstitions and beliefs was that they still had a doleful grip on the minds of her people. No one dared ignore any of them. Leprosy was a disease with which the goddess of the biggest river in Ibuza cursed anyone who dared to flout one of the town's traditions.

Well, Pa and his friends toasted the goddess of the River Oboshi for not allowing Lawyer Nweze to go astray. That Oboshi was strong enough to guide the thoughts of Nweze, demonstrated her power. They toasted her again.

Later, Adah did not know what came over that River Oboshi, though. Oil was discovered very near her, and she allowed the oilmen to dig into her, without cursing them with leprosy. The oilmen were mainly white, which was a surprise. Or perhaps she had long been declared redundant by the greater gods. That would not have surprised Adah, for everybody could be declared redundant these days, even goddesses. If not redundant, then she must have been in a Rip Van Winkle sleep, for she also allowed the Hausa soldiers to come and massacre her sons, and some Ibuza men had married white women without getting leprosy. Only last year an Ibuza girl graduate had married a white American! So Oboshi was faster than most of her sons and daughters at catching up with the times.

Anyway, the talk about Nweze's arrival went on for months and months. Adah talked about him to all her friends at school, telling them that he was her cousin. Well, everybody else talked big, so she might as well. But she made a secret vow to herself that she would go to this United Kingdom one day. Her arrival there would be the pinnacle of her ambition. She dared not tell anyone; they might decide to have her head examined or something. A small girl of her kind, with a father who was only a railwayman and a mother who knew nothing but the Ibo Bible and the Ibo Anglican hymn-book, from the Introduction to the Index, and who still thought that Jerusalem was at the right hand of God.

That she would go to the United Kingdom one day was a dream she kept to herself, but dreams soon assumed substance. It lived with her, just like a Presence.

EMILY PERKINS

Emily Perkins was born in Christchurch, New Zealand in 1970. She acted in New Zealand and also attended Drama School there. She currently lives and works in London. *Not Her Real Name and other stories* (1996) is her first book.

OPTIONS

from *Not Her Real Name*

THE SHARED EXPERIENCE

These are her options.

1. Drive away. The keys are in the ignition. He's in the back of a long queue waiting to pay for the petrol. The car's an expensive one. She could get a lot of money for it. Quietly open her door, take the petrol pump out of the car, get in the driver's side and take off with a full tank. Drive as far as she can, to the nearest port. Sell the car to someone who doesn't want to see the papers. Get on a boat. Disappear.
2. Stay in the car. Go to the hotel. Feign exhaustion. Order food up to her room, have a bath, go to bed alone.
3. Stay in the car. Go to the hotel. Cross the line that's been waiting to be crossed all day. Become the sort of woman who sleeps with her boss.

He comes back to the car, folding the receipt into his wallet. She sits politely in the passenger seat, hands crossed in her lap. Say goodbye to Option 1.

He starts the car and pulls out into the traffic. He jerks his seatbelt over his shoulder. The buckle won't do up.

'Can you?'

She twists in her seat and tries to jam the buckle into the thing it's supposed to jam into. His left hand moves over, as if to help. It's big and dry and covers both of her hands. She feels the flush starting at her throat and moving round to the back of her neck. She has a tendency to go blotchy when embarrassed. She hopes he doesn't notice. The buckle finally clicks into place and he moves his hand back to the steering wheel. She turns round to face front and presses the button to unwind her window. Pushing her sunglasses up on her nose, she sneaks a look at his hands, their casual touch on the wheel. Big hands. Big hands with a big gold wedding ring on one of them. When she went to America she wore a ring on her wedding finger, a cheap imitation number she'd picked up from a street stall. Her sister told her it was bad luck, that if you wore a ring on that finger without being married, it meant you never would be. Her sister's authority on luck was questionable, as she was married at the time to a man called Dwayne who spent all his money on gambling and had no sense of humour. This seemed like a fate far worse than spinsterhood, but she didn't say so to her sister. The fake American wedding ring seems ridiculous now, a flimsy attempt to shield herself from physical or emotional danger. She laughs.

'What's funny?'

She can't tell him she's thinking about wedding rings.

'Nothing.'

'You're a strange one.'

Why did men feel compelled to say things like that to her? Really and truly. What a horrible thing to say. You're a strange one – it's not the kind of thing you'd ever say to someone you considered an equal, is it? Well, so, he's never going to leave his wife for her. It doesn't mean Option 3 couldn't still happen.

He clears his throat. 'Do you mind if I put a tape on?'

'No.'

This'll be it. If it's *Eric Clapton Unplugged* she's definitely not going to bed with him. In fact the list of tapes that would put her off him is potentially endless. *Yodelling Favourites. Ravel's Bolero. Twenty Big Band Hits.* Anything played by Kenny Gee.

'Do you want to find one? They're in the glove box.'

Oh shit. Shit shit shit. This way it's her own taste on the line – at least, her choice of his selection. She opens the glove box and yes, it's her worst nightmare. Next to the maps and a tube of toothpaste (toothpaste?) are five or six tapes of classical music. Does it have to be this way? She knows next to nothing about classical music. It occupies the same place in her head as wine lists, or the inside of car engines. Things she can't concentrate on long enough to ever figure out. OK, don't panic, breathe. What have we got here? Mozart, Mozart, Haydn, Beethoven, Handel. Mozart's nice, isn't he? What's the difference between Haydn and Handel? Opus? What does that even mean? She pulls out a tape at random. Beethoven. The deaf guy. OK then, here we go.

Big dark booming notes bounce around the car.

'Jesus,' says her boss. 'That's a bit grim.'

'Yeah, sorry,' she says, and presses stop. The tape won't eject and she pushes and pushes the button desperately till it pops out.

'I don't know what that tape's doing there,' he says. 'I haven't heard it in years.'

'What one do you want?'

'Oh, you choose.'

This is starting to feel like a challenge. She grabs one of the Mozart tapes and shoves it in the tape deck. She turns to the window again, hot with embarrassment and anger.

'That's nice,' he says, and she feels a bit better. The countryside rolls past and she starts to feel much better. The tape crisis is over, and now they don't have to talk.

They arrive in the town where the meeting is going to be held just as it's getting dark. Standing at the reception desk in the hotel, she is struck by the full force of the romance of the situation. Here they are, checking into a hotel together. Sure, they're getting separate rooms and they're here on business and they're not lying to the receptionist about their last names, but still – anything could happen. She stands just behind her boss while he does the talking with the woman at the desk. He passes her a key. She turns it over and over, feeling the cool outline of its ridges warming up in her hand, the embossed 13F on the tag.

She follows him down the hall, clutching her small weekend bag, trying to take in the old wallpaper and gilt-framed paintings and thick carpets without losing her blasé expression. She could probably count the number of hotels she's stayed in on one hand. She steps into the lift. He presses the button for their floor. The silence in the lift is excruciating. Say something, say something, she tells herself. There must be something to say. The lift stops. They check their keys.

'I think, right ... and the ...' He could be talking to himself. She pretends not to notice.

Her room is right next to his. They stand in front of their respective doors. She looks at her shoes.

'Have you got everything ready for tomorrow?'

'Yes,' she says. 'I've just got to sort some papers together.'

'Mm, yes, I've got a couple of calls I'd better make and then I thought I'd grab a bite. We may as well eat downstairs. Half an hour?'

He's inside his room with the door shut before he's finished talking, before she says, OK. She puts her hand to her face and feels how hot it is. She lets herself into her room.

It's small, just a double bed next to a window looking on to the wall of the next building. There's a door leading to a shower cubicle, basin and toilet. She washes her hands and lies down on the bed. Through the wall by her head she can hear him talking. She shuts her eyes and feels a rush of tiredness, and something like nausea. She sits up and blinks, dizzy. There's not enough oxygen in here. She kicks her shoes off, enjoying the thump they make as they hit the floor. When she was a teenager she used to throw her shoes against the wall of her bedroom just to listen to the sound of it.

Should she change for dinner? The clothes she's been wearing in the car all day feel sticky and gross, but maybe changing would look like she was making too much effort. Perhaps one thing. She decides to keep her skirt and change her top. She takes the papers for tomorrow's meeting out of her bag and spreads them out on the floor. Can't be fucked sorting through them now. Her own company is making her tired. She takes a small bottle of vodka out of her bag and has a couple of mouthfuls. Drinking with inferiors again, she thinks, and laughs. She'd better be careful.

The shower's a dribbly contraption with water that runs only extremely hot or extremely cold. She shivers under it for a minute and gets out. Drying herself, she has an idea. Maybe she shouldn't wear any knickers. Wouldn't it be exciting not to, in a private and slightly scary kind of way? But it would make her even more self-conscious than she already is. She can imagine getting a kick out of it though, feeling powerful and secretive as she toys with her linguine. Though if anything happens between them later, he'll know and he might think she's overly forward. Unless he's the kind of man who likes that. Maybe she'd feel too vulnerable. And then, if nothing does happen, she'll feel like an idiot. Of course, nobody ever needs to know. Option 3, Option 3, she sings to her reflection in the steamed-up mirror. No. It's stupid. He's her boss, for goodness' sake. They've got to work tomorrow. She should be preparing for this meeting instead of fantasising about his big hands and his pin-striped suit. This is just a power displacement thing. She should want to screw him figuratively, get his job or something, not literally. That's not going to get her anywhere. Besides, he's married. How can she even be considering this? Has she got no scruples at all? She could at least pretend to have a moral dilemma about this. But the only dilemma she's having is whether or not to put on her underwear. Well. That settles it. She puts her clothes back on, including her bra and knickers, and brushes her hair.

There, a nicely presented young woman. Competent, attractive, and desperate. She must be desperate, to have fixated on her boss like this. He is good-looking, there's no doubt about that. But surely she should be looking for someone from her own peer group? Well, it's obvious why she isn't. They're all fatuous, self-obsessed, undirected, confused, emotional retards. Whereas her boss, her managing director – she loves those words! – is nothing like that. He's young for his position – he must be driven, focused. And he's interesting, isn't he, and knowledgeable? She lights a cigarette and sits back down on the bed. So what if he is, and so what if he isn't? She's fascinated by him the same way she's mesmerised in the menswear sections of department stores. She can wander around them for hours, hypnotised by the umbrellas and wallets and canes and gloves. The ties, the hats, the pipes. The smell – no, the *idea* of the smell – of tobacco and leather and shoe polish. She loves it. She loves it all, and she wants to get close to it.

She hears his door shut. Stubs out her cigarette and fans the air. There's a knock on her door. 'Coming,' she calls. She looks in the mirror. Fuck it, she's going to take a risk. Why the fuck not? She hitches up her skirt, takes off her knickers, and throws them in the corner of the room. There. She smooths her skirt down and smiles. She's still smiling as she opens the door, looks her managing director straight in the eye, and walks with him down to the restaurant.

It probably started at her interview for the job, the first time she shook his hand and smiled her job-interview smile and asked herself what it was he was looking for. But the moment she knew it was there was when she read back a fax she'd typed for him arranging an appointment. Instead of 'if this suits' she'd written 'if his suits'. And as soon as she saw the words she knew they were a sign. If his suits were under her hands. If his suits were pressed against her cheek. If his suits hung in neat rows in his wardrobe. If his suits ever came off. She didn't talk to anyone about this new way she had of looking at him as he sat behind his desk. Watching him on the telephone, or in meetings. Dressing for him every day. When she went drinking with other girls from work she kept her mouth shut as they speculated about his marriage, his past, his private life. Because she worked the closest with him, they accorded her a certain respect, but she could tell that her silence irritated them. She didn't care. She'd get quietly drunk and go home and get more drunk and go to bed and dream, drunkenly, about him.

'So, tell me how you find the company,' he says.

Her first thought is that he means his company, here tonight, then she realises.

'Oh, it's good,' she says. 'I'm enjoying it.'

'Not too stuffy?'

'Well, they are a bit,' she says. 'Not everyone, I mean. But, mm . . .' She trails off.

'Yes, well,' he says, and laughs. 'Wine?'

'Yes, please.'

'Red all right?'

'Sure.' You choose, she thinks. Just don't ask me.

'Good.' He orders some wine from the sullen waiter. They study the menus.

'This is on the expense account, so have whatever you like.' The writing on the menu blurs in front of her eyes. Expense account. Somehow those words expose the tackiness of the situation more than anything so far, the way they conjure up images of travelling salesmen. Men with moustaches. Wife-swapping parties where the car keys get thrown in the swimming pool. The horror, the horror.

'I'll have steak,' he tells the waiter. 'Rare.'

He says the word as if it's an announcement, a declaration of his hunger. His carnivorous, bare-fanged hunger. She crosses her legs.

'I'll have the salmon, please.'

'With red wine?' He raises his eyebrows.

Who is this man, James Bond? 'Why not?'

Surely this discomfort, this nervousness, this level of tension, means there's something going on? Surely he can feel it too?

He takes off his jacket and hangs it over the back of his chair. This is really too much. She's got to stop staring at his hands, their clipped nails, the thick veins running from his knuckles back into his shirt-cuffs. The thick brown leather band of his watch strap, the thick gold band of his wedding ring.

Their wine arrives. She thanks the waiter. He doesn't. She drinks too quickly, eyes down, nearly emptying her glass.

'Cheers.' He toasts vaguely in her direction. 'Here's to it.'

To what, to what, she wants to say. What is this thing? What is this thing called, love? Watch it – she'll make herself laugh again. Can't have that.

'Well, I must say work's a much more pleasant place to be since you've started with us.'

Did he really say that? Did she hear him right? She smiles.

'Thanks,' she simpers.

'Have you ever been to America?'

It's clear to her that the conversation will go wherever he leads it – it won't be appropriate for her to initiate anything. This is probably OK – it's hard to know what she could think of to say anyway.

'Once,' she says, and clears her throat. Her voice is coming out funny. 'I went to New York, and down to the New Orleans jazz festival. It was great.'

'Yeah, it's a pretty exciting place all right. This is off the record – we're thinking of merging with another company there. In New York City, actually. I'm going over next month to sound it out.'

'Wow. That would be great.'

God, is she reduced to this pathetic sort of platitude after everything he says? She makes herself sit up straighter.

'Yes, it could be exciting. As long as they don't swamp us.'

'Is it a big company?'

'I'd better not say too much. Big enough.' He smiles.

She feels like a child being taught how to add with building blocks. This is the big one, see, and this one – that's smaller. Say something intelligent, she tells herself, furious.

'Would there be a staffing merge as well?'

He raises his eyebrows at her. 'You mean, is there a chance for free trips to the States?'

She goes bright red, pulls her napkin on to her lap and twists it hard. 'No, that's not—'

He laughs. 'I'm teasing. There may be the odd swap – I'm looking into all of that.'

She feels as if she's had a sense of humour bypass. Maybe

she's just too uptight to get a joke any more.

The restaurant begins to fill with other diners. Old people mostly, the odd lone businessman. What are they thinking of the two of them? What do they look like together? She hopes they look like a glamorous couple. They do suit each other, she's sure of that. She wonders what his wife looks like. She imagines blonde and gorgeous. This is daunting, but at least picture-perfect and unreal.

The salmon comes complete with bones. So unfair. She drops her fork. Did that have to happen? It's an effort to stay on her chair as she slides down to retrieve it. She's just lifting it back up to the table when the waiter brings her a new one. Red again. Blotch Girl. Lovely. Her boss eats like a guy, which is reassuring she supposes – he seems completely unselfconscious and in control. Since the fork incident the table has become an obstacle course to her – everything there only to be knocked over, or spilt, or hit against something else with a loud and resonant ping.

They talk about travel: he's done a lot, she very little. And opera – the same. And sailing – that too. She begins to wonder if there is a topic she knows anything about. Asks him if he likes going to the movies. It sounds like a come-on, she knows it even as she's saying it, lets her voice die away, her sentence unfinished.

'Are you all right there?'

'Yes,' she smiles brightly, 'fine.' Pull yourself together, she thinks. At the same time she thinks it's unfair of him to draw attention to her nervousness. She's supposed to be nervous, isn't she? They both know what's in the air, on the agenda, up for grabs. Of course she's bloody nervous. Getting angry has a calming effect. She tackles her salmon again with renewed confidence. Smiles flirtatiously at the waiter when he pours her more wine. Hopes her boss notices. He doesn't. Too busy tucking into his steak. Zoltar, Ruler of the Universe. It's so easy for men.

They somehow muddle through dinner. Her most hopeful moment is when he orders a second bottle of wine. Once their plates have been cleared there is a long silence. All she can think of is touching him. She keeps her eyes down, for safety. What if she made a move? Just reached her hand over to his. She experimentally probes under the table with her foot. Nothing. His feet must be tucked under his chair. Then he leans back, stretches his legs out, and a foot collides with hers. She makes herself keep her foot there. It's a light contact but it's something. Risks a glance at him. He's looking at her. Oh boy, oh boy. She feels giddy. Drunk. Smiles. Looks away. Smiles again. Looks back. He raises his eyebrows. She's entranced by his face, his eyes, his jaw, his mouth. Wants to kiss him. Feels immobile. Opens her mouth to say something. Has no words. Closes it again.

'Didn't you do something funny at university?' he asks. 'Horticulture or something?'

She nods, bewildered. She must have mentioned it at work. 'A couple of papers.'

'I should introduce you to my wife,' he says. 'She's a very keen gardener.'

Jesus, that was out of left field. She manages a smile. 'Oh really.'

'Yes. We have a beautiful garden.'

What is he raving about? 'Excuse me a minute,' she says.

She heads towards the bathroom and at the last minute veers off towards the lifts. She falls into one, back into the corner, mouth open, head throbbing. Turns to face herself in the mirrored wall. Christ. Her lipstick's all eaten off. At least she hasn't got food in her teeth. She staggers to her room, jabs at the lock with her key, gets in, retrieves her knickers from their landing place by the waste-paper basket, drags them on, falling back on her bed in the process – pulls herself up, smears more lipstick on and goes back down to the restaurant.

'Are you OK?'

'Yes, thanks,' she says. How long has she been gone from the table? It felt like seconds but maybe it was unnaturally long. She dabs at the corners of her mouth, hoping he'll attribute her absence to bulimia. She shifts in her chair, feeling happier now that she's fully clothed, feeling stronger.

He pours out the last of the wine. Coughs. Says, 'Do you mind if I smoke?'

'Not at all,' she says with relief. At last she can light up herself. He's not going to pull out a cigar, is he? No. Thank God. He passes her the lighter. Now is her chance. She lets her fingers brush against his. They look at each other. She can feel the pulse knocking in the base of her throat. Don't blotch, she tells herself, just don't. She lights her cigarette with trembling hands. Light-headed. Feels queasy, almost. That salmon was too rich.

'We must get you on some more interesting projects,' he says. 'You're a bright girl.'

Oh, please, she thinks. 'That'd be good.'

Doesn't want to talk about work. Doesn't want to talk at all. The waiter comes over, asks if they'd like anything else.

'Cognac?' he asks her.

What's the right answer? Yes, stay and have more to drink, or no, go straight to his room? They are going to his room, aren't they? This can't end in nothing. She tries to look noncommittal.

'Two cognacs,' he says to the waiter.

And two become four, and four become six. Blurry. Slurring words. A lot of cigarettes. Somewhere between the second and third cognac he reaches under the table and puts his hand on her knee. She's too drunk to blush any more. Blinks slowly. Puts her hand on his hand. Moves her fingers over it, tries to ignore the fucking wedding ring. Just avoids that part of the hand, the way you avoid touching a pimple on someone's back, or a cold sore on their mouth. Watching his two faces, she has to keep herself from squinting in an attempt to bring him into focus.

The waiter hovers. He doesn't even look up.

'Could we have the bill, please.'

He slides his hand out from between her hand and her knee, finds his wallet. Takes out a card, puts it on the table.

'What do you think?' he says.

She smiles. 'What do you think?'

'I asked first.'

'I think . . .' She lights another cigarette, stalling. The waiter brings the receipt back and he signs it.

'I think I'm drunk.' The words don't seem as gauche and uncharming to her now as they will when she remembers them later. If she remembers them.

He smiles. 'So am I. Shall we go?'

Standing up is a bit tricky. She follows him out through the restaurant like an air hostess, steadying herself on the backs of chairs as she passes. Things begin to fragment here. Flashes of consciousness, moments of blankness. It's as if a light some-where is being turned on and off at random. Through the reception area. Slippery floor. Don't slip on the floor. The lift. He kisses her in the lift. She feels tired. The awkwardness of standing outside his door while he tries to find his key.

In his room. They're both in his room. It's dark. What if she throws up? He's unlacing his shoes, unbuttoning his shirt. Isn't she supposed to be doing that for him. 'Come here,' he says, and she sits gingerly on the bed next to him. Did she fall over on the way up here? Her knee hurts. He kisses her. She can smell the aftershave smell of him, and smoke. Then they're, you know, fooling around. She feels very uncoordinated. It's kind of nice though. In a far-off sort of a way. Soon it's all happening, the clothes are off, the sheets are off, she's in an out-of-town hotel room doing it with her boss. Oh boy. Shouldn't there be a condom here somewhere? Oh. There is already. She must have missed that bit. How embarrassing. She must have blacked out because a few minutes later she has a sense of time passing and he's still there on top of her, grinding away. This is excruciating. She makes an effort to wake up and get into it. A brief effort. Why is she so detached? Oh come on, come on, get it over with. This seems like it's been going on for ever.

It does go on for ever, and then it stops. She lies there thinking about her room, thinking she should go back to it. The energy involved in dragging herself out of bed and running to her room with her bundle of clothes seems impossible. She'll just lie here a little bit more. Just a little bit, then she'll go. Her mouth is dry. She's vaguely aware of her boss next to her in the bed, naked, hairy, snoring. How can she ever go back to work for him now? Yuck. As she falls into a stupor, the thought passes through her mind that if he brought condoms, then he must have had some idea of something.

Somewhere in her coma she hears the phone ringing. A light snaps on. Her boss sits bolt upright. He grabs the phone. Doesn't look at her.

'Yes? Hello?'

She can hear a woman's voice, faintly, and a child crying, less faintly.

'All right, put her on. Darling? It's Daddy. Hello. Was it a bad dream?'

This seems like an opportune moment to leave. Keeping her head down, she grabs her clothes and keys from the floor where they're all jumbled in with his. Remembers to get her earrings from the table – a mistake she's made before, losing jewellery – though she has no memory of taking these off. She shuts the door behind her, not looking back at him, feeling like shit.

Now here she is in the hallway with no clothes on. A nightmare made real. Which door is hers? Her eyes can't focus enough to read the letters. Oh bugger, these aren't her room keys. They're his fucking car keys. Oh Christ. Why her? Why? She performs a crouching half-run up and down the hall, checking for any sign of life. Shivering, she knocks lightly on his door. No answer. She can hear him still talking on the phone. Did he hear her knock? – maybe not. But it's so unbearable to have to make a noise. She takes a deep breath and knocks again, slightly louder. This is hell. People go to the theatre to laugh at things like this. A fucking farce. Why doesn't he come to the door? Why? Help me, help me. This is desperate. Her face burning more than ever before in her life, she hammers on the door. She wants to call out, Let me in, but what if someone hears? Her feet are freezing. Then to the right she hears the lift bell ding and knows she's going to be caught naked and drunk and post-sex in the hallway. It's too much. She dives for the door to the stairwell. It bangs shut behind her just in time. Through the smoked glass she sees a couple weaving down the hall, arm in arm, to their room. Kissing. Then she sees his door open and her boss looking out into the hallway. For some reason she shrinks back against the wall so he doesn't spot her. He looks bleary and tired and intensely irritated. Irritated with her. What a mess. How can she go through with it? How can she go through with the meeting tomorrow, with the drive back to the city, with the next days and weeks and months typing that bloody bastard's boring bloody memos? Never able to tell anyone. Never able to relax. She watches as he closes the door.

Shit, it's cold. Her hands are numb. She scrambles into her clothes, skin crawling with the awful itch of putting her legs back into day-old tights, the awkward hooks of her stupid bra, the ashtray stink of her hair as it falls around her face. The taste in her mouth. Her too-tight skirt and her too-high heels. She's never going to wear anything but jeans ever again. She opens the door, wincing as it squeaks. Pushes the button for the lift, checking over her shoulder that no one's coming.

Thirteen floors down and she's feeling nauseous, her head starting to throb in a sharp and painful way. She staggers out into the reception area, nearly going over on her ankle in these mindless shoes. She makes her way to the desk. They must have a spare key to her room. Presses the buzzer, hears it ringing back in the office behind the desk. Waits. So tired. Suddenly hungry. McDonald's. A big greasy hamburger oozing fat and sauce. Chips caked with salt. A Coke. Where are these people? She holds the buzzer down for a few seconds and leans forward on the desk, rests her head on it, arms hanging slackly by her sides. Feels the pulse in her temple against the marble desktop. Oh for God's sake. She thumps the buzzer again, bashes it with her fist, the tinny ringing of it making her more angry every time. What, are they all asleep? Watching the wrestling on TV? Drunk? Hello? Fuck it, she'll sleep in the car. It can't get any worse than this.

She stumbles around the car park as if it's happening to someone else. One day this might be a funny story to tell someone. Not right now, but it probably has potential. Spice up the sexy details a bit. God, she'd have to make it sound worth it. Where is his goddamn car? What she'd like to do now is take her shoe to the paintwork of every one of these big fat sleek self-satisfied automatic four-wheel-drive kiddie-proof stereophonic convertible tinted-window monstrosities. She could do some pretty good damage, scrape them up, put in a couple of dents. She goes to touch one of the cars, feel just what sort of kick it is these guys get out of them, when she gets too close and its alarm goes off, shrill and angry in the darkness. She jumps back as if she's been shouted at. Hits the ground, crawls between two other cars to hide, stockings ripping on the concrete. Shit. Please no one come. Shhh, shhh. The alarm sounds as if it's coming from inside her head. Shut up, shut up. She's too scared to look out over the cars to see if anyone's heard. There must be security guys all over this place. Bangs her head back against the car behind her. Just about brains herself on the door handle. Wait a minute, this is it. His car. Fantastic. She kisses the door. Breathes out at last. Sleep, soon she will be asleep and this will all be over. She controls the shaking in her hand long enough to get the key in the door and open it. Climbs carefully into the passenger seat, locks the door after her. Safe at last. The other car has finally stopped screaming. Maybe she won't be arrested after all. SECRETARY SCREWS BOSS, SMASHES UP SAAB. DRUNKEN DORIS DENTS DAIMLER. AUTO ATTACK BY TIPSY TYPIST. With the headlines of her evening flashing up in lurid colours behind her eyes, she curls up in the front of her boss's car and falls asleep.

When she wakes up she is cold. She has a crick neck. She is unsure where she is. Oh. That's right. She laughs croakily. It is kind of funny. It's going to be one of those things, she can tell already – flashes of memory will come unbidden to her in the street, at work, in the shower – those cringey moments that make you grit your teeth or suck in your breath or rub your hand across your forehead as if to erase what's there. There are a lot of involuntary blushes stored up from this one. She shakes her head. It's getting light outside. Grey misty light. She looks up at the hotel, sees a couple of lights on. Wonders if he's awake yet. Awake, guilty, going through his stuff for the meeting. Or perhaps he's not guilty. Perhaps he's having a shower, planning to knock on her door and invite her downstairs for breakfast. Yeah, likely story. The fuck wouldn't even let her back in his room. Wanker. No, he'll be trying to pretend he hasn't got a hangover, trying not to think about last night, just get through the meeting and get back to his wife. Thinking, Yes! Probably punching the fucking air. He knows she can't afford repercussions at work. He's got away with it, the tinny bastard. A brief aberration and then everything back to his normal in-control I'm-so-powerful life. She's getting worked up now. The energy feels good. Her head's not that bad either. Could be still drunk. Starving.

Something snaps. That fuck. She's not going to go back up there, pretend nothing's happened, pour fucking coffee for the fucking meeting and take notes. Nuh. He can take his own bloody notes. She's taken enough notes to last a bloody lifetime. Shook enough hands, made enough tea, typed enough minutes. Probably sterile from spending so much time standing by a hot photocopier. Probably got sick building syndrome. Repetitive strain injury. Early Alzheimer's, for all she knows. No more. No going back. No way. What she might do instead doesn't seem to matter at this point. She'll think of something. The first thing she's got to do is get something to eat. Get out of this godforsaken shit-heap and get a life. A hamburger as well. She rubs her face. Checks herself out in the rear-vision mirror. Not pretty. Mascara smudges under her eyes, greasy hair, waxy skin. Too bad. No more girly office eyeshadow for her. No more dress code. No more being nice to stupid jerks and stupider cows just because they're more senior than her and make more money.

Money. Damn. It's all back in her room. She's not going to risk going up there. It's not much, she can easily say goodbye to all that old junk. The office clothes she won't be needing any more. The so-called notes she's prepared for the so-called meeting she's supposed to attend, as if she's something more than a glorified secretary. Her reputation. She grins, looking around at the car. Seems like a fair swap. Shoves her hand down the back of the seat till she finds enough coins for breakfast. It's true, she thinks, remembering a conversation from last night, she really hasn't done enough travelling. What a good time to start. She slides over into the driver's seat. Can she handle one of these big cars? A breeze. The key slots into the ignition with a satisfying click. Pulling out of the car park on to the main road, she runs over her options.

DOORSTEP ADVENTURES

ANONYMOUS

The anonymous author of *A Woman in Berlin* was known to her publisher to be 'from a good middle-class family'. She was given an excellent education and soon showed talents allowing her an early independence. Sketching, photographing, studying, she travelled throughout the greater part of Europe. Personal taste and experience prevented her from becoming involved in any of the organisations of the 'Third Reich'. Although free to make decisions, a job she had just accepted kept her tied to Berlin during the last year of the war – until it was too late to leave that city.

When the Russian Army sacked Berlin, which despite the large-scale evacuations, still harboured four million people, the author began her diary. From Friday April 20th 1945 to June 22nd she jotted down in old ledgers and on loose pages what happened to her and the inhabitants of the house where she had taken refuge. Her lot was the lot of practically every female in Berlin, regardless of age. The author assumed, rightly, that there would be a collective forgetting of these months. She was unique in recording, as it happened, the frenzy of rape. Her wisdom and wit lift the diary from social document to literature as she observes from the eye of the cyclone. Like every other woman in Berlin, she had to resume a semblance of normal life after the atrocity – hence her anonymity.

THE COURAGE
TO STAY

from *A Woman in Berlin*

4 P.M., FRIDAY, 20 APRIL, 1945
CHRONICLE BEGUN ON THE DAY BERLIN
SAW BATTLE FOR THE FIRST TIME

No doubt about it, the war is rolling towards Berlin. What yesterday was a distant rumble is today a permanent roar. One inhales the noise of guns. The ear is deafened; all it can hear is the firing of the heaviest artillery. It can no longer detect the direction. We live in a circle of guns which contracts by the hour.

Every now and again lulls of sinister silence. Suddenly one remembers it's spring. Through the fire-blackened ruins the scent of lilac comes in waves from ownerless gardens. The stump of acacia in front of the cinema is bursting with green. Freshly tilled soil surrounds the shacks on the Berliner Strasse: between air raids the allotment owners must have spent some time digging. Only the birds distrust this April; there are no sparrows on the gutter of our roof.

At about three o'clock the newspaper boy arrived at the kiosk. A couple of dozen people had been lying in wait for him. Instantly he was invisible behind heads and hands. Gerda, the janitor's daughter, snatched a handful of night editions and let me have one. No longer a real newspaper, just a single sheet printed on both sides, and still wet. While walking away the first thing I read was the Wehrmacht's report. New place names: Müncheberg, Seelow, Buchholz. Sounds damned near. A fleeting glimpse at news of the Western Front. What's that got to do with us now? Our fate is rolling towards us from the east and is as sure to change our climate as did the Ice Age once upon a time. Why? How on earth did all this happen? One torments oneself with questions. Pointless. I'll think only of today, of immediate problems.

All round the kiosk groups of people, dead-white faces, murmuring:

'God, who'd have thought it would come to this?'

'There goes our last shred of hope.'

And about Western Germany: 'They're all right. They're over the worst.' The word 'Russians' is no longer mentioned. The lips won't pronounce it.

Back again in the garret. It's not my home. I no longer have one. The furnished room which was bombed from under me wasn't mine either. But in the course of six years I had filled it with my atmosphere, with my books and pictures and the hundred odd things one accumulates: starfish from the last summer in Norderney, the *Kelim* which Gerd brought me from Persia. The battered alarm clock. Snapshots, old letters, sketchbooks, my coins from twelve countries, the half-finished knitting – all the souvenirs, layers, skins, deposits, the familiar odds and ends of the years.

Now all that has gone and I've nothing left but a suitcase full of old clothes; I feel naked and light. And as I no longer own anything, everything belongs to me. For instance, this unfamiliar garret . . .

I can't find any peace up here, keep pacing through the two rooms. I've systematically gone through all the cupboards and drawers in search of something useful – i.e. something edible, drinkable, burnable. Alas, found almost nothing. Seems that Frau Weiers, the owner's former char, has already done a thorough job. Nowadays everything belongs to everyone. One is only vaguely connected with things, doesn't distinguish clearly between one's own property and another's.

I found a letter addressed to the owner stuck behind one of the drawers. I felt ashamed to read it, but read it I did. A love letter; I flushed it down the drain. (We still have water most of the time.) Heart, longing, love. Passion. What remote, unfamiliar words. Presumably a refined, fastidious love life presupposes regular and ample meals. My centre, while I'm writing this, is the stomach. All my thinking, feeling, desires, and hopes begin with food.

Two hours later. The gas is burning with a little dying flame. The potatoes have been on it for hours. The country's most miserable potatoes, they disintegrate into a watery pulp and taste of cardboard. I swallowed one of them almost raw. I've been filling myself up since early this morning. Went to Bolle's to use the light-blue milk tickets which Gerd sent me for Christmas. I wasn't a moment too soon. The woman behind the counter was already tipping the can and told me there wouldn't be any more milk coming to Berlin. This will mean death to the children.

I drank a few gulps right there in the street. When I got home I filled my stomach with gruel and followed that up with a crust of bread. Theoretically I'm fuller than I've been for a long time; in reality I'm tormented by bestial hunger. Eating only had the effect of making me really hungry. I'm sure this fact can be explained scientifically – for instance, that food stimulates the secretion of the stomach, making the juices eager to digest. And by the time they are in full swing, the little that was in reserve has already been digested. Then the juices really begin to give trouble.

Which reminds me of something odd. While rummaging through the owner's little library of books here, I opened a novel at random. The following sentence from a description of an upper-class English family: '... threw a furtive glance at the untouched meal, got up and left ...' I had read on a further ten lines when, magnetically attracted, I returned to the words quoted above. After reading them about a dozen times I suddenly caught myself clawing at the words with my nails, as

though I could scratch the untouched meal (previously described in detail) out of the book.

Crazy! Beginning of a slight hunger madness ...

At the baker's this morning there was a rumour: 'When they get
here they'll take everything we have to eat. They won't give us
anything. They've decided to starve the Germans for eight
weeks. In Silesia people are already digging for roots in the
woods. Children are dying right and left. Old people are eating
grass, like animals.'

So much for the *vox populi*. Actually, one knows nothing. The
Völkischer Beobachter no longer lies on the staircase. There's no
Frau Weiers to read to me at breakfast the long list of rapes.
'Seventy-year-old woman ravished. Nun violated twenty-four
times.' (Who counted?) These are the headlines. Are they
meant to encourage the Berlin men to defend and protect us
women? Ridiculous. In reality it only urges more thousands of
helpless women and children to take to the arterial roads
towards the west, there to die of starvation or be killed from the
air.

While reading these reports Frau Weiers's eyes always grew
quite round and shiny. Something in her enjoyed the horror. Or
maybe her subconscious delighted in the fact that she was not
affected. For afraid she is, and determined to get out. Haven't
seen her since the day before yesterday.

The radio has been dead for four days. Once again one
realises what doubtful gifts technology has bestowed on us. They
have no value in themselves, are of use only provided there's a
place to plug them in. Bread is an absolute value. So is coal,
provided I can set fire to it. And gold was gold in Rome or Peru
or Breslau. A radio, on the other hand, a gas stove, central
heating, an electric plate, all the great benefits of modern times
– they're all so much useless ballast when the main breaks
down. We're now on the road back to bygone centuries. Cave
dwellers ...

In any case the cellar tribe in this house is convinced that its cave is one of the safest. There's nothing stranger than a strange cellar. I have belonged to this one for more than three months and still feel a stranger in it. Each cellar has its own taboos, its own tics. In my old cellar they had the extinguishing-water tic; everywhere one bumped into buckets, pitchers, pots and barrels filled with a muddy brew. It didn't prevent the house from burning like a torch. The whole extinguishing brew would have been as much use as spitting into the blaze ...

Here we sit, a motley crowd, the residue whom neither the Front nor the Volksturm can use. Absent: the master baker who, as the only one in this house to have received the red travel permit Class III, has taken the tram to his allotment to bury his silver. Absent: Fräulein Behn, post-office employee, unmarried and daring, who has just dashed upstairs to fetch the daily paper. Absent: a woman at present in Potsdam where she is burying seven members of her family who were killed in the last great air raid. Absent: the engineer from the second floor with wife and son. Last week he boarded a barge which is supposed to take him and his furniture via the Central Canal to Braunschweig, whither his armament works have been transferred. All industry is moving towards the centre. The overcrowding there must create a great strain – provided the Amis haven't got there first.

Midnight. Still no light. The kerosene lamp on the beam above me is smoking, the heavy droning outside increasing. The towel tic has gone into action, all noses and mouths are covered. A ghostly Turkish harem, a gallery of half-veiled death masks. Only the eyes are alive.

2 A.M., SATURDAY, 21 APRIL 1945

Bombs, the walls swayed. My fingers are still trembling round the fountain pen. I'm drenched, as though after heavy work. At one time I used to eat thick sandwiches in the cellar. Ever since I myself was bombed out and during that night had to help rescue the buried, I've been attacked by the fear of death. The symptoms are always the same. The palms of my hands begin to sweat. Then a circle of sweat round the scalp, a boring sensation in the spinal cord, a twitching pain in the neck, the roof of the mouth dries up, the heart beats in syncope, the eyes stare at the chair leg opposite, memorising its carved nobs and curves. To be able to pray now. The brain gropes for fragments of sentences: 'Let the world go by, it's nothing . . . And no one falls out of this world . . . *Noli timere* . . .' Until the wave subsides.

As though by command a feverish babbling broke out. Everyone began to laugh, to outshout the others, to crack jokes. Fräulein Behn stepped forth and read the Goebbels speech in honour of the birthday of the Führer, a day most people seem to have forgotten. She read with a special emphasis, with a new jeering, and malicious voice which until now hadn't been heard down here. 'Golden wheat on the fields . . . People living in peace . . .' Imagine! says the Berliner. And: 'Sure would be nice.' Music out of the past which no longer reaches the ear.

3 a.m. The cellar is dozing. There have been several all clears, but immediately afterwards new alarms; no bombs. I'm writing; it does one good, diverts. And I want Gerd to read it, in case he returns – in case he's still – no, crossed out, one mustn't think of such things.

The young girl who looks like a young man has sidled up to me and asks what I'm writing. I: 'Diary.' She glances inquisitively over my shoulder, is disappointed at seeing nothing but short-hand. I: 'It's of no value – just some private scribbling to give myself something to do.' . . .

9 a.m. Back in the garret. Grey morning, drizzling rain. I'm writing at the windowsill which is my desk. Shortly after three o'clock came the final all-clear. I came upstairs, took off my dress and shoes and fell into bed, which is always ready to be slept in. Five hours of deep sleep. The gas has gone off.

I've just been counting my ready cash – 452 marks; don't know what to do with so much, since the few purchases still possible can be bought with pennies. In addition, there's my account at the bank, approximately a thousand marks, untouched because there has been nothing to spend them on. (When starting this account during the first year of the war, I was still planning for peace and a trip round the world. This seems very long ago.) Nowadays some people rush to the bank, to those that are still functioning, and draw out their money. What for? When we go down, money will also go down the drain. Money, after all, paper money, has only a fictitious value and once the central government collapses, is just so much paper. I leaf through the roll of notes without any emotion whatever. Seems to me that at best this stuff could serve as a souvenir. As little pictures of bygone days. I assume the conquerors will bring along their own money, or they will print some military money – that is, if they let us get that far and we aren't condemned to work for a bowl of soup.

Noon. Endless rain. Went on foot to the Park Strasse and got myself another roll of notes to add to my pile of 'little pictures'. The clerk paid me my last month's salary and gave me a 'vacation'. The whole publishing firm is dissolved. The Labour Exchange has also given up completely; no one is interested any longer in available labour. In this respect we are now all our own masters.

Bureaucracy seems to flourish only in good weather. In any case, all public offices close down as soon as it rains shells. (Right now, by the way, it's very calm – a sinister calm.) We are no longer governed. And yet some kind of order always asserts itself, everywhere, in every cellar. When I was bombed out I noticed how even those who had been buried alive, the wounded, the scared, left the place of action in good order. This cellar is also ruled by some spirit of order and organisation, which must be deeply rooted in human nature. Even in the Stone Age humanity must have functioned on these lines. Instinct of the herd and preservation of the species . . .

On my way back from the Park Strasse I kept pace for a time with the tram; I couldn't board it as I don't have the Class III permit. The tram was almost empty, I counted eight passengers in it. Dozens of people walked past it in pouring rain; the tram could have taken them all, since it had to go anyway. But no – the principle of order has to be adhered to. It's deep inside us. We obey.

I bought some rolls at the baker's. The shelves are still well stocked. So far no signs of hysterical buying. Afterwards I went to the Food Office. Today my letter came up for the stamping of the potato coupons, Numbers 75 to 77. Although only two women were serving, instead of the usual crowd, it went surprisingly fast. They hardly looked at the coupons, just stamped them automatically, like machines. What is all this stamping really for? No one knows, yet everyone trundles there, convinced it must have some deeper meaning. According to an announcement, the letters X to Z are due to come up on 28 April.

Carts came rolling through the rain in the direction of the city, covered by sodden tarpaulins, under them soldiers. Filthy, grey-bearded faces, typical 'front' types, all of them old. All the carts drawn by small Polish horses, black and shiny with rain. Their loads: hay. It no longer looks like a motorised Blitzkrieg.

On my way home I sneaked into Professor K's deserted garden behind the black ruin of his house and picked some crocuses and lilac. I took some of them to Frau Golz, a neighbour in my previous house. We sat opposite one another over her coffee table and chatted – or rather, we bellowed against the newly started barrage. Frau Golz, with breaking voice: 'The flowers, the beautiful flowers . . .' And the tears pour down her face. I too feel miserable. Beauty hurts, nowadays. One is so full of death.

This morning I tried to remember how many dead people I have seen in my life. The first was Herr Schermann. I was five at the time, he seventy – silver-white hair on white silk, candles at his head, dignified and raised. So death was solemn and beautiful. Until 1928 when Hilde and Käte P. showed me their brother Hans who had died the previous day. He was lying on the sofa like a bundle of rags, his jaws held together with a blue handkerchief, the knees bent – a mess, a nothingness. Later on dead relatives, blue fingernails among flowers and rosaries.

Then in Paris the man who had been run over, smashed to a bloody pulp. And the frozen man on the river Moskwa. And lastly Father – angry, hard.

Yes, I have seen dead people, but not dying itself. No doubt this experience too will soon come my way. But I doubt that it will get me, I've so often given death the slip, and feel I'm to be spared. Probably most people have this feeling. How could they be so cheerful otherwise, surrounded as they are by so much death? There's no doubt that the threat to life enhances the will to live. I myself am burning with a more intense and larger flame than before the war of bombs. Each new day of life is a day of triumph. It's a challenge. One raises oneself, so to speak, higher and stands firmer on the ground. That day when we were shaken for the first time by bombs, I wrote in pencil on the walls of my room a Latin couplet which I still happen to remember:

> *Si fractus illabatur orbis,*
> *Impavidum ferient ruinae.*[1]

At that time one could still write to people abroad. I quoted the above lines in a letter to my friends D. in Stockholm, telling them about the intensity of our threatened existence, possibly in order to bolster my own courage. In doing so I also felt a slight pity for them, as though I, now grown up and feeling admitted to the centre of life, were corresponding with innocent children who had to be spared the naked truth.

---

[1] If the world should break and fall on him, its ruins would strike him unafraid. (*Epistles of Horace*)

LOUISE MERIWETHER

A native New Yorker, Louise Meriwether grew up in the Black community of Harlem, which is the locale of her first novel, *Daddy was a Number Runner*. The numbers was a sort of illegal lottery that afforded her father a living. After graduating from New York University Louise Meriwether moved to Los Angeles where she was a reporter for a Black newspaper and later worked in Hollywood at Universal Studios. While attending the University of California at Los Angeles, where she received a masters degree in Journalism, she wrote book reviews for the *Los Angeles Times* and conducted workshops for the Watts Writers Workshop. She has also published a novel on the civil war and three biographical books for children as well as short stories and articles. A former faculty member of Sarah Lawrence College and the University of Houston, she lives in New York City.

THE DREAM BOOK

from *Daddy was a Number Runner*

'I dreamed about fish last night, Francie,' Mrs Mackey said, sliding back the chain and opening the door to admit me. 'What number does Madame Zora's dream book give for fish?'

'I dreamed about fish last night, too,' I said, excited. Maybe that number was gonna play today. 'I dreamed a big catfish jumped off the plate and bit me. Madame Zora gives five fourteen for fish.'

I smiled happily at Mrs Mackey, ignoring the fact that if I stood here exchanging dreams with her, I'd be late getting back to school and Mrs Oliver would keep me in again.

'What more hunch could a body want,' Mrs Mackey grinned, 'us both dreaming about fish. Last night I dreamed I was going under the Bridge to buy some porgies and it started to rain. Not raindrops, Francie, but fish. Porgies. So I just opened up my shopping bag and caught me a bagful. Ain't that some dream?'

She laughed, her cheeks puffing up like black plums, and I laughed with her. You had to laugh with Mrs Mackey, she was that jolly and fat. She waddled to the dining-room table and I couldn't keep my eyes off her bouncing, big behind. When she passed by in the street, the boys would holler, 'Must be jelly 'cause jam don't shake,' and she would laugh with them. They were right. Her behind was a quivering, shivering delight and I hoped when I grew up I would have enough meat on my skinny butt to shimmy like that.

Mrs Mackey sat at the dining-room table and began writing her number slip.

'Mrs Mackey,' I said timidly, 'my father asks would you please have your numbers ready when I get here so I won't have to wait. I'm always late getting back to school.'

'They's ready, lil darlin'. I just wanna add five fourteen to my slip. I'm gonna play it for a quarter straight and sixty cents combination. How is your daddy and your mama, too?'

'They're both fine.'

She handed me her number slip and two dollar bills which I slipped into my middy blouse pocket.

'Them's my last two dollars, Francie, so you bring me back a hit tonight, you hear? I didn't mean to spend so much but I couldn't play our fishy dreams cheap, right?'

We both giggled and I left. I raced down the stairs, holding my breath. Lord, but this hallway was funky, all of those Harlem smells bumping together. Garbage rotting in the dumbwaiter mingled with the smell of frying fish. Some drunk had vomited wine in one corner and peed in another, and a foulness oozing up from the basement meant a dead rat was down there somewhere.

The air outside wasn't much better. It was a hot, stifling day, June 2, 1943. The curbs were lined with garbage cans overflowing into the gutters, and a droopy horse pulling a vegetable wagon down the avenue had just deposited a steaming pile of manure in the middle of the street.

The sudden heat had emptied the tenements. Kids too young for school played on the sidewalks while their mamas leaned out of their windows searching for a cool breeze or sat for a moment on the fire escape.

Knots of men, doping out their numbers, sat on the stoops or stood wide-legged in front of the storefronts, their black ribs shining through shirts limp with sweat. They spent most of their time playing the single action – betting on each number as it came out – and they stayed in the street all day until the last figure was out. I was glad Daddy was a number runner and not just hanging around the corners like these men. People were always asking me if I knew what number was out, like I was somebody special, and I guess I was. Everybody liked an honest runner like Daddy who paid off promptly the same night of the hit. A number runner is something like Santa Claus and any day you hit the number is Christmas.

I turned the corner and raced down forbidden 118th Street because I was late and didn't have time to go around the block. Daddy didn't want me in this street because of the prostitutes, but I knew all about them anyway. Sukie had told me and she ought to know. Her sister, China Doll, was a whore on this very same street. Anyway, it was too early for them to be out hustling, so Daddy didn't have to worry that I might see something I shouldn't.

A half-dozen boys standing in front of the drugstore were acting the fool, as usual, pretending they were razor fighting, their knickers hanging loose below their knees to look like long pants. Three of them were Ebony Earls, for sure, I thought. I tried to squeak past them but they saw me.

'Hey, skinny mama,' one of them yelled. 'When you put a little pork chops on those spareribs I'm gonna make love to you.'

The other boys folded up laughing and I scooted past, ignoring them. I always hated to pass a crowd of boys because they felt called upon to make some remark, usually nasty, especially now that I was almost twelve. So I was skinny and black and bad looking with my short hair and long neck and all that naked space in between. I looked just like a plucked chicken.

'Hey, there goes that yellow bastard,' one of the boys yelled. They turned their attention away from me to a skinny light kid who took off like the Seventh Avenue Express when he saw them. With a wild whoop the gang lit out after him, running over everybody who didn't move out of their way.

'Damn tramps,' a woman muttered, nursing her foot that had been trampled on.

I held my breath, hoping the light kid would escape. The howling boys rounded Lenox Avenue and their yells died down.

I ran down the street and turned the corner of Fifth Avenue, but ducked back when I saw Sukie playing hopscotch by herself in front of my house, not caring whether she was late for school or not. That Sukie. She was a year older than me, but much bigger. I waited until her back was turned to me, then with a burst of energy I ran toward my stoop. But she saw me and her moriney face turned pinker and she took out after me like a red witch. I was galloping around the first landing when I heard her below me in the vestibule.

'Ya gotta come downstairs sometime, ya bastard, and the first time I catch ya I'm gonna beat the shit out of ya.'

That Sukie. We were best friends but she picked a fight whenever she felt evil, which was often, and if she said she was going to beat the shit out of me, that's just what she would do.

I kept on running until I reached the top floor and then I collapsed on the last step, leaning my head against the rusty iron railing. I heard someone on the stairs leading up to the roof and my heart began that crazy tap dancing it does when I get scared.

Somebody whispered: 'Hey, little girl.'

I tiptoed around the railing and peeked up into the face of that white man who had followed me to the movies last Monday. He had tried to feel my legs and I changed my seat. He found me and sat next to me again, giving me a dime. His hands fumbled under my skirt and when he got to the elastic in my bloomers, I moved again. It was the same man, all right, short and bald with a fringe of fuzzy hair around the back of his head. He was standing in the roof doorway.

'Come on up for a minute, little girl,' he whispered.

I shook my head.

'I've got a dime for you.'

'Throw it down.'

'Come and get it. I won't hurt you. I just want you to touch this.'

He fumbled with the front of his pants and took out his pee-pee. It certainly was ugly, purple and wet looking. Sukie said that everybody did it. Fucked. That's how babies were made, she said. I believed the whores did it but not my own mother and father. But Sukie insisted everybody did it, and she was usually right.

'Come on up, little girl. I won't hurt you.'

'I don't wanna.'

'I'll give you a dime.'

'Throw it down.'

'Come on up and get it.'

'I'm gonna tell my Daddy.'

He threw the dime down. I picked it up and the man disappeared through the roof door. I went back around the railing and leaned on our door and the lock sprang open. Daddy was always promising to fix that lock but he never did.

Our apartment was a railroad flat, each small room set flush in front of the other. The door opened into the dining room, so junky with heavy furniture that the room seemed tinier than it was. In the middle of the room a heavy, round mahogany table squatted on dragon-head legs. Against the wall was a long matching buffet with dragon heads on the sideboards. Scattered about were four straight-back chairs with the slats falling out, their tall backs also carved with ugly dragons. The furniture, scratched with scars, was a gift from the Jewish plumber downstairs, and was one year older than God.

'Mother,' I yelled. 'I'm home.'

'Stop screaming, Francie,' Mother said from the kitchen, 'and put the numbers up.'

I took the drawer out of the buffet, and reaching to the ledge on the side, pulled out an envelope filled with number slips. I put in Mrs Mackey's numbers and the money, replaced the envelope on the ledge, and slid the drawer back on its runners. It stuck. I took it out again and shoved the envelope farther to the side. Now the drawer closed smoothly.

'Did you push the envelope way back so the drawer closes good?' Mother asked as I went into the kitchen.

'Yes, Mother.'

I sat down at the chipped porcelain table, tilting crazily

on uneven legs. Absentmindedly I knocked a scurrying roach off the table top to the floor and crunched it under my sneaker.

'If you don't stop racing up those stairs like that, one of these days you gonna drop dead.'

'Yes, Mother.'

I wanted to tell her that Sukie had promised to beat me up again, but Mother would only repeat that Sukie would stop bullying me when I stopped running away from her.

Mother was short and dumpy, her long breasts and wide hips all sort of running together. Her best feature was her skin, a smooth light brown, with a cluster of freckles over her nose. Her hair was short and thin, and she had rotting yellow teeth, what was left of them. In truth, she had more empty spaces in her mouth than she had teeth, but you would never know she was sensitive about it except for the fact that she seldom smiled. It was hard to know what Mother was sensitive about. Daddy shouted and cursed when he was mad, and danced around and hugged you when he was feeling good. But you just couldn't tell about Mother. She didn't curse you but she didn't kiss you either.

She placed a sandwich before me, potted meat stretched from here to yonder with mayonnaise, which I eyed with suspicion.

'I don't like potted meat.'

'You don't like nothing. That's why you're so skinny. If you don't want it, don't eat it. There ain't nothing else.'

She gave me a weak cup of tea.

'We got any sugar?'

'Borrow some from Mrs Caldwell.'

I got a chipped cup from the cupboard and going to the dining-room window, I knocked on our neighbor's window-pane. The Caldwells lived in the apartment building next door and our dining rooms faced each other. They were West Indians and Maude was my best friend, next to Sukie. We were the same age, but where my legs were long, Maude's were bowed just like an O. Maude's father had died last year, and Pee Wee, her oldest brother, had just gone off to jail again, which was his second home. Maude came to the window.

'Can I borrow a half cup of sugar?' I asked.

She took the cup and disappeared, returning in a few minutes with it almost full. 'Y'all got any bread?' she asked. 'I need one more piece to make a sandwich.'

'Maude wants to borrow a piece of bread,' I told Mother.

'Give her two slices,' Mother said.

I gave Maude two pieces of whole wheat.

'Elizabeth's coming back home today with her kids and Robert,' she said. 'Their furniture got put out in the street.'

Elizabeth was her oldest sister and Robert her husband. He used to be a tailor but wasn't working now.

'Y'all gonna be crowded,' I said.

'Yep,' she answered, her head disappearing from the window.

I returned to the kitchen and told Mother Elizabeth was coming home.

'Lord, where they all gonna sleep?' she asked.

Maude and her sister, Rebecca, sixteen, had one bedroom, their mother the other, and their brother, Vallie, slept in the front room.

I sat down at the table and began to sip my tea, looking at the greasy walls lumpy with layers of paint over cracked plaster. Vomit-green, that's what Daddy called its color. The ceiling was dotted with brown and yellow water stains. Daddy had patched up the big leaks but it didn't do much good and when it rained outside it rained inside, too. The last time the landlord had been there to collect the rent Daddy told him the roof needed fixing and that if the ceiling fell down and hurt one of his kids he was going to pitch the landlord headfirst down the stairs. The landlord left in a hurry but that didn't get our leaks fixed.

The outside door slammed and my brother Sterling came into the kitchen and slumped down at the table. He was fourteen, brown-skinned, and lanky, his long, tight face always bunched into a frown, and today was no exception.

'Where's James Junior?' Mother asked.

'I'm not his keeper,' Sterling grumbled. 'I didn't see him at recess.'

James Junior, my oldest brother, was a year older than Sterling,
and good looking like Daddy. He was nicer than Sterling, too, but slow in his studies, always getting left back, and Sterling had already passed him in school and was going to graduate this month.

The door slammed shut again and I could tell from the heavy footsteps that it was Daddy. I jumped up and ran into the dining room hurling myself against him. He laughed and scooped me up in his arms, swinging me off the floor. Mother was always telling me that men were handsome, not beautiful, but she just didn't understand. Handsome meant one thing and beautiful something else and I knew for sure what Daddy was. Beautiful. In the first place he was a giant of a man, wide and thick and hard. He was dark brown, black really, with thick crinkly hair and a wide laughing beautiful mouth. I loved Daddy's mouth.

He sat down at the dining-room table and began pulling number slips from his pocket.

'Get the envelope for me, sugar.'

I removed the drawer and handed him the envelope, smiling. 'I dreamed a big catfish jumped off the plate and bit me, Daddy. The dream book gives five fourteen for fish. And Mrs Mackey dreamed it was raining fish.'

'Great God and Jim,' Daddy cried, and we grinned at each other. 'My chart gives a five to lead today. I'm gonna play a dollar on five fourteen straight and sixty cents combination.'

Daddy said that of all the family my dreams hit the most. If 514 came out today we'd be rich, which would be a good thing 'cause Mother was always grumbling that we were playing all of our commission back on the numbers.

From force of habit I huddled close to the radiator, which was cold now. The green and red checkerboard linoleum around it was worn so thin you couldn't even see its pattern and there was a jagged hole in the floor near the pipe almost big enough to get your foot through. Daddy was always nailing cardboard and linoleum over that hole but it kept wearing out.

'Henrietta,' Daddy called, 'where are the boys?'

Mother came to the kitchen door. 'Sterling's here eating, but James Junior ain't come home yet.'

Daddy's fist hit the table with a suddenness which made me jump. 'If that boy's stayed out of school again it's gonna be me and his behind. Sterling,' he shouted, 'where's your brother?'

'I ain't seen him since this morning,' Sterling answered from the kitchen.

Daddy turned on Mother. 'If that boy gets into any trouble I'm gonna let his butt rot in jail, you hear? I'm warning you. I've done told him time and time again to stop hanging out with those Ebony Earls, but his head is damned hard. All of them's gonna end up in Sing Sing, you mark my words, and ain't no Coffin ever been to jail before. Do you know that?'

Mother nodded. She also knew, as I did, that Daddy would be the first one downtown to see about Junior if anything happened to him.

Junior had started hanging around with the Ebony Earls a few months ago, together with his buddies Sonny and Maude's brother Vallejo. Sterling didn't belong to the gang. He said gangs were stupid and boys who hung out together like that were morons.

Daddy started adding up the amounts of his number slips and counting the money. Mother sat down at the table beside him and said nervously that she heard Slim Jim had been arrested. He was a number runner like Daddy.

'Slim Jim is a fool,' Daddy said. 'His banker thinks he can operate outside the syndicate but nobody can buck Dutch Schultz. The cops will arrest anybody his boys finger, and they did just that. Fingered Slim Jim and his banker.'

'Maybe you'd better stop collecting numbers now before ...' Mother began nervously, but Daddy cut her off.

'For christsakes, Henrietta, let's not go through that again. How many times I gotta tell you it ain't much more dangerous collecting numbers than playing them. As long as the cops are paid off, which they are, they ain't gonna bother me. Schultz even pays off that stupid ass, Dodge, we've got for a district attorney, so stop worrying.'

Mother played the numbers like everyone else in Harlem but she was scared about Daddy being a number runner. Daddy started working for Jocko on commission about six months ago when he lost his house-painting job, which hadn't been none too steady to begin with.

Jocko's name was really Jacques and he was a tall Creole from Haiti. He wore a blue beret cocked on the side of his head and had curly black hair and olive skin. Now, Jocko was handsome but he wasn't beautiful. He ran a candy store on Fifth Avenue and 117th Street as a front and everybody said he was really close to Big Boy Donatelli, his banker, who was real close to Dutch Schultz. Daddy said Jocko was as big a man in the syndicate as a colored man could get since the gangsters took over the numbers. Daddy said the gangsters controlled everything in Harlem – the numbers, the whores, and the pimps who brought them their white trade.

Mother grumbled: 'I thought Mayor La Guardia say he was gonna clean up all this mess.'

'If they really wanted to clean up this town,' Daddy said, 'they would stop picking on the poor niggers trying to hit a number for a dime so they won't starve to death. Where else a colored man gonna get six hundred dollars for one? What they need to do is snatch the gangsters banking the numbers, they're the ones raking in the big money. But the cops ain't about to cut off their gravy train. But you stop worrying now, Henrietta. Ain't nothing gonna happen to me, you hear?'

Mother nodded slowly. Then she looked at me. 'Francie, get up from there and go on back to school before you be late again. Sterling,' she yelled.

'Okay,' he answered from the kitchen. 'I'm comin'.'

'Francie! Don't let me have to tell you again.'

'Okay, Mother. I'm goin'. 'Bye, Daddy.'

''Bye, sugar.'

When I got downstairs I peeked outside but Sukie was nowhere in sight. I ran most of the way back to school but was good and late anyhow.

ELIZABETH VON ARNIM

Elizabeth von Arnim (1866–1941) was born in Sydney, Australia, and brought up in England. In 1894, she and her first husband, Count von Arnim, moved to Nassenheide, in Pomerania, which was wittily encapsulated in her first and most famous novel: *Elizabeth and Her German Garden* (1899). The 21 books she then went on to write were signed 'By the Author of *Elizabeth and Her German Garden*', and later simply 'By Elizabeth'.

After her husband's death in 1910, Elizabeth built the Chateau Soleil in Switzerland where she entertained such friends as H.G. Wells (with whom she had an affair) and Katherine Mansfield (her cousin). On the outbreak of war, she escaped to England with three of her four children, although the fourth was forced to remain in Germany. In London she married again, albeit briefly to the second Lord Russell, brother of Bertrand Russell. This proved to be a disastrous marriage and in 1919 the couple separated. Her novel, *Vera*, draws on the marriage.

A greatly dismissed literary figure of her time, she was described by Alice Meynell as 'one of the three finest wits of her day'. She died at the age of 75.

THE GARDEN IS THE PLACE I GO

from *Elizabeth and Her German Garden*

How happy I was! I don't remember any time quite so perfect since the days when I was too little to do lessons and was turned out with sugar on my eleven o'clock bread and butter on to a lawn closely strewn with dandelions and daisies. The sugar on the bread and butter has lost its charm, but I love the dandelions and daisies even more passionately now than then ...

During those six weeks I lived in a world of dandelions and delights. The dandelions carpeted the three lawns – they used to be lawns, but have long since blossomed out into meadows filled with every sort of pretty weed – and under and among the groups of leafless oaks and beeches were blue hepaticas, white anemones, violets, and celandines in sheets. The celandines in particular delighted me with their clean, happy brightness, so beautifully trim and newly varnished, as though they too had had the painters at work on them ...

There were only the old housekeeper and her handmaiden in the house, so that on the plea of not giving too much trouble I could indulge what my other half calls my *fantaisie déréglée* as regards meals – that is to say, meals so simple that they could be brought out to the lilacs on a tray; and I lived, I remember, on salad and bread and tea the whole time, sometimes a very tiny pigeon appearing at lunch to save me, as the old lady thought, from starvation. Who but a woman could have stood salad for six weeks, even salad sanctified by the presence and scent of the most gorgeous lilac masses? I did, and grew in grace every day, though I have never liked it since. How often now, oppressed by the necessity of assisting at three dining-room meals daily, two of which are conducted by the functionaries held indispensable to a proper maintenance of the family dignity, and all of which are pervaded by joints of meat, how often do I think of my salad days, forty in number, and of the blessedness of being alone as I was then alone!

And then the evenings, when the workmen had all gone and the house was left to emptiness and echoes, and the old housekeeper had gathered up her rheumatic limbs into her bed, and my little room in quite another part of the house had been set ready, how reluctantly I used to leave the friendly frogs and owls, and with my heart somewhere down in my shoes lock the door to the garden behind me, and pass through the long series of echoing south rooms full of shadows and ladders and ghostly pails of painters' mess, and humming a tune to make myself believe I liked it, go rather slowly across the brick-floored hall, up the creaking stairs, down the long whitewashed passage, and with a final rush of panic whisk into my room and double lock and bolt the door!

There were no bells in the house, and I used to take a great dinner-bell to bed with me so that at least I might be able to make a noise if frightened in the night, though what good it would have been I don't know, as there was no one to hear. The housemaid slept in another little cell opening out of mine, and we two were the only living creatures in the great empty west wing. She evidently did not believe in ghosts, for I could hear how she fell asleep immediately after getting into bed; nor do I believe in them, 'mais je les redoute', as a French lady said, who from her books appears to have been strong-minded . . .

How pretty the bedrooms looked with nothing in them but their cheerful new papers! Sometimes I would go into those that were finished and build all sorts of castles in the air about their future and their past. Would the nuns who had lived in them know their little whitewashed cells again, all gay with delicate flower papers and clean white paint? And how astonished they would be to see cell Number 14 turned into a bathroom, with a bath big enough to ensure a cleanliness of body equal to their purity of soul! They would look upon it as a snare of the tempter; and I know that in my own case I only began to be shocked at the blackness of my nails the day that I began to lose the first whiteness of my soul by falling in love at fifteen with the parish organist, or rather with the glimpse of surplice and Roman nose and fiery moustache which was all I ever saw of him, and which I loved to distraction for at least six months; at the end of which time, going out with my governess one day, I passed him in the street, and discovered that his unofficial garb was a frock-coat combined with a turn-down collar and a 'bowler' hat, and never loved him any more.

The first part of that time of blessedness was the most perfect, for I had not a thought of anything but the peace and beauty all round me. Then he appeared suddenly who has a right to appear when and how he will and rebuked me for never having written, and when I told him that I had been literally too happy to think of writing he seemed to take it as a reflection on himself that I could be happy alone. I took him round the garden along the new paths I had had made, and showed him the acacia and lilac glories, and he said that it was the purest selfishness to enjoy myself when neither he nor the offspring were with me, and that the lilacs wanted thoroughly pruning. I tried to appease him by offering him the whole of my salad and toast supper which stood ready at the foot of the little veranda steps when we came back, but nothing appeased that Man of Wrath, and he said he would go straight back to the neglected family. So he went; and the remainder of the precious time was disturbed by twinges of conscience (to which I am much subject) whenever I found myself wanting to jump for joy. I went to look at the painters every time my feet were for taking me to look at the garden; I trotted diligently up and down the passages; I criticised and suggested and commanded more in one day than I had done in all the rest of the time; I wrote regularly and sent my love; but I could not manage to fret and yearn. What are you to do if your conscience is clear and your liver in order and the sun is shining?

10 May – I knew nothing whatever last year about gardening and this year know very little more, but I have dawnings of what may be done, and have at least made one great stride – from ipomæa to tea-roses.

The garden was an absolute wilderness. It is all round the house, but the principal part is on the south side and has evidently always been so. The south front is one-storeyed, a long series of rooms opening one into the other, and the walls are covered with Virginia creeper. There is a little veranda in the middle, leading by a flight of rickety wooden steps down into what seems to have been the only spot in the whole place that was ever cared for. This is a semicircle cut into the lawn and edged with privet, and in this semicircle are eleven beds of different sizes bordered with box and arranged round a sundial, and the sundial is very venerable and moss-grown, and greatly beloved by me. These beds were the only sign of any attempt at gardening to be seen (except a solitary crocus that came up all by itself each spring in the grass, not because it wanted to, but because it could not help it), and these I had sown with ipomæa, the whole eleven, having found a German gardening book, according to which ipomæa in vast quantities was the one thing needful to turn the most hideous desert into a paradise. Nothing else in that book was recommended with anything like the same warmth, and being entirely ignorant of the quantity of seed necessary, I bought ten pounds of it and had it sown not only in the eleven beds but round nearly every tree, and then waited in great agitation for the promised paradise to appear. It did not, and I learned my first lesson.

Luckily I had sown two great patches of sweet-peas which made me very happy all the summer, and then there were some sunflowers and a few hollyhocks under the south windows, with

Madonna lilies in between. But the lilies, after being trans-
planted, disappeared to my great dismay, for how was I to know
it was the way of lilies? And the hollyhocks turned out to be
rather ugly colours, so that my first summer was decorated and
beautified solely by sweet-peas . . .

16 May – The garden is the place I go to for refuge and shelter,
not the house. In the house are duties and annoyances, servants
to exhort and admonish, furniture, and meals; but out there
blessings crowd round me at every step – it is there that I am
sorry for the unkindness in me, for those selfish thoughts that
are so much worse than they feel, it is there that all my sins and
silliness are forgiven, there that I feel protected and at home,
and every flower and weed is a friend and every tree a lover.
When I have been vexed I run out to them for comfort, and
when I have been angry without just cause, it is there that I find
absolution. Did ever a woman have so many friends? And always
the same, always ready to welcome me and fill me with cheerful
thoughts. Happy children of a common Father, why should I,
their own sister, be less content and joyous than they? Even in a
thunderstorm when other people are running into the house I
run out of it. I do not like thunderstorms – they frighten me for
hours before they come, because I always feel them on the way;
but it is odd that I should go for shelter to the garden. I feel
better there, more taken care of, more petted. When it thun-
ders, the April baby says, 'There's *lieber Gott* scolding those angels
again.' And once, when there was a storm in the night, she
complained loudly and wanted to know why *lieber Gott* didn't do
the scolding in the daytime, as she had been so *tight* asleep. They
all three speak a wonderful mixture of German and English,
adulterating the purity of their native tongue by putting in
English words in the middle of a German sentence. It always
reminds me of justice tempered by mercy . . .

3 June – This is such an out-of-the-way corner of the world that
it requires quite unusual energy to get here at all, and I am thus
delivered from casual callers; while, on the other hand, people

I love, or people who love me, which is much the same thing, are not likely to be deterred from coming by the roundabout train journey and the long drive at the end. Not the least of my many blessings is that we have only one neighbour. If you have to have neighbours at all, it is at least a mercy that there should be only one; for with people dropping in at all hours and wanting to talk to you, how are you to get on with your life, I should like to know, and read your books, and dream your dreams to your satisfaction? Besides, there is always the certainty that either you or the dropper-in will say something that would have been better left unsaid, and I have a holy horror of gossip and mischief-making. A woman's tongue is a deadly weapon and the most difficult thing in the world to keep in order, and things slip off it with a facility nothing short of appalling at the very moment when it ought to be most quiet. In such cases the only safe course is to talk steadily about cooks and children, and to pray that the visit may not be too prolonged, for if it is you are lost. Cooks I have found to be the best of all subjects – the most phlegmatic flush into life at the mere word, and the joys and sufferings connected with them are experiences common to us all . . .

7 *December* – I have been to England. I went for at least a month and stayed a week in a fog and was blown home again in a gale. Twice I fled before the fogs into the country to see friends with gardens, but it was raining, and except the beautiful lawns (not to be had in the Fatherland) and the infinite possibilities, there was nothing to interest the intelligent and garden-loving foreigner, for the good reason that you cannot be interested in gardens under an umbrella. So I went back to the fogs, and after groping about for a few days more began to long inordinately for Germany. A terrific gale sprang up after I had started, and the journey both by sea and land was full of horrors, the trains in Germany being heated to such an extent that it is next to impossible to sit still, great gusts of hot air coming up under the cushions, the cushions themselves being very hot and the wretched traveller still hotter.

But when I reached my home and got out of the train into the purest, brightest snow-atmosphere, the air so still that the whole world seemed to be listening, the sky cloudless, the crisp snow sparkling underfoot and on the trees, and a happy row of three beaming babies awaiting me, I was consoled for all my torments, only remembering them enough to wonder why I had gone away at all.

PARIS FRANZ

Paris Franz was born in Ventura, California, and brought up in England, where she spent most of her childhood trying to live down her name. After a series of secretarial jobs, she gave in to the lure of travel and writing, and now lives and works in London as a freelance journalist.

MORE BY ACCIDENT
THAN DESIGN

from *Desert Dancers*

Most of my first two years were spent in my mother's dressing rooms in Las Vegas, surrounded by sequins and feathers, chaos and colour. I've always regretted not being able to remember that time, the time when Sophie, my mother and I were together. There are occasions when I think I do remember it, but I suspect I'm just imagining myself into the photographs Sophie brought with her when we left.

Those dressing rooms have taken on a vivid quality in my imagination. I can see my chubby self crawling across the floor in search of hairpins and feathers and discarded lengths of scarlet silk and jade-green taffeta; I can see dancers scurrying around in various states of undress and a small man popping his head around the door and yelling 'Five minutes to curtain up!' The rooms are full of chatter as make-up is applied and removed, costumes inspected and wriggled into, while the dressing tables are covered in make-up brushes and false eyelashes and sundry aged pots, all exuding that odd, intoxicating odour of greasepaint. The wardrobes are full to bursting and the threadbare dressing gowns hanging from spindly hooks often fall to the floor. Everything, from the multi-coloured sequins sparkling in the harsh fluorescent light to the feather boas and bejewelled wigs, has a life of its own.

I'm told that my high chair served as some kind of clothes

rail, perpetually draped in silks and satins, and that, completely unfazed, I would peep out from the midst of all this material and wrap it around me as though it were my own. (I think I was spoiled by such early exposure to fine fabrics, as I can't stand the feel of polyester.)

There's a photograph of me riding Tanya the elephant backstage at the Casino de Paris at the Dunes Hotel. Sophie is pretty sure it was the Dunes, as the Tropicana was far too chic for animal acts. I was about a year old at the time, maybe less, balanced on the neck of this gigantic beast like a tiny mahout, fascinated by the prickly hairs and slate-grey skin beneath me. Tanya – the star of the opening act – was a well-trained elephant and kept totally still as I was lifted on and a photograph was taken, some half-hour or so before the show began. Everyone wanted their picture taken with Tanya.

The photo shows Sophie holding me steady with her long, pale hands. A statuesque vision in royal-blue ruffles, she and the master of ceremonies are beaming at the camera, and a young man in a black waistcoat and striped shirt is unsuccessfully trying to duck out of the picture. As for me, I am gazing into the distance; I look a little alarmed at being so high up. The photo shows Tanya to be a small elephant, as elephants go, but she must have seemed huge to me. I was on top of the world and nothing could touch me.

My mother went on to frequent a great many stages and dressing rooms over the years, in diverse parts of the world. She was the lead dancer at the Casino du Liban in Beirut for nearly eight years. She was with the Bluebell Girls at the Lido in Paris and the Scala in Barcelona. But Las Vegas would be the only place where I was a part of her life.

Sophie has hung up her fishnet tights now, after a career of over twenty years, and gone to live in a small town in Italy, near the border with Slovenia. It is a strange place for her to have ended up, considering all the places she's been, all the things she's seen. But then, Sophie has always travelled more by accident than by design. She carries her own world around with her wherever she goes, unaware that there is another world outside. She could just as easily be living in Bahrain or Brighton as Friuli-Venezia Giulia. It's all the same to her.

This is, after all, the woman who lived in Lebanon for eight years and never saw the cedars ...

ARRIVAL

It was sixteen years before that the three of us – grandmother, mother and daughter – came together for the first time and in the years to come it was sometimes difficult to tell who was who. In the end, though, it always came down to the same thing: Ginger was Mum, Sophie was Sophie and that was that.

Those early years are little more than a series of snapshots to me now, just photographs and snatches of memory. Ginger says she can remember her mother shaking her fist at the trains which carried prisoners of war as they passed the end of their garden in Peckham, when she was just a year old, but I find it hard to remember that far back. I can't remember Las Vegas, for instance, or even the house in Chapman Road. It seems a shame, as the pictures show a happy baby, oblivious of impending matrimonial disaster, perfectly content to play in Sophie's dressing room. There's a picture of us there, taken before the show at the Casino de Paris. Sophie is wearing a blonde wig, piled very high; it's adorned by a band of sparkling gold and topped with long red feathers. Her earrings are sparkling, too. She's also wearing a black cloak with a fur collar and she's holding me in arms encased in long, cerise gloves. I must have been about seven or eight months old at the time, convinced that it was right that my mother should sparkle so, although unaware that I shared the name of the casino.

I was two and a half when Sophie brought me to England, and Ginger met us at the airport. I didn't know her, but I'm told I ran straight to her anyway, through the mêlée in the arrivals lounge. Everyone runs to Ginger, you see: cats, dogs, babies even stranger than myself. She didn't know me, either – Sophie had never bothered to send a picture – but it didn't matter; Ginger scooped me up in a great big hug, kissed me on the forehead, and our partnership was formed, had we but known it.

It was some moments before Sophie herself emerged from Customs, ambling amiably through the crowd. Ginger spotted her and sighed, looking me up and down once more. She still sighs when she tells the story, even now. Hadn't she always said that Sophie didn't have a clue? Here was more evidence. It was November, a wet and windy and altogether dismal November. Winter had arrived with a vengeance. And what was I wearing? A sleeveless cotton dress and a less than dainty pair of sandals, that's what I was wearing.

Ginger raised her eyebrows as Sophie approached. Ginger's eyebrows were famous for what they could do to people.

'You're not in the desert now,' she said, acidly. 'This is England in November. This child needs warm clothes.'

Sophie ran a hand through her hair – she was blonde then – and did her best to look contrite. It may have been due to the length of the flight on that occasion, but it was fairly safe to assume that the advice followed its customary route, in one ear and out the other.

Ginger gave her another one of those looks of hers, and then we headed out to the car and the stop-start drive through rush-hour traffic to the house in Chapman Road. Ginger turned the heating up and I fell asleep.

Clothes were the first of many things that Ginger bought for me over the years. A woolly sweater, a pair of trousers I would soon outgrow, a coat complete with hood, a pair of boots. She has long had a thing about me being cold.

Sophie had lived in Las Vegas some four years before she bolted, with suitcase and baby in tow. A desert fever – a feeling almost of panic at being confronted by so much space, so much light – had been seeping, unheeded, into her bones all that time, and marriage and motherhood had only added to the strain. Sophie herself could never be sure about the how and the why of it all, but that didn't bother her unduly. Observation, of both herself and others, had never been one of her strong points, and she was happy with that. She would, she once said with a laugh, make a terrible witness.

Excitement, that was what she needed. She couldn't feel bored, she just couldn't. The spotlight at the Tropicana was getting too, too familiar – Sophie had a short attention span long before that became popular – and the wide desert sky was beginning to press in on her with its unending blueness. And so she left, without a plan beyond that of showing the baby – or 'the thing', as she called me – to the relatives on the other side of the pond. Sophie's never been one for planning ahead. There was talk of rehearsals in France, but other than that she really had no idea. All she knew was she was back home with Ginger and, for a while – at least according to a letter she wrote to my father – she felt like she belonged. 'I had no intention of staying when I first got here,' she wrote, 'but I just don't want to leave so soon.'

I think she genuinely enjoyed life in Las Vegas, at least to begin with. An oasis of neon and chrome slap bang in the middle of a landscape of scrub and rock, it was a new playground to explore, a beacon for gamblers and thrill-seekers and entrepreneurs. When she first went there, she'd had to change planes in New York, then fly into Vegas on the same flight as the Rat Pack. Her picture appeared in the paper, beneath a picture of Dean Martin and Sammy Davis Jr. It's a grainy black and white shot, but she still manages to look stunning, with her miniskirt and white ankle boots, all round smiling face and long, long legs. She was in demand from the start, at the Tropicana with its imported Folies Bergères, and the Dunes, where diners could eat at the Sultan's Table with Arturo Romero and his Magic Violins.

But she was off sick the night Elvis was in the audience, and maybe that was when the rot set in.

All things considered, I probably should have gone on the stage too, and I did consider it once, but I think the surrounding desert has proved to be a more lasting influence. Unlike Sophie, I love big skies and sparse vegetation and landscapes older than time. I feel at home with space on every side.

Sophie brought a lot of photographs with her when we left Las Vegas, and sometimes I can't look at them without thinking I must be looking at photographs of strangers, in some alternate universe. There's the photograph of Sophie backstage at the Lido in Paris, shortly after she'd arrived to join the Bluebells. She's sitting on a stool, her hair dyed red, and she's looking glum. There's the shot of Sophie, posing haughtily on stage at the Tropicana in Las Vegas, blonde hair peeping out from underneath a head-dress inspired by ancient Egypt. She's wearing long, white gloves and fishnet tights and her costume – what there is of it – is adorned with jewels. An outfit to pose in, not dance in, that's for sure: with those heels and that head-dress, she must have been a good seven feet tall. And the eye make-up is very sixties.

There's also the black and white eight-by-ten of the three of us together – mother, father and child. A family, in other words. It's a curious notion. Scrubbed of make-up, Sophie looks barely more than a child herself. My father looks young, too, with his dark hair neatly brushed back. Then there's the shot of Sophie and me outside what I assume to be our apartment. We're smiling, I'm wearing her sunglasses, and she's wearing a floppy hat, and everything looks hard and bright in the glare of the desert sun.

My parents were, I discovered, better left unmentioned. If I should be asked about them, I had a stock of answers ready. Life was much easier that way. My name, however, was not so easily dealt with. Called out every morning at registration, it was out there for everyone to hear. I thought, hoped, prayed that, just once, someone else would bear the brunt of the bullying, for whatever perceived deformity – glasses, a stutter, a constant need to go to the loo – but no, my name ensured I stayed in the spotlight. I would sit at my small wooden desk, with its ink-stains and scratches, and study the specks of chalk which hung suspended in the air, all the while wishing my name was Susan or Jane. There were a lot of Susans and Janes in my class.

Even the teachers and the people who worked in the office could be less than helpful when it came to my name. Once, when I wasn't well, Ginger rang the school to tell them I wouldn't be in that day. 'I'm calling for Paris Franz,' she said. 'From where?' said the voice on the other end of the line.

School could be a contradictory place. Fate and social ineptitude meant that playtime was something to be endured rather than enjoyed, but an eagerness to learn meant that the classroom was more than a simple place of refuge. It was a place of knowledge, a place where I could satisfy my curiosity, or at least try to. Unlike Sophie, I wanted to see the cedars. I wanted to see everything.

It only made things worse, of course. Scholarly endeavour was frowned upon almost as much as having a strange name and parents across the sea. Eggheads were definitely beyond the pale.

Most lessons held my attention, although I have to admit that arithmetic wasn't one of them. Arithmetic and home economics were both a dead loss as far as I was concerned. The concept of cooking was one I instinctively shied away from and the blackboard scrawled with sums was already becoming a blur. So I sat at the back as the teacher lectured us about fractions and let my mind wander far away from the heavy desks and whitewashed walls, and hoped the teacher wouldn't ask me anything. I hated it when that happened. One of my English reports said that I was very good but, when asked to read aloud, I had a tendency to rush in order to end the ordeal.

My mind wandered far and wide, as I daydreamed there at the back of the class. I daydreamed about Great-Uncle Bill on the frozen waters of the Crooked River, dressed in furs and fishing for salmon with a harpoon; I daydreamed about Sophie doing the can-can, her long legs encased in fishnet tights, like in the picture we had at home; I daydreamed about the postcard from Baalbek.

It had taken almost a month to reach us – post from Lebanon

always took a long time – and it showed the Great Temple, overlaid with a picture of a large, majestic tree, a cedar of Lebanon. I asked if there were any cedars in Croydon, and Ginger said she didn't think so.

Sophie had been to see Comédie Française at the Baalbek Festival. She and Marco had stayed at the Palmyra Hotel, a hotel which was said to have a Roman theatre buried beneath its floors and had over the years played host to everyone from Louis Napoleon to the Empress of Abyssinia. 'It was great!' Sophie wrote. 'There were singers and musicians and dancers – anyone who is anyone is here!'

I looked at the photo of the Temple, with its columns and monumental stairs, and imagined dancers pirouetting from column to column and men in white robes striding across the stone. I saw myself running from pillar to pillar, trying to catch a glimpse of Sophie in hew new costume, whirling like a dervish. I imagined camels munching tufts of stubbly grass at the foot of the steps. It wasn't such a big leap of the imagination – I had recently seen camels on television, loping across endless sand dunes, and Ginger had said that they lived in the Middle East. I knew Lebanon was in the Middle East, and that Baalbek was in Lebanon. Therefore, camels were at Baalbek.

And then, at last, the bell would ring and I would be back in the classroom, transported from my desert temple in time to join the daily stampede to leave. And Ginger would be there at the gates, smart in her dark green trouser suit, waiting to take me home . . .

THE DOCUMENTARY

I never did get to see Sophie on stage. The documentary was the closest I came. I was seven years old by that time, old enough to know that it didn't do to stand out from the crowd yet secretly rather glad all the same. My moment of glory, brief though it would be, had come.

'My mum's going to be on television!'

The announcement was enough to silence my fellow pupils, temporarily at least, which was something of an achievement in itself.

The documentary was to be about Beirut, that playpen of the filthy rich as it still was in those days. It was the first of many which would appear in the years to come. This time, though, it wouldn't be about street battles and car bombs and hostages, it would be about the Casino du Liban, along with its clientele of international businessmen and decorous women with lots of hair. The cameras would record all aspects of the show, from the belly dancers to the ice spectacle to the Dancers of the Nile. Sophie would take centre stage, dancing the Jungle Story and modelling the long black and white cape she wore when riding the elephants which didn't go anywhere, and I knew she would look stunning.

She had been in Lebanon some time by then, and was enjoying every minute. True, the heat could sometimes be unbearable and she did once have to tell a sheikh to get stuffed, but she had a flat which looked out on to the Mediterranean and a job which meant she didn't have to get up early. What more did she need?

The incident with the sheikh always made her laugh. He was a regular in the audience, and one night he sent a note backstage asking if she'd like to go to dinner with him after the show. She'd never been to dinner with a sheikh before and wasn't at all sure. It was Callie, the flame-haired showgirl from Guildford, who dared her to accept.

'Go on,' she said. 'Go for it.'

'Oh, all right,' Sophie replied, as much to shut Callie up as anything else.

Sauntering into the lobby, over six foot in her heels, she towered above the sheikh, which didn't get things off to a good start. He looked quite splendid in his robes, but it couldn't be denied he also looked short. This was the tail-end of the sixties – Sophie had the miniskirt and the messy hairdo, the whole bit. There was an awkwardness neither could overcome. The sheikh tried a gallant smile but went on to burn his boats when he asked

– no, told – her to walk three paces behind him. That's when she told him to get stuffed.

Chauvinist sheikhs apart, Sophie had a good time in Lebanon. She was earning a packet and she didn't have me to worry about. She didn't have anything to worry about. Life was jolly. She rehearsed and she danced; she sipped cocktails on the terrace of the Saint George's Hotel, from where she could see a fleet of ships riding at anchor, waiting their turn to be unloaded; she swam in the Mediterranean and went skiing up in the mountains at Faraya, just like it said in the tourist brochures. Well, perhaps it would be more accurate to say that she posed on skis at Faraya.

It would all come crashing down before long, of course. Refugee camps were an established part of the landscape, and the Falangists were already marching, like sinister Boy Scouts, in the foothills of Mount Lebanon. A newspaper report said that 'bandits' had shot up the souk in Tripoli. But the restaurants were still full, the water-skiers were out in force and the lights of the Casino du Liban lit up the coast as the sun went down. The signs of what was to come were all around, but no one wanted to know, Sophie least of all.

As things turned out, the Casino would remain open during much of the mayhem and the roof, so Sophie said, was a good place from which to watch the action, rather like a matinée at the Odeon.

The fate of the documentary was perhaps the first indicator of events to come, for those who knew no better. It was just before the programme was due to go on the air that a bus was attacked on the coast road, and all hell broke loose. Neither the Casino nor Sophie was able to compete and both ended up on the cutting-room floor, along with my aspirations to social acceptability at West Thornton Primary School. Having a mother on the stage was bad enough, but it was even worse to have that mother fail to appear on television when she's supposed to.

Lebanese events formed the backdrop to my early childhood, and I prided myself on my knowledge of Maronites and Druze.

The Maronites were Syrian Christians, I read; persecuted for heresy in the seventh century they retreated into the mountains of north Lebanon, where they'd remained ever since, taking on all comers. The Druze, with their secret faith and belief in reincarnation, were regarded as heretics, too. Once allies, now enemies, the Druze and the Maronites had that in common, if nothing else. It has to be said such knowledge wasn't of much use to me, certainly not at primary school, where a particular group of girls held sway by virtue of their belligerence. Deeply suspicious of the slightest eccentricity, they struck fear into the heart of every bespectacled misfit who crossed their path, but it's doubtful whether they knew Al Fatah from Al Capone.

My school had a number of entrances and exits, which was a useful feature as it sometimes paid to vary my route home. There were, it seemed to me as the years passed, some parallels between Beirut and the educational establishments of south London: one had to know the correct passwords, belong to the right group, in order to proceed unscathed.

MARILYNNE
ROBINSON

Housekeeping, Marilynne Robinson's first novel, was acclaimed by the critics and later filmed by Bill Forsyth. She is also the author of a non-fiction title, the controversial *Mother Country*. Marilynne Robinson now lives in New England.

HOUSEKEEPING

from the novel

We spent the whole of that week at the lake. At first we tried to decide how to get ourselves back into school – for the difficulty was no longer just Lucille's. The problem of inventing excuses for us both baffled us, and after the third day, when, in theory, both of us would need doctor's excuses, we decided that we had no choice but to wait until we were apprehended. It seemed to us that we were cruelly banished from a place where we had no desire to be, and that we could not return there of our own will but must wait to return under duress and compulsion. Of course our Aunt Sylvie knew nothing of our truancies, and so there would be her to face. All of this was too dreadful to consider, and every aspect of the situation grew worse with every day that passed, until we began to find a giddy and heavy-hearted pleasure in it. The combined effects of cold, tedium, guilt, loneliness and dread sharpened our senses wonderfully.

The days were unnaturally lengthy and spacious. We felt small in the landscape, and out of place. We usually walked up a little sheltered beach where there had once been a dock, and there were still six pilings, upon which, typically, perched five gulls. At intervals the gull on the northernmost piling departed with four cries, and all the other gulls fluttered northward by one piling. Then the sojourner would return and alight on the southern-most piling. This sequence was repeated again and again, with only clumsy and accidental variations. We sat on the beach just above the place where the water wet it and sorted stones (Fingerbone had at the best a rim or lip of sand three or four feet wide – its beaches were mostly edged with little pebbles half the size of peas). Some of these stones were a mossy and vegetable green, and some were as white as bits of tooth, and some of them were hazel, and some of them looked like rock candy. Farther up the beach were tufts of grasses from the year before, and leafless vines, and sodden leaves and broken ferns, and the black, dull, musky, dormant woods. The lake was full of quiet waves, and smelt cold, and smelt of fish.

It was Thursday that we saw Sylvie at the shore. She did not see us. We were sitting on a log talking about this and that, and waiting for another cold hour to be gone, when we saw her down the beach, very near the water, with her hands in her coat pockets. 'She's looking for us,' Lucille said, but she only looked across the lake, or up at the sky if a gull cried, or at the sand and the water at her feet. We sat very still. Nevertheless, she should have seen us. We were almost accustomed by that time to the fact that Sylvie's thoughts were elsewhere, but having waited so many days for someone to come for us, we found her obliviousness irksome. She stood looking at the lake for a long time, her hands deep in the pockets of her big, drab coat and her head to one side, and lifted, as if she hardly felt the cold at all. We heard a train whistle across the lake, and then we saw the train creep out of the woods and on to the bridge, its plump wide plume tilted and smeared a little by the wind. From such a distance it seemed a slight thing, but we all watched it, perhaps struck by the steady purpose with which it moved, as methodical as a caterpillar on a straw. After the train had crossed the bridge and sounded its whistle one last, long time, just when it would have been passing behind our house, Sylvie began to walk back toward the bridge. We followed, very slowly because Sylvie walked very slowly, and at a distance behind her. She nodded at two men in plaid jackets and dusty black pants who were sitting on their heels under the bridge, and they exchanged pleasant-sounding words we could not hear. She walked up the bank, and stood looking across the bridge for a moment, and then she began carefully, tie by tie, out on to it. Slowly she walked on and on, until she was perhaps fifty feet out over the water. Lucille and I stopped and watched our aunt, with her fisted hands pushed against the bottoms of her pockets, glancing up now and then at the water and at the sky. The wind was strong enough to press her coat against her side and legs, and to flutter her hair. The elder of the hoboes stepped out from under the bridge and looked up at her.

'Ain't our business,' the younger one said. They picked up their hats and strolled off down the beach in the other direction.

Sylvie stood still and let the wind billow her coat. She seemed to become more confident of her balance after a moment. She peered cautiously over the side of the bridge where the water slapped at the pilings. Then she glanced up the shore and saw us watching her. She waved. Lucille said, 'Oh.' Sylvie made her way back to the shore a little hurriedly, smiling. 'I had no idea it was so late!' she called as we walked toward her. 'I thought it would be an hour or so until school was out.'

'School isn't out,' Lucille said.

'Well, I was right after all, then. The 1.35 just went through a little while ago, so it must be pretty early still.' We walked with Sylvie along the railroad tracks toward home. She said, 'I've always wondered what it would be like.'

'What was it like?' Lucille asked. Her voice was small and flat and tensely composed.

Sylvie shrugged and laughed. 'Cold. Windy.'

Lucille said, 'You just did it to see what it was like?'

'I suppose so.'

'What if you fell in.'

'Oh,' Sylvie said. 'I was pretty careful.'

'If you fell in, everyone would think you did it on purpose,' Lucille said. 'Even us.'

Sylvie reflected a moment. 'I suppose that's true.' She glanced down at Lucille's face. 'I didn't mean to upset you.'

'I know,' Lucille said.

'I thought you would be in school.'

'We didn't go to school this week.'

'But, you see, I didn't know that. It never crossed my mind that you'd be here.' Sylvie's voice was gentle, and she touched Lucille's hair.

We were very upset, all the same, for reasons too numerous to mention. Clearly our aunt was not a stable person. At the time we did not put this thought into words. It existed between us as a sort of undifferentiated attentiveness to all the details of her appearance and behaviour. At first this took the form of sudden awakening in the middle of the night, though how the sounds that woke us were to be interpreted we were never sure. Sometimes they occurred in our heads, or in the woods, and only seemed to be Sylvie singing, because once or twice we had awakened in the middle of the night when most assuredly we did hear Sylvie singing, though the next morning we disagreed about what the song had been. We thought we sometimes heard her leave the house, and once when we got out of bed, we found her playing solitaire in the kitchen, and once we found her sitting on the back porch steps, and once we found her standing in the orchard. Sleep itself compounded our difficulties. The furtive closing of a door is a sound the wind can make a dozen times in an hour. A flow of damp air from the lake can make any house feel empty. Such currents pull one's dreams after them, and one's own dread is always mirrored upon the dread that inheres in things. For example, when Sylvie looked over the bridge she must have seen herself in the water at the foot of the trestle. But as surely as we tried to stay awake to know for certain whether she sang, or wept, or left the house, we fell asleep and dreamed that she did.

Then there was the matter of her walking out on to the bridge. How far might she have gone had she not seen us watching her? And what if the wind had risen? And what if a train had come while she was still on the bridge? Everyone would have said that Sylvie had taken her own life, and we would not have known otherwise – as, in fact, we still did not know otherwise. For if we imagined that, while we watched, Sylvie had walked so far away that the mountains rose up and the shore was diminished, and the lake bellied and under her feet the water slid and slapped and shone, and the bridge creaked and teetered, and the sky flowed away and slid over the side of the earth, might she not have carried the experiment a step further? And then imagine that same Sylvie trudging up from the lake bottom, foundered coat and drowned sleeves and marbled lips and marble fingers and eyes flooded with the deep water that gleamed down beneath the reach of light. She might very well have said, 'I've always wondered what that would be like.'

We spent Friday at the shore, watching the bridge. Saturday and Sunday we spent at home with Sylvie. She sat on the floor and played Monopoly with us and told us intricate and melancholy tales of people she had known slightly, and we made popcorn. Sylvie seemed surprised and shyly pleased by our attention. She laughed at Lucille for hiding her 500-dollar bills under the board, and for shuffling the Community Chest cards so thoroughly that the backs broke. I spent much of several games in jail, but Sylvie prospered, and she was full of her good fortune, and she made us each a gift of three hotels.

Monday Lucille and I went back to school. No one questioned us. Apparently it had been decided that our circumstances were special, and that was a relief, although it suggested that Sylvie had already begun to draw attention to herself. We spent the day waiting to go home, and when we came home Sylvie was there, in the kitchen, with her coat off, listening to the radio. Days and weeks passed the same way, and finally we began to think of other things.

I remember Sylvie walking through the house with a scarf tied around her hair, carrying a broom. Yet this was the time that leaves began to gather in the corners. They were leaves that had been through the winter, some of them worn to a net of veins. There were scraps of paper among them, crisp and stained from their mingling in the cold brown liquors of decay and regeneration, and on these scraps there were sometimes words. One read *Powers Meet*, and another, which had been the flap of an envelope, had a pencilled message in an anonymous hand: *I think of you*. Perhaps Sylvie when she swept took care not to molest them. Perhaps she sensed a Delphic niceness in the scattering of these leaves and paper, here and not elsewhere, thus and not otherwise. She had to have been aware of them because every time a door was opened anywhere in the house there was a sound from all the corners of lifting and alighting. I noticed that the leaves would be lifted up by something that came before the wind, they would tack against some impalpable movement of air several seconds before the wind was heard in the trees. Thus finely did our house become attuned to the orchard and to the particularities of weather, even in the first days of Sylvie's housekeeping. Thus did she begin by littles and perhaps unawares to ready it for wasps and bats and barn swallows. Sylvie talked a great deal about housekeeping. She soaked all the tea-towels for a number of weeks in a tub of water and bleach. She emptied several cupboards and left them open to air, and once she washed half the kitchen ceiling and a door. Sylvie believed in stern solvents, and most of all in air. It was for the sake of air that she opened doors and windows, though it was probably through forgetfulness that she left them open. It was for the sake of air that on one early splendid day she wrestled my grandmother's plum-coloured davenport into the front yard, where it remained until it weathered pink.

Sylvie liked to eat supper in the dark. This meant that in summer we were seldom sent to bed before ten or eleven o'clock, a freedom to which we never became accustomed. We spent days on our knees in the garden, digging caves and secret passages with kitchen spoons for our dolls, mine a defrocked bride with a balding skull and Lucille's a filthy and eyeless Rose Red. Long after we knew we were too old for dolls, we played out intricate, urgent dramas of entrapment and miraculous escape. When the evenings came they were chill because the mountains cast such long shadows over the land and over the lake. There the wind would be, quenching the warmth out of the air before the light was gone, raising the hairs on our arms and necks with its smell of frost and water and deep shade.

Then we would take our dolls inside and play on the floor in the circle of chairs and couches, by the refracted, lunar light of the vacant sky, while darkness began to fill the room, to lift the ice-blue doilies from the sodden sleeves of chairs. Just when the windows went stark blue Sylvie would call us into the kitchen. Lucille and I sat across from each other and Sylvie at the end of the table. Opposite her was a window luminous and cool as aquarium glass and warped as water. We looked at the window as we ate, and we listened to the crickets and nighthawks, which were always unnaturally loud then, perhaps because they were within the bounds that light would fix around us, or perhaps because one sense is a shield for the others and we had lost our sight.

The table would be set with watermelon pickles and canned meats, apples and jelly doughnuts and shoestring potatoes, a block of pre-sliced cheese, a bottle of milk, a bottle of catsup, and raisin bread in a stack. Sylvie liked cold food, sardines aswim in oil, little fruit pies in paper envelopes. She ate with her fingers and talked to us softly about people she had known, her friends, while we swung our legs and ate buttered bread.

Sylvie knew an old woman named Edith who came to her rest crossing the mountains in a boxcar, in December. She was wearing, besides her rubbers and her hunting jacket, two dresses and seven flannel shirts, not to keep off the cold, Sylvie said, but to show herself a woman of substance. She sailed feet first and as solemn as Lincoln from Butte to Wenatchee, where she was buried at public expense. It was such a winter, Sylvie said, so cold, that the snow was as light as chaff. Any wind would blow a hill bare and send the snow drifting, as placeless as smoke. In the face of such hard weather the old woman had grown formal and acquiescent. She had crept off to the freight yard one morning in the dark, leaving no word but a pearl ring which had never before been known to leave her hand. The pearl was brown as a horse's tooth and very small. Sylvie kept the ring in a little box with her hairpins.

Edith found her boxcar and composed herself in it, while the trainmen went about the jamming and conjoining of cold metal parts. In such weather one steps on fossils. The snow is too slight to conceal the ribs and welts, the hollows and sockets of the earth, fixed in its last extreme.

LONGING TO
BE SOMEONE
ELSE

RAFFAELLA BARKER

Raffaella Barker was born in 1964. She grew up, mostly in Norfolk in the literary household of her father, the poet George Barker. Out of this bohemian youth she wrote *Come and Tell Me Some Lies*. She lives in Norfolk with her husband and three children. *The Hook* is her second book.

SMALL GLAMOURS

from *The Hook*

Christy walked around Mick's garden and the midges swooped lower than swallows in the dusk. Above her the trees creaked and expanded towards the clearing, casting a veil of deciduum through their branches. There were no trees outside the house in Lynton where she had grown up, and at the lake they were still saplings. Unused to the creaking voices of old trees, she shivered, clasping her arms close to her as she looked up to a canopy of leaves. Mick's lawn was as wild as the wood beyond and Christy wove a patch back and forth to skirt the brambles leaning in from the wall. A damp scent of nettles hung across the gateway, their green a bright blur in the dying light. Arms bare, hair a blunt gleam on her back, Christy was out of place and small in this wilderness. She was not good at being alone, her steps were hesitant, her body tensed against imagined terrors. At home if Frank was out she spent the evening on the telephone to Maisie or a friend because she didn't really believe she existed if no one was there to see her.

Her dress danced out of the evening when she turned back towards the cottage; in the kitchen steam rolled up to the ceiling from a pan on top of the chipped stove.

Mick was muttering a line of the recipe he was reading, repeating it like a mantra.

' "Blanch and pour, blanch and pour." Here, sweetheart, have a drink for me.' He passed Christy a cloudy glass and went on chanting, ' "Blanch and pour, blanch and pour." '

The wine stung her throat and she felt it sliding down,

weighty and rotund as if she were swallowing an oyster. Suffocation crept over her again and she kicked off her shoes and lay on the sofa. She knew what was really troubling her. It was Friday, she wasn't working on Saturday, although she often did, and neither was Mick. She had no way of getting home unless Mick decided to take her. She was stuck and she was going to sleep with him. That was why she was here. It wasn't that she didn't want to do it, she had come knowing this would happen. She crushed a cushion against herself and longed for it to be over, to have done it so it could never be the first time again.

Mick laid the table with candles while Christy sat like a stone, Hotspur's head resting on her lap. The scar on Mick's forehead turned red as the sun lingered on the front window. It was already dark on the other wall and the last rays waned, shrinking the room towards Mick and Christy facing one another in the glowing window. Mick ate her food as well as his own, holding his fork like a shovel as she had been taught never to do, wiping the plate clean with bread and rubbing his hands across his mouth when he had finished; she half expected him to burp and push his plate back but he leaned his elbows on the table and picked his teeth instead. Christy pushed some grains of rice around her plate then smoked four cigarettes in a row. She could never eat with Mick. His vast appetite swallowed hers, and his energetic pursuit of every morsel repelled her, making food something too physical for her to bear.

Mick finished cleaning his teeth and left the table to light the fire. He crouched on the hearth breaking kindling, light as a cat on his feet even though he was filling the whole fireplace with his body. Christy tiptoed past Mick's turned back and tucked herself into the chair by the fire.

'What do you think of this place, sweetheart? Do you like it out here in the sticks?' His voice was smooth as glass to steady her now they had moved from the table.

In the half-light he loomed and Christy receded sinking back in monochrome shadows, her pink dress the only colour in the room. She didn't answer.

Mick laughed.

'Are you still here, Christy? I can't see you now, and I can't hear you. You're scared as all hell, aren't you?'

'I'm not scared, I'm nervous.'

'Same thing,' said Mick and he stretched out on the sofa, leaning back to look at her bolt upright on her chair near the fireplace.

She wished he would turn the lights on. The heap of him merged with the heap of sofa, spreading across the whole room. Neither of them spoke. And then Mick was holding her hands and his hands were so warm she realised hers were frozen. And he was putting his arms around her, unbending her clamped elbows and wrapping her arms around him. And he was kissing her, making her feel so wanted that she did not notice that she wasn't nervous any more.

Christy woke up stretching in warm morning light. She was in Mick's bedroom and the telephone was ringing downstairs. She heard him answer it, his voice clear at first then rumbling indistinct but constant like a train passing. She couldn't help smiling, thinking that even at 7.30 he couldn't stop talking.

He appeared in the bedroom, dressed and wide awake.

'You get up early.' Christy pulled the sheets up to her face, self-conscious at being naked in daylight when Mick had clothes on. He smelt of coffee when he kissed her. 'I thought you'd be asleep. I have to collect something now, so I'll be seeing you later, sweetheart.' He stroked her hair and was gone.

Christy rolled over and closed her eyes, listening to the car roar away until the sound was so distant it mingled with the moving trees.

From the beginning of the trial everyone knew I was Mick's girlfriend. The policemen with macho guns who guarded every entrance, the court clerks, even the traffic warden, who had stopped giving me tickets when a constable told him who I was. They smiled at me with sad sympathy in their eyes and whispered 'Poor love' when I passed.

Mick was delighted.

'It'll really help the atmosphere with the jury and their mood and all that if everyone feels sorry for you, sweetheart,' he told me during one of our visits.

'But I don't know if they're sorry for me because of what might happen to you or because I'm involved with you.'

Mick stretched his fingers under the glass screen and touched my hand.

'It doesn't matter what they're thinking. Just look tragic and wronged as often as you can and be drop-dead sexy the rest of the time. They'll love you, Christy, they'll love you.'

He pressed his palm flat against the glass and I did the same, my hand fitting into his so it looked as though I'd drawn round it. This was how we held hands now.

Mick liked being in court. Right from the first day he had power even though he was handcuffed. The security around his case was crazy. Even the barristers were searched with metal detectors, once at the front door and once outside the courtroom.

Mick applied to the judge to have the handcuffs removed a week after the case was opened. His arm was sore from the days spent tethered to a shifting rota of police officers.

'It's not as though I'm going to do anything, Your Honour,' he said to the judge with a grin. I thought he shouldn't be smiling, he should be pleading, but Mick wasn't like that and anyway the judge almost smiled back. 'I'd have to be crazy, wouldn't I, to think about escaping with two dozen men with guns crawling around this building?' He lifted his right arm, dragging the policeman beside him to reluctant attention. 'I'll be ending up deformed, Your Honour. I'm already blistered and bruised enough – you can see the bandage right here.' He pointed with his unyoked hand at the greying fabric on his captive wrist.

The judge considered him, head on one side, wig awry, heaped up like suet.

'No, I don't think we'll uncuff you, Mr Fleet.'

Mick scratched his scalp and ran his fingers through his hair slowly; the policeman's hand hovered useless above his own.

'I suppose it might be prejudicial to the prosecution,' said

Mick. 'For sure it's prejudicial to the defence that I am handcuffed.'

The judge straightened up in his chair shaking his head and shuffled small hands among his papers.

'No, Mr Fleet. I cannot allow that. You cannot talk like that in the courtroom.'

I didn't see why it mattered. The jury were always sent out when the judge and Mick, interrupting his barrister, had this sort of conversation, and they had it often. Mick couldn't help treating the judge like someone he knew. He was always demanding reasons and explanations for the way things worked. The judge allowed far more than I expected. He seemed to like Mick, even though Mick was fired up and emotional sometimes.

'This is the rest of my life being debated, Your Honour. I need to know what you all think you're doing with it in here.'

The judge was like a slap of water in his responses.

'Yes, yes, but you cannot go against the legal structure,' he explained time after time.

Mick had a talent for making other people feel important. He gave me a role when all I really needed was to be there. But maybe he was right to. He sucked me into his trial so deep that I could not have got out if I had wanted to. I didn't want to. I was his route to the outside world, and I was vital. Mr Sindall, Mick's barrister, had a team of solicitors who darted around me nipping information from me before returning to their notes and files. Members of the public who came to watch the trial smiled at me; one or two spoke, just making conversation: 'It's a lovely day', 'Traffic's bad on the ring road, I hear', 'Do you know when the canteen opens?' I knew what they were doing. Each sentence came with a searching gaze, their ears flared when I responded and they tucked my words into their gloating minds and hoarded them to tell their friends later. 'I spoke to his girlfriend. She was friendly, not like you'd expect one of them to be.' I could hear them marvelling as if I was with them, back in their safe worlds where court was a source of excitement and glamour. I was a part of that glamour and it would have been a lie to say I didn't love it.

JESSIE KESSON

Jessie Kesson was born Jessie Grant McDonald in Inverness in 1915. She soon moved to Elgin with her mother where they were forced to live off their own resources until, aged nine, she was forcibly removed to an orphanage. As a teenager she entered service, then worked as an indentured farm labourer. In 1934 she settled on a croft with her husband Johnnie. Those early years have inspired much of her work: the novels, *The White Bird Passes* (1958), *Glitter of Mica* (1963) and *Another Time Another Place* (1985). She also wrote short stories, poetry and over ninety radio plays. She is one of Scotland's best loved writers, but little known beyond except through the prize-winning film of *Another Time Another Place*; she wrote and lived with passion and a profound understanding of human nature. Her collected novels were republished in 1998. She died in London in 1994.

A WOMAN OF THE WORLD

from *Glitter of Mica*

'Fiona!' Sue Tatt shouted upstairs in warning, to her eldest daughter. 'If you go mucking up all my new cleaned bedroom, I'll land you one. You'll go flying straight through the wall. And that's a promise!'

Having got this off her chest, Sue made her way back to the kitchen again, pausing in the doorway as though she were some complete stranger come to pay a visit to herself, and, standing there, took in every aspect of her newly turned-out room. Sue, a woman of many parts, was equal to many roles, and Fridays always brought out the house-proud in her.

True, her household would rough it contentedly enough all the rest of the week, when Sue would be absorbed in some other role, though she would always justify her muddle to anyone who crossed her threshold uninvited, with the dubious welcome, 'You're just about the last one I was looking for. But come on away inside. The clartier the cosier! Or so they say' – accompanied by a slap on the back that would have flung you flat on your face if you hadn't been expecting it. But, when the pendulum swung the *other* way, as now, a tiny speck of dust in any corner of her house was enough to send Sue up in smoke, and was more than a little unfair on her family, who could never quite adjust themselves to the suddenness of their mother's change of role. And doubly unfair tonight, when Sue was combining two roles.

She would let days pass on end, giving her face a lick and a promise, and her hair a rough redd through. But today a sudden beautifying spasm had seized her; a visit to the town and Woolworth's had become a Must. Descending on the cosmetic counter, Sue had bought up everything that promised anything: a face pack which 'erased tell-tale wrinkles', a highlight rinse which 'brought out hidden golden glints', a lipstick which 'carried a breath of spring'. And, miser-like, Sue was now preparing to lock herself away in the bathroom, with all her little packages, and looking forward to lying, soaking herself leisurely, and reading the instructions on her Beauty Aids as lovingly as if they were the word of God – though with more faith.

'I'll be in the bathroom if I'm wanted,' she reminded Fiona. 'And don't any of you lot go mucking all my place up,' she warned again.

'Forget it, Mam,' Fiona advised casually from the bedroom. 'Don't let it go and get your wick.'

'I'll tell you what does get my wick' – Sue turned to survey her kitchen again – 'and that's just the sight of a pair of sharny boots lying on my new-brushed rug. You would think,' she added in pained protest, 'that we all lived in a pigsty.'

'We do, too.' Young Beel dodged Sue's aim, but gave her the cue for another role.

'I work my fingers to the bone for you all,' she complained, 'slaving to bring you up, and that's all the thanks I get.' She made her way to the bathroom almost tearfully, remembering now that she was 'a widow woman, bringing up a young family, all on her own'.

And indeed it was a kind of truth. Though Sue did whiles confuse the names of the mythical husbands who had widowed her, certain it was that she worked with a fair degree of regularity to bring up her bairns. '*Drag* them up' was Caldwell's private interpretation of her efforts. But, then, Caldwell was seldom charitable towards its own. For though they accepted Sue as their own, they condoned neither Sue nor themselves for this acceptance.

The role of Self-Supporting Widow was dear to Sue's heart. Mounting her bicycle two or three times a week to do the wash for surrounding farmers' wives, Sue was aware of the heightened interest she aroused both in them and in their daily helps, who were forever making some excuse to pop into the washhouse for a news with Sue. And the selfsame thing with the farm-workers' wives. Sue Tatt was well aware that their attitude to herself veered between superiority and a kind of envy. And their approach towards her was transparency itself.

Meeting any one of them alone on the Ambroggan road it would simply be as housewife to housewife: newsing together of this and that; the cost of food, exchanging a recipe maybe, or a cleaning hint. In such moments, Sue would become so enthusiastic over the preserving qualities of beeswax and turpentine, that she would deceive even herself and, mounting her bicycle, would take down the road a glow of goodness over her, and the assurance within her – I, Sue Tatt, am just an ordinary housewife after all. And what is more, I am accepted as such by the Plunger's wife.

When Sue Tatt ran into a group of farm-workers' wives, things took a different turn altogether.

'Aye! But it's another fine night, again,' the Plunger's wife would shoot out of the side of her mouth in hurried passing, the remembered mutual addiction to beeswax and turpentine simply forcing the salutation out of her, while the other wives would just keep going, their gaze fixed steadily on the road ahead, their mouths clamped down in firm disapproval. Such an attitude always had the effect of bringing out the worst in Sue towards womankind – 'A drab-like lot! All gone to seed. Not one amongst them would have seen their feet if they hadn't been all gripped in with brassières and stays': while she, Sue Tatt, could stand, and sometimes did, as now, as firm mother-naked as other women in all their harness; and standing so, she would think, 'Oh, the pity of it! And the waste. To grow old. And there's the whole wide world. And all of them that's in it. And I have never seen the world. Nor half of them that's in it. And what is *more* the pity is that *they* have never seen *me* so!'

Sue would have stripped herself at any time, and just for that. The way a child might rush from school, its crayoned drawing held aloft, and shouting, 'Look what I've got. It's all my own!' ... And, just as the praise of some loving observer would ring in its mind for a long time after, so would some lover's praise, when he himself and all his intimacy were long forgotten, bell in Sue's mind – 'God, Sue! But you're a bonnie woman right enough.'

It was when Sue Tatt ran into two wives on the road that she really came into her own, for they held the fallacy that two could keep a secret. And, having taken the risk of a friendly encounter with Sue Tatt, two wives would become bolder still, skipping hastily over the polite preliminaries like bairns, weather and neighbours, till at last they landed warily but with relief on basic ground; drawing gradually from the well of Sue's reputed experience ... For men were just a perfect nuisance – wasn't that so, now? My goodness me! No wonder women always aged much quicker than their menfolk, considering all they had to put up with, one way or another. A man could go on being a man till he dropped into his grave; but a woman had to call a halt, some time or other. 'Oh, it was all right when you were young and daft,' the Plunger's wife had once confessed. 'Though even then,' she had admitted, 'I got to just wanting my good night's sleep. And now, to tell the truth, it's gotten like a cup of cold water.'

Oh, but to tell truth was always so much easier than to *be* truth. At least, Sue Tatt had found that so; for she met so many sweet deceptions in herself, and each seemed genuine truth. As in times like that, when Sue would find herself in entire agreement with the wives; with, all the time, the other side of it badgering her inwardly for a hearing – 'But I never felt like that about a man, in all my born days. Well, maybe I did. But only once or twice. And even then, I always managed to put a face on it. For I could never let any man feel that he was other than the best man ever.' Sue knew instinctively that a man in bed was as vulnerable as his own nakedness, and that only by covering his failure for him, could she reveal her own completeness.

'There are some men, though,' she had once assured Lil and the Plunger's wife – only because she felt she owed them some little comfort and confidence for all that they had confided in her – 'There are some men, though,' Sue had informed them, 'and I have met one or two of them, that whiles feel the same way about it all as you and me. They go so off themselves when it's all over, that they could just cut their throats.'

Still and on, it was fine to be looked upon as something of a woman of the world, but overburdening whiles, and more like myth than truth; then it was finer to dissolve the burden in the washtub, for the sight of their washing blowing high and white along the lines seldom failed to produce the comment from the farmers' wives:

'Let Sue Tatt be what she likes. One thing is sure. She never fails to hang out a bonnie white washing!'

The same thing when they sent for her to help out with the spring cleaning.

'I never found anybody could get the grain of that wood as white as you can scrub it, Sue,' Kingorth's wife had confessed to her just the other week. And coming from Kingorth's wife that was praise, for she was a tight woman, and had she been a ghost, would have grudged giving you a fright.

Such praise was sweet to Sue, for she cared. At least, one of the many parts of her cared. So often Sue Tatt felt the conflicting burden of all her various potentialities bearing down on her. For Oh, but it was a terrible thing to have within you the power to be a plain woman or a beauty, a slut or house-proud, a respectable body or a light of love. All of which Sue had been at some time, and could be at another, for she always grasped the immediate potential.

'From now on,' she had vowed, under the impetus of Kingorth's wife's praise, 'from now on, I'm always going to clean my own little house as thoroughly as I clean other folks' big houses.' And she did – for nearly a week. A week in which she almost drove her family mad; confiding sadly to Fiona, when the cleaning mood had deserted her:

'Do you know something, Fiona? I could be one of the most house-proud women in all Caldwell, if I just wasn't *Me!*'

It was true too. And Fiona, although she was only fourteen, understood the truth of it. Fiona was the only one of her children that Sue Tatt really liked; and then simply as one human being likes another. She had named her daughter, even before she was born, after the heroine of the serial she had been perusing – a favourite occupation of Sue in her carrying times.

'Fiona' – for that dark, willowy girl who strode the heathery hills of Scottish 'Family Fiction'. Tweed clad and windswept. Her head flung back. Her eyes always 'set wide apart and grey' – scanning the far horizons of loch and hill, against whose background stood the ancient but fast-decaying House of the noble but impoverished laird, loved by and at last won by Fiona, despite all the intrigues of that wealthy London blonde, who never really cared about each stick and stone of the Ancient House. Not as Fiona did, her eyes set wide apart and grey.

It was some flaw in Sue Tatt's nature, made her accept Fiona – a flaw she shared with many of her like. Even those in Caldwell who had never known their Scotland so, preferred their image of it thus – a fable-flowering land. But, even so, their need of the 'rowan tree' was such, it could cause the antrin bush to bloom unpruned within their minds. Only an alien, and then perhaps out of a need as urgent as their own, had ever attempted to deprive them of their illusions.

Even God Knows himself could laugh about that, now. 'Yon Italian prisoner of war was one I'll never forget. For Oh, but he had a right ill will to Scotland. "Nothing for look," was always yon one's cry. "In Scotland. Nothing for look. Tatties, turnips. Rain and wind. And no divertiment. In Italy now! Plenty for

look. Plenty sun. Plenty divertiment. Plenty plenty sun." God
Almighty. The way he spoke about that country of his was
enough to set you thinking that the sun itself had a hard time
of it getting around to get its blink in anywhere else on the
face of the earth. According to yon one, it just bided in Italy.
Aye, but he had a right sore grudge against Scotland. Still, like
the Poles, he apparently found our women much to his liking.
For I never saw a man so set on women. He had even gotten
the length of teaching Sue Tatt Italian. And whatten a waste
yon was. Sue could have understood what he was seeking in
any tongue! Still, if his taste in countries was anything like his
taste in women, Scotland lost nothing at all through his opinion
of it.'

But there had been those whose tastes had been worth taking
all the care in the world for. Sue Tatt remembered that as she
stood surveying the result of all her beautifying efforts in the
bathroom mirror. It had taken a Second World War to bring
Sue one tithe of the admiration which she had always felt was
her due.

The curious thing about wars was that you were born in
the remembrance of your parents' wars, and grew up within
their constant recollections of an age, alluring as myth,
'Before the War', so that you got the feeling it were better
never to have been born at all than to live in the dull eras
'After the War' when 'Times have changed', and always 'For
the worst'.

Sue Tatt had reached her prime during the Second World
War. She now knew why the period of one's life, lived through
wartime, never became relegated to the past, and, though
foreshadowing the future, stood in the present, like the Celtic
cross in front of Caldwell's Old Established Church, erected to
'The Memory of the Men of This Parish' who had fallen in
battles as near in time and far in distance as the Dardanelles
and Libya. Despite that, there still was room for the names of
men who might fall in future battles, since war was never the
countryman's first urgency nor last loyalty. A glance at the
names on the Celtic cross would have convinced you that, by

and large, it was the countryside's artisans who 'fell' – its labourers and tradesmen, and sometimes farmers' only sons, not old enough for their first heritage, side by side with crofters' younger sons who had none, since the croft ever provided for but one heir.

Maybe the flatness of 'After the War' was but in natural contrast to its years of heightened tempo. Sue Tatt could see it all, as clear as yesterday, without today impinging. The first hot flush of patriotism. 'All in it Together.' China and Russia swinging into their orbit. Aid for them both. Knitting bees, plain and purl; socks and balaclavas; picking up dropped stitches side by side with the Misses Lennox, and Miss McCombie of the Whins, while Colonel McCombie, resurrected from retirement, manœuvred up on Soutar Hill with a platoon of tractormen and cattlemen who formed Home Guard. The sudden prestige of men in uniform, particularly their own regiment, the Gordon Highlanders. But, though you sang 'Scots Wha Hae' and 'Highland Laddie', the paradox remained: the soldier, except in times of war, in moments of high sentimental fervour, in retrospect or in song, was regarded as the lowest form of life. 'Where's my mam?' ... 'She's run off with a sodger!'

In peacetime, few girls kept company with soldiers. Sue Tatt herself had drawn the line at them, and had hitherto ignored all mating calls from Kilties. This prejudice may have had its roots in 'old, unhappy far-off things', when paternity claims could be avoided by the simple expedient of enlisting. Certain it was that a strong prejudice against the soldier prevailed in country places; until wars came, of course. And then the girl not clinging to the arms of a soldier became an oddity, and an object of pity.

Sue Tatt herself had clung to not a few. The Fusiliers, when the boast on everyone's tongue was 'We're going to hang out our washing on the Siegfried Line'. The Tank Corps, when the prophecy was 'There'll be bluebirds over the white cliffs of Dover'. And when the war was in its closing stages, Sue had vowed to the music in the sergeant's mess 'This is my lovely day, this the day I will remember the day I am dying'.

When the first high tension of war had passed, Caldwell had settled down again to minding its own business. For its business was a total war effort – or so the government ruled, by bringing out the Stand Still Order, which forbade all in reserved occupations to leave their jobs. But, since your born farm-worker would never have dreamed of doing so anyhow, the Stand Still Order was not only superfluous, but unsettling! As the Plunger had observed at the time, 'It just never dawned on me before to leave Darklands. But then I suppose I always knew I could leave, if I so desired. And that's how it should be! I don't like the idea of this Stand Still Order. I don't like it at all.'

Men who had even less control of themselves, or more within themselves, saw in the Order something against which they could test their initiative, and left their jobs on the land for no other reason than to prove it could be done. But, by and large, Caldwell had settled down again, and subsidies began to roll in – subsidies for bull calves and potatoes. Farm-workers' wages began to rise, and with them their status. The two term days of the year became a thing of the past. No longer could the townsman, half affectionately, half con-temptuously, instantly recognise the 'Country Geordie' walking his streets, for the farm-workers' uniform – navy blue suit and bonnet – began to disappear, too. Nor was such prosperity confined to farmers and their workers. Even the tinkers wandering the countryside began to benefit. For, though they had always sold their all, their all had now increased – clothing coupons, sweet coupons, food 'points' – so that Caldwell itself was moved to protest. 'The world is coming to a pretty fine pass when you can no longer tell whether it's the farmers or the tinkers that are driving round the countryside in brakes.'

Sue Tatt had also shared in the rising prosperity, though, strangely enough, not in any material way. It had been sufficient for Sue to feel that she 'lived' at last. She began to roll distinguishing abbreviations off her tongue – RSM, CSM, QMS, warrant officer, sarn't and simply Lance Jack – with an expertise which impressed before it shocked those in Caldwell whose acquaintance with the military within their gates remained long-distance and objective towards anyone under the rank of lieutenant. Sue had moved from one intense emotional crisis to another with Lofty, Shorty, Nobby, Bootlace, Snudge, retaining her resilience, recovering from their postings, and even surviving their overseas drafts.

There had been an element of competition in those war years which had presented a challenge to Sue Tatt, for, having no fellow-like in Caldwell, Sue had lived in a Crusoe kind of loneliness. But when the war came, it had revealed that all the surrounding parishes had, unknowingly, harboured at least one of Sue's kind; submerged for years, but rising to the surface, and suffering some great sea change at Bugle Call.

Sue could still remember the excitement of getting ready, and making up, with all her little clique, in this same bathroom, their children skirling in and out amongst their feet, small nightmares interrupting large dreams, and silenced only by a sixpence, or quietened with a curse.

None of the female friendships Sue had made in those years had lasted, of course. For, although all were of the pack, each had remained a lone wolf. Now and again Sue would run into one such crony from those years, submerged once more into respectability and beyond personal recognition, so that they would have less to say to each other than utter strangers, since some kinds of memories shared ever make for mutual silence.

Oh, but there had been no holding of them in those years. It was as if all the world had joined hands and were rushing together towards the end of the war, and nothing had mattered in between. The end of the war. The very phrase had conjured up within itself the magic and escape of some Open Sesame to a new and different world. But anticipation, once so keen, had now dissolved itself, though, for some months after V-Day, Sue had still cast searching, disappointed eyes over Caldwell, seeking some kind of transformation, and finding it only as an exile, after long absence from his country, might find that the mountains of his memory were but hills.

Caldwell itself, though, had gradually become aware of some change in Sue Tatt. She had become 'more choosy' after the war, 'more particular' – or so they said. And small wonder! For whatever else she had learned from the war years, Sue had learned comparison. While never being unaware of her own needs, nor contemptuous of the needs of men, she had simply discovered that there were ways and means of supplicating for them. It had been better to lie down on the windswept target range up at Balwhine, thinking it was for love, than to stand up against Kingorth's byre door, knowing it was simply out of good nature. Nothing put Sue so clean off now as Caldwell's matter-of-fact approach ... 'Well, Sue. What about it then?'

There was the exception, though. And, once again, Sue had created it for herself, in her relationship with Hugh Riddel; for once deceiving herself only in small externals, knowing instinctively that any other woman could have served his purpose, though even then the relationship for Sue had to become one of acquisition. 'Anyone *could* have him. But it is *I*, Sue Tatt, who has gotten him.'

'You stink of stuff, Mam,' was all that young Beel could find to say, when Sue, her elaborate toilette completed, stood once again on the threshold of her kitchen, pausing this time for appreciative acclamation.

'You just stink of stuff.'

Coarse, that was what young Beel was! Just like the father of him. Unlike mothers in wedlock, Sue Tatt seldom associated herself with her children at all, but had acquired a rare degree of parental objectivity. Coarse. It always came out.

'That lipstick doesn't look too bad on you, Mam,' Fiona conceded. 'Can I have it when you're done with it?'

'No. You can *not*.' Sue advanced into her kitchen, conflicting roles battling within her – Helen of Troy and Widow Woman Bringing up Young Family. 'What you *can* do,' she suggested, looking at Fiona as though seeing her for the first time, 'is to take that muck off your face, and give that neck of yours a right good scrub. The pores of your skin are going to all clog up for the want of plain soap and water.'

'Skip it, Mam,' Fiona shrugged, certain in the knowledge that she would fall heir to all the little pots of stuff anyhow, when her mother had got tired of them.

'What do you mean ... *skip it*?' Sue demanded ominously. There were moments when her comprehensive methods of rearing her family suddenly backfired on herself. And this was blowing up into one of those moments. Sue felt an old inexplicable anger falling down over herself and her daughter, and cloaking them in awful proximity. Her eyes took in each detail of Fiona, with the cruel, confining clarity of temper. 'Dolling yourself up there in my best shoes! *And* my new bracelet. Eyebrow pencil too. And eyeshadow. You look' – it was either this, or slap the girl until all rage was eased out of herself – 'just like a little whore. That's what you look like.'

It was true too, Sue assured herself, her eyes still fixed on her daughter's face. But now the concentrated image was diffusing. Sue turned her attention to the mantelpiece and started rearranging her ornaments. 'You can keep the bracelet if you like.' Her offer came rough and jerky, acquiring smoothness only in its enlargement. 'But those shoes of mine will ruin your feet. I was thinking of taking out another Provident check. You can have a pair of shoes for yourself off it.'

'What about *me*?' Young Beel had sniffed out the favourable drift of his mother's mood. 'I'm needing a new pair of trousers.'

'I'll get a Provident check big enough for all of us, then,' Sue promised, suddenly feeling capable of bequeathing the moon in gratitude for the lightness within her.

'Got a fag on you, Mam?' Beel was taking every ounce out of the advantageous wind.

'Try my cardigan pocket,' Sue acquiesced, equably enough. 'But you'll have to run down to Davy for fags later on. And you can have the price of a packet for yourself.'

'Ta, Mam.' Beel's interpretation of the offer equalled his mother's casual bribery. 'I'll nip down for them when Hugh Riddel comes!'

The kitchen and its occupants now settled down into an intimacy of a kind which was rarely experienced in more orthodox homes.

'I saw Hugh Riddel this morning,' Fiona said, waving her newly acquired bracelet in front of the fire till it reflected its light.

'Oh, did you now? What time would that have been about?' Sue asked, as if the answer didn't concern her.

'I don't right remember what time it was.' Fiona felt stubborn. 'Early though,' she added for safety's sake, her eyes still fixed on the changing lights of her bracelet.

'What time's early?' Sue demanded, irritation creeping into her voice.

'First bus.' Fiona, apprehensive of stretching her mother's patience too far, was yet reluctant to reveal too much too soon. 'He had driven Isa Riddel down to catch it.'

'She must have been for the town the day, then?'

'Must have,' Fiona agreed absently.

'*Was* she, or was she *not*?' Sue demanded impatiently. 'Surely you know what bus she got on to?'

'The town bus, of course!'

'Well then! Couldn't you have said that in the first place? How did she look? Was she all dressed up for the town?'

'No. The same old usual,' Fiona admitted at last.

'An awful-looking frump of a wifie yon,' young Beel said, getting the mood of the thing at last.

'Did Hugh Riddel himself seem in good bone?' Sue's interest almost defied discernment.

'Never him! He's a right dour dook yon. But he's coming

here the night,' Fiona remembered. Her bracelet, reflected by the firelight, glowed like the jewels of story-book memory. 'He's definitely coming here the night.' Fiona handed her ace to her mother at last. 'I'm sure of that. I heard him telling Wylie the blacksmith that he'd call in by for the bottling lever tonight, because he'd be passing this way anyhow.'

'That will just depend on the weather,' Sue said irrelevantly and, rising, made her way out to the gate to have a look at the weather.

'It's as bright as day, and as quiet's the grave.'

'Aye. It's going to be a right fine night, Mam,' Fiona assured her mother, finding her hand and squeezing it, the only demonstration of affection they ever allowed, or needed between them. 'It's going to be a fine night, Mam,' Fiona insisted, as they stood looking out on a night that their wish had willed.

You would never have thought that a moon on the wane like this would give such light. But with it was ground frost, and in your mind the promise of the lengthening nights. The quietness over it might well be known to the dead, where every sound was in itself an interruption, and lights snapped up like noise upon the landscape.

'I'd know the Plunger's wife's skirl anywhere.' Sue broke their own silence.

'It's all the Darklands' cottar wives making for the Rural,' Fiona said.

'So it is,' Sue remembered. 'God help us. They'll all be singing "And Did Those Feet" and "Land Of Our Birth" the night, then.'

'I know. Grown-up women seem terrible gowkit when they're all together,' Fiona reflected, as they laughed together in the darkness, adding for good measure, in the great good will of their togetherness, 'But *you're* never like that, Mam.'

'Fiona!' The pressure of Sue's hand indicated the urgency of her question. 'The *truth*, now. Say you had never once set eyes on me or on Isa Riddel in all your life, and suddenly you met us both together on the road, which one of us would you say was the bonniest?'

'You, Mam.' The answer was unhesitating and sincere. 'You are far younger looking and bonnier than Isa Riddel.'

LIANE DE POUGY

Liane de Pougy was one of the last great French courtesans. The scandal and notoriety that surrounded her for two decades in Paris as she indulged her passion for both men and women while consuming legendary fortunes made her one of the most famous women in France. Her horizontal career, in the true courtesan fashion, included loves and liaisons with heads of state, crown princes, magnates and stars.

When she married Georges, a Rumanian prince, she gave up her career, embracing the life of a chatelaine while attempting, with varying degrees of success, to transform herself from sinner to saint. *My Blue Notebooks* are a combination of her philosophical, social and erotic musings.

IT WAS
ONE LOVELY PARTY

from *My Blue Notebooks*

13 July. Sunday, eve of the victory parade. Oh, my country! My first country, because now I have become a Romanian.

Georges is deeply hurt if anyone says, by way of a compliment, that he has a tiny (!) trace of a charming foreign accent. He thinks they must be deaf or trying to insult him, draws himself up and replies with a barrage of 'I have a horrrrror of everrrrrything Rrrrromanian!' Georges is an angel, a love, an exquisite little boy, an ancient sage, a boring philosopher, an erudite scholar, etc. etc. He is sometimes accused of being – too handsome. People are rather beastly to him. After we were married, the first time we went to a first night, which is my way of going out and about, I caught glances, spiteful smiles in our direction, whispers. So in front of those three powerful, widely distributed news-sheets known as Henry Bernstein, Pierre Mortier and Pierre Frondaie, when one of them asked me how I was: 'I am happy and enviable, my dear. I live with the two bravest men in the world.'

'???'

'Yes, my son who is a famous aviator, and my husband who had the courage to marry me.'

It was at the Théâtre-Français, a performance of *Primerose*: it went the rounds in a flash, and I had won the mockers over to our side ...

*

15 July. Dreamed about Blanche d'Arvilly, a friend of my theatre days who went all over the place with me. She used to pick up the crumbs of my frivolous glory, was often very useful to me and more often treacherous and disagreeable. When I had my serious motor-car accident and was immobilised in the hospital at Beaujon, I saw her approaching my bed. Instinctively I shut my eyes. She came right up to the bed and bent over me – I could feel her breath on my face – and then she turned to the nurse and said in a tone of voice quite impossible to describe: 'So she is not disfigured?'

How can I hold it against her when we shared so much laughter? . . .

4 August. Have seen the new honours list in the papers. Henry Bernstein has been made a *chevalier* of the Legion of Honour. At last! Yes, but Pierre Wolf has been made a *commandeur.* Oh dear!

Pierre Wolf was once brought to see me, Liane of the Folies-Bergère, at lunchtime. I invited him to stay to lunch. Wolf was in bicycling clothes, britches and leggings, which put me off to start with. My mother was lunching with me that day, and four or five close friends. The witty Wolf elected to show off his gift of the gab on dirty stories, sparing us no obscene detail or word. I was seething. I controlled myself as best I could, and he noticed nothing. As we waited in the hall for coffee after the meal, convinced of his success, he suddenly remembered that as well as being the star of the Folies, I was his hostess. So he came over to me all smiling and gracious, still quite tipsy on his own talk and my wine: 'Liane, my lovely Liane, what an exquisite lunch! How delighted I am to have met you. Tell me, tell me – what can I do in my turn to give you pleasure?'

At these words I jumped: 'Give me pleasure? You would like to do that, really?'

'Yes,' he said, surprised.

'But really?'

'Of course.' Already a bit nervous.

'Well, that's simple. You can give me enormous pleasure this very minute.'

'How?' and he leaned towards me, his lips pursed.

'You can get the hell out of here!' And I called to the footman who happened to be passing: 'Get M. Wolf's hat and stick. He's in a hurry. Goodbye, Monsieur.' And I left him standing there. Flabbergasted, he grabbed his stick and made off. That evening I received a magnificent potted palm wrapped in rich Japanese embroideries, with an apologetic note. We became the best of friends. He remembers that little incident and often tells the story...

23 August. Am I vain? At bottom, yes. Not outwardly. I am aware of my beauty, naturally enough – the nation's Liane could hardly have remained unaware of it – but age is here. I often say 'Every age has its happiness and its beauty.' So my vanity finds words to console itself. I know that I am not a fool. I am prouder of my friendship with Salomon than of my husband's love. I am immensely and painfully proud of being Marco's mother. But I have a persistently naive side which makes my first reaction to anything one of delighted amazement, whether it's a dress, a painting, a house, a piece of furniture, a book, a poem, a gesture, a face. On second thoughts I return to reality. So I seem very changeable and in fact I *am* changeable, oh dear yes, tremendously so. I'm always turning coats completely, and doing it with the utmost sincerity. So I have intelligence, but it has holes in it! And I never get to the bottom of anything, I have neither the time nor the inclination. I learn nothing. It's like wearing a watch, which I've never dreamed of doing. If I want to know the time I ask whoever happens to be at hand. In the same way, if I want to know something – all right, I'll ask the encyclopedia, or Georges, or above all Salomon. The Gascon's prayer would be the prayer for me: 'Give me not wealth, oh Lord, but the company of those who possess it.'

Wit? I am quite quick-witted. It still comes spontaneously when I write but it is slower when I'm speaking. My attention is drawn and held by exterior objects and I don't even think about what I am going to say. As soon as I start thinking, there's the repartee, easy and clever – and biting, too.

I am kind, really instinctively kind. I can be devoted but only to special people. Then I am infinitely so. I'm generous too. I like doing without in order to give – the old Catholic side of me, says Georges. I can't refuse anything if I'm asked for it, yet I'm afraid of being deprived. I keep accounts. Like an American, I want to get value for my money. I'm careful over five francs and spend five thousand without a thought. I'm never wasteful in little everyday matters – the good order of a household depends on that. I haven't always been rich so I take money seriously as a means to an end and to liberation. I save it when I can. I can seem miserly even to myself, and that disgusts me! I pause to question myself, I examine the facts in detail, I calculate. No, I am not miserly, I am prudent. I have profited from some hard lessons and from the example of other people's experience. But it's just as well to examine oneself from time to time, because it's a slippery slope: method leads to economy, economy leads to avarice – and that is really dreadful!

That and laziness. I abominate idleness. I like to have plenty to do, to organise and to look after. On days when I've trailed lazily hither and thither and nothing special has happened, I feel uncomfortable when I examine my conscience in the evening, as though I had done wrong. There are heaps of little daily duties to be performed, that's where one should turn for occupation. How can one ask everything from those around one if one gives nothing oneself? Before the war everything was so easy and abundant. In this big house where now I have two little maids and a cleaning woman, I used to have four Arab servants, a cook, a lady's maid, a scrubber and a housekeeper! I never put my hand to a thing. It was one long party! Everyone talked at the top of his voice, swore, frittered, guzzled, had a good time. Sometimes I used to pull myself up and tell myself: 'Life is too good, it can't last! It's against nature. Georges loves me, our health is more or less all right, my son is famous, I have charming friends, almost enough money . . . any change would ruin it.' The war came . . . catastrophes, sorrows . . .

26 August. The other day someone asked me how old Emilienne d'Alençon is. Fifteen years ago I heard people saying she must be fifty, and she is not that even now. There is just a year between us. How pretty she used to be! Enormous golden eyes, the finest and most brilliant complexion! A proud little mouth, a tip-tilted nose you could eat, an oval face rather in the style of my own.

We were friends, she was my leading light in the ways of the theatre and of our pleasures. She could be beastly, but was really so pretty that one couldn't hold it against her. For instance, she said to me: 'I know you are going to be at this big dinner tonight. Don't dress, I shall be wearing just a coat and skirt and a blouse and one row of pearls. You do the same, so that we'll be alike – and send your carriage away, I'll take you home.' So at eight o'clock there I am in my simple little suit and one row of pearls – and at nine o'clock in sweeps my Emilienne resplendent in sumptuous white and gold brocade, dripping with diamonds, pearls and rubies, no hat, her curls full of sparkling jewels. 'Oh dear – am I late?', with a delicious little pretence at absent-mindedness! One careless, hardly even teasing, glance at me, and she doesn't speak to me for the rest of the evening. But as she leaves she says goodbye and offers me her lips with the choicest nonchalance. And I go home in a cab, confused and cross, brooding bitterly on these lines which I found in a notebook belonging to my grandmother Olympe:

> *In each young girl with gentle eyes you see*
> *A sister, not a rival . . .*

Two days later and it might never have been, on my side as well as hers. With an impudence as great as her beauty she had moved in on me, had installed herself in my bed, at my table, in my carriages, in my theatre boxes – and all, I must confess, to my great pleasure. I couldn't be strict with her. But forewarned is forearmed, and I no longer believed what she said.

We went to Nice together, to the casino and to fancy-dress balls. We gambled together at Monte Carlo. Everyone admired us and ran after us; we were fêted, we were spoilt. Darling little Mimi! Last year, at the Majestic, she came to spend an afternoon with me. It was very moving to see each other again after twelve or thirteen years, and we were pleased to find each other still so beautiful. Her face is still ravishing, mine too. We cheered each other up. Our lives have gone completely different ways. She laughs, she dances, she stays up all night, she smokes (opium), she enjoys everything just as she used to do. She is rich, she has lots of friends. Bad friends – but that doesn't worry her. Her expression is still childlike and amused. When you tell her a joke she chuckles like a delightful chicken. She has become a woman of letters and has published a collection of sensitive and well-turned verse. She never stops falling in love, following her whim for better or for worse. She is adored, she's always changing lovers. They weep for her a little – too little – and console themselves rather too soon, but they are proud that she was there. How often have I heard someone drop her name into a conversation with a smug little look! She used to be my favourite model, vicious and ravishing, not like the others. Nothing about her was banal or vulgar, not her face, nor her gestures, nor the things she dared to do. It was she who made me cut my hair. She turned up with a pair of scissors and 'snip', it was done. Then she said: 'Come along, we'll try some henna.' Three months later, we were corn-coloured. Then in a flash we became brunette. We did have such fun with ourselves – and how we laughed at others, both men and women. And then, little Mimi, your lips were so soft, your gestures were so coaxing and ... but here we are, my dear, a pair of nice little old ladies ...

I have been beastly, I have failed to practise Christian charity today. Georges wanted the door between our rooms to be shut during the night so that if I had the luck to fall asleep I wouldn't be woken. I shouted: 'You know that I can't sleep, you know that I'm alone and I'm frightened.' He persisted – ponderously, as he does everything. So then I slammed his door and locked the second door. I refused to go in to see him, and I can tell from the hundred thousand devils inside me that nothing and no one will be able to make me set foot in there this evening, and perhaps not tomorrow either, for the whole day. Not a nice character, Liane ...

29 December. Gaby Deslys becomes iller and iller. Perhaps it will be her fate to be spared old age and an actress's retirement, which is like burial.

I am reading Pascal's *Pensées*. I have begun his 'conversion of a sinner'. It could well be applied to me ... but why are these pages, and all writing concerning religion, so full of exhortations to humble and abase yourself, to fall on your knees and smite your breast? Does God really want that from His creatures?

They say that D'Annunzio, like Napoleon, has been abandoned by all his friends. He continues, nevertheless, to live in Fiume ...

Confession bores me, and the Mass, too, costs me an effort – I am not making progress on that road; I reproach myself for it. I am a poor soldier, at the least excuse I swing the lead. I don't rally properly to my flag, and I take the punishment for it inside myself: I am not happy ...

23 January. This day, the anniversary of the death of Louis XVI, brings back memories of my childhood in that corner of Brittany where all the old, right-minded families indicated their respectful mourning by keeping their shutters closed all day, going to Mass dressed in black and doing penance to compensate for France's criminal gesture. My mother, my old aunts and their friends set the example. My youth and cheerfulness were put to a hard test. Faces had to be long. Only the humble folk were allowed the privilege of passing this day comfortably, but they were regarded with an indulgent and disdainful pity.

I once knew an indirect descendant of Louis XVI, even knew him quite intimately. He was the eldest son of the Duc de Chartres, that charming Prince Henri d'Orléans who went exploring in Africa in the direction of Abyssinia. Sadly enough, he died down there, like the young Duc Jacques d'Uzès who preceded him by some years. Henri d'Orléans pursued me and loved my beauty, my wit and my delicacy. True descendant of Henri IV that he was, he had heaps of passions, but his faithful friendship gave the little dancer-mime at the Folies-Bergère a sort of halo. He used to write to me from those distant lands, tell me his exotic experiences, give me his books (he published several accounts of his travels). One day he sent me some heavy bronze rings and some circlets of old yellow ivory, saying: 'I have brought you back bracelets from your Abyssinian sisters, you won't think them very elegant. Use them for paper-weights.' I still have them at Roscoff; they are precious on the days when the wind rages.

Another time he gave me a white poodle from Syracuse, bought from a circus trainer. I couldn't keep it, it was so vicious. The mountebank must have beaten it dreadfully. Henri sent it to me washed, combed and tied with sky-blue ribbon, accompanied by these words in a letter: 'I belong to Liane de Pougy. I want to live for her. I know how to jump very high through a hoop of flaming paper, climb a ladder and count to twenty.' At first I was enchanted – then I had to think twice. The animal went for people's throats. It knocked down Emilienne d'Alençon and bit my butler. He opened the door for it and the animal flew out and ran away – to the house of the Duc de Chartres! Henri caught it and sent it back, thinking that it had escaped. Then I told him everything and begged him to rid me of it. He took it back, a little vexed I think, and after that gave me easier presents . . .

30 January. Something strange is up: for some time the wireless telegraph has been registering mysterious signals. Our learned men wonder whether we are in communication with a planet – Mars, it would be. Oh, how wonderful it would be to see that in one's lifetime! There are people who laugh and think it's a hoax, but I prefer the explanation which gives my imagination play . . .

10 February. At this moment I adore Max Jacob. I will be judged inconsistent, changeable, crazy. I have fulminated against the poor devil in my time ... Everything is different. I am sensitive to a fault, influenced by the day and the event. This poor, crushed Max, I love! I began to love him when I saw him again last year and he had risen somewhat above his material misfortunes, had started to earn his living – and his socks. Before that he used to wear his friends' socks and underwear, their old clothes. I was sorry for him but I found that ignoble and it hurt me to see a gifted man so bogged down. I found him repugnant and turned away from him angrily. Now he has freed himself from Picasso and his charity, from Poiret and his old neckties. Since his painting sells, he has been painting and has thus been able to continue the philosophical and poetic lucubrations which bring him in nothing beyond admiration. His accident has moved me very much and I am going to prepare a pretty, sunny, white and red bedroom for him on my second floor, for a sweet, affectionate convalescence in the fresh air. I will plan meals and flower arrangements for him, delights, instant satisfactions; in fact I will take – with a great deal of pleasure – a lot of trouble for him and he will not feel the effort in it ...

13 February. Gaby Deslys is dead. Never will she know the wrinkles of old age, and all they bring, and all they drive away ...

22 April. Long talk with Georges last night, from bed to bed. I made my way of thinking perfectly clear to him. It will do no good: Georges is a stupid and ceaseless bungler. He becomes more like Mariette every day. I really can't stand any more of this dismal, bad-tempered, discontented, hostile and disapproving spirit of contradiction. When he assured me of his profound and faithful love I ended with these true and conciliating words: 'I don't mind about your love, just give me a little sympathy and kindness. That is what I need and that is what my conduct, my bearing and my efforts have earned me.' Sympathy and kindness! Those two words contain the whole secret of domestic happiness.

Royal Dutch have fallen to 61,000 francs after having risen to

66,400! We are very dejected. Georges telephoned Lazarus who doesn't care a jot for us. These fluctuations are the coquettishness of value, allowing clever speculators to play with it and grow rich. The carrot is dangled, then withdrawn ...

7 June. Tumultuous day yesterday. My menu was phenomenal. Our guests were Bouchor, unexpected; Max Jacob, appearing like a jack-in-the-box with a beautiful bouquet of roses; Lucienne Rouveyre; Raoul de Galland, who came by car bringing his camera; Margot de La Bigne and all my shopping. For tea we were joined by our future tenants who have signed the agreement, my Uncle and Aunt Burguet, Steinilber and Lazarus with his little Pierre. Lazarus – oh dear, not so good. He was embarrassed and uncomfortable in my presence. On my side I smiled too much and couldn't help feeling hostile, also embarrassed and uncomfortable. Oh dear, money! Damnable and necessary money, up to its tricks.

Last but not least we opened our big gates to a ravishing grey motor car from which Andrée de La Bigne emerged, all golden in a dress of blue Japanese silk – really stunning, that girl – and loaded with chocolate caramels. She was followed by André Germain, resolute but staggering under the immense weight of his literary productions. Finally a delicious little grey night-moth came flitting out of the car, alighted beside me, fixed me with its tender and luminous gaze, full of childlike curiosity. It was Madame Clauzel, and I was conquered. Our arms linked, our hands met, our enchanted thoughts mingled. She is exquisite, gentle, authoritarian.

The friends left, the night-moth stayed – the night-moth and the clothes-moth. André Germain is a domesticated clothes-moth, we choose to spare him. He read us his articles on Dadaism, on D'Annunzio. Meanwhile the night-moth was in my arms: delicate touches, caresses, kisses, nips and scratches. This morning I still have little marks on my wrist. Like me, she adores Salomon, loves Flossie, admires Pauline. We evoked them, we compared our pearls and the textures of our skins. There were ripples of laughter, exclamations. Stern André Germain came to a halt and drilled us with a coldly indignant look; his nose became even more pointy and he told us: 'I can't go on reading while you talk.' So we kept quiet and our hands squeezed each other with increased intensity. She is like Eva Palmer, my Yvée, recalls a slender Liane from those bygone days of fragility and delicacy. I gave my *Idylle saphique* to the night-moth, who opened enormous eyes at the idea of reading something which, she says, Salomon has forbidden her. Oh, Salomon!

My 'Maintenon' dress exhausted me, I was the slave of that white collar which crushes so easily. Lianon! Organdie's victim! It's impossible to lean back. Poiret is decidedly impractical, doesn't know how to combine elegance with comfort.

FLORA TRISTAN

Flora Tristan was born in Paris in 1803, the daughter of a French mother and a Peruvian-Spanish father. Her first publication was a pamphlet, *Nécessité de faire un bon accueil aux femmes étrangères* (1835). This was followed in 1838 by her autobiography, *Pérégrinations d'une paria*, which made her famous, and in the same year she published her only novel, *Méphis*. In 1839 Flora Tristan visited England for the fourth time and wrote her *London Journal* which was published in French in 1840 and 1842 as *Promenades dans Londres* and ran to four editions.

In 1843 Flora Tristan published her manifesto, *L'Union ouvrière*, calling for a world-wide Workers' International. Many of the ideas formulated in it were used by Marx in his 1848 *Manifesto*. The following year she travelled through France addressing workers' meetings, making a record of this in her *Tour de France* which remained unpublished until 1973. While on her journey, Flora Tristan contracted typhoid fever and died at Bordeaux at the age of forty-one and was mourned throughout France as 'the worker's saint'. Her last book, *L'Emancipation de la femme*, was completed by Alphonse Constant and published posthumously in 1845.

IN ANOTHER GUISE

from *London Journal, 1840*

The honourable Members of Parliament loll on the benches, like so many tired and bored men; several of them are completely stretched out and actually asleep. The English, who are always zealous martyrs to the rules of etiquette, who attach so much importance to dress that even in the country they do not fail to change three times a day, who are so stiff and who take offence at the slightest social blunder, at the least oversight, affect in the Chamber nothing but contempt for the courtesy which good manners require. It is good parliamentary form to come to the session bespattered with mud, an umbrella under one's arm, in morning dress: or to come on horseback, to enter the Chamber with spurs on, riding whip in hand, and dressed in hunting clothes.

Insignificant people, of which there are so many in the British Parliament, hope in this way to give the impression of having important business, or having just come from some fashionable pastime, and although, I assume, none of these gentlemen would venture to visit any of his colleagues without taking his hat off, each one of them makes a point of keeping it on in the Chamber. To tell the truth, they demand no more courtesy from others than they have toward one another! No one in the galleries takes off his hat. In France this mark of respect is required in all public meetings; one must assume that in England the House of Commons does not believe itself entitled to it.

When a Member speaks, he takes off his hat, leans on his cane or umbrella, puts his thumbs in his waistcoat or in his watch pocket. In general, orators are very long-winded, they are accustomed to not being listened to at all, and appear to be not particularly interested themselves in what they are saying. Of course, a deeper silence prevails there than in our assembly: most of the Members are either asleep or reading their newspapers. We had spent more than one hour in the hall, two orators had spoken in turn without attracting the slightest attention, and I was beginning to feel quite tired. I did not understand English well enough to follow the discussion, and had I understood it better, the monotonous voices of those wooden figures would not have jarred any the less on my nerves. We were just about to go to the House of Lords when O'Connell stood up, whereupon everyone awoke from his parliamentary torpor; those who had been lying down sat up, rubbed their eyes and snapped to attention, the others left off reading their newspapers and all whispering stopped. Their pale and impassive faces took on an expression of rapt attention.

O'Connell is a short fat man, thickset and common looking; his face is ugly, all wrinkled, red and pimply. His gestures are jerky and rather commonplace, his clothes complete the picture. He wears a wig and a broad-brimmed hat, his umbrella has become a part of him, it never leaves him, and resembles by its size those carried by the kings of the Congo. Seeing him on the street one would take him for a coachman in his best Sunday clothes, but I hasten to say that under that coarse exterior there is a being full of spirit and poetry, heaven-sent to Ireland! Seeing him walking in the street one would never believe that there goes the champion of the people! . . .

The people's spokesman is, in appearance, no way different from the people themselves, and that partially explains the power he exerts, for, in this corrupt society, elegant manners cast suspicion on pureness of heart and sincerity. When he champions the cause of the people or speaks in the name of his religious beliefs, he is stirring and superb! He makes the oppressor quake! His ugliness disappears, and his countenance is as impressive as his words. His small eyes flash, his voice is expressive, clear and sonorous, his speech is forceful, it goes straight to the heart and arouses the most violent as well as the sweetest of motions; at meetings, he stirs up at one and the same time anger, tears, enthusiasm and revolt! I can think of nothing so marvellous as this man. If Queen Victoria could rely on such a powerful auxiliary ... she would complete in a few years what Louis XI was not able to do during his whole reign, and her emancipated people would bless her name.

We went on to the House of Lords. There also they guessed my sex; but the manners of these gentlemen were quite different from those I was exposed to in the House of the representatives of shopkeepers and financiers. They did not crowd around me to get a better look, they exchanged amused whispers, but I heard no improper or discourteous remark. I saw that I was in the presence of true gentlemen, tolerant of ladies' whims which they felt honour bound to respect. The refined manners and courtesy of the English nobility, haughty though it may be, are not to be found among the lords of finance or in any other class.

As we entered, the Duke of Wellington was speaking; his delivery was cold, colourless and languid. His words were received with some deference, but they failed to produce any effect. Lord Brougham proffered two or three broad jokes which were greeted with guffaws by their lordships.

The Chamber of Lords is scarcely any better than that of the Commons; it is built on the same plan: massive architecture without adornment.

The lords behave with no more decorum than the Members of the House of Commons. They too keep their hats on, but in their case it is not lack of manners, but pride of rank, and they require spectators and witnesses, even Members of the other House, to bare their heads. After Lord Wellington had finished speaking, he stretched out, nay sprawled on his bench with his feet up on the bench above so that his legs were higher than his head; a truly grotesque position.

I came away from the two Houses far from edified by the spectacle they had offered me and most certainly more shocked

by the behaviour of the gentlemen of the House of Commons
than they had been by my attire.

FACTORY WORKERS

Alerte, alerte, alerte, enfants
De la grande patrie;
Soldats de l'industrie,
Garde à vous, à vos rangs!
 Va, c'est en vain
 Qu'en son dédain,
 L'oisif raille
 De qui travaille;
  Toi seul es roi,
  Réveille-toi,
 Producteur, impose ta loi,
 Montre par la pratique,
 Au siècle écrivailleur,
 L'avenir pacifique
 Qui s'ouvre pour le travailleur.
Alerte, alerte, alerte, etc.

'Appel'
(a song by Vinçard, worker and follower of Saint-Simon)

Workers nowadays are the pariahs of society; no mention is ever
made of them in Parliament, unless it be to propose measures that
impinge upon their freedom and interfere with their pleasures.
        London and Westminster Review

Slavery appears in the early stages of all society; the harm it
engenders makes it fundamentally transitory, and its duration is
in inverse proportion to its harshness. If our fathers had treated
their serfs with no more humanity than manufacturers in
England treat their workers, slavery would not have endured
throughout the Middle Ages. The worker, under English rule,
no matter what his trade, leads such a dreadful existence that

the Negroes who have left the sugar plantations of Guadalupe and Martinique in order to enjoy English 'freedom' in Dominica and Santa Lucia return, when they can, to their masters. Far be it from me to entertain the sacrilegious thought of attempting to defend any kind of slavery! I only wish to demonstrate by this fact that the worker is more harshly treated by the law than the Negro by the whim of his French master. The slave of English property has, in order to earn his bread and pay the taxes imposed on him, a far more burdensome task.

The Negro is only exposed to the whims of his master, whereas the life of the English worker, his wife and children are at the mercy of the manufacturer. Should the price of calico or any other product drop, immediately those affected by the drop, spinner, cutler, potter, etc., lower wages in concert, without any thought as to whether the new wages they have decided upon are sufficient to feed the worker; they also increase the working hours. For piece-work, they demand better-quality work but for less pay, and work which does not meet all the requirements is not paid for. Cruelly exploited by his employer, the worker is also squeezed dry by the tax collector and starved to death by the landlords; he almost always dies young; his life is cut short by excessive work or by the nature of his work. His wife and children do not survive him for long; harnessed to factory work, they succumb for the same reasons; if they are not employed in the factories in winter, they starve to death on the street corner.

Division of labour, which has been pushed to the extreme and has brought tremendous progress to manufacturing, has destroyed intelligence and reduced men to mere cogs in the machinery. If at least a worker was trained to perform the various steps in one or more manufacturing processes, he would enjoy more independence; his master's cupidity would have fewer means of tormenting him; the organs of his body would retain enough energy to combat the harmful effects of an occupation he would be engaged in for only a few hours at a time. Tool grinders in English factories do not live beyond thirty-five years of age; the use of the grinding stone has no pernicious effects on our workers in Châtellerault, because grinding is only a part of their trade; and takes up only a small amount of their time, whereas in English workshops, tool grinders do nothing else. If the worker could work at various aspects of manufacturing, he would not be overwhelmed by his own insignificance, by the perpetual inactivity of his mind, while doing over and over again the same things all day long; strong spirits would not become necessary to arouse him from the stupor in which the monotony of his work plunges him, and drunkenness would not add the final touch to his misery.

Without having visited the manufacturing towns, without having seen the workers in Birmingham, Manchester, Glasgow, Sheffield, in Staffordshire, etc., one cannot get a true idea of the physical suffering and moral degradation of this class of the population. It is impossible to form an opinion about the lot of the English worker from that of the French worker. In England, life is half again as expensive as in France, and since 1825 there has been such a drop in wages that almost without exception, to support his family, the worker is obliged to ask the parish for assistance; and since parishes are hard-pressed because of the amount of assistance they give, they determine the share to be given in proportion to the wages of the worker and the number of his children, not according to the price of bread but according to the price of potatoes; for the English worker, bread is a luxury. The elite among the working class, excluded from parish assistance because of their wages, are scarcely better off. The average wage they earn, I am told, does not exceed three or four shillings a day, and they have on average four children. By comparing these two figures to the cost of living in England it is easy to understand their distress.

Most workers have no clothes, no bed, no furniture, fuel or nourishing food, and often not even potatoes to eat! . . . They are confined for twelve to fifteen hours a day in low rooms, where they breathe in, with the foul air, fibres from cotton, wool, linen, particles of copper, lead, iron, etc., and frequently try to compensate for an insufficient diet by excessive drink: in consequence, the wretches are all sickly, rachitic, debilitated; they are thin and stooped, with weak limbs, pale complexions and lifeless eyes; it is as if they were all suffering from consumption. I know not whether the painful expression to be seen on the faces of almost all the workers should be attributed to permanent exhaustion or to the dark despair which feeds upon their souls. It is difficult to get them to meet your glance, they constantly keep their eyes lower and will only look at you furtively, with sly sidelong glances which give a stupid, savage and thoroughly vicious expression to their cold, impassive faces impregnated with profound sadness;[1] English factories are unlike ours in that no singing, chatter or laughter is heard. The master wants no reminder of the world to distract, for a single minute, his workers from their task; he demands silence, and a deathlike silence reigns, such is the power of hunger that the master's word becomes law! There exists between the worker and his employer none of the ties of familiarity, courtesy and interest to be seen in France: ties which lull the hatred and envy which the disdain and hard-heartedness of the exacting, luxury-loving rich foster in the hearts of the poor. In English work-shops, the master is never heard to say to the worker: 'Hello, Baptiste, old man; well, well, and how is your wife doing? And the little one? Indeed, that's splendid. Let us hope that its mother will soon be better; tell her to come and see me as soon as she is up and about.' Any master would think it demeaning to talk to his workers in this way. In every factory owner the worker sees a man who can have him thrown out of the shop where he works, so he slavishly doffs his cap to every factory owner he meets; but the latter would feel compromised if he returned the courtesy.

Since I have become acquainted with the English working class, slavery is no longer, to my mind, the greatest human misfortune; the slave is sure of his daily bread as long as he lives and he is sure of being cared for when he is ill; whereas there is no bond whatsoever between the worker and the English master. If the employer has no work to offer, the worker starves; if he is ill, he succumbs on his wretched cot unless, on the point of death, a hospital will take him in: for it is a special favour to be admitted to one. If he gets too old, if he is crippled in an accident, he is dismissed and takes to begging stealthily for fear of being arrested. This situation is so horrible that in order to bear it, the worker must be possessed of superhuman courage or total apathy.

Cramped premises are common to English factories; the space allotted to the worker is parsimoniously measured out. The yards are small, the stairways narrow; he is obliged to sidle around the machines and the looms; it is easy to see, upon visiting a factory, that the builder has given no thought to the comfort, well-being or even the health of the men destined to occupy it. Little attention is paid to cleanliness, the most effective means of assuring salubriousness; the machines are as carefully painted, varnished, cleaned and polished as the yards are filthy, full of stagnant water, the floors dusty, the windows dirty. In truth, if the buildings and the workshops were clean, tidy and well-kept as are the factories in Alsace, the tattered clothes of the English workers would seem all the more hideous. It matters little whether it be negligence or design: this lack of cleanliness nonetheless adds to the worker's ills.

England has no greatness left except in her industry, but she is a giant in respect to the instruments devised by the mathematical genius of modern times, magical instruments which petrify everything around them! The docks, the railroads, the enormous dimensions of factories give an idea of the importance of British commerce and industry.

The power of the machines and their universal application are astonishing and stun the imagination! Human science incorporated into a thousand shapes has taken the place of the functions of the intellect; with machines and the division of labour, only motors are needed, reasoning and reflection are useless.

I have seen a steam engine with the strength of five hundred horses![2] Nothing is more formidable than the sight of the motion imparted to these iron masses whose colossal proportions frighten the imagination and seem to surpass the power of man! This motor of hyperbolical power is located in a vast building where it runs a considerable number of machines which work iron and wood. Its enormous polished iron bars go up and down forty or fifty times a minute and impact a backward and forward motion to the tongue of the monster which seems to suck in everything in order to swallow it up, the awesome groans it utters, the rapid turning of the enormous wheel which emerges from the abyss to plunge immediately back again, never revealing more than half of its circumference to the eye, fills one's soul with terror. In the presence of the monster one sees nothing else, one hears nothing but its breathing.

Upon recovering from your stupefaction and your terror, you look around for man; he almost escapes notice, reduced to the size of an ant by the dimensions of all that surrounds him, he is busy placing under the cutting edge of two large blades, shaped like the jaws of a shark, enormous iron bars which the machine cuts with the precision of a Damascus blade slicing a turnip.

Notes

1. This look, which I also noticed in America among the slaves, is not, in the British Isles, peculiar to factory workers. It is found everywhere among those who are dependent, subservient; it is one of the distinguishing characteristics of 20 million workers. There are nonetheless exceptions, and it is almost always among women that they are to be found.
2. I saw it in Birmingham. The owners of the factory assured me that the power of this steam engine could be estimated as that of 500 horses; it turns more than 200 pulleys, and runs saws, metal cutters, flatting mills of all sizes, an assortment of machines for making zinc spoons, etc. A sixpence coin was set under a press to give me an idea of its power and I watched as a narrow band of silver paper 42 yards long and thin as the skin of an onion emerged from the machine.

MARSHA HUNT

Marsha Hunt was born in Philadelphia and studied at the University of California during the student riots of the 1960s but soon left for Europe. In London she made her name in the hit musical *Hair*. She has been an actress, singer and, more recently, an acclaimed novelist. Her autobiography, *Real Life*, was published in 1986, and her first novel, *Joy*, in 1990. Her latest book is *Repossessing Ernestine*.

WORK TO EAT,
EAT TO WORK

from *Free*

Across town in that dusty dead end where the sun was less happy to shine Aunt Em was in a rage. 'You been to school with them white crackers so long, you gettin' lazy like 'em,' she ranted. But Atlanta hardly heard. In an effort to taunt, Atlanta was singing 'fat tub of lard' under her breath and had both hands cupped over her ears.

'Heifer! Who you callin' a fat tub of lard? Don't you know I'll take and maul your head against the wall?'

As they normally had a major stand-off early Saturday evening, Atlanta was ready for threats, insults and minor shoving. But since a lifetime battling Aunt Em had taught her the dangers of shifting her resolve, she knew better than to let up. 'Fat tub of lard,' her murmuring singsong went on.

'Sitting there like the Queen of Sheba with your good dress on!' charged Aunt Em.

After the interview with Mrs Tewksbury Atlanta hadn't changed out of her Sunday best.

'And I told you last time you slipped out of here without going to do for them Klabbers.'

'Klabber,' hissed Atlanta. 'Their name is Kleber! So ignorant you can't even talk right.'

Such disparagements riled Aunt Em more than anything else. But she was deafened by the sound of her own voice. It ricocheted off the kitchen walls over the issue which had started the fracas. 'Talkin' 'bout you free and it's a free country. The only thing a nigger's free to do is die.'

The 'fat tub of lard' singsong rose in blatant challenge; Atlanta's fear of Aunt Em made her so crazy she was incapable of backing down, though she knew Aunt Em lacked her usual bluster, having missed a night's sleep listening to a barking hound.

The old woman's rabble-rousing belied her homespun image. Wide as a barrel, wrapped in a navy skirt which was supposed to reach her bare feet but stopped above the ankle, Aunt Em looked motherly. But that didn't stop her saying, 'Don't come in my face with no mess, 'cause I'll ram a knife in your gut.'

With her two hundred pounds leaning against the aluminium sink, she jutted both hands on her hips to rant, 'I done four shirts while you got the nerve to set with your head in a book … Claimin' you read one page and I done heard you turn don't know how many.' The ABC had been her master's exclusive code and she couldn't abide it in her kitchen. 'Next you be telling me you late for somebody's choir and ain't gonna cart that bundle to Miz Holloway's.'

As it was, Atlanta had managed to slip through an entire week without scrubbing or ironing. She'd been trying to soften the skin on her hands, in the hope that Hernando Lopez might grab hold of one. Since he'd moved to town, she'd refused to be seen in the streets balancing washloads on her head.

'You ain't good for nothin',' accused Aunt Em. 'Talkin' 'bout school this and school that.' Tired or not, she was a steel-driving man when her dander was up. 'Girl, don't you know I'd ruther see you dead in the gutter than let your narrow behind slip out this house without hitting tap at a snake.'

Atlanta turned the page.

Her face was as stony as Lincoln's on Rushmore. But underneath the table, her right hand nervously twisted her petticoat round and round. Round and round, practically cutting off the circulation in her forefinger.

Her dream was to speak softly, change the tablecloth twice a week and be included in some pastor's social rounds. Other girls she knew hadn't been raised among smelly socks constantly boiling and strangers' long johns strewn around their kitchen floor.

In fourth grade Atlanta began claiming that her father was an elevator operator, and all through fifth she'd prayed that her real parents would come for her. When she was ten, being so much taller than Teenotchy made her able to convince herself he wasn't her real brother. But by the sixth grade she had to accept that they had the exact same noses and stubby toes and arched eyebrows. And he could remember their mother nursing Atlanta and imitate the way he remembered Derwent Simms hobbling with his cane.

Aunt Em saw Atlanta's mind drift from the book, so she reared. 'I let you get away with your mess last Sat'day 'cause Tessie was laid up, but I'm ready for you now. I'll beat you till you black and blue!' She parroted every threat her slave owners had hurled at her. But whereas she only struck with belt or birch switch, she'd survived whips and the cat o' nine tails.

However provoked the old woman was, her rages were simply tornadoes that whirled up from past hurts and furies. They left a deathly hush within her once they'd passed.

Atlanta noticed the vein throbbing down the centre of Aunt Em's forehead. It was the sign that any minute she would quit shouting to calm her nerves. So Atlanta closed her book upon the stained tablecloth. Having made it in her home economics class, she'd vowed never to make another for Aunt Em to ball up in the windowsill. Trying to turn the Klebers' converted stable into a home was impossible, she'd concluded, because Aunt Em refused to notice and Teenotchy refused to help.

'You ready to tote these things to Miz Holloway's?' Aunt Em asked in her normal voice. Sparrows could be heard again in the yard.

Atlanta stood to unravel her long limbs. 'Guess Teenotchy's over in his plot.' To share the news with Aunt Em about the Women's Auxiliary job and possible work for Teenotchy at the Tewksburys' would've been like passing secrets to the enemy. So she was saving it for him or Beulah ... or Hernando Lopez, assuming she could think of an excuse to start a conversation with him at Glee Club.

Teenotchy'd advised Atlanta about her crush on Hernando Lopez. 'Doesn't matter that he's as black as my boot. He's still over there on Coulter Street. And anyway, I saw him walking with Erlethia Robinson!' Erlethia's father had his own catering business and for two generations both sides of her family, so she bragged, had been born free.

Until Hernando arrived in Germantown, Atlanta'd resolved on a spinster life teaching, she was so sure that nobody decent would marry her. But standing behind Hernando in Glee Club and studying the way his hair grew down the back of his neck resurrected her passion for boys.

With her contralto rising above his bass, she could think only of running her fingers along the rim of his collar while their 'Onward Christian Soldiers' rang out in descant.

Hernando's black eyes galvanized Atlanta and talking about him constantly to Beulah let her believe that his failed attempts to explain himself in English were practically marriage proposals.

With him on her mind, she bounded upstairs blurting, 'I need to change.' Her plan was to slip out to Glee Club before church bells chimed seven.

Aunt Em huffed over to her curtained-off corner where she slept to avoid the rickety stairs. In a jar on the dresser was a chunk of bread pudding she'd been hoarding. Careful not to make a sound, she unscrewed the jar and, hearing Atlanta tiptoe out, she gobbled an edge, relieved to savour it in peace.

'You ain't so slick,' mumbled Aunt Em, with her mouth full.

Her swollen feet shuffled to the door. 'Teenotchy'll have to take them things 'cause I ain't studdin' her. One o' these days I'll stick her and her rags in the street.'

Staring out at the three clothes-lines sagging with dried sheets, her mind was on the bread tin, where she kept the stale bakery goods that Tessie brought her Thursdays.

Although she regretted that Tessie suffered diabetes and couldn't have sugary treats, Aunt Em was grateful for the broken three-day-old cookies and other items Tessie got free, working for the Jewish baker. These large crumbs, exchanged for laundry services, found their way to Aunt Em's tin. Without them she could never have appeased her belly god.

Some nights, no sooner than she'd collapsed on her cot, belly god would nudge, 'Feed me', and drag her from her bed in search of something, anything, to nibble. Wednesdays were the worst. Wednesdays Aunt Em needed more night feeds than a newborn, since on Thursdays she collected Miz Llewellyn's things. Not that Miz Llewellyn complained or short-changed more than the others, but she always searched Aunt Em's face for clues. 'You sure, Auntie, that I don't know you from somewhere? You look *so* familiar to me. Where you from?' she'd pry. 'What's your last name? Who'd you say you worked for?'

Aunt Em hadn't said, having vowed to live a lie from the day she laid eyes on Teenotchy's grey ones, which haunted her and made her remember what she needed to forget.

'You ain't Emma no more,' Aunt Em recalled the straggly-haired young mother informing her the day she bought her, aged thirteen, plus a sick cow, from the dairy farm by the river.

'Emma can't be a nigger's name. It's my name. Miz Emma,' she'd accentuated.

So the African girl who'd become Emma with her first slave-master wept under her horse blanket that February night without name or number.

Next morning Miz Emma said, 'Lottie, the baby needs to be changed,' and passed her a beefy one-year-old with a big head and big feet, grinning to show off his baby teeth. 'This here's your mammy, James,' she announced to her son. 'Her name's Lottie.'

Until then Aunt Em had spent her hostage years cow-herding and milking. She wasn't good with words, having spent all her time with the animals, and had never been trained for house-work, having never been inside a house. But Miz Emma believed a good hiding was the surest way to train slaves. She expected a switch of birch to show 'Lottie' the way to iron and knead bread and fold back the corners of the bed. And when that didn't work she tried the cat o' nine tails, only relying on the old horse whip as a last resort. 'Don't make me beat'cha till ya bleed,' Miz Emma used to warn the girl, as if baby-minding came easy and mending wasn't a science.

'Lottie' waited for spring to try to find the dairy farm, but Miz Emma's dogs soon tracked her on the road by morning. Beating her back to the barn, where the hatchet waited, Miz Emma said, 'This time I'm taking a finger, but you try to run off again and it'll be your big toe.'

Aunt Em, remembering, opened and shut her four-fingered left hand. One less for her rheumatics, she always told Tessie, but it didn't make the washing any easier.

'Lottie,' she said, shaking her head on the way to the cookie tin. But the Lottie in her refused to be buried. The piles of stale cookies and bread puddings couldn't shake off memories that clung like a noose ...

While other Germantowners rubbed down their souls at Sunday prayer meetings that morning, Aunt Em shook herself from one of her daytime nightmares. She'd been catnapping in the kitchen until a blonde voice in her dream shrieked, 'Lottie! I gotta take the whip to you ag'in. Don't look like you done that outhouse!'

Eleven o'clock, judging from the chorus of church bells that gonged. Not that it mattered.

By eight, Aunt Em'd pressed Teenotchy's good shirt for him (though he'd refused to tell her that he was going to Upper Germantown to see about the Tewkesburys' stable job) and had already boiled a kettle of lacy handkerchiefs, a tub of Miz Brandauer's snuggies and the bank-teller's white shirts.

The washerwoman's bunions ached worse than her knuckles, knotted from rheumatism and cracking them most of her life. So, snatching her clothes-peg bag, she could just about do a lead-footed shuffle to the door.

The line of dress shirts had to be taken down and ironed, which she did year in and out, never complaining that for all the men she sent to work clean not one had ever laboured for her.

When she came north, Thanksgiving of '96, she'd considered it an honour that what she called 'high-class folk' trusted her to wash their finery. She marvelled at the crocheted doilies, delicate silk stockings and hand-embroidered collars. But she'd given up admiring other people's fancy goods. They didn't change her life. If anything they made it more difficult, since she was expected to note when they needed repairing.

Work to eat. Eat to work. Aunt Em was a washing machine, scared the three of them would end up starving in the poorhouse if she idled and believing she had no right to more.

Her soul sustenance had been an annual Good Friday revival meeting, until she and her neighbour Tessie went to one where the preacher, possessed of a great pair of lungs and fancy patter, damned all fornicators. That sermon convinced Aunt Em that God served only the sinless, so she refused to go again, telling Tessie, 'I'm too crippled up to walk anywhere that I ain't *got* to.' She knew she was damned and needed no reminders.

But even without revivals, her body and mind stayed too busy for reflection until the Chinese laundry opened on Bringhurst, taking some customers and leaving enough time for her memory to taunt her.

Whether she sidled back in daydreams or got jostled back in a nightmare, she couldn't forget the Van Zandts' decrepit homestead by the river, or her mistress, Miz Emma. Or Miz Emma's son, James, whose grey, almond-shaped eyes stayed the same though everything else about him, particularly the size of his hands and feet, changed in those seventeen years she was their hostage, or slave, as they called her.

James Van Zandt was three before he could say Lottie.

'Thick-tongued and dumb like his damned daddy,' explained Miz Emma, never having a kind word for the Dutchman who'd abandoned her and the baby boy before Lottie arrived.

From the moment the thirteen-year-old African girl was

purchased, baby James curled his plump toddler's arms around her bird-like black neck and burrowed his mass of straw-coloured curls on her shoulders, because he could resist her innocence no more than she could his. And at seven, he still made her his refuge and she, starved of hugs, all but his, was glad to have somebody to hold. They made a handsome portrait, especially when he was perched on her shoulders, which was as often as not.

'You can't hang about all day on that wench,' his red-faced mother would quip, resentfully noticing that her son had found comfort while she had none. 'Time you got over to that schoolhouse, so they can learn you the alphabet.'

But James wouldn't sit still in the brick room they called 'school' unless he was sure Lottie was outside on the steps. Through all inclement weather, the scrawny figure could be seen shifting from one foot to the other beside the school steps. Her fingers were number than ice cubes in winter and her round ebony head would soak up sun and sweat in the long Southern summers.

The older schoolchildren were quick to tease and taunt once they realised that the frail figure was James's mammy, stationed to escort him. And they were quick to chant, 'Jimmy Van Zandt's a mammy's boy,' whenever they saw her walking back through the trees along the dusty old road that touched the Mississippi.

From time to time he'd demand that she showed him where she'd planted her baby finger, but she couldn't remember where she'd buried it, and the stick marking its grave had been blown away by the years.

It was only due to the fact that his mother had nothing to give James for his eighth Christmas that she handed over Lottie's papers to stop him whining. Lottie was chopping wood when the long-limbed boy rushed out, wielding her bill of sale.

'I own you,' he said, and he danced up and down, slinging chickenfeed at her from a pail beside the rooster's pen.

WAITING FOR
MY LIFE

JANET FRAME

Janet Frame was born in 1923 in New Zealand and is that country's best known living writer. In addition to her autobiography she has written eleven novels, short stories and poems. She has been awarded numerous international prizes for her work. *To The Is-land* is the first of Janet Frame's three-volume autobiography. It chronicles her childhood and adolescence spent in a materially poor but intellectually intense railway family in the 1920s and 30s.

KEEPING MYRTLE'S MEMORY GREEN

from *To the Is-Land*

IN THE SECOND PLACE

From the first place of liquid darkness, within the second place of air and light, I set down the following record with its mixture of fact and truths and memories of truths and its direction always toward the Third Place, where the starting point is myth.

TOWARD THE IS-LAND

The Ancestors – who were they, the myth and the reality? As a child, I used to boast that the Frames 'came over with William of Orange'. I have since learned that this may have been so, for Frame is a version of Fleming, Flamand, from the Flemish weavers who settled in the Lowlands of Scotland in the fourteenth century. I strengthen the reality or the myth of those ancestors each time I recall that Grandma Frame began working in a Paisley cotton mill when she was eight years old; that her daughters Polly, Isy, Maggie spent their working lives as dressmakers and in their leisure produced exquisite embroidery, knitting, tatting, crochet; and that her son George Samuel, my father, had a range of skills that included embroidery (or 'fancywork', as it was known), rug-making, leatherwork, painting in oils on canvas and on velvet. The Frames had a passion for making things. Like his father, our Grandad Frame, a blacksmith who made our firepokers, the boot-last, and even the wooden spurtle smoothed with stirring the morning porridge, my father survives as a presence in such objects as leather workbag, a pair of ribbed butter pats, a handful of salmon spoons.

As children, we heard little of our father's ancestors, the Frames and the Patersons, only that most had immigrated to the United States of America and to Canada, where 'Cousin Peg' became a schoolteacher. And none remains now of that Frame family of eight sons – John, Alex, Thomas, Robert, William Francis, Walter Henry, George Samuel, Charles Allan – and four daughters – Margaret, Mary, Isabella Woods. The fourth, my namesake, died at thirteen months.

Mother's family, the Godfreys, had long been established in Wairau and Blenheim and Picton, where Mother, Lottie Clarice, was born and brought up in a family of three brothers – Charles, Lance, William – and five sisters – May, Elsie, Joy, Grace, Jessie (who died in her twenty-first year). Mother's father, Alfred Godfrey, also a blacksmith, was the son of John Godfrey, a political character known as 'The Duke', who owned the Sheepskin Tavern in Wairau Valley and was later editor of the *Marlborough Press*. We heard from Mother of John Godfrey's brother Henry and of their father, an Oxford doctor, whose 'Godfrey's Elixir' was known in Great Britain in the early nineteenth century; of Mother's mother, Jessie Joyce, from a Jersey Islands family of French origin and her mother, Charlotte, formerly Charlotte Nash, author of the poems in a small book with an engraved cover and sweet-pea-coloured pages, written at eighteen, before her emigration from Harlbedown, Kent, to New Zealand – Charlotte, whose second marriage was to James or 'Worser' Heberley, of Worser Bay, Wellington, given to him by the tribe of his first wife (Te Ati Awa).

Mother and Father, then. Mother leaving school early to become a dental nurse at Mr Stocker's rooms in Picton, later to be a housemaid in various homes in Picton and Wellington – the Beauchamps, the Loughnins – and, during the Great War, in the early years of her marriage, in the home of Wili Fels in Dunedin;

Mother, a rememberer and talker, partly exiled from her family through her marriage out of the Christadelphian faith and her distance from Marlborough, remembering her past as an exile remembers her homeland; Mother in a constant state of family immersion even to the material evidence of the wet patch in front of her dress where she leaned over the sink, washing dishes, or over the copper and washtub, or, kneeling, wiped the floor with oddly shaped floorcloths – old pyjama legs, arms and tails of worn shirts – or, to keep at bay the headache and tiredness of the hot summer, the vinegar-soaked rag she wrapped around her forehead: an immersion so deep that it achieved the opposite effect of making her seem to be seldom at home, in the present tense, or like an unreal person with her real self washed away. Perhaps we were jealous of the space that another world and another time occupied in our mother's life; and although, perhaps fearing immersion in this foreign world, we struggled to escape, we were haunted by her tales of the Guards, the Heberleys, Dieffenbach, shipwrecks in the Sounds, life in Waikawa Road and down the Maori pa, family life at the Godfreys', remembered as paradisal. We came to know by heart incidents reported with exact conversations at school, at home, in the dentist's rooms, and in the homes where Mother worked – from her excitement on her first day at school at seeing a weta crawling on brother Willy's knee ('Oooh, look on Willy's knee!') to the words of Mr Loughnin the magistrate as he (in nightshirt and nightcap) lured his wife to his bed with 'Letty, I want you . . .'

When Mother talked of the present, however, bringing her sense of wondrous contemplation to the ordinary world we knew, we listened, feeling the mystery and the magic. She had only to say of any commonplace object, 'Look, kiddies, a stone' to fill that stone with a wonder as if it were a holy object. She was able to imbue every insect, blade of grass, flower, the dangers and grandeurs of weather and the seasons, with a memorable importance along with a kind of uncertainty and humility that led us to ponder and try to discover the heart of everything. Mother, fond of poetry and reading, writing, and reciting it, communicated to us that same feeling about the world of the written and spoken word.

Father, known to us as 'Dad', was inclined to dourness with a strong sense of formal behaviour that did not allow him the luxury of reminiscence. One of the few exceptions was his tales of 'the time we had the monkey', told with remembered delight and some longing. When his family left Oamaru, where he was born, to live in Port Chalmers (where his mother, Grandma Frame, became known as midwife), Grandad Frame brought home from the pub a monkey left by one of the sailors. 'Tell us,' we used to say to Dad, 'about the time you had a pet monkey.'

Dad, too, left school early, although he was a good student, as the class photos of 'Good Workers at Albany Street School' testify. His first job was making sound effects (horses galloping and wild storm sounds) at the local theatre, and his first adventure was his attempt to fly from the roof of the family house in Dunedin. Later he began work on the railway as a cleaner, progressing to fireman, second-class engine driver, which was his occupation when I first met him, later to first-class engine driver, following the example of his brothers who spent their lives with engines and movement – Alex, who became a taxi driver; Wattie, a sea captain, later a harbour master in Newport, Melbourne; Charlie, who was for a time a motor mechanic and chauffeur to Sir Truby King. Brother Bob became a baker in Mosgiel.

Mum and Dad (Mother was known as 'Mum' until I considered myself grown up enough to acknowledge her as a separate personality) were married at the Registry Office in Picton three weeks before Dad sailed to the Great War. When Dad returned from the war, he and Mother set up house in Richardson Street, St Kilda, Dunedin, helped by a rehabilitation loan of £25, with which they bought one wooden kerb, one hearth-rug, two Morris dining chairs, one *duchesse*, one oval dining table, one iron bedstead and flock mattress, one kitchen mat, these items being listed on the document of loan with a chilling reminder that while the loan remained unpaid, the King's representative (the agreement was between 'His Majesty the King and George Samuel Frame') had the right to enter the Frame household to inspect and report on the condition of the 'said furniture and fittings'. The loan was repaid after a few years, and the document of discharge kept by my parents in their most hallowed keeping place – the top right-hand drawer of the King's duchesse – where were also kept my sister Isabel's caul, Mother's wedding ring, which did not fit, her upper false teeth, which also did not fit, Myrtle's twenty-two-carat gold locket engraved with her name, and Dad's foreign coins, mostly Egyptian, brought home from the war.

There were the ancestors, then, given as mythical possessions – your great-grandmother, your great-grandfather, did this, was this, lived and died there and there – and the living parents, accumulating memories we had not shared. Then on 15 December 1920 a daughter, Myrtle, was born, and on 20 April 1922 a son, Robert, or Bruddie; in 1923 another son, stillborn, unnamed, was buried, and on 28 August 1924 I was born, named Janet Paterson Frame, with ready-made parents and a sister and brother who had already begun their store of experience, inaccessible to me except through their language and the record, always slightly different, of our mother and father, and as each member of the family was born, each, in a sense with memories on loan, began to supply the individual furnishings of each Was-Land, each Is-Land, and the hopes and dreams of the Future.

A DEATH

The school year began. The schools were not to reopen. We were to have lessons by correspondence. My school tunic arrived from Aunty Polly. It fitted closely, with two instead of three pleats, but I was satisfied enough to let Dad take my photo to send to Aunty Polly.

As if school holidays and summer had been destined to go hand in hand, yet another summer came, with hot winds, nor'westers burning from the Canterbury Plains, copper

sulphate or 'blue-stone' skies, and no place for comfort except
the water, the sea or the baths, with us going back and forth from
both. And on the last Friday before the book lists and the first
school lessons were to arrive, Myrtle suggested we go swimming
first and then go downtown to look at the boys, but I refused,
interested now in my lessons, how to get my new books without
too much pleading and argument, wondering whether I'd like
senior high, thinking, too, of the notebooks I would fill with
poetry. Myrtle and I quarrelled about my refusal to go with her;
only the quarrel was really about me as 'Dad's pet' because I'd
been Dux, and I was now going to senior high, to be a teacher
like Dad's Cousin Peg, who immigrated to Canada; I was
entering the world that Myrtle had once shared with Joan of Arc
and the Prince of Sleep, with the promise of many more
wonderful characters lost; besides, Dad was cruellest to Myrtle,
who was rebellious, daring, openly disobedient, always under
the threat of being sent to the industrial school at Caversham,
whereas I who wanted only to be 'good' and approved of, was
timidly obedient except where I could deceive with a certainty
of not being caught.

As a result of that afternoon quarrel, Myrtle went with
Marguerite and Isabel to the baths while I stayed home, dutifully
preparing myself for the new school year. It was late afternoon
when someone knocked at the door, and Mother, thinking it was
a salesman, opened the door, said quickly, 'Nothing today, thank
you', and was about to shut the door in the man's face when he,
like the stereotype of a salesman, wedged his foot in and forced
his way into the kitchen, while Mother, who had told us tales of
such actions, prepared herself to, in her usual phrase, 'floor
him'. I was standing by the door into the dining room. The man
glanced at me and said sharply, 'Send that child away.' I stayed
and listened. 'I'm a doctor,' the man said, 'I've come to tell you
about your daughter Myrtle. She's been drowned. They've taken
her body to the morgue.'

I stared, able only to absorb the news, 'They've taken her
body to the morgue.' We children had always fancied we knew
which building was the morgue, a small, moss-covered stone hut

down by the post office, near where the Oamaru creek rolled green and slimy over an artificial waterfall. We used to frighten one another by referring to the morgue as we passed it on our shortcut through Takaro Park toward Tyne Street and the beach, and sometimes we tried to look through the small barred window ('for air, so the bodies don't smell') to see within. The place was so small, sealed, inaccessible that we knew it must be the morgue, and when we spoke of it at home, Mother had always shown fear, which encouraged us, after the many examples from our teasing father, to repeat the word.

'Morgue, morgue.'

'Don't say that word, kiddies.'

Now, when the doctor had delivered his news and gone, Mum herself spoke the word, for it had convinced her, too, that Myrtle was dead, drowned. At first I was glad, thinking there'd be no more quarrels, crying, thrashings, with Dad trying to control her and angry with her and us listening frightened, pitying, and crying, too. Then the sad fact came home to me that there might be a prospect of peace, but the cost was the entire removal of Myrtle, not just for a holiday or next door or downtown or anywhere in the world, but off the face of the earth and out of the world, a complete disappearance and not even a trial, just to see how it worked. And where would be the fun-loving, optimistic, confiding, teasing Myrtle with the scar on her knee and her grown-up monthlies, and the ambition to go to Hollywood to be a film star, to tap-dance with Fred Astaire, singing and dancing her way to fame and fortune? Where would be the Joan of Arc with her painted silver armour and helmet, the wireless performer who recited 'over the air':

> *I met at eve the Prince of Sleep,*
> *His was a still and lovely face.*

Myrtle's entire removal was stressed when she didn't come home that night to do the things she ordinarily did, to finish what she had begun in the morning, bring in the shoes cleaned with white cleaner and left to dry on the washhouse windowsill in the sun. Dad came home early and put his arms around Mum and cried, and we'd never seen him cry before. And everyone seemed to forget about Isabel, and it was quite late, almost dark, when Isabel came in, her fair hair still wet and bedraggled from swimming in the baths, her small, scared face telling everyone where she had been and what she had seen.

That night we cuddled in bed together, and as the next day passed and the next, with the grown-ups talking about inquests and coroners and undertakers and Mother naming each with a sharpness of tone that allowed them to take a share of the 'blame'; and the talk of the funeral and the mechanics of burial, I gradually acquired a new knowledge that hadn't reached me through the other deaths in the family; but this was Myrtle, her death by drowning, her funeral notice, her funeral, her flowers, her coffin, her grave; she had never had so many possessions all at once.

After the inquest, when they brought her home in her coffin into the Sturmer-smelling front room and Mum asked, 'Do you want to see Myrtle?' I said no. 'We'll see her on Resurrection Day,' Mum said, conjuring once again in my mind the turmoil of Resurrection Day, the crowds, the wild scanning of faces, the panic as centuries of people confront each other and only a miracle provides room for all.

Myrtle was buried, her grave covered with wreaths from many people in Oamaru, including the swimming club where she had been a member, and some of the boys that we'd watched showing off with their muscles and their togs. And soon the rain rained on the flowers, and the ink on the cards was smudged, and the coloured ribbons frayed and rotted, and the grave itself sank until it was level with the earth. 'It always sinks, you know,' they said.

And one afternoon, when I was putting fresh flowers on Myrtle's grave and crumbling Aspros into the water in the jam jar because 'they' had said Aspros made the flowers last, I saw Miss Lindsay nearby visiting her mother's grave, Miss Lindsay of the 'jewelled sword Excalibur and the hand clothed in white samite mystic, wonderful'.

'Is Myrtle there?' Miss Lindsay asked.

I nodded.

'What are you putting in the water?'

'Aspros,' I said. Miss Lindsay's suddenly gentle tone and her ooze of understanding infuriated me.

'They won't bring her back,' she said gently.

'I know,' I said coldly, explaining the reason for the Aspros.

I had lately learned many techniques of making flowers and other things 'last', for there had suddenly been much discussion at home and amongst people who came to the house to offer their sympathy in our 'sad loss'. They were obsessed with means of preventing the decay of their 'floral tributes', of preserving the cards and ribbons. They spoke of Myrtle, too, of keeping her memory 'green'.

'And you'll have photos of her, too, Lottie,' they said to Mother (as they sat patting and arranging their 'permanent' waves). And that was so, for when we finally realised that Myrtle had really collapsed in the water and been drowned, that she was never coming home again to wear her clothes and sleep in the bed and just be there, everyone searched for recent photos and found only the 'ghost' photo taken at Rakaia and one other, with us all in our bathing suits, I with a beginning titty showing where my shoulder strap had slipped; but it was Myrtle's photo that was needed. The photographer downtown was unable to extract Myrtle entirely from that family group, although he was forced to leave behind one of Myrtle's arms that had been around Marguerite. Undaunted, the photographer fashioned for Myrtle a new photographic arm and at last presented us with a complete enlarged photo of Myrtle. Everyone said how lucky we were to have a recent photo, and only those who knew could discern the grafted arm.

HELEN GARNER

Helen Garner was born in 1942 in Geelong, Victoria, and was educated there and at Melbourne University. She has worked as a high-school teacher and freelance journalist. Her first novel, *Monkey Grip*, appeared in 1977. It won the Australian National Book Council Award in 1978. She lives in Melbourne where she writes film scripts, non-fiction and novels.

LOOK WHERE
I AM NOW

from *Postcards from Surfers*

---

*One night I dreamed that I did not love and that night, released
from all bonds, I lay as though in a kind of soothing death.*

Colette

We are driving north from Coolangatta airport. Beside the road
the ocean heaves and heaves into waves which do not break. The
swells are dotted with boardriders in black wetsuits, grim as
sharks.

'Look at those idiots,' says my father.

'They must be freezing,' says my mother.

'But what about the principle of the wetsuit?' I say. 'Isn't there
a thin layer of water between your skin and the suit, and your
body heat ...'

'Could be,' says my father.

The road takes a sudden swing round a rocky outcrop. Miles
ahead of us, blurred in the milky air, I see a dream city: its cream,
its silver, its turquoise towers thrust in a cluster from a distant
spit.

'What – is that Brisbane?' I say.

'No,' says my mother. 'That's Surfers.'

My father's car has a built-in computer. If he exceeds the
speed limit, the dashboard emits a discreet but insistent pinging.
Lights flash, and the pressure of his right foot lessens. He
controls the windows from a panel betwee in the two front seats-

We cruise past a Valiant parked by the highway with a FOR SALE sign propped in its back window.

'Look at that,' says my mot her. 'A WA number-plate. Probably thrashed it across the Nullarbor and now they reckon they'll flog it.'

'Pro'ly stolen,' says my father. 'See the sticker? ALL YOU VIRGINS, THANKS FOR NOTHING. You can just see what sort of a pin'ead he'd be. Brain the size of a pea.'

Close up, many of the turquoise towers are not yet sold. 'Every conceivable feature,' the signs say. They have names like Capricornia, Biarritz, the Breakers, Acapulco, Rio.

I had a Brazilian friend when I lived in Paris. He showed me a postcard, once, of Rio where he was born and brought up. The card bore an aerial shot of a splendid, curved tropical beach, fringed with palms, its sand pure as snow.

'Why don't you live in Brazil,' I said, 'if it's as beautiful as this?'

'Because,' said my friend, 'right behind that beach there is a huge military base.'

In my turn I showed him a postcard of my country. It was a reproduction of that Streeton painting called *The Land of the Golden Fleece* which in my homesickness I kept standing on the heater in my bedroom. He studied it carefully. At last he turned his currant-coloured eyes to me and said, 'Les arbres sont rouges?' Are the trees red?

Several years later, six months ago, I was rummaging through a box of old postcards in a junk shop in Rathdowne Street. Among the photos of damp cottages in Galway, of Raj hotels crumbling in bicycle-thronged Colombo, of glassy Canadian lakes flawed by the wake of a single canoe, I found two cards that I bought for a dollar each. One was a picture of downtown Rio, in black and white. The other, crudely tinted, showed Geelong, the town where I was born. The photographer must have stood on the high grassy bank that overlooks the Eastern Beach. He lined up his shot through the never-flowing fountain with its quartet of concrete wading birds (storks? cranes? I never asked my father: they have long orange beaks and each bird holds one leg bent, as if about to take a step); through the fountain and out over the curving wooden promenade, from which we dived all summer, unsupervised, into the flat water; and across the bay to the You Yangs, the double-humped, low, volcanic cones, the only disturbance in the great basalt plains that lie between Geelong and Melbourne. These two cards in the same box! And I find them! Imagine! 'Cher Rubens,' I wrote, 'Je t'envoie ces deux cartes postales, de nos deux villes natales ...'

Auntie Lorna has gone for a walk on the beach. My mother unlocks the door and slides open the flywire screen. She goes out into the bright air to tell her friend of my arrival. The ocean is right in front of the unit, only a hundred and fifty yards away. How can people be so sure of the boundary between land and sea that they have the confidence to build houses on it? The white doorsteps of the ocean travel and travel.

'Twelve o'clock,' says my father.

'Getting on for lunchtime,' I say.

'Getting towards it. Specially with that nice cold corned beef sitting there, and fresh brown bread. Think I'll have to try some of that choko relish. Ever eaten a choko?'

'I wouldn't know a choko if I fell over it,' I say.

'Nor would I.'

He selects a serrated knife from the magnetised holder on the kitchen wall and quickly and skilfully, at the bench, makes himself a thick sandwich. He works with powerful concentration: when the meat flaps off the slice of bread, he rounds it up with a large, dramatic scooping movement and a sympathetic grimace of the lower lip. He picks up the sandwich in two hands, raises it to his mouth and takes a large bite. While he chews he breathes heavily through his nose.

'Want to make yourself something?' he says with his mouth full.

I stand up. He pushes the loaf of bread towards me with the back of his hand. He puts the other half of his sandwich on a green bread and butter plate and carries it to the table. He sits with his elbows on the pine wood, his knees wide apart, his belly relaxing on to his thighs, his high-arched, long-boned feet planted on the tiled floor. He eats, and gazes out to sea. The noise of his eating fills the room.

My mother and Auntie Lorna come up from the beach. I stand inside the wall of glass and watch them stop at the tap to hose the sand off their feet before they cross the grass to the door. They are two old women: they have to keep one hand on the tap in order to balance on the left foot and wash the right. I see that they are two old women, and yet they are neither young nor old. They are my mother and Auntie Lorna, two institutions. They slide back the wire door, smiling.

'Don't tramp sand everywhere,' says my father from the table.

They take no notice. Auntie Lorna kisses me, and holds me at arm's length with her head on one side. My mother prepares food and we eat, looking out at the water.

'You've missed the coronary brigade,' says my father. 'They get out on the beach about nine in the morning. You can pick 'em. They swing their arms up really high when they walk.' He laughs, looking down.

'Do you go for a walk every day too?' I ask.

'Six point six kilometres,' says my father.

'Got a pedometer, have you?'

'I just nutted it out,' says my father. 'We walk as far as a big white building, down that way, then we turn round and come back. Six point six altogether, there and back.'

'I might come with you.'

'You can if you like,' he says. He picks up his plate and carries it to the sink. 'We go after breakfast. You've missed today's.'

He goes to the couch and opens the newspaper on the low coffee table. He reads with his glasses down his nose and his hands loosely linked between his spread knees. The women wash up.

'Is there a shop nearby?' I ask my mother. 'I have to get some tampons.'

'Caught short, are you?' she says. 'I think they sell them at the shopping centre, along Sunbrite Avenue there near the bowling club. Want me to come with you?'

'I can find it.'

'I never could use those things,' says my mother, lowering her voice and glancing across the room at my father. 'Hazel told me about a terrible thing that happened to her. For days she kept noticing this revolting smell that was ... emanating from her. She washed and washed, and couldn't get rid of it. Finally she was about to go to the doctor, but first she got down and had a look with the mirror. She saw this bit of thread and pulled it. The thing was *green*. She must've forgotten to take it out – it'd been there for days and days and *days*.'

We laugh with the tea-towels up to our mouths. My father, on the other side of the room, looks up from the paper with the bent smile of someone not sure what the others are laughing at. I am always surprised when my mother comes out with a word like 'emanating'. At home I have a book called *An Outline of English Verse* which my mother used in her matriculation year. In the margins of *The Rape of the Lock* she had made notations: 'bathos; reminiscent of Virgil; parody of Homer.' Her handwriting in these pencilled jottings, made forty-five years ago, is exactly as it is today: this makes me suspect, when I am not with her, that she is a closet intellectual.

Once or twice, on my way from the unit to the shopping centre, I think I see roses along a fence and run to look, but I find them to be some scentless, fleshy flower. I fall back. Beside a patch of yellow grass, pretty trees in a row are bearing and dropping white blossom-like flowers, but they look wrong to me, I do not recognise them; the blossoms too large, the branches too flat. I am dizzy from the flight. In Melbourne it is still winter, everything is bare.

I buy the tampons and look for the postcards. There they

are, displayed in a tall revolving rack. There is a great deal of blue. Closer, I find colour photos of white beaches, duneless, palmless, on which half-naked people lie on their backs with their knees raised. The frequency of this posture, at random through the crowd, makes me feel like laughing. Most of the cards have GREETINGS FROM THE GOLD COAST or BROADBEACH or SURFERS PARADISE embossed in gold in one corner: I search for pictures without words. Another card, in several slightly differing versions, shows a graceful, big-breasted young girl lying in a seductive pose against some rocks: she is wearing a bikini and her whole head is covered by one of those latex masks that are sold in trick shops, the ones you pull on as a bandit pulls on a stocking. The mask represents the hideous, raddled, grinning face of an old woman, a witch. I stare at this photo for a long time. Is it simple, or does it hide some more mysterious signs and symbols?

I buy twelve GREETINGS FROM cards with views, some aerial, some from the ground. They cost 25 cents each.

'Want the envelopes?' says the girl. She is dressed in a flowered garment which is drawn up between her thighs like a nappy.

'Yes please.' The envelopes are so covered with coloured maps, logos and drawings of Australian fauna that there is barely room to write an address, but something about them attracts me. I buy a packet of licorice chews and eat them all on the way home. I stuff them in two at a time: my mouth floods with saliva. There are no rubbish bins so I put the papers in my pocket. Now that I have spent money here, now that I have rubbish to dispose of, I am no longer a stranger. In Paris there used to be signs in the streets that said, LE COMMERCE, C'EST LA VIE DE LA VILLE. Any traveller knows this to be the truth.

The women are knitting. They murmur and murmur. What they say never requires an answer. My father sharpens a pencil stub with his pocket knife, and folds the paper into a pad one-eighth the size of a broadsheet page.

'Five down, spicy meat jelly. Aspic. Three across, counterfeit. Bogus! Howzat.'

'You're in good nick,' I say. 'I would've had to rack my brains for Bogus. Why don't you do harder ones?'

'Oh, I can't do those other ones, the cryptic.'

'You have to know Shakespeare and the Bible off by heart to do those,' I say.

'Yairs. Course, if you got hold of the answer and filled it out looking at that, with a lot of practice you could come round to their way of thinking. They used to have good ones in the *Weekly Times*. But I s'pose they had so many complaints from cockies who couldn't do 'em that they had to ease off.'

I do not feel comfortable yet about writing the postcards. It would seem graceless. I flip through my mother's pattern book.

'There's some nice ones there,' she says. 'What about the one with the floppy collar?'

'Want to buy some wool?' says my father. He tosses the finished crossword on the coffee table and stands up with a vast yawn. 'Oh – ee – oh – ooh. Come on, miss. I'll drive you over to Pacific Fair.'

I choose the wool and count out the number of balls specified by the pattern. My father rears back to look at it: this movement struck terror into me when I was a teenager but I now recognise it as long-sightedness.

'Pure wool, is it?' he says. As soon as he touches it he will know. He fingers it, and looks at me.

'No,' I say. 'Got a bit of synthetic in it. It's what the pattern says to use.'

'Why don't you—' He stops. Once he would have tried to prevent me from buying it. His big blunt hands used to fling out the fleeces, still warm, on to the greasy table. His hands looked as if they had no feeling in them but they teased out the wool, judged it, classed it, assigned it a fineness and destination: Italy, Switzerland, Japan. He came home with thorns embedded deep in the flesh of his palms. He stood patiently while my mother gouged away at them with a needle. He drove away at shearing time in a yellow car with running boards, up to the big sheds in the country; we rode on the running boards as far as the corner of our street, then skipped home. He went to the Melbourne Show for work, not pleasure, and once he brought me home a plastic trumpet. 'Fordie,' he called me, and took me to the wharves and said, 'See that rope? It's not a rope. It's a hawser.' 'Hawser,' I repeated, wanting him to think I was a serious person. We walked along Strachan Avenue, Manifold Heights, hand in hand. 'Listen,' he said. 'Listen to the wind in the wires.' I must have been very little then, for the wires were so high I can't remember seeing them.

He turns away from the fluffy pink balls and waits with his hands in his pockets for me to pay.

'What do you do all day, up here?' I say on the way home.

'Oh ... play bowls. Follow the real estate. I ring up the firms that advertise these flash units and I ask 'em questions. I let 'em lower and lower their price. See how low they'll go. How many more discounts they can dream up.' He drives like a farmer in a ute, leaning forward with his arms curved round the wheel, always about to squint up through the windscreen at the sky, checking the weather.

'Don't they ask your name?'

'Yep.'

'What do you call yourself?'

'Oh, Jackson or anything.' He flicks a glance at me. We begin to laugh, looking away from each other.

'It's bloody crook up here,' he says. 'Jerry-built. Sad. "Every conceivable luxury"! They can't get rid of it. They're desperate. Come on. We'll go up and you can have a look.'

The lift in Biarritz is lined with mushroom-coloured carpet. We brace our backs against its wall and it rushes us upwards. The salesman in the display unit has a moustache, several gold bracelets, a beige suit, and a clipboard against his chest. He is engaged with an elderly couple and we are able to slip past him into the living room.

'Did you see that peanut?' hisses my father.

'A gilded youth,' I say. '"Their eyes are dull, their heads are flat, they have no brains at all."'

He looks impressed, as if he thinks I have made it up on the spot. '*The Man from Ironbark*,' I add.

'I only remember *The Geebung Polo Club*,' he says. He mimes leaning off a horse and swinging a heavy implement. We snort with laughter. Just inside the living-room door stand five Ionic pillars in a half-moon curve. Beyond them, through the glass, are views of a river and some mountains. The river winds in a plain, the mountains are sudden, lumpy and crooked.

'From the other side you can see the sea,' says my father.

'Would you live up here?'

'Not on your life. Not with those flaming pillars.'

From the bedroom window he points out another high-rise building closer to the sea. Its name is Chelsea. It is battleship grey with a red trim. Its windows face away from the ocean. It is tall and narrow, of mean proportions, almost prison-like. 'I wouldn't mind living in that one,' he says. I look at it in silence. He has unerringly chosen the ugliest one. It is so ugly that I can find nothing to say.

It is Saturday afternoon. My father is waiting for the Victorian football to start on TV. He rereads the paper.

'Look at this,' he says. 'Mum, remember that seminar we went to about investment in diamonds?'

'Up here?' I say. 'A *seminar*?'

'S'posed to be an investment that would double its value in six days. We went along one afternoon. They were obviously con-men. Ooh, setting up a big con, you could tell. They had sherry and sandwiches.'

'That's all we went for, actually,' says my mother.

'What sort of people went?' I ask.

'Oh . . . people like ourselves,' says my father.

'Do you think anybody bought any?'

'Sure. Some idiots. Anyway, look at this in today's *Age*. "The Diamond Dreamtime. World diamond market plummets." Haw haw haw.'

He turns on the TV in time for the bounce. I cast on stitches as instructed by the pattern and begin to knit. My mother and Auntie Lorna, well advanced in complicated garments for my sister's teenage children, conduct their monologues which cross, coincide and run parallel. My father mumbles advice to the footballers and emits bursts of contemptuous laughter. 'Bloody idiot,' he says.

I go to the room I am to share with Auntie Lorna and come back with the packet of postcards. When I get out my pen and the stamps and set myself up at the table my father looks up and shouts to me over the roar of the crowd, 'Given up on the knitting?'

'No. Just knocking off a few postcards. People expect a postcard when you go to Queensland.'

'Have to keep up your correspondence, Father,' says my mother.

'I'll knit later,' I say.

'How much have you done?' asks my father.

'This much.' I separate thumb and forefinger.

'Dear Philip,' I write. I make my writing as thin and small as I can: the back of the postcard, not the front, is the art form. 'Look where I am. A big red setter wet from the surf shambles up the side way of the unit, looking lost and anxious as setters always do. My parents sent it packing with curses in an inarticulate tongue. Go orn, get orf, gorn!'

'Dear Philip. THE IDENTIFICATION OF THE BIRDS AND FISHES. *My father*: "Look at those albatross. They must have eyes that can see for a hundred miles. As soon as one dives, they come from everywhere. Look at 'em dive! Bang! Down they go." *Me*: "What sort of fish would they be diving for?" *My father*: "Whiting. They only eat whiting." *Me*: "They do not!" *My father*: "How the hell would *I* know what sort of fish they are."'

'Dear Philip. My father says they are albatross, but my mother (in the bathroom later) remarks to me that albatross have shorter, more hunched necks.'

'Dear Philip. I share a room with Auntie Lorna. She also

is writing postcards and has just asked me how to spell "too".
I like her very much and *she likes me*. "I'll keep the stickybeaks
in the Woomelang post office guessing," she says. "I won't put
my name on the back of the envelope."'

'Dear Philip. OUTSIDE THE POST OFFICE. My father, Auntie
Lorna and I wait in the car for my mother to go in and pick
up the mail from the locked box. *My father*: "Gawd, amazing,
isn't it, what people do. See that sign there, ENTER, with the
arrow pointing upwards? What sort of a thing is that? Is it
a joke, or just some no-hoper foolin' around? That woman's
been in the phone box for half an hour, I bet. How'd you
be, outside the public phone waiting for some silly coot to
finish yackin' on about everything under the sun, while you
had something important to say. That happened to us, once,
up at—" My mother opens the door and gets in. "Three
letters," she says. "All for me."'

Sometimes my little story overflows the available space and
I have to run over on to a second postcard. This means I
must find a smaller, secondary tale, or some disconnected
remark, to fill up card number two.

'*Me* (opening cupboard): "Hey! Scrabble! We can have a
game of Scrabble after tea!" *My father* (with a scornful laugh):
"I can't wait."'

'Dear Philip. I know you won't write back. I don't even
know whether you are still at this address.'

'Dear Philip. One Saturday morning I went to Coles and
bought a scarf. It cost four and sixpence and I was happy with
my purchase. He whisked it out of my hand and looked at
the label. "Made in China. Is it real silk? Let's test it." He
flicked on his cigarette lighter. We all screamed and my
mother said, "Don't *bite*! He's only teasing you."'

'Dear Philip. Once, when I was fourteen, I gave cheek to
him at the dinner table. He hit me across the head with
his open hand. There was silence. My little brother gave a
high, hysterical giggle and I laughed too, in shock. He hit
me again. After the washing-up I was sent for. He was
sitting in an armchair, looking down. "The reason why we

don't get on any more," he said, "is because we're so much alike." This idea filled me with such revulsion that I turned my swollen face away. It was swollen from crying, not from the blows, whose force had been more symbolic than physical.'

'Dear Philip. Years later he read my mail. He found the contraceptive pills. He drove up to Melbourne and found me and made me come home. He told me I was letting men use my body. He told me I ought to see a psychiatrist. I was in the front seat and my mother was in the back. I thought: If I open the door and jump out, I won't have to listen to this any more. My mother tried to stick up for me. He shouted at her. "It's your fault," he said. "You were too soft on her."'

'Dear Philip. I know you've heard all this before. I also know it's no worse than anyone else's story.'

'Dear Philip. And again years later he asked me a personal question. He was driving, I was in the suicide seat. "What went wrong," he said, "between you and Philip?" Again I turned my face away. "I don't want to talk about it," I said. There was silence. He never asked again. And years after *that*, in a café in Paris on my way to work, far enough away from him to be able to, I thought of that question and began to cry. Dear Philip. I forgive you for everything.'

Late in the afternoon my mother and Auntie Lorna and I walk along the beach to Surfers. The tide is out: our bare feet scarcely mark the firm sand. Their two voices run on, one high, one low. If I speak they pretend to listen, just as I feign attention to their endless, looping discourses: these are our courtesies: this is love. Everything is spoken, nothing is said. On the way back I point out to them the smoky orange clouds that are massing far out to sea, low over the horizon. Obedient, they stop and face the water. We stand in a row, Auntie Lorna in a pretty frock with sandals dangling from her finger, my mother and I with our trousers rolled up. Once I asked my Brazilian friend a stupid question. He was listening to a conversation between me and a Frenchman about our

216

countries' electoral systems. He was not speaking and thinking to include him, I said, 'And how do people vote *chez toi*, Rubens?' He looked at me with a small smile. 'We don't have elections,' he said. Where's Rio from here? 'Look at those clouds!' I say. 'You'd think there was another city out there, wouldn't you, burning.'

Just at dark the air takes on the colour and dampness of the sub-tropics. I walk out the screen door and stand my gin on a fence post. I lean on the fence and look at the ocean. Soon the moon will thrust itself over the line. If I did a painting of a horizon, I think, I would make it look like a row of rocking inverted Vs, because that's what I see when I look at it. The flatness of a horizon is intellectual. A cork pops on the first-floor balcony behind me. I glance up. In the half-dark two men with moustaches are smiling down at me.

'Drinking champagne tonight?' I say.

'Wonderful sound, isn't it,' says the one holding the bottle.

I turn back to the moonless horizon. Last year I went camping on the Murray River. I bought the cards at Tocumwal. I had to write fast for the light was dropping and spooky noises were coming from the trees. 'Dear Dad,' I wrote. 'I am up on the Murray, sitting by the camp fire. It's nearly dark now but earlier it was beautiful, when the sun was going down and the dew was rising.' Two weeks later, at home, I received a letter from him written in his hard, rapid, slanting hand, each word ending in a sharp upward flick. The letter itself concerned a small financial matter, and consisted of two sentences on half a sheet of quarto, but on the back of the envelope he had dashed off a personal message: 'P.S. Dew does not rise. It *forms*.'

The moon does rise, as fat as an orange, out of the sea straight in front of the unit. A child upstairs sees it too and utters long werewolf howls. My mother makes a meal and we eat it. 'Going to help Mum with the dishes, are you, miss?' says my father from his armchair. My shoulders stiffen. I am, I do. I lie on the couch and read an old *Woman's*

Day. Princess Caroline of Monaco wears a black dress and a wide white hat. The knitting needles make their mild clicking. Auntie Lorna and my father come from the same town, Hopetoun in the Mallee, and when the news is over they begin again.

'I always remember the cars of people,' says my father. 'There was an old four-cylinder Dodge, belonging to Whatsis-name. It had—'

'Would that have been one of the O'Lachlans?' says Auntie Lorna.

'Jim O'Lachlan. It had a great big exhaust pipe coming out the back. And I remember stuffing a potato up it.'

'A *potato*?' I say.

'The bloke was a councillor,' says my father. 'He came out of the council chambers and got into the Dodge and started her up. He only got fifty yards up the street when BA-BANG! This damn thing shot out the back – I reckon it's still going!' He closes his lips and drops his head back against the couch to hold in his laughter.

I walk past Biarritz, where globes of light float among shrubbery, and the odd balcony on the half-empty tower holds rich people out into the creamy air. A barefoot man steps out of the take-away food shop with a hamburger in his hand. He leans against the wall to unwrap it, and sees me hesitating at the slot of the letterbox, holding up the postcards and reading them over and over in the weak light from the public phone. 'Too late to change it now,' he calls. I look up. He grins and nods and takes his first bite of the hamburger. Beside the letterbox stands a deep rubbish bin with a swing lid. I punch open the bin and drop the postcards in.

All night I sleep safely in my bed. The waves roar and hiss, and slam like doors. Auntie Lorna snores, but when I tug at the corner of her blanket she sighs and turns over and breathes more quietly. In the morning the rising sun hits the front windows and floods the place with a light so intense that the white curtains can hardly net it. Everything is pink and golden. In the sink a cockroach lurks. I try to swill it down the drain with a cup of water but it resists strongly. The air is bright, is milky with spray. My father is already up: while the kettle boils he stands out on the edge of the grass, the edge of his property, looking at the sea.

SHENA MACKAY

Shena Mackay was born in Edinburgh in 1944 and grew up in Kent and London, where she now lives. She has three daughters and two grandchildren. Her first two novellas, *Dust Falls on Eugene Schlumberger* and *Toddler on the Run* appeared in 1964. Since then she has written eight novels and three volumes of short stories, *Babies in Rhinestones*, *Dreams of Dead Women's Handbags* and *The Laughing Academy* which was the winner of a Scottish Arts Council Book Award. Her novels include *Music Upstairs*, *Old Crow*, *An Advent Calendar*, *A Bowl of Cherries*, *Redhill Rococo* (winner of the Fawcett Society Prize), *Dunedin*, *The Orchard on Fire* (which was shortlisted for the 1996 Booker Prize and the McVitie's Prize) and The Artist's Widow (1998). Her work has been widely anthologised and was the subject of a BBC *Bookmark* film in 1993. She has served on the London Arts Board, been a judge for several literary prizes and has edited two anthologies. A new collection of stories, *The World's Smallest Unicorn* will be published in 1999.

DREAMS BEACHED ON THE MORNING

from *Dreams of Dead Women's Handbags*

It was a black evening bag sequined with salt, open-mouthed under a rusted marcasite clasp, revealing a black moiré silk lining stained by sea water; a relic stranded in the wrack of tarry pebbles and tufts of blue and orange nylon string like garish sea anemones, crab shells and lobster legs, plastic detritus, oily feathers, condoms and rubbery weed and clouded glass, the dry white sponges of whelk egg cases, and a brittle black-horned mermaid's purse. This image, the wreckage of a dream beached on the morning, would not float away; as empty as an open shell, the black bivalve emitted a silent howl of despair; clouds passed through its mirror.

Like Webster, Susan Vigo was much possessed by death. Sitting on a slow train to the coast, at a table in the compartment adjacent to the buffet car, she thought about her recurring dream and about a means of murder. A book and a newspaper lay in front of her, and as she inserted the word 'limpid' in the crossword, completing the puzzle, she saw aquamarine water in a rock pool wavering limpidly over a conical white limpet shell. Her own id was rather limp that morning, she felt; the gold top of her pen tasted briny in her mouth. The colour of the water was the precise clear almost-green of spring evening skies when the city trembled with the possibility of love. She wondered dispassionately if she would ever encounter such a sky again, and as she wondered, she saw a handbag half submerged on the bottom of the pool among the wavering weeds, green and encrusted with limpets, as though it had lain there for a long time, releasing gentle strings of bubbles like dreams and memories. A mermaid's purse, she remembered her father teaching her, as she made her way to the buffet, was the horny egg case of a skate, or ray or shark, but to whom the desolate handbag in her dreams had belonged, she had no idea, only that its owner was dead.

The buffet car steward seemed familiar, but perhaps the painful red eyes were uniform issue, along with the shiny jacket spattered by toasted sandwiches; his hair had been combed back with bacon grease and fell in curly rashers on his collar, his red tie was as slick as a dying poppy's petal. As Susan waited in the queue she told herself that he could have no possible significance in her life, and reminded herself that she made many journeys and had probably encountered him before, leering over the Formica counter of another train. Nevertheless she watched him, it was her habit to stare at people, with an uneasy notion that he was Charon ferrying her across the Styx – but Charon would not be the barman, but the driver of this InterCity train, sitting at the controls in his cab, racing them down the rails to the Elysian fields, and she was almost certain that she and her fellow passengers were still alive and their coins were for the purchase of refreshments and not the fees of the dead. The barman's years of bracing himself on the swaying floors of articulated metal snakes had given him the measure of his customers. The woman in the simulated beige mink, in front of Susan in the queue, asked for two gins and tonics, one for an imaginary friend down the corridor, and was given two little green bottles, two cans of tonic, and one plastic cup with a contemptuous fistful of ice-cubes. Her eyes met the barman's and she did not demur. One of his eyes closed like a snake's in a wink at Susan as the woman fumbled her purchases from the counter. It takes one to know one, thought Susan, refusing to be drawn into complicity by the reptilian lid of his red eye as she ordered her coffee. Her face in the mirror behind the bar, her shirt, her scarf, her brooch, the cut of her jacket spoke as quietly of success as the fur-coated woman's screeched failure.

Failure. That was a word Susan Vigo hated. She saw it as a sickly plant with etiolated leaves, flourishing in dank unpleasant places, a parasite on a rotting trunk, or a pot plant on the windowsills of houses of people she despised. If she had cared to, she could have supplied a net curtain on a string as a backcloth and a plaster Alsatian, but she had a horror of rotting window frames and rented rooms, and banished the image. Susan Vigo was not the sort of woman who would order two gins for herself on a train. She was not, like some she could name, the sort of writer who would arrive to give a reading with a wine-splashed book and grains of cat litter in her trouser turn-ups, having fortified herself with spirits on the journey for the ordeal, who would enter in disarray and stumble into disrepute. The books in her overnight bag were glossy and immaculate with clean white strips of paper placed between the pages, to mark the passages which she would read. She did not regard it as an ordeal; she had memorised her introductory speech, and was looking forward to the evening. She had done her homework, and would have been able to relax with a book by another author had consciousness of the delivery date of her own next crime novel not threatened like a migraine at the edge of her brain. The irony was that the title of her book was *Deadline* and for the first time in her life, she feared that she would not meet hers. Notice of it had appeared already in her publisher's catalogue and she had not even got the plot. It was set on the coast, she knew that; it involved a writer – yes, and horned poppy and sea holly and viper's bugloss, stranded sea-mice leaking rainbows into the sand, and of course her Detective Inspector Christopher Hartshorn, an investigator of the intellectual, laconic school; a body – naturally; a handbag washed up on the beach – the sort of handbag that had foxtrotted to Harry Roy, or a flaunting scarlet patent number blatant as a stiletto heel, a steel-faceted purse, a gondola basket holding a copy of *Mirabelle* or *Roxy* – she didn't even know in which period to set her murder – a drawstring leather bag which smelled of raw camel hide, a satchel with a wooden pencil box, a strap purse, containing a threepenny bit, worn across the front of a gymslip – old handbags like discarded lovers. She sifted desperately through the heap of silk and plastic, leather and wicker – it had to be black, like the handbag in her dream . . .

Susan lived in Hampstead, on a staple diet of vodka and asparagus, fresh in season, or tinned. It made life simple; she never had to think about what food to buy except when she had guests, which was not very often; she was more entertained than entertaining. She loved her flat and lived there alone. She had once been given two love-birds but had grown jealous of their absorption in each other and had given them away. Trailing plants now entwined the bars of the cage where the pink and yellow birds had preened, kissing each other with waxy bills; she preferred their green indifference. There was not a trace of a plaster Alsatian. The man who had seduced her had introduced her to asparagus, its tender green heads swimming in butter, with baked beans – her choice. Professor Bruno Rosenblum, lecturer in poetry who although his juxtaposed names conjured up withered roses on their stems, had once strewn the bed with roses while she slept. Waking in the scent and petals, she had wept. 'Ah, as the heart grows older, it will come to such sights colder,' she thought now, in the train, remembering, as the past, like the dried petals of pot-pourri exhaled a slight sad scent, and, Perhaps G.M. Hopkins got it right – it is always ourselves for whom we are grieving – enough of this. She turned from the dirty window slashed with rain that obscured the flat landscape and the dun animals in the shabby February fields, to her book. She wondered if she could, perhaps, take its central situation or *donnée*, and by changing it subtly, and substituting her own characters, manufacture a convincingly original work . . .

*

' "If you want to know about a woman, look in her purse." ' The detective dumped the clues to the dead dame's life into a plastic bag and consigned it to Forensic. Susan's own handbag, if studied, would have told of an orderly life and mind, or of an owner who had dumped all her old make-up in the bin and dashed into an expensive chemist's on the way to the station: no sleazy clutter there, no circle of foam rubber tinged with grimy powder, no sweating stubs of lipstick and broken biros leaking into the lining, or tobacco shreds or dog-eared appointment cards for special clinics or combs with dirty teeth or minicab cards acquired on flights through dawn streets from unspeakable crises. Susan could see as clearly in her mind the contents of the handbag of the woman who had bought the two gins as she could see her black stilettos resting on the next seat, and the fall of fake fur caressing her calf. She saw her lean forward and open a compact the dark blue of a mussel shell, and peer into a mirror, and her imagination supplied a crack zigzagging across the glass, presaging doom. The man directly opposite Susan was reading a report and was of as little interest as he had been at the start of the journey; on the other side of the aisle a family, parents and two children, finished their enormous lunch and settled down to a game of three-dimensional noughts and crosses, which involved plastic tubes and marbles, clack clack clack. The marbles bounced off Susan's brain like bullets. 'Why can't they just use pencil and paper?' she thought irritably: the extra dimensions added nothing but cost and noise to the game. She put her hands over her ears, and, resting her book on the table, tried to read, but her concentration was shot to pieces. She closed her eyes, and the handbag in her dream returned like a black shell, which if held to the ear would whisper her own mortality.

There was this handbag washed up on the beach – what next? She waited for a whole narrative to unwind and a cast of characters to come trooping out, but nothing happened. There was this crime writer travelling on a train, panicking about a deadline when suddenly ... a single shot passed through the head of the buffet car attendant's head, shattering the glass behind him ... Susan's fascination with firearms dated from a white double holster studded with glass jewels and two fancy guns with bluish shining barrels and decorated stocks; she had loved them more than any of her dolls, taking them to bed with her at night, loving the neat round boxes of pink caps. She could smell them now, and the scent of new sandals with crêpe soles like cheese.

Dreams of dead women's handbags: the click of a false tortoise-shell clasp, the musty smell of old perfume from the torn black moiré lining, and powder in a shell, lipstick that would look as ghastly on a skull as it did on the mouths of the little white flat fish on the seaside stall, skate smoking cigarettes through painted mouths, the glitter of saliva on a pin impaling whelks. She saw a man and a woman walking on a clifftop starred with pink thrift, a seagull's white scalloped tail feathers; the woman wore a dress patterned in poppies and corn and the man had his shirt-collar open over his jacket, in holiday style. A child skipped between them on that salty afternoon when the world was their oyster.

Amberley Hall, where Susan was heading, was a small private literary foundation where students of all ages attended courses and summer schools in music, painting and writing. She had been invited to be the guest reader at one of their creative writing courses, and was looking forward to seeing again the two tutors, both friends, and renewing her acquaintance with Amberley's directors whom she had liked very much when she met them the previous year when she herself had been a co-tutor. The house was white and stood on a cliff; reflections of the sea and sky met in its windows. Susan hoped that she would be given the room in which she had slept before, with its faded blue bedspread and shell-framed looking-glass and vase of dried flowers beside the white shells on the windowsill, sea lavender faded by time, like a dead woman's passions and regrets. The clatter of marbles became intolerable. Susan strode towards the buffet car. The train seemed to be going very slowly. She began to worry about the time and wish that she had accepted her host's offer to meet her at the station.

'Going all the way?' the barman asked as he sliced a lemon with a thin-bladed knife. The other woman had not been offered lemon.

'I bet your pardon?'

'Going all the way?'

'No. Not quite.'

'Business or pleasure?'

Susan had never seen why she should answer that question, so often asked by strangers on a train.

'A bit of both,' she replied.

Again his eyelid flickered in a wink.

'Ice?'

'Please.' She hoped her tone matched the cubes he was dropping into her glass with his fingers, one of which was girdled with a frayed plaster. Stubble was trying to break through the red nodules of a rash on his neck; he looked as though he had shaved in cold water in the basin in the blocked toilet, with his knife. The arrival of two other customers brought their conversation to an end.

As she approached her seat with her vodka and tonic she stopped in her tracks. That woman in the fur coat had Susan's overnight bag down on the seat and was going through her things.

'What do you think you're doing?' She grabbed her furry arm; her hand was shaken from it.

'I'm just looking for a tissue.'

'But that's my bag. Those are my things!'

The woman was pulling out clothes and underclothes and dumping them on the seat while the noughts and crosses clicked and clacked, tic tac toe. She scrabbled under the books at the bottom of the bag.

'Stop it, do you hear?'

'She's only looking for a tissue,' said the man opposite mildly, looking up from his report.

'I'm going to get the guard. I'm going to pull the emergency cord.'

The other woman's full lips shook and she started to cry.

The man took a handkerchief from his breast pocket, shook it out and handed it to her.

'Have a good blow.'

She did.

'I'll give you a good blow!' said Susan, punching her hard in the chest, at the top of a creased *décolletage* where a gilt pendant nestled in the shape of the letter M. The lights went out. The train almost concertinaed to a stop.

'Now look what you've done, pulling the communication cord.'

'I didn't touch it,' Susan shouted. 'What's going on? What's the matter with everybody? I didn't go near it.'

She felt the woman move away, and sat down heavily on her disarranged bag, panting with affront and rage, the unfairness of it all and the fact that nobody had stood up for her. Tears were rolling down her face as she groped for her clothes and crammed them back into the bag. Marbles rolled across the table and ricocheted off the floor. The tips of cigarettes glowed like tiny volcanoes in the gloom and someone giggled, a high nervous whinny. Susan began to sweat. Rain was drumming on the windows like her heartbeats, and she knew that she had died and was to be locked for eternity in this train in the dark with people who hated her. This was her sentence: what was her crime? Battalions of minor sins thronged her memory. Her hand hurt where she had punched the woman; she sucked her knuckle and tasted blood. The lights came on. Susan screamed.

The barman stood in the doorway, his knife in his hand.

'Nearly a nasty accident,' he said. 'Car stalled on the level crossing.'

People started to laugh and talk.

'Could've been curtains for us all,' he said as the train brayed and the orange curtains at the black windows swayed as it started to move.

The woman in the fur coat came sashaying down the aisle, reeled on a marble, and plonked herself down beside Susan.

'Sorry about that little mistake, only I mistook it for my bag. They're quite similar. Here, let me help you put it up.'

They swung it clumsily on to the rack, next to a dirty tapestry bag edged in cracked vinyl. Susan looked into her eyes, opaque as marbles, and perceived that she was mad. She picked up her book.

'Like reading, do you?'

'When I get the chance.'

'I know what you mean. There's always something needs doing, isn't there? I expect you're like me, can't sit idle. What with my little dog, and my crocheting and the telly there's always something, isn't there?'

'Crocheting?' Susan heard herself ask.

'Yes, I've always got some on the go. I made this.'

She pulled open her lapels to show a deep-throated pink filigree garment.

'It was a bolero in the pattern, only I added the sleeves.'

Susan smiled and tried desperately to read, but it was too late: she saw in vivid detail the woman's sitting room, feet in pink fluffy slippers stretched out to the electric fire that was mottling her legs, the wheezy Yorkshire terrier with a growth on its neck, the crochet hook plying in a billowy sea of pink and violet squares; a bedspread for a wedding present to a niece, who would bundle it into a cupboard.

She almost said, 'I'm sorry about your little dog', but stopped herself in time, and before she was tempted to advise her to abandon her bedspread, the guard announced that the train was approaching her station. She gathered her things together with relief and went to find an exit. As she passed the bar the steward, who had taken off his jacket and was reading a newspaper, did not raise his head. She saw how foolish she had been to fear him.

'Thank God that's over,' she said aloud on the platform as she took deep breaths of wet dark air which although the station was miles inland, tasted salty, and the appalling train pulled away, carrying the barman and the deranged woman to their mad destinations. She came out into the forecourt in time to see the rear lights of a taxi flashing in the rain. She knew at once that it was the only one and that it would not return for a long time. She saw a telephone box across the road, and shielding with her bag her hair that the rain would reduce to a nest of snakes, hurried through the puddles. At least, being in the country, the phone would not have been vandalised. A wet chip paper wrapped itself round her ankles; the receiver dangled from a mess of wires, black with emptiness roaring through its broken mouth, like a washed-up handbag.

A pub. There must be a pub somewhere near the station that would have a telephone. Susan stepped out of the smell of rural urine and started to walk. She would not let herself panic, or let the lit and curtained windows sheltering domesticity make her feel lonely. Perhaps she could hire a car, from the pub. She imagined the sudden silence falling on the jocular company of the inn and a fearful peasant declaring, 'None of us villagers dare go up to Amberley Hall. Not after dark', and a dark figure in a bat-winged cloak flying screeching past the moon.

Mine host was a gloomy fellow who pointed her to a pay phone. The number was engaged. Temporarily defeated, Susan ordered a drink and sat down. It was then that she realised that her overnight bag had been transformed into a grubby tapestry holdall with splitting vinyl trim. A cold deluge of disbelief engulfed her and then hot pricking needles of anger. She drowned the words that rose to her lips; this wasn't Hampstead. How could it have happened – that madwoman – Susan was furious with herself; she would have scorned to use the device of the switched luggage in one of her own books, and here she was, lumbered, in this dire pub, with this disgusting bag, and worse, worse, all her own things, her books – the reading ... She was tempted to call it a day then, and order another drink, and consign herself to fate, propping up the bar until her money ran out and they dumped her in the street, but she made another attempt at the telephone, and this time got through. Someone would be there to pick her up in twenty minutes. She thought of ordering a sandwich but the knowledge of the meal, the refectory table heaped with bowls of food awaiting her, restrained her, and she sat there half listening to the jukebox, making her drink last, wishing she was at home doing something cheerful like drinking vodka and listening to Bessie Smith, or Billie Holiday singing 'Good Morning Heartache'.

She thought she had found her murder victim, a blonde woman with a soft white face and body and a pendant in the shape of the letter M and a stolen bag; she lolled in death, her black shoes stabbing skywards, on a clifftop lying in the thrift that starred the grass and was embossed on a threepenny bit, tarnished at the bottom of an old handbag. Threepence, that was the amount of pocket money she had received; a golden hexagonal coin each Saturday morning. The early 1950s: a dazzle of red, white and blue; father, mother and child silhouetted against a golden sunburst in a red sky like figures on a poster, marching into Utopia.

The dead woman's dress was splashed with poppies and corn – no, that was wrong – it must be black. Her mother had had a dress of poppies and corn, scarlet flowers and golden ears and sky-blue cornflowers on a white field; Ceres in white peep-toe shoes, the sun sparkling off a Kirbigrip in her dark gold hair. Her father's hair was bright with brilliantine and he wore his shirt-collar, white as vanilla ice cream, open over his jacket. Susan's hair was in two thin plaits of corn and gripped on either side with a white hair-slide in the shape of Brumas the famous polar bear cub. Susan sat in the pub, becoming aware that it was actually a small hotel and staring at a red-carpeted staircase that disappeared at an angle, leading to the upper guest rooms. In a flash she realised why the barman in the train looked familiar, and blind and deaf to the music and flashing lights she sat in a waking dream.

*

The child woke in the hotel bedroom and found herself alone. Moonlight lay on the pillows of the double bed her parents shared. The bed was undisturbed. They had come up from the bar to tuck her in. 'You be a good girl now and go to sleep. We're just popping out for a stroll, we won't be gone more than a few minutes.' Her father's eyes were red – she turned her face away from his beery kiss. Her mother's best black taffeta dress rustled as she closed the door behind them. She pulled a sweater over her nightdress and buckled on her holster and her new white sandals and tiptoed to the door. A gust of piano playing and singing and beer and cigarette smoke bellied into the bedroom. She closed the door quietly behind her and slid slowly down the banister, so as not to make any noise. She was angry with them for leaving her alone. She bet they were eating ice creams and chips without her. She crept to the back door and let herself out into the street. Although she had never been out so late alone, she found that it was almost light – girls and boys come out to play, the moon doth shine as bright as day – she would burst into the café and shoot them dead – Susan saw her in the moonlight, a small figure in a white nightdress in the empty street with a gun in each hand. The café was closed.

She turned on to the path that led to the cliffs. Rough grass spiked her bare legs and sand filled her new sandals and rubbed on her heels. She holstered her guns because she had to use her hands to scramble up the steep slope, uttering little sobs of fear and rage. She reached the top and flung herself panting on to the turf. At the edge of the cliff sat two figures, from this distance as black as two cormorants on a rock against the sky. The sea was roaring in her ears as she wriggled on her belly towards them. As she drew nearer she could see the woman's arms, white as vanilla in her black taffeta dress and the man's shirt-collar. She stood up and drew her guns and took aim but suddenly she was frightened at herself standing there against the sky and just wanted them to hold her, and shoved the guns back in the holster and as she did the man put his arm round the woman's shoulder and kissed her. The child was running towards them, to thrust herself between their bodies shouting joyfully 'Boo!' as she thumped them on their backs and the woman lost her balance and clutched the man and they went tumbling over and over and over and the woman's handbag fell from her wrist and went spiralling after them screaming and screaming from its open black mouth.

When the landlady, impatient at the congealing breakfast, came to rouse the family in the morning she found the child asleep, cuddled up to a holster instead of a teddy. The parents' bed was undisturbed. It seemed a shame to wake the little girl. She looked so peaceful with her fair hair spread out on the pillow. She shook her gently.

'Where are your mummy and daddy, lovey?'

The child sat up, seeing the buckle of her new sandal hanging by a thread. Mummy would have to sew it on.

'I don't know,' she answered truthfully.

'Susan. Hi.' Tom from Amberley Hall was shaking her arm. 'You look awful. Have you had a terrible journey? You must have.'

'Perfectly bloody,' said Susan.

'I'm afraid you've missed supper,' said Tom, in the car, 'but we'll rustle up something for you after the reading. I think we'd better get straight on with it if you don't mind. Everybody's keen to meet you. Quite an interesting bunch of students this time . . .'

His voice went on. Susan wanted to bury her face in the thick cables of his sweater. As they entered the house she explained about the loss of her bag.

'Just like Professor Pnin, eh, on the wrong train with the wrong lecture?' he laughed. Susan wished then profoundly to be Professor Pnin, Russian and ideally bald; to be anybody but herself in her creased clothes with her hair snaking wildly round her head and a tapestry bag in her hand containing the crocheted tangle of that woman's mad life.

'It was the right train,' she said, 'but I haven't got anything to read.'

'I did get in touch with your publishers to send some books

to sell, but I'm afraid they haven't arrived. Never mind though, some of the students have brought their own copies for you to sign so you could borrow one. Five minutes to freshen up, OK? We've put you in the same room as last time.'

'No bloody food. No bloody wine. Not even any bloody books,' said Susan behind the closed door of her room. She aimed a kick at the bookcase: each of those spines faded by sea air representing somebody's futile bid to hold back eternal night. Precisely five minutes later she stepped, pale, poised and professional, into the firelit room to enchant her audience.

When she had finished reading, a chill hung over the room for a moment and then someone started the clapping. As the appreciative applause flickered out, bottles of wine and glasses were brought, and the evening was given over to informal questions and discussion. A gallant in corduroys bowed as he handed her a glass.

'You're obviously very successful, Miss Vigo, or may I call you Susan? Could you tell us what made you decide on writing as a career in the first place? I mean I myself have been attempting to—'

'I wanted to be rich,' interrupted Susan quickly before he could launch on his autobiography. The firelight striking red glints on her hair, and her charming smile persuaded her listeners that she was joking. 'You see, I was always determined to succeed in whatever career I chose. I came from a very deprived background. My parents died tragically when I was young and I was brought up by relatives.' Her lip trembled slightly; a plaster Alsatian barked in corroboration.

'What was your first big breakthrough?'

'I was very lucky in that I met a professor at university, a dear old soul, who took an interest in my youthful efforts and who was very helpful to me professionally. He's dead now, alas.' She became for a moment a pretty young student paying grateful tribute to her crusty old mentor. Most of the audience were half in love with her now.

'What made you turn to crime, as it were, Susan, instead of to any other fictional form?'

Susan's slender body rippled as she giggled, 'I don't know really – I developed a taste for murder at an early age, and I've never looked back, I suppose.'

'Can I ask where you get your ideas from?'

The frail orphan sipped her wine before replying.

'From "the foul rag-and-bone shop of the heart".'

DOROTHY PARKER

Dorothy Parker was born in West End, New Jersey, in 1893 and grew up in New York. In 1916 she sold some of her poetry to the editor of *Vogue* and was subsequently given an editorial position on the magazine, writing captions for fashion photographs and drawings. She then became drama critic of *Vanity Fair* and the central figure of the celebrated Algonquin Hotel Round Table. Famous for her outspoken wit, she showed the same trenchant commentary in her book reviews for the *New Yorker* and *Esquire* and in her poems and sketches. She plunged in and out of severe depression, made several suicide attempts and had a long love affair with alcohol. Her writing was said to capture the spirit of her age. She was said to be a 'masochist whose passion for unhappiness knew no bounds'. One of the most talked about writers of her day, rich and gifted, she has been described as 'a Sappho who could combine a heartbreak with a wisecrack'.

WORLD WEARY

from *The Portable Dorothy Parker*

FROM THE DIARY OF A NEW YORK LADY: DURING DAYS OF HORROR, DESPAIR AND WORLD CHANGE

Monday. Breakfast tray about eleven; didn't want it. The champagne at the Amorys' last night was *too* revolting, but what *can* you do? You can't stay until five o'clock on just *nothing*. They had those *divine* Hungarian musicians in the green coats, and Stewie Hunter took off one of his shoes and led them with it, and it *couldn't* have been funnier. He is *the* wittiest number in the *entire* world; he *couldn't* be more perfect. Ollie Martin brought me home and we both fell asleep in the car – *too* screaming. Miss Rose came about noon to do my nails, simply *covered* with *the* most divine gossip. The Morrises are going to separate *any minute*, and Freddie Warren *definitely* has ulcers, and Gertie Leonard simply *won't* let Bill Crawford out of her sight even with Jack Leonard *right there in the room*, and it's all *true* about Sheila Phillips and Babs Deering. It *couldn't* have been more thrilling. Miss Rose is *too* marvellous; I really think that a lot of times people like that are a lot more intelligent than a lot of people. Didn't notice until after she had gone that the damn fool had put that *revolting* tangerine-coloured polish on my nails; *couldn't* have been more furious. Started to read a book, but too nervous. Called up and found I could get two tickets for the opening of *Run like a Rabbit* tonight for 48 dollars. Told them they had *the* nerve of the world, but what *can* you do? Think Joe said he was dining out, so telephoned some *divine* numbers to get someone to go to the theatre with me, but they were all tied up. Finally got Ollie Martin. He *couldn't* have more poise, and what do *I* care if he *is* one? *Can't* decide whether to wear the green crêpe or the red wool. Every time I look at my fingernails, I could *spit*. *Damn* Miss Rose.

Tuesday. Joe came barging in my room this morning at *practically nine o'clock. Couldn't* have been more furious. Started to fight, but *too* dead. Know he said he wouldn't be home to dinner. Absolutely *cold* all day; couldn't *move*. Last night *couldn't* have been more perfect. Ollie and I dined at Thirty-Eight East, absolutely *poisonous* food, and not one *living* soul that you'd be seen *dead* with, and *Run like a Rabbit* was *the* world's worst. Took Ollie up to the Barlows' party and it *couldn't* have been more attractive – *couldn't* have been more people absolutely *stinking*. They had those Hungarians in the green coats, and Stewie Hunter was leading them with a fork – everybody simply *died*. He had *yards* of green toilet paper hung around his neck like a lei; he *couldn't* have been in better form. Met a *really new number,* very tall, *too* marvellous, and one of those people that you can *really* talk to them. I told him sometimes I get so *nauseated* I could *yip*, and I felt I absolutely *had* to do something like write or paint. He said why didn't I write or paint. Came home alone; Ollie passed out *stiff*. Called up the new number three times today to get him to come to dinner and go with me to the opening of *Never Say Good Morning*, but first he was out and then he was all tied up with his mother. Finally got Ollie Martin. Tried to read a book, but couldn't sit still. *Can't* decide whether to wear the red lace or the pink with the feathers. Feel *too* exhausted, but what *can* you do?

Wednesday. The most terrible thing happened *just this minute*. Broke one of my fingernails *right off short*. Absolutely *the* most horrible thing I ever had happen to me in my life. Called up Miss Rose to come over and shape it for me, but she was out for the day. I do have *the* worst luck in the *entire* world. Now I'll have to go around like this all day and all night, but what *can* you do? *Damn* Miss Rose. Last night *too* hectic. *Never Say Good Morning too* foul, *never* saw more poisonous clothes on the stage. Took Ollie up to the Ballards' party; *couldn't* have been better. They had those Hungarians in the green coats and Stewie Hunter was leading them with a freesia – *too* perfect. He had on Peggy Cooper's ermine coat and Phyllis Minton's silver turban: *simply* unbelievable. Asked simply *sheaves* of *divine* people to come here Friday night; got the address of those Hungarians in the green coats from Betty Ballard. She says just engage them until four, and then whoever gives them another 300 dollars, they'll stay till five. *Couldn't* be cheaper. Started home with Ollie, but had to drop him at his house; he *couldn't* have been sicker. Called up the new number today to get him to come to dinner and go to the opening of *Everybody Up* with me tonight, but he was tied up. Joe's going to be out; he didn't *condescend* to say *where of course.* Started to read the papers, but nothing in them except that Mona Wheatley is in Reno charging *intolerable cruelty.* Called up Jim Wheatley to see if he had anything to do tonight, but he was tied up. Finally got Ollie Martin. *Can't* decide whether to wear the white satin or the black chiffon or the yellow pebble crêpe. Simply *wrecked* to the *core* about my fingernail. Can't *bear* it. *Never* knew *anybody* to have such *unbelievable* things happen to them.

Thursday. Simply *collapsing* on my *feet.* Last night *too* marvellous. *Everybody Up too* divine, *couldn't* be filthier, and the new number was there, *too* celestial, only he didn't see me. He was with Florence Keeler in that *loathsome* gold Schiaparelli model of hers that every *shopgirl* has had since *God* knows. He must be out of his *mind*: she wouldn't *look* at a man. Took Ollie to the Watsons' party; *couldn't* have been more thrilling. Everybody simply *blind.* They had those Hungarians in the green coats and Stewie Hunter was leading them with a lamp, and, after the lamp got broken, he and Tommy Thomas did adagio dances – *too* wonderful. Somebody told me Tommy's doctor told him he had to absolutely get *right out of town*, he has *the* world's worst stomach, but you'd *never* know it. Came home alone, couldn't find Ollie *anywhere*. Miss Rose came at noon to shape my nail, *couldn't* have been more fascinating. Sylvia Eaton can't go *out the door* unless she's had a hypodermic, and Doris Mason *knows every single word* about Douggie Mason and that girl up in Harlem, and Evelyn North won't be *induced* to keep away from those three acrobats, and they don't *dare* tell Stuyvie Raymond *what* he's got the matter with him. *Never* knew anyone that had a more simply *fascinating* life than Miss Rose. Made her take that *vile* tangerine polish off my nails and put on dark red. Didn't notice until after she had gone that it's practically *black* in electric light; *couldn't* be in a worse state. *Damn* Miss Rose. Joe left a note saying he was going to dine out, so telephoned the new number to get him to come to dinner and go with me to that new movie tonight, but he didn't answer. Sent him three telegrams to *absolutely surely* come tomorrow night. Finally got Ollie Martin for tonight. Looked at the papers, but nothing in them except that the Harry Motts are throwing a tea with Hungarian music on Sunday. Think will ask the new number to go to it with me; they must have meant to invite me. Began to read a book, but too exhausted. *Can't* decide whether to wear the new blue with the white jacket or save it till tomorrow night and wear the ivory moiré. Simply *heartsick* every time I think of my nails. *Couldn't* be wilder. Could *kill* Miss Rose, but what *can* you do?

Friday. Absolutely *sunk*; *couldn't* be worse. Last night *too* divine, movie *simply* deadly. Took Ollie to the Kingslands' party, *too* unbelievable, everybody absolutely *rolling*. They had those Hungarians in the green coats, but Stewie Hunter wasn't there. He's got a *complete* nervous breakdown. Worried *sick* for fear he won't be well by tonight; will absolutely *never* forgive him if he doesn't come. Started home with Ollie, but dropped him at his house because he *couldn't* stop crying. Joe left word with the butler he's going to the country this afternoon for the weekend; *of course* he wouldn't *stoop* to say, *what* country. Called up *streams* of marvellous numbers to get someone to come dine and go with me to the opening of *White Man's Folly*, and then go somewhere after to dance for a while; can't *bear* to be the first one there at your own party. Everybody was tied up. Finally got Ollie Martin. *Couldn't* feel more depressed; never should have gone *anywhere near* champagne and Scotch together. Started to read a book, but too restless. Called up Anne Lyman to ask about the new baby and *couldn't* remember if it was a boy or girl – *must* get a secretary *next week*. Anne *couldn't* have been more of a help; she said she didn't know whether to name it Patricia or Gloria, so then of course I knew it was a girl *right away*. Suggested calling it Barbara; forgot she already had one. Absolutely *walking the floor* like a *panther* all day. Could *spit* about Stewie Hunter. Can't *face* deciding whether to wear the blue with the white jacket or the purple with the beige roses. Every time I look at those *revolting* black nails, I want to absolutely *yip*. I really have *the* most horrible things happen to me of anybody in the *entire* world. *Damn* Miss Rose.

HARRIET WILSON

It is not known for sure when Harriet E. Wilson was born, although it is believed she was born Harriet Adams, a free black, in New Hampshire in 1827 or '38 or, in Federicksburg, Virginia, in 1807 or 1808. Either way, she is known to have lived between 1850 and 1860 with a white family in Milford, New Hampshire. In 1837 she married Thomas Williams. In 1852 her only child, George M. Wilson, was born.

In 1859, on August 18th, Harriet E. Wilson registered the copyright of *Our Nig* at the District Clerk's Office at Boston. The novel was then printed for the author by George C. Band of Boston, rather than published by a commercial house. It was the first novel written by a black woman and yet it passed relatively unnoticed in its day and has continued to be somewhat neglected ever since, despite both its content and its historical significance. The author subtitled her narrative: 'Sketches from the life of a Free Black, in a Two-Storey White House, North, Showing That Slavery's Shadows Fall Even There, By "Our Nig"'. She died sometime between February 1860 and the summer of 1860.

BLACK, WHITE AND YELLER

from *Our Nig*

MY FATHER'S DEATH

Misery! we have known each other,
Like a sister and a brother,
Living in the same lone home
Many years – we must live some
Hours or ages yet to come.

Shelley

Jim, proud of his treasure – a white wife – tried hard to fulfil his promises; and furnished her with a more comfortable dwelling, diet and apparel. It was comparatively a comfortable winter she passed after her marriage. When Jim could work, all went on well. Industrious, and fond of Mag, he was determined she should not regret her union to him. Time levied an additional charge upon him, in the form of two pretty mulattos, whose infantile pranks amply repaid the additional toil. A few years, and a severe cough and pain in his side compelled him to be an idler for weeks together, and Mag had thus a reminder of bygones. She cared for him only as a means to subserve her own comfort; yet she nursed him faithfully and true to marriage vows till death released her. He became the victim of consumption. He loved Mag to the last. So long as life continued, he stifled his sensibility to pain, and toiled for her sustenance long after he was able to do so.

A few expressive wishes for her welfare; a hope of better days for her; an anxiety lest they should not all go to the 'good place'; brief advice about their children; a hope expressed that Mag would not be neglected as she used to be; the manifestation of Christian patience; these were *all* the legacy of miserable Mag. A feeling of cold desolation came over her, as she turned from the grave of one who had been truly faithful to her.

She was now expelled from companionship with white people; this last step – her union with a black – was the climax of repulsion.

Seth Shipley, a partner in Jim's business, wished her to remain in her present home; but she declined, and returned to her hovel again, with obstacles threefold more insurmountable than before. Seth accompanied her, giving her a weekly allowance which furnished most of the food necessary for the four inmates. After a time, work failed; their means were reduced.

How Mag toiled and suffered, yielding to fits of desperation, bursts of anger, and uttering curses too fearful to repeat. When both were supplied with work, they prospered; if idle, they were hungry together. In this way their interests became united; they planned for the future together. Mag had lived an outcast for years. She had ceased to feel the gushings of penitence; she had crushed the sharp agonies of an awakened conscience. She had no longings for a purer heart, a better life. Far easier to descend lower. She entered the darkness of perpetual infamy. She asked not the rite of civilisation or Christianity. Her will made her the wife of Seth. Soon followed scenes familiar and trying.

'It's no use,' said Seth one day; 'we must give the children away, and try to get work in some other place.'

'Who'll take the black devils?' snarled Mag.

'They're none of mine,' said Seth; 'what you growling about?'

'Nobody will want any thing of mine, or yours either,' she replied.

'We'll make 'em p'r'aps,' he said. 'There's Frado's six years old, and pretty, if she is yours, and white folks 'll say so. She'd be a prize somewhere,' he continued, tipping his chair back against the wall, and placing his feet upon the rounds, as if he had much more to say when in the right position.

Frado, as they called one of Mag's children, was a beautiful mulatto, with long, curly black hair, and handsome, roguish eyes, sparkling with an exuberance of spirit almost beyond restraint.

Hearing her name mentioned, she looked up from her play, to see what Seth had to say of her.

'Wouldn't the Bellmonts take her?' asked Seth.

'Bellmonts?' shouted Mag. 'His wife is a right she-devil! and if—'

'Hadn't they better be all together?' interrupted Seth, reminding her of a like epithet used in reference to her little ones.

Without seeming to notice him, she continued, 'She can't keep a girl in the house over a week; and Mr Bellmont wants to hire a boy to work for him, but he can't find one that will live in the house with her; she's so ugly, they can't.'

'Well, we've got to make a move soon,' answered Seth. 'If you go with me, we shall go right off. Had you rather spare the other one?' asked Seth, after a short pause.

'One's as bad as t'other,' replied Mag. 'Frado is such a wild, frolicky thing, and means to do jest as she's a mind to; she won't go if she don't want to. I don't want to tell her she is to be given away.'

'I will,' said Seth. 'Come here, Frado?'

The child seemed to have some dim foreshadowing of evil, and declined.

'Come here,' he continued; 'I want to tell you something.'

She came reluctantly. He took her hand and said: 'We're going to move, by-'m-bye; will you go?'

'No!' screamed she; and giving a sudden jerk which destroyed Seth's equilibrium, left him sprawling on the floor, while she escaped through the open door.

'She's a hard one,' said Seth, brushing his patched coat sleeve. 'I'd risk her at Bellmont's.'

They discussed the expediency of a speedy departure. Seth

would first seek employment, and then return for Mag. They would take with them what they could carry, and leave the rest with Pete Greene, and come for them when they were wanted. They were long in arranging affairs satisfactorily, and were not a little startled at the close of their conference to find Frado missing. They thought approaching night would bring her. Twilight passed into darkness, and she did not come. They thought she had understood their plans, and had, perhaps, permanently withdrawn. They could not rest without making some effort to ascertain her retreat. Seth went in pursuit, and returned without her. They rallied others when they discovered that another little coloured girl was missing, a favourite play-mate of Frado's. All effort proved unavailing. Mag felt sure her fears were realised, and that she might never see her again. Before her anxieties became realities, both were safely returned, and from them and their attendant they learned that they went to walk, and not minding the direction soon found themselves lost. They had climbed fences and walls, passed through thickets and marshes, and when night approached selected a thick cluster of shrubbery as a covert for the night. They were discovered by the person who now restored them, chatting of their prospects, Frado attempting to banish the childish fears of her companion. As they were some miles from home, they were kindly cared for until morning. Mag was relieved to know her child was not driven to desperation by their intentions to relieve themselves of her; and she was inclined to think severe restraint would be healthful.

The removal was all arranged; the few days necessary for such migrations passed quickly, and one bright summer morning they bade farewell to their Singleton hovel, and with budgets and bundles commenced their weary march. As they neared the village, they heard the merry shouts of children gathered around the schoolroom, awaiting the coming of their teacher.

'Halloo!' screamed one. 'Black, white and yeller!' 'Black, white and yeller,' echoed a dozen voices.

It did not grate so harshly on poor Mag as once it would. She did not even turn her head to look at them. She had passed into an insensibility no childish taunt could penetrate, else she would have reproached herself as she passed familiar scenes, for extending the separation once so easily annihilated by steadfast integrity. Two miles beyond lived the Bellmonts, in a large, old-fashioned, two-storey white house, environed by fruitful acres, and embellished by shrubbery and shade trees. Years ago a youthful couple consecrated it as home; and after many little feet had worn paths to favourite fruit trees, and over its green hills, and mingled at last with brother man in the race which belongs neither to the swift or strong, the sire became grey-haired and decrepit, and went to his last repose. His aged consort soon followed him. The old homestead thus passed into the hands of a son, to whose wife Mag had applied the epithet 'she-devil', as may be remembered. John, the son, had not in his family arrangements departed from the example of the father. The pastimes of his boyhood were ever freshly revived by witnessing the games of his own sons as they rallied about the same goal his youthful feet had often won; as well as by the amusements of his daughters in their imitations of maternal duties.

At the time we introduce them, however, John is wearing the badge of age. Most of his children were from home; some seeking employment; some were already settled in homes of their own. A maiden sister shared with him the estate on which he resided, and occupied a portion of the house.

Within sight of the house, Seth seated himself with his bundles and the child he had been leading, while Mag walked onward to the house leading Frado. A knock at the door brought Mrs Bellmont, and Mag asked if she would be willing to let that child stop there while she went to the Reeds' house to wash, and when she came back she would call and get her. It seemed a novel request, but she consented. Why the impetuous child entered the house, we cannot tell; the door closed, and Mag hastily departed. Frado waited for the close of day, which was to bring back her mother. Alas! it never came. It was the last time she ever saw or heard of her mother.

TRAVELLING
THROUGH
LOVE

ELIZABETH SMART

Elizabeth Smart was born in Ottawa, Canada, in 1913. She was educated in private schools in Canada and for a year at King's College, University of London. One day, while browsing in a London bookshop, she chanced upon a slim volume of poetry by George Barker and fell passionately in love with him through the printed word. Eventually they communicated directly and, as a result of Barker's impecunious circumstances, Elizabeth Smart flew both him and his wife to the United States. Thus began one of the most extraordinary, intense and ultimately tragic love affairs of our time. They never married but Elizabeth bore George Barker four children and their relationship provided the impassioned inspiration for this moving and immediate chronicle of a love affair: *By Grand Central Station I Sat Down and Wept*. Originally published in 1945, this remarkable book is now widely recognised as a classic work of poetic prose which, more than four decades later, has retained all of its searing poignancy, beauty and power of impact.

After the war, Elizabeth Smart supported herself and her family with journalism and advertising work. In 1963 she became literary and associate editor of *Queen* magazine but subsequently dropped out of the literary scene to live quietly in a remote part of Suffolk, where her garden at The Dell was also a masterpiece. She died in 1986.

WAITING FOR
MY BUS TO COME IN

from *By Grand Central Station I
Sat Down and Wept*

I am standing on a corner in Monterey, waiting for the bus to come in, and all the muscles of my will are holding my terror to face the moment I most desire. Apprehension and the summer afternoon keep drying my lips, prepared at ten-minute intervals all through the five-hour wait.

But then it is her eyes that come forward out of the vulgar disembarkers to reassure me that the bus has not disgorged disaster: her madonna eyes, soft as the newly-born, trusting as the untempted. And, for a moment, at that gaze, I am happy to forgo my future, and postpone indefinitely the miracle hanging fire. Her eyes shower me with their innocence and surprise.

Was it for her, after all, for her whom I had never expected nor imagined, that there had been compounded such ruses of coincidence? Behind her he for whom I have waited so long, who has stalked so unbearably through my nightly dreams, fumbles with the tickets and the bags, and shuffles up to the event which too much anticipation has fingered to shreds.

For after all, it is all her. We sit in a café drinking coffee. He recounts their adventures and says, 'It was like this, wasn't it, darling?', 'I did well then, didn't I, dear heart?', and she smiles happily across the room with a confidence that appals.

How can she walk through the streets, so vulnerable, so unknowing, and not have people and dogs and perpetual calamity following her? But overhung with her vines of faith, she is protected from their gaze like the pools in Epping Forest. I see she can walk across the leering world and suffer injury only from the ones she loves. But I love her and her silence is propaganda for sainthood.

So we drive along the Californian coast singing together, and I entirely renounce him for only her peace of mind. The wild road winds round ledges manufactured from the mountains and cliffs. The Pacific in blue spasms reaches all its superlatives.

Why do I not jump off this cliff where I lie sickened by the moon? I know these days are offering me only murder for my future. It is not just the creeping fingers of the cold that dissuade me from action, and allow me to accept the hypocritical hope that there may be some solution. Like Macbeth, I keep remembering that I am their host. So it is tomorrow's breakfast rather than the future's blood that dictates fatal forbearance. Nature, perpetual whore, distracts with the immediate. Shifty-eyed with this fallacy, I plough back to my bed, up through the tickling grass.

So, through the summer days, we sit on the Californian coast, drinking coffee on the wooden steps of our cottages.

Up the canyon the redwoods and the thick leaf-hands of the castor-tree forebode disaster by their beauty, built on too grand a scale. The creek gushes over green boulders into pools no human ever uses, down canyons into the sea.

But poison oak grows over the path and over all the banks, and it is impossible even to go into the damp overhung valley without being poisoned. Later in the year it flushes scarlet, both warning of and recording fatality.

Between the canyons the hills slide steep and cropped to the cliffs that isolate the Pacific. They change from gold to silver, grow purple and massive from a distance, and disintegrate downhill in avalanches of sand.

Round the doorways double-size flowers grow without encouragement: lilies, nasturtiums in a bank down to the creek, roses, geraniums, fuchsias, bleeding-hearts, hydrangeas. The sea booms. The stream rushes loudly.

When the sea otters leave their playing under the cliff, the kelp in amorous coils appear to pin down the Pacific. There are rattlesnakes and widow-spiders and mists that rise from below. But the days leave the recollection of sun and flowers.

Day deceives, but at night no one is safe from hallucinations. The legends here are all of blood feuds and suicide, uncanny foresight and supernatural knowledge. Before the convict workers put in the road, loneliness drove women to jump into the sea. Tales were told of the convicts: how some went mad along the Coast, while others became hypnotised by it, and, when they were released, returned to marry local girls.

The long days seduce all thought away, and we lie like the lizards in the sun, postponing our lives indefinitely. But by the bathing pool, or on the sandhills of the beach, the Beginning lurks uncomfortably on the outskirts of the circle, like an unpopular person whom ignoring can keep away. The very silence, the very avoiding of any intimacy between us, when he, when he was only a word, was able to cause me sleepless nights and shivers of intimacy, is the more dangerous.

Our seeming detachment gathers strength. I sit back impersonally and say, I see human vanity, or feel myself full of gladness because there is a gentleness between him and her, or even feel irritation because he lets her do too much of the work, sits lolling whilst she chops wood for the stove.

But he never passes anywhere near me without every drop of my blood springing to attention. My mind may reason that the tenseness only registers neutrality, but my heart knows no true neutrality was ever so full of passion. One day along the path he brushed my breast in passing, and I thought, Does this efflorescence offend him? And I went into the redwoods brooding and blushing with rage to be stamped so obviously with femininity, and liable to humiliation worse than Venus's with Adonis, purely by reason of my accidental but flaunting sex.

Alas, I know he is the hermaphrodite whose love looks up through the apple tree with a golden indeterminate face. While we drive along the road in the evening, talking as impersonally as a radio discussion, he tells me, 'A boy with green eyes and long lashes, whom I had never seen before, took me into the back of a printshop and made love to me, and for two weeks I went around remembering the numbers on bus conductors' hats.'

'One should love beings whatever their sex,' I reply, but withdraw into the dark with my obstreperous shape of shame, offended with my own flesh which cannot metamorphose into a printshop boy with armpits like chalices.

Then days go by without even this much exchange of metaphor, and my tongue seems to wither in my throat from the unhappy silence, and the moons that rise and set unused, and the suns that melt the Pacific uselessly, drive me to tears and my cliff of vigil at the end of the peninsula. I do not beckon to the Beginning, whose advent will surely strew our world with blood, but I weep for such a waste of life lying under my thumb.

His foreshortened face appears in profile on the car window like the irregular graph of my doom, merciless as a mathematician, leering accompaniment to all my good resolves. There is no medicinal to be obtained from the dried herbs of any natural hill, for when I tread those upward paths, the lowest vines conspire to abet my plot, and the poison oak thrusts its insinuation under my foot.

From the corner where the hill turns from the sea and goes into the secrecy and damp air of forbidden things, I stand disinterestedly examining the instruments and the pattern of my fate. It is a slow-motion process of the guillotine in action, and I see plainly that no miracle can avert the imminent deaths. I see, measuring the time, regarding equably the appearance, but I am as detached as the statistician is when he lists his thousands dead.

When his soft shadow, which yet in the night comes barbed with all the weapons of guilt, is cast up hugely on the pane, I watch it as from a loge in the theatre, the continually vibrating I in darkness. Swearing invulnerability, I measure mercilessly his shortcomings, and with luxurious scorn, ask who could be ensnared there.

But that huge shadow is more than my only moon, more even than my destruction: it has the innocent slipping advent of the next generation, which enters in one night of joy, and leaves a meadowful of lamenting milkmaids when its purpose is grown to fruit.

Also, smoothed away from all detail, I see, not the face of a lover to arouse my coquetry or defiance, but the gentle outline of a young girl. And this, though shocking, enables me to understand, and myself rise as virile as a cobra, out of my loge, to assume control.

He kissed my forehead driving along the coast in evening, and now, wherever I go, like the sword of Damocles, that greater never-to-be-given kiss hangs above my doomed head. He took my hand between the two shabby front seats of the Ford, and it was dark, and I was looking the other way, but now that hand casts everywhere an octopus shadow from which I can never escape. The tremendous gentleness of that moment smothers me under; all through the night it is centaurs hoofed and galloping over my heart: the poison has got into my blood. I stand on the edge of the cliff, but the future is already done.

It is written. Nothing can escape. Floating through the waves with seaweed in my hair, or being washed up battered on the inaccessible rocks, cannot undo the event to which there were never any alternatives. O lucky Daphne, motionless and green to avoid the touch of a god! Lucky Syrinx, who chose a legend instead of too much blood! For me there was no choice. There were no crossroads at all.

I am jealous of the hawk because he can get so far out of the world, or I follow with passionate envy the seagull swooping to possible cessation. The mourning doves mercilessly coo my sentence in the woods. They are the hangmen pronouncing my sentence in the suitable language of love. I climb above the possessive clouds that squat over the sea, but the poison spreads. Naked I wait ...

I am overrun, jungled in my bed, I am infested with a menagerie of desires: my heart is eaten by a dove, a cat scrambles in the cave of my sex, hounds in my head obey a whipmaster who cries nothing but havoc as the hours test my endurance with an accumulation of tortures. Who, if I cried, would hear me among the angelic orders?

I am far, far beyond that island of days where once, it seems, I watched a flower grow, and counted the steps of the sun, and fed, if my memory serves, the smiling animal at his appointed hour. I am shot with wounds which have eyes that see a world all sorrow, always to be, panoramic and unhealable, and mouths that hang unspeakable in the sky of blood.

How can I be kind? How can I find bird-relief in the nest-building of day-to-day? Necessity supplies no velvet wing with which to escape. I am indeed and mortally pierced with the seeds of love.

Then she leans over in the pool and her damp dark hair falls like sorrow, like mercy, like the mourning weeds of pity. Sitting nymphlike in the pool in the late afternoon her pathetic slenderness is covered over with a love as gentle as trusting as tenacious as the birds who rebuild their continually violated nests. When she clasps her hands happily at a tune she likes, it is more moving than I can bear. She is the innocent who is always the offering. She is the goddess of all things which the vigour of living destroys. Why are her arms so empty?

In the night she moans with the voice of the stream below my window, searching for the child whose touch she once felt and can never forget: the child who obeyed the laws of life better than she. But by day she obeys the voice of love as the stricken obey their god, and she walks with the light step of hope which only the naive and the saints know. Her shoulders have always the attitude of grieving, and her thin breasts are pitiful like Virgin shrines that have been robbed.

How can I speak to her? How can I comfort her? How can I explain to her any more than I can to the flowers that I crush with my foot when I walk in the field? He also is bent towards her in an attitude of solicitude. Can he hear his own heart while he listens for the tenderness of her sensibilities? Is there a way at all to avoid offending the Lamb of God?

*

Under the waterfall he surprised me bathing and gave me what I could no more refuse than the earth can refuse the rain. Then he kissed me and went down to his cottage.

Absolve me, I prayed, up through the cathedral redwoods, and forgive me if this is sin. But the new moss caressed me and the water over my feet and the ferns approved me with endearments: My darling, my darling, lie down with us now for you also are earth whom nothing but love can sow.

And I lay down on the redwood needles and seemed to flow down the canyon with the thunder and confusion of the stream, in a happiness which, like birth, can afford to ignore the blood and the tearing. For nature has no time for mourning, absorbed by the turning world, and will, no matter what devastation attacks her, fulfil in underground ritual, all her proper prophecy.

Gently the wood sorrel and the dove explained the confirmation and guided my return. When I came out of the woods on to the hill, I had pine needles in my hair for a bridal wreath, and the sea and the sky and the gold hills smiled benignly. Jupiter has been with Leda, I thought, and now nothing can avert the Trojan Wars. All legend will be born, but who will escape alive?

But what can the wood sorrel and the mourning dove, who deal only with eternals, know of the thorny sociabilities of human living? Of how the pressure of the hours of waiting, silent and inactive, weigh upon the head with a physical force that suffocates? The simplest daily pleasantries are torture, and a samson effect is needed to avoid his glance that draws me like gravity.

For excuse, for our being together, we sit at the typewriter, pretending a necessary collaboration. He has a book to be typed, but the words I try to force out die on the air and dissolve into kisses whose chemicals are even more deadly if undelivered. My fingers cannot be martial at the touch of an instrument so much connected with him. The machine sits like a temple of love among the papers we never finish, and if I awake at night and see it outlined in the dark, I am electrified with memories of dangerous propinquity.

The frustrations of past postponement can no longer be restrained. They hang ripe to burst with the birth of any moment. The typewriter is guilty with love and flowery with shame, and to me it speaks so loudly I fear it will communicate its indecency to casual visitors.

How stationary life has become, and the hours impossibly elongated. When we sit on the gold grass of the cliff, the sun between us insists on a solution for which we search in vain, but whose urgency we feel unbearably. I never was in love with death before, nor felt grateful because the rocks below could promise certain death. But now the idea of dying violently becomes an act wrapped in attractive melancholy, and displayed with every blandishment. For there is no beauty in denying love, except perhaps by death, and towards love what way is there?

To deny love, and deceive it meanly by pretending that what is unconsummated remains eternal, or that love sublimated reaches highest to heavenly love, is repulsive, as the hypocrite's face is repulsive when placed too near the truth. Farther off from the centre of the world, of all worlds, I might be better fooled, but can I see the light of a match while burning in the arms of the sun?

No, my advocates, my angels with sadist eyes, this is the beginning of my life, or the end. So I lean affirmation across the café table, and surrender my fifty years away with an easy smile. But the surety of my love is not dismayed by any eventuality which prudence or pity can conjure up, and in the end all that we can do is to sit at the table over which our hands cross, listening to tunes from the Wurlitzer, with love huge and simple between us, and nothing more to be said.

So hourly, at the slightest noise, I start, I stand ready to feel the roof cave in on my head, the thunder of God's punishment announcing the limit of His endurance.

She walks lightly, like the child whose dancing feet will touch off gigantic explosives. She knows nothing, but like autumn birds feels foreboding in the air. Her movements are nervous, there are draughts in every room, but less wise than the birds whom small signs send on three-thousand-mile flights, she only looks vaguely out to the Pacific, finding it strange that heaven has, after all, no Californian shore.

I have learned to smoke because I need something to hold on to. I dare not be without a cigarette in my hand. If I should be looking the other way when the hour of doom is struck, how shall I avoid being turned into stone unless I can remember something to do which will lead me back to the simplicity and safety of daily living?

IT is coming. The magnet of its imminent finger draws each hair of my body, the shudder of its approach disintegrates kisses, loses wishes on the disjointed air. The wet hands of the castor-tree at night brush me and I shriek, thinking that at last I am caught up with. The clouds move across the sky heavy and tubular. They gather and I am terror-struck to see them form a long black rainbow out of the mountain and disappear across the sea. The Thing is at hand. There is nothing to do but crouch and receive God's wrath.

LISA ST AUBIN
DE TERÁN

Lisa St Aubin de Terán was born in London in 1953 of half-Jersey and half-South American parents. Aged sixteen she married a Venezuelan political exile and spent two years travelling in Italy until sailing to his sugar plantation in the Venezuelan Andes. There, for the next seven years, she found inspiration for her writing, returning to Europe in 1979. She has written eight novels and five non-fiction books which have been translated into over a dozen languages. She lives in Italy with her third husband, the painter Robbie Duff-Scott, and her three children.

RAZING THE SAINTS

from *The Marble Mountain and Other Stories*

ANNE OF THE RAGGED LACE

Anne

Summer always came late to the fens, it was mostly water there, and mist and mud. The sun can rise and set over the fields and flood-drains in the Saints, and people hardly notice it. It would have taken more than that pale sun to stir the solid surface of our village. I used to like to look up at that frail disc in the sky. Grandad said it was dangerous to stare at the sun. He said you could go blind. But he'd been out in India, and it must have been different there. The only fire in our sky was diluted and as colourless as I, with my too blonde hair and my too pale skin. I'm quite strong, though; I just look weak.

I loved the way the sunlight was sifted through the clouds into pale streaks. I liked them best filtered through the ragged patterns of the cow-parsley, the Queen Anne's lace that grew as thick as planted barley. Whenever I lay down under the canopy of flowers, I felt I was in my world, a queen, at last, in all her finery. 'Anne of the ragged lace' was what my grandad called me.

I'd go missing from the village, and I'd always be there, on the bank of the thin brown river, lying under the white parasols of flowers. It bound me to the village: my title, and the magic growth of stalks and leaves and the white haze. Whatever lacked

in me, I found in them. I didn't talk much about my discovery.
I told my grandad, and Tommy, and that was all.

Most of the village talk was about stoves and beet and barley,
and water levels and the bus times to Lynn. Or it was about boys
and clothes and Saturday outings. Sometimes we talked about
swish jobs over the horizon, knowing that there could be
nothing there because the Saints were so flat and no one had
gone beyond them, except old soldiers. Yet the talk continued,
and every boy in the Saints cut a vicarious dash describing this
or that detail of his luxury flat-to-be in the city. The fantasy was
part of our chemistry, as important to the village as the Spar
supermarket or running water or soap operas.

The only things that actually happened in the village took
place on television or in the back of a car, or, much more usually,
behind the bus stop. The seasons came and went so slowly that
few of us noticed the change. There'd be a new baby at Hangar
Lane, or a funeral from Number 5. They were just the natural
things of a place given over to reaping and sowing.

In every front room or kitchen, the television spoke as from
another planet. Our world was guided by 'the box'. When we
weren't watching it, we discussed its goings on at the bus shelter,
'the stop'. It stood out on the windiest part at the edge of the
housing estate. It was like a boat in a sea of mud. It was our life-
support. The two lurching double-deckers that passed there
twice a day were almost irrelevant to its importance. Life was not
what lay beyond our windswept huddle of houses, it was life as
discussed, observed or brooded on from the stop. Nothing ever
changed, it just slowly mutated towards its inevitable return to
the dark clay around us.

I was born there, on Hangar Lane, and I grew up there, like
we all did, sorting out and discarding the twentieth century from
the grim safety of the bus stop. No one ever questioned the way
we lived, or tried to break away or even disrupt it, no one, that
is, until Tommy. I used to think that as long as the ragged lace
continued to flower, year after year, I would be happy staying
there, having a cottage of my own, or one of the new bungalows,
and a family, competing a little with my friends, and doing

things well. I belonged there, in the Saints' country, between the five churches that we rarely used: St Peter's, St German's, St Mary the Virgin, St Mary Magdalen and St Clement's. I loved it more than anything except Tommy Watkins.

I'd known Tommy all my life, and I'd watched him growing away from us all like a giant hogweed in a patch of beet. We went to school together, and read the same books and poems and failed the same geography exams, but the words were different inside my head. They were always different, and so was Tommy, but no one minded because everyone had their ways. Mine were with the flowers. Johnny Gotobed had a kitchen garden full of fridges; dozens of them rusting into heaps like sculptured shrubs, and none of them working or ever would. Harry kept ferrets, and slept with them in his bed; and even Mum had a thing about folding. So, when Tommy took to his drums, nobody cared. He still met his mates at the stop.

His drumming always reached its peak in the summer, and gradually it began to compete with my collaged skies. At other times the north-easterly winds drowned out his restless pounding. All the Saints' country lived a prey to the wind, so no wonder Tommy couldn't compete with it. Not that he didn't think he could. Tommy thought that everything had been created expressly to set him off, even the wind and the rain. I can't remember when I started to believe it too, but I did.

Tommy was always popular, especially with the girls. Not even my own folk could understand why he had his eye on me. They used to joke that I was only half-made. Me being the eldest, they said they hadn't got the hang of how to make babies when it came to me, and that was why I'd turned out so insipid. The only thing I ever had to boast of was my closeness to the Queen Anne's lace and Tommy. It made me special, special enough to have been happy there in the Saints for always.

Every day Tommy grew more restless to get away. He hated Hangar Lane, hated the Saints, even the fens themselves. I never understood that, because I loved them. But then I never understood him, and I loved him too. He was obsessed by the city. It wasn't even Lynn he wanted, it was London. He said that he despised Lynn. He actually wanted to go to London. He wanted to be a star. When he talked of it, his eyes changed colour, from dull brown to clear.

'Can't you see it?' he'd say.

I couldn't, I had my world, my place, my ragged lace. To go to the city seemed as likely a thing to do as to climb inside a television set and block out the characters with my bulk. But he talked sweet words to me, and he stroked my hair. My mum used to stroke my hair as well, but she used to touch it with a kind of wonder, that she, who was so complete, could have produced me, who wasn't. Sometimes, when she started folding, I used to think that her lips weren't pursed against Dad's old jokes any more, but brooding on the transparency of my hair and the paleness of my eyes. My brothers used to call me Red Eyes, because I cried a lot and it made me look like an albino. Tommy never called me that, he didn't even see it. I was his princess, heiress to the kingdom of Queen Anne's lace.

I had my long plantations of feathery leaves, and my ivory brocade of petal stars so I didn't need the rhythm of other people's drums. Tommy used to say that what I had was too ephemeral to be real. I didn't know what I had, except that it was what I wanted. And then, suddenly, it wasn't enough, although nothing much had changed. I suppose nothing ever changed in the Saints, or could, or would. It was just a landscape of mildew and mud into which the pale sun dripped its filtered sweetness intravenously, and I carried some of its sweetness in my blood.

The last summer before I left the Saints, I lay under the highest Queen Anne's lace by the river, and all I could think of was Tommy, Tommy, Tommy and pray to the tall stalks that he wouldn't go away.

Tommy

I was born here, but I hate it. I started drumming to annoy my dad. That's how I found out I was a drummer. I'd always been a dreamer. For years it was the drums that kept me going, that and hearing the daily calls for Anne of the ragged lace. She used to lose herself in the fields, and I loved hearing them all hunting for her, calling her name, like a character from a play. I used to dream about her. She'd be my queen, and I'd be the greatest rock star in the world with all of London at my feet and my pale lover in tow, paler than anyone, and smiling with whatever secret it was that she culled from the fields.

She never really understood what glitter was about. It was all pale sun with her, and that killed me. If she'd stayed in the Saints, they would have swallowed her up, put her to sleep, planted and gathered her until there was nothing left but husk. Every autumn, when my dad dug the garden, I felt he was burying me bit by bit in his clay. And what I hated him for most was he couldn't even see he was doing it. He was always so bloody ready to talk and change, so understanding, but he didn't understand the first thing. When they heard from somewhere that I wanted to go to the city, they started bunging me full of some government training scheme.

If I hadn't been born in the fens, things would have been different. Its mud sticks. I knew that if I played hard enough, loud enough, someone would hear me and give me a break. That was all I needed, just one break and everything would have been different, one break from the city. The trouble was, people could see that I came from the fens. I didn't belong there, ever, but it must be like having webbed feet or something, real city people can just look at you and tell.

I mean, we're almost into the twenty-first century. People have space ships and Porsches. The days of the hoe are over. Stuff the sugar beets. I hate them. I never eat sugar. I gave it up when I was eight – I didn't want any part of it. Oh, and then the highlight of the week, the one that we were supposed to look forward to, a trip to the dole office on the bus, a beer, a game of darts and six more evenings hanging round the shelter. Even during the war people used to crawl under their shelters and something would happen on top. Dad used to say, 'It's not like that, son, you've got lots of alternatives.' And of course, I had.

I could have worked in the sugar beet factory, been a success, and dug my garden, like my dad.

Tom tom tom tom. I tried to raze the Saints, I hated them. I was in love with Anne of the ragged lace. I tried to explain how things were, but she just didn't understand. She'd got this thing about belonging on the land and nothing changing. She wasn't thick, just brainwashed. There was no way I was going to vegetate. I'd have gone anyway, even if I hadn't got my talent.

Anne

I had to go, Tommy would have gone without me. I tried to tell my mum, but I couldn't turn it into the kind of words she'd understand. I wanted to tell my dad as well, but I knew he'd say, 'Sixteen and no job is no good in London.' He'd have tried to stop me, and I didn't want to hurt him, because I had to go. Tommy said in six months we'd have a big apartment and he'd be signed up with a record company, and I'd have a wardrobe like Krystle in *Dynasty*. I didn't want that, though, not any of it, just Tommy. He had a mate in London, someone who'd come to the Saints for holidays, and we went to stay with him in Notting Hill Gate.

I'd never seen so many faces or so many motors. Tommy said the fens were grey, and yet the day we got to London, I felt a greyness crawl all over me, and it has never gone away. Even my hair picked up the grime. It was like another country. I didn't have the heart to say much, and I didn't need to, because Tommy talked enough for everyone, describing the band he was going to form, and the gear they were going to wear, how often they'd go on tour, and that sort of thing.

His friend didn't like me, he said I gave him the willies, being so pale and quiet. Tommy used to call him Boxer. I don't know if that was his name, he didn't look strong enough to be a boxer. He was more of a traveller, really. He told Tommy he was going to the Philippines soon, he talked about it a lot. He had a poster over his bed of a place called Jakarta. I tried to like Boxer because he looked after Tommy. He knew that the one thing that made Tommy nervous was sticking out in the city, so he helped him to merge in. He even gave him some of his H for free and he never charged us rent. I tried to imagine what Mum would do if two people turned up on her doorstep. She would probably have done the airing cupboard a couple of times and then folded herself in despair.

Tommy kept telling me that I wasn't trying to be nice to Boxer. I suppose he complained about it. He just made me feel uneasy, and although he was helping Tommy, it seemed that he was just changing him into someone I understood even less than I had before. Tommy said that was what happened in the city; people changed and things started to happen and that was right. That was what we had come for. Boxer even changed my name. He said that Queen Anne of the ragged lace was hick, and he changed it to Queer Gladys. Somehow, that was the one that stuck: it became my city name.

That was the first summer that Tommy couldn't play. Boxer was worse than his father. He hated drumming and noise in general, and Tommy's in particular. I thought that Tommy would be lost without his drums, I hoped it would make him feel as lost as me, so that we could go home. But he said it didn't matter. It was better to absorb our surroundings, change our style, drop the hick. For music, we used to go to Waterloo to hear the buskers, and I would watch the dirty water swirling under the bridge.

Tommy

There are ways into a city, it's like crawling into a wasps' nest really. You have to know how to do it. How not to stand out for the wrong reasons. I should have gone to the city on my own. It was a responsibility being in love, a liability. Anne kept saying that we should go back to the Saints, and she shouldn't have said that. Saying things can make them happen. It alters the pattern, changes the rhythm. It's a jinx. Even thinking things is like that. It's like with murder: there is malice aforethought.

We had to grow a new skin. Boxer didn't really understand me either, which was strange, considering he understood such a lot. Boxer was a travelling man. He said travel stretches your awareness. Well, I know it does. I mean, we got out of the fens and it changed our whole perception. But we weren't hicks, not inside. And I'm not just saying this, but I'm good on the drums. Better than good, I'd say, bloody brilliant. We had to pawn the set, and I miss them. I just rattle out my ideas now on Coca-Cola cans.

If Boxer had really listened to my music, I just know he would have felt differently about us. I mean, nobody tells Mick Jagger who to screw. Boxer kept telling me to ditch Anne/Gladys. He said I was a loner. He was wrong though, I needed Anne, and I've never liked being on my own. I get bad dreams. I used to get them at home. An artist needs his public. Anne of the ragged lace used to be my best fan. What kind of a name is Gladys? It sounds more like my gran.

She and her cronies have to be the most boring morons ever born, but they did have something with all their yakking about the war, and waiting for years for their soldiers to return. You'd think Anne could have had a bit more loyalty; stood by me; tried. But no, she just turned out as bad as all the rest, spoonfed on telly. She expected everything to happen in one go. You have to sink to its depths to know what life's about. You go down, and then you go up. I could have made it if she'd had more guts. It was my day. I could feel it coming, a big break was on the way.

Boxer was right, though. She was a watery person. She had the little thin mind of an eel. She started saying she didn't know me any more. She always nagged me about the H, she hated it. If she'd had an ounce of intelligence, she would have seen that H was just camouflage. It brought me friends. They didn't call me hick in the Underground. I could score and a whole load of people would say, 'Hey man, Tommy.'

They knew my name in the city! My own name. Strangers would talk to me like friends. Only Gladys, who was meant to be my best friend, went off me.

Nag nag nag. Nag nag nag. What did she expect? Of course it cost a lot to stay on H. No one was going to give me money if I asked them, it takes a girl to do that. I pawned my drums, for Christ's sake, what more did she want! The other girls did it at Waterloo, dozens of them. And Gladys got a lot of money when she set her mind to it, fifties, pounds, even fivers. But she didn't care if I was in pain. She'd turned against me by then. I could tell. I never thought she'd be like that. She used to be sort of different, nicer. Boxer tipped me off, right from the start, he said that queer Gladys was mean.

Anne

We started to make friends after Boxer chucked us out. We slept under the arches at the station. It was quite nice because it was warm and I'd always liked Waterloo. I liked the river, it reminded me of the fens. There were a lot of us there, and no one called me a kid or said I was too pale to stay with them. We were all pale there, I don't know if it was the hamburgers or the H, but everyone had an ashen look, even the dark ones. The city made everyone grey.

When it started to get cold, we used newspapers for blankets, and the print came off them and stained our skin. It made me feel really old being covered like that with yesterday's news.

Tommy said I didn't love him any more, but I did. He'd get really vicious when I didn't help him. He said that I'd lost faith in him just because we didn't have the apartment and he hadn't bought me any diamonds. He didn't seem to understand that I'd only ever wanted *him*. I just wanted to unpawn his drums. I told him he couldn't get a break without his drums, but he called me a hick and a moron.

We were the cream of the station. It was ours. Outside, under the bridge, all the old tramps and winos lived in cardboard boxes. We didn't mix with them, though. They used to stink.

There was a girl called Gail who did the ticket queues with me. She was my friend, she came from Dumfries. Gail said the station was like a hotel compared to where she came from, and she was going to stay there for ever. The gangs came sometimes and stole all our things, but Gail said it didn't matter. Sometimes she'd even come to the Embankment Gardens with me, where there were flowers, but they didn't have any Queen Anne's lace. I asked about it, once, but a man told me it was only a weed, and they pull weeds out in the city. Gail was so nice to me that I told her my real name, and she said she thought it was really pretty. Tommy never used it any more, he didn't want his mates to think we were hicks.

I went down to the river every day. Tommy said it was pathetic, at first, and then he changed his mind. He actually made me go and get money from the bridge. Later, it was Gail who told me that Tommy was carrying on with another girl. Of course, I didn't believe her. All we had was each other, Tommy and me, and Tommy's future.

When I first saw them together, I went to the Ladies' and cried. Then I waited until he was on his own, and I asked him why. He wouldn't talk to me. He said, 'Shut up, Red Eyes,' and after that he just ignored me. I waited for a few days, sort of hanging around and it was really embarrassing. We were living in the same 'hotel', and we still had the same patch. I couldn't move away, you had to fight to get your space. So I had to watch them and hear them and it made me sick. The boy from the heel-bar had a crush on me. He offered to look after me, but I was in love with Tommy. I did take a fiver from him for my bus fare home. I didn't have the heart to beg, you see, not for myself. I'd only ever done it for Tommy.

All the way back I kept my forehead pressed against the glass, looking at the grey houses and then the rain and the mud and the trees. It was December and I didn't know if my mum and dad would want to see me. They liked Christmas. I didn't know if I would spoil it for them, going home. But I thought that if I had to freeze by a river I'd rather do it in the Saints, beside the Ouse, with my own name.

I took the bus from Lynn, and they were glad when I came

home. Dad told me that I belonged there. I didn't tell the Watkins about Tommy. I said I didn't know where he'd gone. Then I waited, all winter, for my flowers. No winter has ever felt so long. I didn't go to the stop any more, even though my old mates all invited me. They treated me like someone famous, and they didn't call me Red Eyes again, but nothing else seemed to have changed. The fens still stretched out into the clouds, and I could see for miles. I could count the square towers of three of the five churches.

I'm sure Mum thought I was pregnant because she perked up when the months passed and she could see that I wasn't. And she didn't sigh too much, or push me to get work at the beet factory, and Dad was very sweet to me. He kept telling me that the cow-parsley would be up soon. He knew that I was waiting, just waiting for my life to come back to me. Marking time. When the first leaves came through in April, and then the first flowers, in May, I knew I would survive. But, when summer came, and the lace made a high haze along the riverbank, I realised that my old pleasure was gone. I was no longer queen of the fields. A part of me belonged to Tommy, and it was grey and musty and confused.

After the barley was in, I started hanging round the stop again. I knew that I would find a boyfriend there eventually, and settle down, even though it wasn't what I wanted. Sometimes, when I thought about how I had messed up in the Saints and in the city, I felt my lips purse, a bit like my mum's. I started watching her as she folded and refolded everything in the house that would bend itself in her restless hands. I felt closer to her than I'd ever been. And I wondered what she had or hadn't done when she was young that had left that streak of unspent bitterness in her.

I missed Tommy and his drums. I kept hoping that he'd come back and find me; but then Grandad died, and I never heard my proper name again. I hid by the riverbank, but no one ever called me Anne of the ragged lace. So I knew that Tommy wouldn't ever come back for me, because it was my name he'd loved, and not my pallid face.

ROMAINE BROOKS

Romaine Brooks was born in a hotel in Rome in 1874. She was brought up by her mother who neglected her and devoted her life to Romaine's mentally unstable brother St. Mar. Her mother, Ella Waterman Goddard, died in 1902 and Romaine, after ten years of bohemia in Paris and Rome, suddenly became enormously wealthy. She decided to remain in Europe, and the glittering society of the years just before and after the First World War welcomed her. Gertrude Stein, Somerset Maugham, André Gide, Jean Cocteau, Compton Mackenzie, Colette, Radclyffe Hall and her lover Una, Lady Trowbridge, were among her many friends and acquaintances. She made a brief and disastrous marriage before forming a lasting relationship with the heiress and writer, Natalie Barney – an attachment which survived their separate infidelities for fifty years. Pre-eminent among her lovers were Gabriele D'Annunzio, the Italian poet and national hero, and Ida Rubinstein, the dancer, whom she snatched from D'Annunzio and who was the inspiration for some of her most important pictures. Critics such as Robert de Montesquiou and Guillaume Apollinaire judged her to be an important artist and a portrait painter of exceptional power.

Her long life – she died a recluse in 1970 aged 96 – was dramatic, intriguing and above all unconventional. In the artistic world she was acclaimed as one of her generation's finest painters, in her private life she struggled to free herself from her mother's domination, which extended beyond her grave, and the nightmare of her own mad brother.

I NEVER FORGOT
THAT MY FATE WAS
WITH THESE MAD
ONES

from *Between Me and Life:*
A Biography of Romaine Brooks

'The atmosphere she [Romaine's mother] created was that of a court ruled over by a crazy queen; and before my brother showed definite and incurable signs of madness, she treated me either as one of royal blood – since I was descended from her – or else as a page in waiting, rather than a little girl. There was even a time when she dressed me up in replicas of the clothes my brother had worn as a very small boy. But she never failed to remind me that I was not good-looking like St Mar, and indeed, my pale face and dark hair could in no way compare with his angelic blondness'...

'Some higher dispensation makes madmen of those who lose their way and fail to return with their riches'...

'My brother, crouched on the [piano] stool in his great overcoat, would close his eyes as if in pain. Then spreading his limp hands flat on the keys, he would move the fingers as though groping for sound.

'But suddenly he would awake as if in anger. Then the din of fifty madhouses could not have competed with the deafening sounds which he ... drew from the piano,' while our mother, her finger on her lips to enforce silence, stood beside her son in an ecstasy of delight '... At last, like a deflated accordion, he would collapse to his former limp self and remain quietly on the stool until we had left the room.' ...

'Even now any loud, discordant sounds can bring palpitations and send waves of blood to my head' ...

'One of his favourite pastimes, when he could escape my vigilance, was to throw bottles from a balcony on the heads of passers-by. An incident of this kind in a terminus hotel in Paris caused the arrival of the police. My brother was caught red-handed, his pockets bulging with bottles. Only the evident state of his mind averted proceedings against him' ...

'In his crazy fashion, his was the only protection I could hope to find ... On occasions when my mother's mad mood would seek in me a victim, he would intervene on my behalf. These interventions were so unexpected that from mere astonishment my mother instantly calmed down.

My brother would walk slowly forward and stand in silence between us, his limp, stooping figure facing my mother. It was eloquent and sufficient to turn the scale in my favour.

When I went away, I was told that he sought my mother, an unusual thing for him to do, and with shut eyes stood silent and motionless before her. It was his way of protesting against my departure' ...

'Physically I reacted favourably enough, but I am now convinced that mentally the effects of slum life were never effaced. In some dark corner of my inner consciousness these experiences had sown what would soon take the form of a secret craving for the negative exultation of those who are solitary and adrift' ...

'As I grew older I was fortunate enough to be sent away from time to time; but ... I never forgot that my fate was with these mad ones, and on my return I would find them again and be dragged precisely as before into their crazy round of existence' . . .

'We leap into dangerous waters. Lucky is he who, with the return of a wave, is landed higher than he was before' . . .

INTERLUDE: 'HELL,' A SHORT SHORT STORY BY ROMAINE BROOKS

I was watching a tiny little girl seated on the low stone ledge of a building. Her hands, which she held up in front of her, were being slapped very hard by her mother.

The slapping went on more and more violently and the little hands were very red. It must have hurt a great deal, but curiously enough the child was not crying. Her small face was pale and tense and she was gazing as though fascinated into the eyes of her angry parent; there evidently she saw something that forbade her crying.

I was wondering what the misdeed could have been to merit such punishment, when the young mother glanced in my direction. The expression of her eyes startled me for I saw in them the glitter of madness. Her anger had been promoted by her own demon.

And the little girl . . . She belonged to that terrifying other side of things; that child's hell on earth – the mad parent . . .

'The other, the melancholy self, will sleep as long as I live here. These were my thoughts as I drove up the dusty road that runs between old walls and powdered oleander trees, or along the vineyards that looped with green the sea and Vesuvius paled in distant blue.

My mother was only a phenomenon I had been watching fearfully all my life. Death, the climax . . . nothing more' . . .

'I am painting a sad and comical little being and while working I talk to myself in this fashion: "Romaine, you are a great artist.

All your powers and all your thoughts are in your art. How is it that you are now attempting another role whose outcome will mean slavery and imbecility? By taking refuge in your art, you can get the better of nature's traps. Now you are descending from your throne to mingle in the intrigues of the crowd. Romaine you are an elect of the gods, yet you become an ordinary female and concern yourself with the things the least tart in the street knows and always will know better than you. I talk this way, dear friend, probably with a lot of vanity but also with a little sadness, because I would have liked to sit down on a stool beside a throne higher than my own. Alas! The king is almost never there ... it seems he descends every night to give dreams to a woman beside the dunes and when he comes back, he sleeps all the time with his feet on the footstool ... It's sad."'

She would never come back to him, she said, because 'Your destructive power is stronger than you and everything that comes near you is annihilated. I had hoped that because I had so much respect for your art, you would have had a little for mine ... But it was not so; I was for you only another female to destroy' ...

'It now astonishes me that I was not more wary of people. I had no need of them and besides so much real trouble had come my way that though petty scandals and malicious intrigues could not harm me, they did make me extremely angry at times.

Indeed it was with the very stones that were finally flung at me that I built up the strong walls of this inner sanctuary' ...

'I shut myself up for months without seeing a soul, and give shape in my painting to my visions of sad and grey shadows ... I want to have enthusiasm and when it dies I feel as if a part of myself had died ... I fear those shadows most that start from my own feet.'

WHERE I WAS ALWAYS MEANT TO BE

KAREN BLIXEN

Karen Blixen (1885–1962) was born in Rungstedlund, Denmark. She rebelled against bourgeois Danish society and studied English at Oxford and art in Paris and Rome. She married her cousin and with him set up a coffee plantation in Kenya, which she continued to manage after their divorce. After her return to Denmark in 1931 she wrote the bestseller *Out of Africa*.

KAMANTE

from *Out of Africa*

In Kamante's mouth now it [the word 'Msabu'] was a cry for help, but also a word of warning, such as a loyal friend might give you, to stop you in a proceeding unworthy of you. I thought of it with hope afterwards. I had ambition as a doctor, and I was sorry to have put on the poultice too hot, but I was glad all the same, for this was the first glimpse of an understanding between the wild child and myself. The stark sufferer, who expected nothing but suffering, did not expect it from me.

As far as my doctoring of him went, things did not, however, look hopeful. For a long time I kept on washing and bandaging his leg, but the disease was beyond me. From time to time he would grow a little better, and then the sores would break out in new places. In the end I made up my mind to take him to the hospital of the Scotch Mission.

This decision of mine for once was sufficiently fatal, and had in it enough possibilities, to make an impression on Kamante – he did not want to go. He was prevented by his career and his philosophy from protesting much against anything, but when I drove him to the Mission, and delivered him there in the long hospital building, in surroundings entirely foreign and mysterious to him, he trembled.

I had the Church of Scotland Mission as a neighbour twelve miles to the north-west, five hundred feet higher than the farm; and the French Roman Catholic Mission ten miles to the east, on the flatter land, and five hundred feet lower. I did not sympathise with the Missions, but personally I was on friendly terms with them both, and regretted that between themselves they should live in a state of hostility.

The French Fathers were my best friends. I used to ride over with Farah, to hear Mass with them on Sunday morning, partly in order to speak French again, and partly because it was a lovely ride to the Mission. For a long way the road ran through the Forest Department's old wattle plantation, and the virile fresh pinaceous scent of the wattle-trees was sweet and cheering in the mornings.

It was an extraordinary thing to see how the Church of Rome was carrying her atmosphere with her wherever she went. The Fathers had planned and built their church themselves, with the assistance of their Native congregation, and they were with reason very proud of it. There was here a fine big grey church with a bell-tower on it; it was laid out on a broad courtyard, above terraces and stairs, in the midst of their coffee plantation, which was the oldest in the colony and very skilfully run. On the two other sides of the court were the arcaded refectory and the convent buildings, with the school and the mill down by the river, and to get into the drive up to the church you had to ride over an arched bridge. It was all built in grey stone, and as you came riding down upon it, it looked neat and impressive in the landscape, and might have been lying in a southern canton of Switzerland, or in the north of Italy.

The friendly Fathers lay in wait for me at the church door, when Mass was over, to invite me to *un petit verre de vin*, across the courtyard in the roomy and cool refectory; there it was wonderful to hear how they knew of everything that was going on in the colony, even to the remotest corners of it. They would also, under the disguise of a sweet and benevolent conversation, draw from you any sort of news that you might possibly have in you, like a small lively group of brown, furry bees – for they all grew long, thick beards – hanging on to a flower for its store of honey. But while they were so interested in the life of the colony, they were all the time in their own French way exiles, patient and cheerful obeisants to some higher orders of a mysterious nature. If it had not been for the unknown authority that kept them in the place, you felt they would not be there, neither would the church of grey stone with the tall bell-tower, nor the arcades, the school or any other part of their neat plantation and mission station. For when the word of relief had been given, all of these would leave the affairs of the colony to themselves and take a bee-line back to Paris.

Farah, who had been holding the two ponies while I had been to church, and to the refectory, on the way back to the farm would notice my cheerful spirits – he was himself a pious Mohammedan and did not touch alcohol, but he took the Mass and the wine as co-ordinant rites of my religion.

The French Fathers sometimes rode on their motor-bicycles to the farm and lunched there, they quoted the fables of La Fontaine to me, and gave me good advice on my coffee plantation.

The Scotch Mission I did not know so well. There was a splendid view, from up there, over all the surrounding Kikuyu country, but all the same the mission station gave me an impression of blindness, as if it could see nothing itself. The Church of Scotland was working hard to put the Natives into European clothes, which, I thought, did them no good from any point of view. But they had a very good hospital at the Mission, and at the time when I was there, it was in charge of a philanthropic, clever head-doctor, Dr Arthur. They saved the life of many of the people from the farm.

At the Scotch Mission they kept Kamante for three months. During that time I saw him once. I came riding past the Mission on my way to the Kikuyu railway station, and the road here for a while runs along the hospital grounds. I caught sight of Kamante in the grounds, he was standing by himself at a little distance from the groups of other convalescents. By this time he was already so much better that he could run. When he saw me he came up to the fence and ran with me as long as it was following the road. He trotted along, on his side of the fence, like a foal in a paddock when you pass it on horseback, and kept his eyes on my pony, but he did not say a word. At the corner of the hospital grounds he had to stop, and when as I rode on, I looked back, I saw him standing stock still, with his head up in the air, and staring after me, in the exact manner of a foal when you ride away from it. I waved my hand to him a couple of times, the first time he did not react at all, then suddenly his arm went straight up like a pump-spear, but he did not do it more than once.

Kamante came back to my house on the morning of Easter Sunday, and handed me a letter from the hospital people who declared that he was much better and that they thought him cured for good. He must have known something of its contents for he watched my face attentively while I was reading it, but he did not want to discuss it, he had greater things in his mind. Kamante always carried himself with much collected or re-strained dignity, but this time he shone with repressed triumph as well.

All Natives have a strong sense for dramatic effects. Kamante had carefully tied old bandages round his legs all the way up to the knee, to arrange a surprise for me. It was clear that he saw the vital importance of the moment, not in his own good luck, but, unselfishly, in the pleasure that he was to give me. He probably remembered the times when he had seen me all upset by the continual failure of my cures with him, and he knew that the result of the hospital's treatment was an astounding thing. As slowly, slowly, he unwound the bandages from his knee to his heel there appeared, underneath them, a pair of whole smooth legs, only slightly marked by grey scars.

When Kamante had thoroughly, and in his calm grand manner, enjoyed my astonishment and pleasure, he again renewed the impression by stating that he was now a Christian. 'I am like you,' he said. He added that he thought that I might give him a rupee because Christ had risen on this same day.

He went away to call on his own people. His mother was a widow, and lived a long way away on the farm. From what I heard from her later I believe that he did upon this day make a digression from his habit and unloaded his heart to her of the impressions of strange people and ways that he had received at the hospital. But after his visit to his mother's hut, he came back to my house as if he took it for granted that now he belonged there. He was then in my service from this time till the time that I left the country – for about twelve years.

Kamante when I first met him looked as if he were six years old, but he had a brother who looked about eight, and both brothers agreed that Kamante was the elder of them, so I suppose he must have been set back in growth by his long illness; he was probably then nine years old. He grew up now, but he always made the impression of being a dwarf, or in some way deformed, although you could not put your finger on the precise spot that made him look so. His angular face was rounded with time, he walked and moved easily, and I myself did not think him bad-looking, but I may have looked upon him with something of a creator's eyes. His legs remained forever as thin as sticks. A fantastic figure he always was, half of fun and half of diabolism; with a very slight alteration, he might have sat and stared down, on the top of the Cathedral of Notre Dame in Paris. He had in him something bright and live; in a painting he would have made a spot of unusually intense colouring; with this he gave a stroke of picturesqueness to my household. He was never quite right in the head, or at least he was always what, in a white person, you would have called highly eccentric.

He was a thoughtful person. Perhaps the long years of suffering that he had lived through, had developed in him a tendency to reflect upon things, and to draw his own conclusions from everything he saw. He was all his life, in his own way, an isolated figure. Even when he did the same things as other people he would do them in a different way.

I had an evening school for the people of the farm, with a Native schoolmaster to teach them. I got my schoolmasters from one of the Missions, and in my time I have had all three – Roman Catholic, Church of England and Church of Scotland schoolmasters. For the Native education of the country is run rigorously on religious lines; so far as I know, there are no other books translated into Swahili than the Bible and the hymnbooks. I myself, during all my time in Africa, was planning to translate Æsop's fables, for the benefit of the Natives, but I never found time to carry my plan through. Still, such as it was, my school was to me a favourite place on the farm, the centre of our spiritual life, and I spent many pleasant evening hours in the long old storehouse of corrugated iron in which it was kept.

Kamante would then come with me, but he would not join the children on the school benches, he would stand a little away from them, as if consciously closing his ears to the learning, and exulting in the simplicity of those who consented to be taken in, and to listen. But in the privacy of my kitchen, I have seen him copying from memory, very slowly and preposterously, those same letters and figures that he had observed on the blackboard in the school. I do not think that he could have come in with other people if he had wanted to; early in his life something in him had been twisted or locked, and now it was, so to say, to him the normal thing to be out of the normal. He was aware of this separateness of his, himself, with the arrogant greatness of soul of the real dwarf, who, when he finds himself at a difference with the whole world, holds the world to be crooked.

Kamante was shrewd in money matters, he spent little, and did a number of wise deals with the other Kikuyu in goats, he married at an early age, and marriage in the Kikuyu world is an expensive undertaking. At the same time I have heard him philosophising, soundly and originally, upon the worthlessness of money. He stood in a peculiar relation to existence on the whole; he mastered it, but he had no high opinion of it.

He had no gift whatever for admiration. He might acknowledge, and think well of the wisdom of animals, but there was, during all the time that I knew him, only one human being of whose good sense I heard him speak approvingly; it was a young Somali woman who some years later came to live on the farm. He had a little mocking laughter, of which he made use in all circumstances, but chiefly towards any self-confidence or grandiloquence in other people. All Natives have in them a strong strain of malice, a shrill delight in things going wrong, which in itself is hurting and revolting to Europeans. Kamante brought this characteristic to a rare perfection, even to a special self-irony, that made him take pleasure in his own disappointments and disasters, nearly exactly as in those of other people.

I have met with the same kind of mentality in the old Native women who have been roasted over many fires, who have mixed blood with Fate, and recognise her irony, wherever they meet it, with sympathy, as if it were that of a sister. On the farm I used to let my houseboys deal out snuff – *tombacco* the Natives say – to the old women on Sunday mornings, while I myself was still in bed. On this account I had a queer lot of customers round my house on Sundays, like a very old, rumpled, bald and bony poultry yard; and their low cackling – for the Natives will very rarely speak up loudly – made its way through the open windows of my bedroom. On one particular Sunday morning, the gentle lively flow of Kikuyu communications suddenly rose to ripples and cascades of mirth; some highly humorous incident was taking place out there, and I called in Farah to tell me about it. Farah did not like to tell me, for the matter was that he had forgotten to buy snuff, so that today the old women had come a long way, as they say themselves, *boori* – for nothing. This happening was later on a source of amusement to the old Kikuyu women. Sometimes, when I met one of them on a path in the maizefield, she would stand still in front of me, poke a crooked bony finger at me, and, with her old dark face dissolving into laughter, so that all the wrinkles of it were drawn and folded together as by one single secret string being pulled, she would remind me of the Sunday when she, and her sisters in the snuff, had walked and walked up to my house, only to find that I had forgotten to get it, and that there was not a grain there – Ha ha Msabu!

The white people often say of the Kikuyu that they know nothing of gratitude. Kamante in any case was not ungrateful, he even gave words to his feeling of an obligation. A number of times, many years after our first meeting, he went out of his way to do me a service for which I had not asked him, and when I questioned him why he had done it, he said that if it had not been for me he should have been dead a long time ago. He showed his gratitude in another manner as well, in a particular kind of benevolent, helpful or perhaps the right word is, forbearing, attitude towards me. It may be that he kept in mind that he and I were of the same religion. In a world of fools, I was, I think, to him one of the greater fools. From the day when he came into my service and attached his fate to mine, I felt his watchful penetrating eyes on me, and my whole *modus vivendi* subject to clear unbiased criticism; I believe that from the beginning he looked upon the trouble that I had taken to get him cured as upon a piece of hopeless eccentricity. But he showed me all the time great interest and sympathy, and he laid himself out to guide my great ignorance. On some occasions I found that he had given time and thought to the problem, and that he meant to prepare and illustrate his instructions, in order that they should be easier for me to understand.

Kamante began his life in my house as a dog-toto, later he became a medical assistant to me. There I found out what good hands he had, although you would not have thought so from the look of them, and I sent him into the kitchen to be a cook's boy, a *marmiton*, under my old cook Esa, who was murdered. After Esa's death he succeeded him, and he was now my chef all the time that he was with me.

Natives have usually very little feeling for animals, but Kamante differed from type here, as in other things: he was an authoritative dog-boy, and he identified himself with the dogs, and would come and communicate to me what they wished, or missed, or generally thought of things. He kept the dogs free of fleas, which are a pest in Africa, and many times in the middle of the night, he and I, called by the howls of the dogs, have, by the light of a hurricane lamp, picked off them, one by one, the murderous big ants, the *Siafu*, which march alone and eat up everything on their way.

He must also have used his eyes at the time when he had been in the mission hospital – even if it had been as was ever the case with him, without the slightest reverence or prepossession – for he was a thoughtful, inventive doctor's assistant. After he had left this office, he would at times appear from the kitchen to interfere in a case of sickness, and give me very sound advice.

But as a chef he was a different thing, and precluded classification. Nature had here taken a leap and cut away from the order of precedence of faculties and talents; the thing now became mystic and inexplicable, as ever where you are dealing with genius. In the kitchen, in the culinary world, Kamante had all the attributes of genius, even to that doom of genius – the individual's powerlessness in the face of his own powers. If Kamante had been born in Europe, and had fallen into the hands of a clever teacher, he might have become famous, and would have cut a droll figure in history. And out here in Africa he made himself a name, his attitude to his art was that of a master.

I was much interested in cookery myself, and on my first visit back to Europe, I took lessons from a French chef at a celebrated restaurant, because I thought it would be an amusing thing to be able to make good foo in Africa. The chef, Monsieur Perrochet, at that time made me an offer to come in with him in his business of the restaurant, for the sake of my devotion to the art. Now when I found Kamante at hand, as a familiar spirit to cook with, this devotion again took hold of me. There was to me a great perspective in our working together. Nothing, I thought, could be more mysterious than this natural instinct in a Savage for our culinary art. It made me take another view of our civilisation; after all it might be in some way divine and predestinated. I felt like the man who regained his faith in God because a phrenologist showed him the seat in the human brain of theological eloquence: if the existence of theological eloquence could be proved, the existence of theology itself was proved with it, and, in the end, God's existence.

Kamante, in all cooking matters, had a surprising manual adroitness. The great tricks and *tours de force* of the kitchen were child's play to his dark crooked hands; they knew on their own everything about omelettes, vol-au-vents, sauces, and mayonnaises. He had a special gift for making things light, as in the legend the infant Christ forms birds out of clay and tells them to fly. He scorned all complicated tools, as if impatient of too much independence in them, and when I gave him a machine for beating eggs he set it aside to rust, and beat whites of egg with a weeding knife that I had had to weed the lawn with, and his whites of eggs towered up like light clouds. As a cook he had a penetrating, inspired eye, and would pick out the fattest chicken out of a whole poultry yard, and he gravely weighed an egg in his hand, and knew when it had been laid. He thought out schemes for improvement of my table, and by some means of communication, from a friend who was working for a doctor far away in the country, he got me seed of a really excellent sort of lettuce, such as I had myself for many years looked for in vain.

He had a great memory for recipes. He could not read, and he knew no English so that cookery-books were of no use to him, but he must have held all that he was ever taught stored up in his ungraceful head, according to some systematisation of his own, which I should never know. He had named the dishes after some event which had taken place on the day they had been shown to him, and he spoke of the sauce of the lightning that struck the tree, and of the sauce of the grey horse that died. But he did not confound any two of these things. There was only one point that I tried to impress upon him without any success, that was the order of the courses within a meal. It became necessary to me, when I had guests for dinner, to draw up for my chef, as if it were a pictorial menu: first a soup-plate, then a fish, then a partridge, or an artichoke. I did not quite believe this short-coming in him to be due to a faulty memory, but he did, I think, in his own heart, maintain that there is a limit to everything, and that upon anything so completely immaterial, he would not waste his time.

It is a moving thing to work together with a demon. Nominally the kitchen was mine, but in the course of our co-operations, I felt not only the kitchen, but the whole world in which we were co-operating, pass over into Kamante's hands. For here he understood to perfection what I wished of him, and sometimes he carried out my wishes even before I had told him of them; but as to me I could not make clear to myself how or indeed why he worked as he did. It seemed to me a strange thing that anyone could be so great in an art of which he did not understand the real meaning, and for which he felt nothing but contempt.

Kamante could have no idea as to how a dish of ours ought to taste, and he was, in spite of his conversion, and his connection with civilisation, at heart an arrant Kikuyu, rooted in the traditions of his tribe and in his faith in them, as in the only way of living worthy of a human being. He did at times taste the food that he cooked, but then with a distrustful face, like a witch who takes a sip out of her cauldron. He stuck to the maize cobs of his fathers. Here even his intelligence sometimes failed him, and he came and offered me a Kikuyu delicacy – a roasted sweet potato or a lump of sheep's fat – as even a civilised dog, that has lived for a long time with people, will place a bone on the floor before you, as a present. In his heart he did, I feel, all the time, look upon the trouble that we give ourselves about our food, as upon a lunacy. I sometimes tried to extract from him his views upon these things, but although he spoke with great frankness on many subjects, on others he was very close, so that we worked side by side in the kitchen, leaving one another's ideas on the importance of cooking, alone.

I sent Kamante into the Muthaiga Club to learn, and to the cooks of my friends in Nairobi, when I had had a new good dish in their house, and by the time that he had served his apprenticeship, my own house became famous in the colony for its table. This was a great pleasure to me. I longed to have an audience for my art, and I was glad when my friends came out to dine with me; but Kamante cared for the praise of no one. All the same he remembered the individual taste of those of my friends who came most often to the farm. 'I shall cook the fish in white wine for Bwana Berkeley Cole,' he said, gravely, as if he were speaking of a demented person. 'He sends you out white wine himself to cook fish in.' To get the opinion of an authority, I asked my old friend Mr Charles Bulpett of Nairobi, out to dine with me. Mr Bulpett was a great traveller of the former generation, themselves a generation away from Phineas Fogg; he had been all over the world and had tasted everywhere the best it had to offer, and he had not cared to secure his future so long as he could enjoy the present moment. The books about sport and mountaineering, of fifty years ago, tell of his exploits as an athlete, and of his mountain climbings in Switzerland and Mexico, and there is a book of famous bets called *Light Come Light Go*, in which you can read of how for a bet he swam the Thames in evening clothes and a high hat – but later on, and more romantically, he swam the Hellespont like Leander and Lord Byron. I was happy when he came out to the farm for a tête-à-tête dinner; there is a particular happiness in giving a man whom you like very much, good food that you have cooked yourself. In return he gave me his ideas on food, and on many other things in the world, and told me that he had nowhere dined better.

The Prince of Wales did me the great honour to come and dine at the farm, and to compliment me on a Cumberland sauce. This is the only time that I have seen Kamante listening with deep interest when I repeated the praise of his cooking to him, for Natives have very great ideas of kings and like to talk about them. Many months after, he felt a longing to hear it once more, and suddenly asked me, like a French reading-book, 'Did the son of the Sultan like the sauce of the pig? Did he eat it all?'

Kamante showed his good will towards me, outside of the kitchen as well. He wanted to help me, in accordance with his own ideas of the advantages and dangers in life.

One night, after midnight, he suddenly walked into my bedroom with a hurricane lamp in his hand, silent, as if on duty. It must have been only a short time after he first came into my house, for he was very small; he stood by my bedside like a dark bat that had strayed into the room, with very big spreading ears, or like a small African will-o'-the-wisp, with his lamp in his hand. He spoke to me very solemnly, 'Msabu,' he said, 'I think you had better get up.' I sat up in bed bewildered; I thought that if anything serious had happened, it would have been Farah who would have come to fetch me, but when I told Kamante to go away again, he did not move. 'Msabu,' he said again, 'I think that you had better get up. I think that God is coming.' When I heard this, I did get up, and asked him why he thought so. He gravely led me into the dining room which looked west, towards the hills. From the door-windows I now saw a strange phenomenon. There was a big grass-fire going on, out in the hills, and the grass was burning all the way from the hilltop to the plain; when seen from the house it was a nearly vertical line. It did indeed look as if some gigantic figure was moving and coming towards us. I stood for some time and looked at it, with Kamante watching by my side, then I began to explain the thing to him. I meant to quiet him, for I thought that he had been terribly frightened. But the explanation did not seem to make much impression on him one way or the other; he clearly took his mission to have been fulfilled when he had called me. 'Well yes,' he said, 'it may be so. But I thought that you had better get up in case it was God coming.'

ELAINE DUNDY

Elaine Dundy was born and raised in New York. She worked as an actress in Paris and London where she met her husband, Kenneth Tynan. After the birth of her first child, she turned to writing. Her first novel, *The Dud Avocado* (1958), based on the year she spent in Paris, was an immediate best-seller on both sides of the Atlantic. Two more novels and two plays followed. In 1964, divorced from Tynan, she returned to America where she wrote extensively for magazines before moving to Massachusetts where she directed and acted. She is the author of several biographies, including *Elvis and Gladys* (1985). Elaine Dundy lives in Los Angeles. Her autobiography, *Life Itself*, will be published by Virago in 2000.

In *The Dud Avocado*, Sally Jay Gorce is a woman with a mission. It's the 1950s, she's young, she's in Paris, she's dyed her hair pink, she's wearing an evening dress at eleven o'clock in the morning and she's seldom had more fun.

DRIFTING INTO THE STREET LIT WITH LOVE

from *The Dud Avocado*

It was a hot, peaceful, optimistic sort of day in September. It was around eleven in the morning, I remember, and I was drifting down the Boulevard St. Michel, thoughts rising in my head like little puffs of smoke, when suddenly a voice bellowed into my ear: 'Sally Jay Gorce! What the hell? Well, for Christ's sake, can this really be our own little Sally Jay Gorce?' I felt a hand ruffling my hair and I swung around, furious at being so rudely awakened.

Who should be standing there in front of me, in what I immediately spotted as the Left Bank uniform of the day, dark wool shirt and a pair of old Army suntans, but my old friend Larry Keevil. He was staring down at me with some alarm.

I said hello to him and added that he had frightened me, to cover any bad-tempered expression that might have been lingering on my face, but he just kept on staring dumbly at me.

'What *have* you been up to since . . . since . . . when the hell *was* it that I last saw you?' he asked finally.

Curiously enough I remembered exactly.

'It was just a week after I got here. The middle of June.'

He kept on looking at me, or rather he kept on looking over me in that surprised way, and then he shook his head and said, 'Christ, Gorce, can it only be three short months?' Then he grinned. 'You've really flung yourself into this, haven't you?'

In a way it was exactly what I had been thinking, too, and I was on the point of saying, 'Into what?', very innocently, you know, so that he could tell me how different I was, how much I'd changed and so forth, but all at once something stopped me. I knew I would have died rather than hear his reply.

So instead I said, 'Ah well, don't we all?' which was my stock phrase when I couldn't think of anything else to say. There was a pause and then he asked me how I was and I said fine how was *he*, and he said fine, and I asked him what he was doing, and he said it would take too long to tell.

It was then we both noticed we were standing right across the street from the Café Dupont, the one near the Sorbonne.

'Shall we have a quick drink?' I heard him ask, needlessly, for I was already halfway across the street in that direction.

The café was very crowded and the only place we could find was on the very edge of the pavement. We just managed to squeeze under the shade of the awning. A waiter came and took our order. Larry leant back into the hum and buzz and brouhaha and smiled lazily. Suddenly, without quite knowing why, I found I was very glad to have run into him. And this was odd, because two Americans re-encountering each other after a certain time in a foreign land are supposed to clamber up their nearest lamp-posts and wait tremblingly for it all to blow over. Especially me. I'd made a vow when I got over here never to *speak* to anyone I'd ever known before. Yet here we were, two Americans who hadn't really seen each other for years; here was someone from 'home' who knew me *when*, if you like, and, instead of shambling back into the bushes like a startled rhino, I was absolutely thrilled at the whole idea.

'I like it here, don't you?' said Larry, indicating the café with a turn of his head.

I had to admit I'd never been there before.

He smiled quizzically. 'You should come more often,' he said. 'It's practically the only non-tourist trap to survive on the Left Bank. It's *real*,' he added.

Real, I thought ... whatever that meant. I looked at the Sorbonne students surging around us, the tables fairly rocking under their pounding fists and thumping elbows. The whole vast panoramic carpet seemed to be woven out of old boots, checkered wool and wild, fuzzy hair. I don't suppose there is anything on earth to compare with a French student café in the late morning. You couldn't possibly reproduce the same numbers, noise, and intensity anywhere else without producing a riot as well. It really was the most colourful café I'd ever been in. As a matter of fact, the most *coloured* too; there was an especially large number of Singalese, Arab and African students, along with those from every other country.

I suppose Larry's 'reality' in this case was based on the café's internationality. But perhaps all cafés near a leading University have that authentic international atmosphere. At the table closest to us sat an ordinary-looking young girl with lank yellow hair and a grey-haired bespectacled middle-aged man. They had been conversing fiercely but quietly for some time now in a language I was not even able to *identify*.

All at once I knew that I liked this place, too.

Jammed in on all sides, with the goodish Tower of Babel working itself up to a frenzy around me, I felt safe and anonymous and, most of all, thankful we were going to be spared those devastating and shattering revelations one was always being treated to at the more English-speaking cafés like the Flore.

And, as I said, I was very glad to have run into Larry.

We talked a little about the various cafés and he explained carefully to me which were the tourist traps and which weren't. Glancing down at my Pernod, I discovered to my astonishment that I'd already finished it. Time was whizzing past.

I felt terribly excited.

'White smoke,' said Larry clicking his tongue disapprovingly at my second Pernod. His hand twirled around the stem of his own virtuous glass of St. Raphael. 'You keep that up,' he said, tapping my glass, 'and it'll blow your head off – which may be a good thing at that. Why pink?' he asked, studying my new coiffure carefully. 'Why not green?'

As a matter of fact I'd had my hair dyed a marvellous shade of pale red so popular with Parisian tarts that season. It was the first direct remark he made about the New Me and it was hardly encouraging.

Slowly his eyes left my hair and travelled downwards. This time he really took in my outfit and then that Look that I'm always encountering; that special one composed in equal parts of amusement, astonishment and horror came over his face.

I am not a moron and I can generally guess what causes this look. The trouble is, it's always something different.

I squirmed uncomfortably, feeling his eyes bearing down on my bare shoulders and breasts.

'What the hell are you doing in the middle of the morning with an *evening* dress on?' he asked me finally.

'Sorry about that,' I said quickly, 'but it's all I've got to wear. My laundry hasn't come back yet.'

He nodded, fascinated.

'I thought if I wore this red leather belt with it people wouldn't actually notice. Especially since it's such a warm day. I mean these teintureries make it so difficult for you to get your laundry to them in the first place, don't they, closing up like that from noon till three? I mean, my gosh, it's the only time I'm up and around over here – don't you think?'

'Oh sure, *sure*,' said Larry, and murmured, 'Jesus' under his breath. Then he smiled forgivingly. 'Ah well, you're young, you're new, you'll learn, Gorce.' A wise nod of the head. 'I know your type all right.'

'My type?' I wondered. 'My type of what?'

'Of tourist, of course.'

I gasped and then smiled cunningly to myself. Tourist indeed! Ho-ho! That was the last thing I could be called – did he but know.

'Tell me about this,' I said. 'You seem to have tourists on the brain.'

He crossed his legs and pulled out of his shirt-pocket a crumpled pack of cigarettes as du pays as possible – sort of Gauloises Nothings – offered one to me, took one himself, lit them both and then settled back with pleasure. This was obviously one of his favourite subjects.

'Basically,' he began, 'the tourist can be divided into two categories. The Organised – the Disorganised. Under the Organised you find two distinct types: first, the Eager-Beaver-Culture-Vulture with the list ten yards long, who *just* manages to get it all crossed off before she collapses of aesthetic indigestion each night and has to be carried back to her hotel; and second, the cool suave Sophisticate who comes gliding over gracefully, calmly, and indifferently. But don't be fooled by the indifference. This babe is determined to maintain her incorruptible standards of cleanliness and efficiency if the entire staff of her hotel dies trying. She belongs to the take-your-own-toilet-paper set. Stuffs her suitcases full of nylon, Kleenex, soapflakes, and D.D.T. bombs. Immediately learns the rules of the country. (I mean what time the shops open and close, and how much to tip the waiter.) Can pack for a weekend in a small jewel-case and a large handbag and still have enough room for her own soap and washrag. Finds the hairdresser who speaks English, the restaurant who knows how she likes her steak, and the first foreign word she makes absolutely sure of pronouncing correctly is the one for drugstore. After that she's all set and the world is her ashtray. If she's got enough money she's got no trouble at all. On the whole, I rather like her.'

So far so good, I told myself. They neither one had the slightest, smallest, remotest connection with me. Then a thought caught me sharply.

'And the Disorganised?' I asked rather nervously.

'The Disorganised?' He considered me carefully for a moment, narrowing his eyes.

'Your cigarette's gone out,' he said finally. 'You have to *smoke* this kind, you know, they won't smoke themselves.' He lit it for me again and blew out the match without once taking his eyes off my décolletage, which was slipping quite badly. I gave it a tug and he resumed the discourse.

'Yes. The Disorganised. They got split into two groups as well. First of all the Sly One. The idea is to see Europe casually, you know, sort of vaguely, out of the corner of the eye. All Baedekers and Michelins and museum catalogues immediately discarded as too boring and too corny. Who wants to see a pile of old stones anyway? The general "feel" of the country is what she's after. It's even a struggle to get her to look at a map of the city she's in so she'll know where the hell she is, and actually it's a useless one since this type is constitutionally incapable of reading a map and has no sense of direction to begin with. But, as I say, she's the sly one – the "Oh, look, that's the Louvre over there, isn't it? I think I'll drop in for a second. I'm rather hot. We'd better get out of the sun anyway…" or "Tuileries did you say? That sure strikes a bell. Aren't those flowers pretty over there? Now haven't I heard something about it in connection with the – what was it – French Revolution? Oh yes, *of course* that's it. Thank you, hon."'

I laughed – a jolly laugh – to show I was with him.

'The funny thing,' he continued, 'is, scratch the sly one and out comes the *real* fanatic, and what begins with "Gosh, I can never remember whether Romanesque was *before* or *after* Gothic" leads to secret pamphlet-readings and stained-glass studyings, and ends up in wild aesthetic discussions of the relative values of the two towers at Chartres. Then all restraint is thrown to the wind and anything really *old* enough is greeted with animal cries of anguish at its beauty. In the final stage small discriminating lists appear about her person – but they only contain, you may be damn sure, the good, the pure and the truly worthwhile.'

Larry paused, took a small, discriminating sip of his St. Raphael, and puffed happily away at his cigarette.

I swallowed the last of my Pernod, folded my arms seductively on the sticky table and took a long pull on my own French cigarette. It had gone out, of course. I hid it from Larry but he hadn't noticed. He was lost in reverie.

Blushingly I recalled a night not so long before when I had suddenly fallen in love with the Place de Furstenberg in the moonlight. I had actually – Oh Lord – I had *actually* kissed one of the stones at the fountain, I remembered, flung my shoes off, and executed a crazy drunken dance.

The September sun was blazing down on us and the second Pernod was beginning to have a pleasant soporific effect on me. A couple of street arabs came up and listlessly began to try selling us silver jewellery and rugs. After a while they drifted away. I began studying Larry closely. The mat of auburn hair curling to his skull, the grey-green eyes now so blank and far away, the delicate scar running down the pale skin of his forehead, the well-shaped nose covered with a faint spray of freckles, and his large mouth so gently curved, all contributed to give his face, especially in repose, a look of sappy sweetness that was sharply at odds with – and yet at the same time enhanced – his tough, wise-guy manner. Maybe because I had been out very late the night before and was not able to put up my usual resistance, but it seemed to me, sitting there with the sound of his voice dying in my ears, that I could fall in love with him.

And then, as unexpected as a hidden step, I felt myself actually *stumble* and *fall*. And there it was, I *was* in love with him! As simple as that.

He was the first real person I'd ever been in love with. I couldn't get over it. What I was trying to figure out was why I had never been in love with him *before*. I mean I'd had plenty of chance to. I'd seen him almost daily that summer in Maine two years ago when we were both in a Summer Stock company. I had decided to be an actress at the time. Even though we were about the same age, he was already a full-fledged Equity member and I had been a mere apprentice. He was always rather nice to me in his insolent way, but there was also, I now remembered with a passing pang, an utterly ravishing girl, a model, the absolute epitome of glamour, called Lila. She used to come up at weekends to see him.

Then I heard from someone that he'd quit college the next winter and gone abroad to become a genius. I'd met him again when I first landed in Paris. He'd been very nice, bought me a drink, taken down my telephone number and never called me.

You're a dead duck now, I told myself, as I relaxed back into my coma. You're gone. I looked at him smiling idly. I tried to imagine what was going on in his mind. I gave up and I thought of his tourists.

I had no trouble imagining the girl with all the Kleenex and Tampax or whatever. Cool, blonde and slender, she was only too easy to picture, but the thought of all that unruffled poise somehow had the opposite effect on my own – so I drove her away and began concentrating on the last one. What did he call her? The sly one. Here, happily, in my pleasantly drowsy state, I was able to dress up a little grey furry mouse with tail and whiskers in a black bombazine coat and bonnet. She was clutching a small discriminating list in her white-gloved claws and uttering animal squeals of anguish at the beauty of – what? The Crazy Horse Saloon? Oh dear, I really was too ignorant and too lazy to know what was on that list . . . something old . . . those Caves, I thought idly, the word conjuring up no picture whatever. Those Caves *anyway*, I persevered, in . . . Southern France? No, Spain: someplace with an A. Ha! Altamira, that's it. Yes, the Caves, I decided, framing the mouse in the doorway, or rather Caveway. Yes. They're very old . . . very, very old.

'The last type,' said Larry, his voice suddenly snapping me out of my trance, his green eyes fixing me with a significant glare that made my heart lurch, 'the last type is the Wild Cat. The I-am-a-fugitive-from-the-Convent-of-the-Sacred-Heart. Not that it's ever really the case. Just seems so from the violence of the reaction. Anyhow it's her first time free and her first time across and, by golly, she goes native in a way the natives never had the stamina to go. Some people think it's those stand-up toilets they have here – you know, the ones with the iron footprints you're supposed to straddle. After the shock of that kind of plumbing something snaps in the American girl and she's off. The desire to bathe somehow gets lost. The hell with all that, she figures. Then weird haircuts, weird hair-colours, weird clothes. Then comes drink and down, down, down. Dancing in the streets all night, braying at the moon, and waking up in a different bed each morning. Yep,' he polished off his St. Raphael with a judicious smack of his lips, 'that's the lot. Hmm,' a long studying glance, 'now *you*, I'd say, you are going to be a combination of the last two types.'

'Why you utter bastard,' I gasped. 'That's a dirty lie,' I heard myself saying, the phrase dug up from heaven knows what depths of my childhood. Then in an effort to regain my dignity: '*Really*, of all the stupefyingly inaccurate accusations. It's a pretty safe bet I bathe about sixty times as often as *you* . . .' He burst out laughing. To accuse the American male of not bathing in Paris is merely to flatter him.

The Pernod was having quite a different effect on me now. I was wide-awake, and sputtering, and so angry I could almost feel the steam rising from my shoulders.

He put his hand over mine, the one with the dead cigarette crumbled in it, and gave me a wonderful smile. 'Easy, child, easy. I'm only teasing you. Don't think I *disapprove* for Christ's sake. Live it up, I say. Don't say no to life, Gorce, you're only young once.'

We were on last name terms, Keevil and I.

'I'm finding your Grand Old Man just as hard to take as your Scientific Researcher,' I said as nastily as I could, and withdrew my hand.

'I like you, Gorce,' he said. 'I mean it. Had my eye on you that summer. High-spirited.' He laughed but at the same time I knew by the way his motor had started up (you could actually *see* the engine chugging through his body) and the way he was vaguely looking around for a waiter, that the interview, as far as he was concerned, was over. And he was on his way.

'Please order me another Pernod,' I said quickly.

Raised eyebrows.

'Oh, for goodness sake, I'm all right. And have one yourself. Please. Let me pay for this round.' He was the sort of person whose financial circumstances were impossible to guess at, and the quick cynical look he gave me made me start to apologise, but as he didn't refuse I went on. 'Please. I simply must talk to you. I'm in the most awful mess,' and I sighed and buried my head in my hands, stalling for time.

He signalled the waiter and ordered another round.

'OK,' he said. 'Let's have it. What's it all about?'

'Give me a minute,' I pleaded desperately. 'I can't just jump in like that.' My thoughts were chasing each other all over the place, but nothing seemed to sort itself out. Advice, I thought. Ask his advice. On love? Finance? Career? Better stick to love, I decided, it's what's on your mind anyway.

And with that my mind went blank.

Only one small irrelevancy finally appeared. 'Why are all your tourists *she*?' I finally asked.

'Because all tourists are she,' he replied promptly.

'No males at all? Don't be silly.'

'Nope. No males at all. The only male tourists – though naturally there are men visitors – you know, men visiting foreign countries,' he explained maddeningly, 'the only male tourists are the ones loping around after their wives. A tourist is a she all right,' he said, finishing it off with a lot of very reminiscent laughter.

'I can see you've made quite a study of them,' I snarled scornfully.

'I get around, Gorce, I get around.'

And you, I told myself, are just one of the mob.

It was no joke being in love with Larry, I could see that now; it really hit me for the first time. The waiter had brought us fresh drinks and was pouring the water into my Pernod, and ordinarily this would have had quite a cheering effect on me – its changing colour usually reminded me of chemistry-sets and magic potions, but now the cloudy green liquid looked merely poisonous and the strong liquorice smell reminded me of nothing so much as a bottle of Old Grandma's Cough Remedy, hold-your-nose-and-have-a-piece-of-chocolate-quickly-afterwards. I found that the previous drinks had turned icy cold and heavy in my stomach. I felt terribly sober and the inside of my mouth tasted sour. I sighed and picked up the chits. 120 francs.

'It's cheap anyway,' I said, giving him the money. I sat staring at the drink, trying to get up enough courage to down it.

'What's eating you, Gorce? Come on, let's have it.'

His words rang out like coins in the emptiness and I suddenly noticed how still everything around us had become. The students had stopped surging and gone to lunch; the Arab vendors were asleep in the sun; and the waiters, even as we watched, stopped waiting and began drifting back to their stations where they came to a standstill – or as near a standstill as they ever got – still rocking gently back and forth on their heels: heart-beats of perpetual motion gently rocking back and forth, their napkins fluttering in the breeze.

The sun shone on: the shade of the shade of the awning vanished in the hot, white, shadowless midday. In that blaze of heat I was loving Paris as never before.

And there sitting opposite me, stretching himself luxuriously in the sun, his eyes lazily examining his half-empty drink, was Larry, the one I loved the best . . . sensationally uninterested.

All at once I sat bolt upright and let out a yelp.

I suddenly remembered what I was doing in that arrondisse-ment in the first place. I had been in fact on my way to the Sorbonne to meet my lover, who was attending an International Students Conference there for his Embassy. And at that very moment, as if I myself had conjured him (though I supposed I must have unconsciously registered him in the corner of my eye) he came striding along the boulevard large as life: Teddy – Alfredo Ourselli Visconti himself, looking suave and Latin and livid.

I glanced at my watch. Wow! I was just an hour too late. Then, stupidly, I tried to hide my head with my hands. It was too late, of course, and the worst of it was he had also caught me trying to hide. Being a Latin, seeing me there with a young and handsome man, he naturally put two and two together and for once in his life arrived at the right answer about me.

In a panic I knew that he must not sit down with us; if he did, he would stay and Larry would go. And that would be that. There wasn't a moment to be lost. Without explanation, I dashed over to the street-corner to intercept him.

'So I've caught you at last, have I?' he said, in that half-serious half-teasing man-of-the-world voice he always reserved for matters of the heart. Whatever guilt I felt vanished in my exasperation.

'We can't all lead a triple life as successfully as you do,' I replied coolly, and saw a really desperate, haggard look come over his face. 'He's an old, old friend,' I added hastily. 'He's brought me news of home. Very important news.'

'I see,' he said stiffly. 'Very well. We must talk of all this tonight. At the Ritz?'

'Yop.' He always brought out the succinct in me.

'Shall we say at eleven o'clock then, as usual?'

'Not later?' He was always up to a half an hour late.

'It may be difficult to get away,' he said, 'but I shall certainly try to be on time if I can.'

He looked so pleased I could have killed him.

If I hadn't been in such a hurry to get back to Larry, I would have told him then and there, as I'd been vaguely planning to do for about a week, how hellishly bored I was with all his sophisticated manœuvres. It was partly out of necessity, of course, having both a wife *and* a mistress, as well as myself, that he jammed and juggled his days and nights with arranged and rearranged rendezvous. But that was not the only reason he always turned up so late. There was another one, as I suspected when he formed the habit of meeting me around eleven at the Ritz bar: it was that he simply refused to do anything in a straightforward way. He felt that his unpunctuality increased his mystery and desirability.

The unfortunate thing was that he had reckoned without my naivety. I was honestly so thrilled at being at the Ritz in the first place that I didn't mind how long I was kept waiting. There were so many marvellous new things to look at and so many marvellous new drinks to experiment with; sazaracs and slings and heaven knows what else, so that at first I never even noticed the passing of time. But then as the novelty wore off and I took to bringing magazines and novels along with me, I noticed how really put out he was when instead of discovering me ceaselessly scanning the horizon for him, he found me deep in *Paris-Match*.

As I hurriedly said goodbye to Teddy, meekly apologising for not meeting him at the Sorbonne, and promising to see him at the Ritz that evening, I had a sinister premonition of how embarrassing an homme fatal could be when his charms are no longer fatale to you.

I turned round to find Larry quietly taking in the scene. When he caught my eye he began grinning from ear to ear. I felt my ankles wobble under me.

'Watch out,' he shouted as I walked towards him, 'you're going to knock over that chair!'

But of course it was too late.

Larry was really enjoying himself now. He laughed and laughed when I returned. 'Gorce, oh Gorce,' he chortled, neighing like a barnyard in uproar, 'if you're his mistress, and I *think* you are, you've skipped a grade, honey.' A waggle of his forefinger. 'That's not for first-year tourists, that's for the second-year ones, you know.'

At this point, I now realise, there were several things I could have done. For instance, I could have nodded sheepishly or good-naturedly, or whatever one does with 'good grace'. I could have said, 'Well, there you have me, I guess,' and he would have said, 'Now never mind, and what was it you wanted to tell me?' and I would have said, 'Nothing, forget it' and he would have replied, 'Well, cheer up, see you around sometime' and he *would* have, I suppose – sometime. Our Paris, after all, was really very small. And I would have at least been spared one of the most embarrassing moments of my life. No honestly, I don't think *anything* has embarrassed me so much since.

It's crazy but I wonder if all the rest of it – and I mean *all* the rest of it – would have happened if our meeting had ended then and there and in that way. Who knows? But, anyway, seeing myself and the affair with Teddy suddenly through Larry's eyes, and realising that whatever I had done, however original I had thought of it as being before, I was only remaining strictly within the tourist pattern, and having Larry *know* this – well, at the time it was too much to bear.

To have an affair with a man, and one's very *first* affair at that, just because he picks you up under rather romantic circumstances on the Champs-Elysées, takes you to the Ritz and things, and above all, because you're impressed with the fact that he has a wife *and* a mistress already, what could be more predictable? Tourist Second-Year Disorganised.

No, dammit, I wasn't going to be stuffed into that category no matter what. Not in Larry's mind anyway.

'Here's my advice to you, and you're old enough to give it to yourself,' Larry was saying sagely. 'Stay away from married men. I mean it, stay away.'

'How *can* you think such things of me? It's not that way at all,' I moaned. 'We love each other. There's no wife in this at all. How *could* you think such a thing of me? There's something much worse though. A crackpot at the Italian Embassy who's always hated Teddy. Do you know what he's done? He's broken into Teddy's flat and burned some important papers so that Teddy got into the most awful trouble and he's been recalled! He has to leave any day now. God knows if he'll ever be able to straighten this out. It's torture. We can never meet except briefly like you saw us now, and in the open, as if there were nothing to it, for fear of getting that man on to *my* trail. Lord knows how he'd use me against Teddy! All I know is that Teddy is going back to Italy and that I'll probably never see him again.' I was getting worked up by then. 'And I love him so much, Larry, I really do. What shall I do?' Lies, from beginning to end.

'You poor kid,' said Larry. He said it so nicely, so sincerely. I was absolutely staggered by the difference in his tone. I was feeling more than a little sorry for myself at this point, but I was also feeling more than a little elated at the way I had cleared myself of the dreaded tourist charge, at the same time getting rid of Teddy so neatly, or at any rate disposing of him in the near future.

'We've been desperate these last months. We try not to see each other but it's no good. I'll . . . I'll die when he goes.' By now I was really moved. My eyelids stung and tears began to roll slowly down my cheeks.

'Poor kid, poor kid,' he kept repeating. How nice Larry was now. Not mocking, not bored, not restless. I looked into his eyes, soft eyes, interested and sympathetic. He gave a short little laugh of encouragement. It stirred me to my roots. I took a long heady swig of Pernod right into the hot molten sun, and brother, that was my undoing.

'Take it easy, take it easy,' he was saying. 'Everything's going to be all right.' He took my hand away from my drink and held it gently in his own. By now I was maybe drunk, I don't know, but in such a state of uncontrolled passion that the mere touch of his hand on mine charged through my body like a thousand volts.

You know how it is. Some people can hack and hack away at you and nothing happens at all and then someone else just touches you lightly on the arm and it happens . . . yes, I mean I came. I mean that's what happened.

I remember looking down at the table and seeing my fingers clinging and curling around his. I remember being quite aware of this but at the same time quite unable to stop myself. Then I put his hand up to my cheek and caressed his knuckles with my mouth. A split second suspended itself into infinity in the air while my heart pounded furiously and I kept kissing and kissing his knuckles. And then it was over.

I jerked my head back sharply. I tried to pull my hand away from his. He held on tightly. His voice was very close to me, mocking and smooth. 'Why you little fraud.' Very softly, very clearly. 'You shabby little fraud. You'll die when he goes, will you? Now how do I know you've been lying?' He was quite simply torturing me.

My eyes dug a hole in the table, unfortunately not large enough to crawl into. 'You *don't* know—' I began but the whole thing was too much for me. There was one moment while I counted the seconds and then I resigned myself. With a sigh I forced myself to look at him and he looked back at me hard and down and through and I yielded up without a struggle my badly kept secret.

'Isn't it awful?' I said, my voice faltering into a miserably insincere little giggle.

He held his head on one side. He was, I could see, over-whelmingly puzzled. And so, in a word, was I. Had playing with fire for so long without getting burned heated me up for this almost spontaneous combustion? Why, why, *why*, was the question burning in his face. As there was no reason that I could figure out, he wasn't going to get an answer. And maybe he didn't really want one anyway. At any rate he let go of my hand. And his motor started up again. The implications of these acts should have made me feel worse but somehow they cooled me down, and I reached around for my tattered cloak of carelessness. I said casually, 'I saw this stinking little Art film last night. All about the simple life on a barge up and down the Seine. How about that? Not a bad idea.' I was really talking to myself. In times of stress when I'm not coming out of things too well the simple life has a tremendous appeal for me. Picking strawberries off a deserted wind-swept coast on the Atlantic ocean when I was seven is an image I frequently and yearningly return to.

We began talking of other things. Although I had been the one to make such a fool of myself I was the calmer. It was Larry who was flapping about, searching for conversation.

At one point I noticed his eyes had found their way back to my bosom again. 'I think that dress needs something or other around the neck, you know,' he was saying helpfully. 'Haven't you got anything?'

'I had a pearl necklace,' I answered, by now really wishing he would go. 'I lost it or something. Anyway it's gone. The hell with it.'

'What a shame. It wasn't real, I hope?' he asked with a sympathy he couldn't feel.

'As a matter of fact it was. Who cares? The hell with it I said.' I was really getting annoyed at the trivial turn in the conversation.

'Oh come now,' he persisted. 'You don't often lose things, do you?'

'All the time,' I said defiantly, wondering how long we were going to toss this around. 'I don't like possessions. I travel light so I can make my getaway.' Bitterly I was thinking that he was going to incorporate this, too, in his tourist research. OK OK. I was it all right. I was practically the prototype. Getting drunk, having affairs, losing money, losing jewellery, losing God knows what. Whoopee, twenty-three skidoo, and Oh you kid!

'You don't give a damn, do you?' he said finally.

'No. I don't.'

A long pause. 'Gorce, I'll tell you something. You know what? You've got to stop all this drifting. You've got brains and looks and talent. Things could really happen to you. What's become of your acting? You weren't bad. You'd be sensational if you could project that off-beat thing that's you – really you. And what are you doing instead? Wasting your time bumming around with a tourist-trap Casanova!'

'Well, but *living* you know...' I said warily, at the same time trying to project that off-beat thing, whatever it was.

'Oh no. Not that please,' he cut me off briskly. 'Look, I tell you what. I'm going to direct a programme of one-act plays at the American Theatre. You know, that little one around Denfert-

Rochereau they keep trying to get started. It's just possible that you might be right for something. You might fit into the Saroyan play. We're playing safe and starting off with the usual stuff: Saroyan, Shaw, Tennessee Williams—'

'Which ones?' I asked breathlessly.

'Haven't decided yet. Anyway, come over there sometime. We'll be casting soon.'

Then, having made this decision and having wasted enough of his precious time that should no doubt have been spent geniusing, he shot to his feet and faced the cluster of waiters with such imminent departure in his manner that two of them came running.

But I didn't care any more. The whole flock of them could have come. The Pernods melted in my stomach in one glorious swooshing splash and all was gaiety and song and dance.

Larry paid the bill and stood up, looking down at me and grinning.

'Gosh, I'd love to act again,' I said. 'I really would. I'm dying to – but when?'

'As soon as you get your laundry back,' he said, and left.

Larry had gone. I drifted into the street lit with love and began turning imaginary handsprings. I hadn't the faintest idea where I was going. I found myself in front of the Métro Odéon and began playing with the metro map, pushing the buttons en toutes directions. Porte des Lilas-Châtelet, Mairie d'Issy-Porte de la Chapelle, Vincennes-Neuilly . . . how beautiful they sounded. 'To the end of the line,' I murmured. A virtuous thought crossed my mind that in this new life dedicated to Art I should take the metro, not taxis. But I found I couldn't bear to go underground into the dark. Not on a day like that.

A taxi came by and I hailed it, suddenly knowing where I had to go. I told him to go directly to the American Library in Saint-Germain. There I would get out the Collected Works of Tennessee Williams and William Saroyan. Then I would go and see about my laundry. As if to emphasise the miracle of the day the taxi-driver actually conceded the quartier to be in his route.

With many a 'bon, bon, ça va' to commemorate our fellow-feelings we drove off. Upon arrival I glanced at my watch and saw that it was one o'clock. Everything would be closed until three. The little hotel to which I had recently moved was on the Rue Jules Chaplain in Montparnasse, and so was the teinturerie where my laundry was marking time. It was a matter of three minutes away. Three minutes *au maximum*, a mere flicker in the eternity of a taxi-driver's life, you would think, but the doughty old Parisian at the wheel refused to budge another inch with me in the cab.

One o'clock. Two hours to go.

I found a table at the Royal Saint-Germain, ordered an omelette au jambon and a café noir, and stared across at the church with its towers encased in scaffolding. I wondered why I'd never seen any workmen on it. Maybe I *was* up and about for only a few hours every day, after all. Boy, I'd better pull myself together.

I made a mark with my knife on the paper table-cloth to underline my decision: *Teddy would have to go.* I probably really didn't have the true courtesan spirit anyway. How in hell had I got into all this in the first place? I tried to figure out how the whole thing started. Well, first of all, of course, I came to Paris. And the reason I had a chance to come to Paris was because of dear old Uncle Roger...

The week before I became thirteen – two days after I'd run away for the fourth time – my uncle Roger had sent for me. He was then living in lofty majesty, in a big, white clapboard house overlooking the Hudson Valley, and spending most of this time in the enormous living-room he'd had converted into an observatory. A giant telescope was rigged up right smack in the middle of the room, the original idea being that it would give him something to do when he got bored at one of his parties, but gradually it had come to obsess him and he was never far away from it. He even began using it to punctuate his conversations, to gesture with, the way other people use their spectacles and pipes. Uncle Roger had invented a special kind of screw which made him very, very rich, and a special kind of oracular noblesse oblige in distributing his largesse, which made him very, very godlike. The telescope helped too. He was hard at it when I was announced.

'They tell me you were heading down Mexico way this time. What for?' he asked me over his shoulder, apparently unable even for a minute to tear himself away from the stars, or whatever you see through a telescope in broad daylight.

'I wanted to be a bullfighter,' I mumbled.

'What were you going to be last time?'

'You mean last year when I ran away?'

'Yes.'

'A singer in a jazzband. Why?'

'Nothing, nothing. Just curious.' He twiddled a few knobs and had another look at – the sun – I suppose, and finally turned round and looked at me. I was staring down at my saddle shoes. One shoelace had been badly tied and I was trying to re-tie it in my mind.

'My dear child, what a face! What a face to put on. Why so broody?'

'I am in mourning for my life,' I said, still staring at my shoes, wishing they were black, at least, and wondering if he'd ever read the play. He hadn't.

'Good heavens, is that what they teach you at that school?'

'No.'

'Well, never mind. Let's see what we can do to cheer you up, shall we? The reason I've asked you to come – now don't be afraid, I won't scold you. I'm sure you've been scolded quite enough – sit down, child, sit down anywhere, just throw all that camera stuff on the floor, we're shooting Venus tonight, getting her quarter phase – the reason I asked you to come, is to find out what you'd like for your birthday this year.'

'I want my freedom!' I said, tears stinging my eyes at the word.

'Your freedom? Ah yes, of course. What are you planning to do with it?'

I hesitated. I had to think for a moment. I hadn't really put it into words before.

'I want to stay out as late as I like and eat whatever I like any time I want to,' I said finally.

'Is that all?'

'No. I think if I had my freedom I wouldn't allow myself to get introduced to all the mothers and fathers and brothers of the girls at school. And all that junk. I wouldn't get introduced to anyone. I've never wanted to meet anyone I've been introduced to. I want to meet all the other people . . . I can't explain . . .'

'Try. There must be some reason for your ambulatory urges.'

'It's just that I *know* the world is so wide and full of people and exciting things that I just go crazy every day stuck in these institutions. I mean if I don't get started soon, how will I get the chance to sharpen my wits? It takes lots of training. You have to start very young. I want them to be so sharp that I'm always able to guess right. Not *be* right – that's much different – that means you're going to do something about it. No. Just guessing. You know, more on the wing.'

Uncle Roger went back to the telescope and swung it around a bit, back and forth. Finally he came over and sat down beside me. For the first time he spoke to me man to man. 'I think I understand your predilection for being continually on the wing, or rather, to put it more precisely, on the lam,' he said seriously. 'It's difficult to know nowadays where adventure lies. There are no more real frontiers. Funny how these things work out. I came roaring out of the Middle West, you know, and my greatest ambition was to conquer – that's how I saw it – to conquer New York; New York and the mysterious, civilised East. Now my father before me had set his sights on conquering the Middle West. That was his adventure. I wonder what you will try to conquer? Europe, I suppose, since our family seems to be going backwards.'

I don't know why but at this moment I had one of those aberrations where people say one thing to you and you take it to mean something quite different. I fully expected Uncle Roger to put a steamship ticket in one of my hands, a bouquet of flowers in the other, and wish me Bon Voyage.

I drew myself to attention, trying to look alert, composed, above all trustworthy, and I said, 'I should like to go to Europe very much, Uncle Roger. Could you write to my school and explain that you've decided to send me away?'

'Good God, this is impossible!' exclaimed my uncle, horrified. 'See here, young lady the world may be very wide, but you also are very young and don't you forget it. Now then,' he said, and he took me by the elbows and looked earnestly into my eyes, 'I have a proposition to make to you. The more I see of the world the more I realise how much we are haunted by our childhood dreams. We have been having a serious conversation just now, whether you know it or not. I want you to remember every word. And when you've graduated from college—'

'Oh no!'

'—graduated from college, and if you haven't run away in the meantime, I'll give you your freedom. Two years of it. Upon graduation you'll receive in monthly sums enough money for you to go anywhere you like and do anything you like during that period. No strings. I don't even want to hear of you in those two years. Afterwards come back and tell me what it was like . . .'

When I first arrived in Paris I got sick. Then I got well and began walking everywhere round and round and round, crossing and re-crossing the river, hardly knowing where I was going or where I'd been. Hardly caring, it all seemed so fine.

And then one day, one memorable day in the early evening, I stumbled across the Champs-Elysées. I know it seems crazy to say, but before I actually stepped on to it (at what turned out to be the Etoile) I had not even been aware of its existence. No, I swear it. I'd heard the words 'Champs-Elysées', of course, but I thought it was a park or something. I mean that's what it sounds like, doesn't it? All at once I found myself standing there gazing down that enchanted boulevard in the blue, blue evening. Everything seemed to fall into place. Here was all the gaiety and glory and sparkle I knew was going to be life if I could just grasp it.

I began floating down those Elysian Fields three inches off the ground, as easily as a Cocteau character floats through Hell. Luxury and order seemed to be shining from every street-lamp along the Avenue; shining from every window of its toy-shops and dress-shops and car-shops; shining from its cafés and cinemas and theatres; from its bonbonneries and parfumeries and

313

nighteries.... Talk about seeing Eternity in a Grain of Sand and Heaven in a Wild Flower; I really think I was having some sort of mystic revelation then. The whole thing seemed like a memory from the womb. It seemed to have been waiting there for me.

For some people history is a Beach or a Tower or a Graveyard. For me it was this giant primordial Toy Shop with all its windows gloriously ablaze. It contained everything I've ever wanted that money can buy. It was an enormous Christmas present wrapped in silver and blue tissue paper tied with satin ribbons and bells. Inside would be something to adorn, to amuse, and to dazzle me forever. It was my present for being alive.

As I say, I'd started at the Etoile and was working my way down to the Place de la Concorde. Somewhere around the Rond-Point I floated off the kerb and into an oncoming car. The scream of brakes that had at first seemed so dim and irrelevant was now screeching into my ears. All in all it was a very near miss. The driver leapt out of the car and rushed over to the lamp-post against which I was limply draped. 'Are you all right?' he asked anxiously. I could have kissed him for not yelling why the hell hadn't I looked where I was going. I nodded and started to leave but found that it was quite impossible to put one foot in front of the other. The upshot of the matter was that this extremely charming man, his arm firmly under my elbow, suggested we both take a spin in his car for a little while to unwind.

The next thing I knew I was ankle deep in martinis at the Ritz Bar, and he was calling me Sally Jay and I was calling him Teddy.

I sighed nostalgically, drained my coffee to the grounds, and unrolled l'addition from the tight little scroll in my hand. If I was going to break off with Teddy it wouldn't do at all to remember those early days and what fun they'd been. After all, he was madly attractive dans sa façon. No question. Was I being wise or merely rash? Oh dear. By now I was completely uncertain. Two of les boys flitted past. They certainly wore their jeans with a difference. One of the differences between Saint-Germain and Montparnassse, I decided, was that Saint-Germain was queerer. And that was the only decision I seemed likely to make for the time being.

COPYRIGHT
ACKNOWLEDGEMENTS

Other Virago Books of Interest

THE VIRAGO BOOK OF
WOMEN TRAVELLERS

Edited by Mary Morris
with Larry O'Connor

'An excellent collection'
– *Sunday Times*

'A volume in which rich and unexpected seams of precious
minerals await discovery'
– *Guardian*

'From the acerbic wit of Freya Stark to the raw courage of
Dervla Murphy, over three hundred years of the best and
bravest women's travel writing is gathered here in a collection of
stunning journeys we can all take – on the page and in the
imagination'
– *The List*

THE VIRAGO BOOK OF
WICKED VERSE

Edited by Jill Dawson

This wonderfully sharp and witty collection of poems feisty,
bawdy, erotic, irreverent, is an illuminating comment on
women's ability to transform poetry into a medium of
subversiveness. There are jibes at hypocrisy and prejudice, plenty
of sexiness and sauciness, and a riotous turning of the 'Lady
Poet' image on its head. With poets spanning continents and
centuries, this anthology demonstrates lavishly the myriad ways
in which women can be 'wicked' by their definition and wilfully
so!

**Poems by: Aphra Behn, Wendy Cope, Emily Dickinson, Carol
Ann Duffy, Suniti Namjoshi, Grace Nichols, Vicki Raymond,
Ntozake Shange, Izumi Shikibu, Anna Wickham and many more**

THE VIRAGO BOOK OF
SPIRITUALITY
OF WOMEN AND ANGELS

Edited by Sarah Anderson

'A beautiful book' – *Times Literary Supplement*

This anthology looks at spirituality in its broadest sense and includes extracts from fiction and poetry as well as writings by women known for their search for spiritual fulfilment, women whose inner journeys were often very different from those of men. Crossing all religious boundaries, disciplines and ages, this represents not just Christianity, Judaism, Buddhism, Hinduism, Sufism but also women who do not conform to any mainstream orthodox religion. Some of the writers included are: Simone Well, St Teresa of Avila, Julian of Norwich, Emily Brontë, Iris Murdoch, Lady Mary Herbert, Kathleen Raine, Alice Walker, Hildegard of Bingen, Rabiah Balhki, Emily Dickinson, Nangsa Obum, Virginia Woolf and many more.

THE VIRAGO BOOK OF
FAIRY TALES

Angela Carter

'Angela Carter's imagination was one of the most dazzling this century . . . For her, fantasy always turns back its eyes to stare hard at reality, never losing sight of material conditions. She once remarked, "A fairytale is a story where one king goes to another king to borow a cup of sugar."' – Marina Warner

Fairy tales are a shorthand way of describing the marvellous narratives that have been passed down through the generations by word of mouth. We don't know the names of the people who made up the stories, but there's a mythical figure, 'Mother Goose', who knows *all* the stories. *The Virago Book of Fairy Tales* contains the pick of Mother Goose's feathers. Lyrical tales, bloody tales, hilariously funny, ripely bawdy, stories that show the dark and the light side of life – from Europe, the Arctic, the USA, Africa, the Middle East and Asia.

THE VIRAGO BOOK OF
LOVE AND LOSS

Edited by Georgina Hammick

Elizabeth Bowen, Janette Turner Hospital, Doris Lessing, Shena
Mackay, Alice Munro, Grace Paley, Dorothy Parker and Sylvia
Townsend Warner are among the writers whose considerable
talents feature in this memorable exploration of love and loss.
Here is the subterfuge and yearning of an illicit relationship,
the intolerable oppression of summer in the face of a loved
one's death and a mother who obscures her loneliness with
irascible complaints to her son. Alongside stories of love's
frailties are those shadowed by lost opportunities, lingering
regrets and the bruising of age. This seductive collection brings
together some of the foremost writers of this century. Whether
devastating or poignant, or glistening with wry humour, these
stories reach into the corners of the heart.

THE VIRAGO BOOK OF LOVE LETTERS

Edited by Jill Dawson

'As we head down the super-highway of e-mail and fax, we shall all need instruction in this old-fashiond art' – Aisling Foster, *Times Literary Supplement*

Passion, longing, the desolation of unrequited love or the end of an affair are some of the consuming emotions in this ravishing compendium which reveals the enduring power of the love affair to produce ardent and often unguarded personal writing. From Emily Dickinson to Anaïs Nin, Anne Boleyn to the Empress Josephine, a miner's wife writing to her dead husband to prisoners of war in a Russian jail writing to friends and family, as well as contemporary figures such as Winnie Mandela and poets Suniti Namjoshi and Gillian Hanscombe, all wrote marvellous, highly charged love letters. With the promise of intimate glimpses into the writers' hearts, this anthology delivers Virginia Woolf at her wittiest, Colette in ardent and dreamy mood, Simone de Beauvoir at her most private and provocative, and many others.

THE VIRAGO BOOK OF
LOVE POETRY

Edited by Wendy Mulford

'Feisty selection of anthems with attitude . . . a noisy throng of impressively dissimilar voices . . . A book to treasure'– *Irish Times*

For centuries women have written about love with passion, humour, frustration and despair; but never before have their voices come together as in this exhilarating and timeless compendium. Here are love poems in all their true, subversive drama, delicately arranged according to a balance of moods and modes: of argument and lyric, joke and passionate utterance, rejection, rage and ecstacy. Poets, well-known and obscure, ancient and modern – from Sappho to Akhamotova, Patti Smith to Selima Hill, Sylvia Plath to Alice Walker – all challenge the traditional perception of women as muse and object of desire, and magnificently transcend it.

Now you can order superb titles directly from Virago

☐	The Hacienda	Lisa St Aubin de Terán	£6.99
☐	Joanna	Lisa St Aubin de Terán	£6.99
☐	The Virago Book of Women Travellers	Mary Morris (ed)	£8.99
☐	The Virago Book of Wicked Verse	Jill Dawson (ed)	£8.99
☐	The Virago Book of Spirituality	Sarah Anderson (ed)	£6.99
☐	The Virago Book of Fairy Tales	Angela Carter (ed)	£7.99
☐	The Virago Book of Love and Loss	Georgina Hammick (ed)	£6.99
☐	The Virago Book of Love Letters	Jill Dawson (ed)	£6.99
☐	The Virago Book of Love Poetry	Wendy Mulford (ed)	£6.99

Please allow for postage and packing: **Free UK delivery.**
Europe; add 25% of retail price; Rest of World; 45% of retail price.

To order any of the above or any other Virago titles, please call our credit card orderline or fill in this coupon and send/fax it to:

Virago, 250 Western Avenue, London, W3 6XZ, UK.
Fax 0181 324 5678   Telephone 0181 324 5516

☐ I enclose a UK bank cheque made payable to Virago for £ ....
☐ Please charge £.............. to my Access, Visa, Delta, Switch Card No.

☐☐☐☐☐☐☐☐☐☐☐☐☐☐☐☐☐☐☐

Expiry Date ☐☐☐☐   Switch Issue No.   ☐☐

NAME (Block letters please) ....

ADDRESS ....

....

....

Postcode ....Telephone ....

Signature ....

Please allow 28 days for delivery within the UK. Offer subject to price and availability.

Please do not send any further mailings from companies carefully selected by Virago ☐